ANGEL FIRE

Mary Marshall

ANGEL FIRE

Mary Marshall

Published by
CCC of America
Irving, Texas 75063

Published in Irving, Texas by CCC of America.

Library of Congress Cataloging-in-Publication Data

Marshall, Mary.
    Angel Fire / Mary Marshall.

ISBN 1-56814-525-X (pbk.)

Printed in the United States of America.

ACKNOWLEDGMENTS

I would like to thank the following people who said the right things at the right times and whose encouragement gave me the springboard that I needed, (in order of appearance in my times of need); Beth Feia, Father Michael Scanlan, T.O.R., Ann Spangler, Penelope Stokes, Anne Martin, Jackie Zick, my brother Greg Kissel, Pat and Tim Miller and Bert Ghezzi. My thanks to Rhonda DeLong, Colleen Morgan and Suzie Ackerman for the generosity of their time and talents in making up for my lack of computer skills.

My very special thanks to Alan Napleton, John Williams, and Bob Angelotti who had the faith in God's provision, in me and in my book to publish it.

I don't know how to adequately thank my husband, Marshall, for his unselfish love, support and encouragement as I went through the labor and delivery of *Angel Fire*. For the courage he showed in reading my rough draft in 1990. For the kindness he showed me as he read revision after revision. For his unfailing computer expertise and the hours I took advantage of it. For his tolerance when I scrutinized every nuance of my revisions. For his genius in understanding my thinking and in reading my long-hand writing. And finally for his faithfulness in sharing my vision and in trusting in God for the publication of *Angel Fire*. For all these things and for the day to day joy he gives me I thank my husband, Marshall.

And to the Lord our God, Jesus Christ, be all thanksgiving and praise. To Jesus, who is my Anchor and my Sail.

For Marshall, my husband and my best friend. And for Clare, my daughter, and my inspiration.

"Some men see things as they are and ask 'why?' But I see things that never were and ask 'why not?'"

George Bernard Shaw

CHAPTER
ONE
SORN

Today he would have sold his soul for one good whiff of the future. To survive for the moment without a future was not survival at all. It was a tease.

Today he felt a dozen hungers, hungers which had always driven him. Perhaps all of life was just a tease. Human souls hungering for love and finding only crumbs. Hungering to keep the taste of joy for more than just an instant. Hungering for truth, and when you thought you had the truth, skeptical that it was a trick. His father always told him that he was too skeptical.

Today the flower died. Each morning he had watched the purple stalk thicken and sprout. It had actually formed a flower bud. Somewhere between Tethra and the destitute nothingness of space, something new had grown in the sterile coldness of his solitary starship. The Ytar plant was supposed to be vigorous and resilient, bred for space and for the anemic lighting of a military starship. But today it had died. He should never have let himself care.

Today he knew that he would die soon. Every breath of oxygen drew him closer to his last. The ship had lost the bulk of its life support system in its escape maneuver. In six more weeks the oxygen would run out. Now his starship traveled through the void of uncharted space, going nowhere, needing everything. They had not spotted a planet or an asteroid anywhere in sensor range. And even if they discovered a planet today, they could barely reach it in six weeks. They were traveling at only one-tenth the speed of light. Kollann, of the great Sorn family, had been brought to his knees, adrift in empty space. Sorn was grateful that there was no one here to read his mind. To see his weakness. In fact, he did kneel as he touched the plant and examined its stem. And then he fingered his Captain's insignia, worn proudly on his left sleeve. Both the plant and the Starfleet commission, they stood for something. He had to know just what. On the surface there were many things to believe in. And he believed in them all. He fought for Chadran ideals and was pledged to protect the defenseless. He served the monarch of free Chadra, the greatest nation on the planet Tethra. On the surface it all sounded good. But deep inside he was empty.

Sorn stood up straight and walked away from the drooping plant. He looked outside the porthole window of his private cell. The severe beauty of the stars used to excite him. Not now. Nothing did. Eighteen weeks of losing hope had drained him. It had not occurred to him eighteen weeks ago that Starfleet would abandon him in deep space. That they could not send an escort to help him return to the strings. Today he knew what it was to be powerless and stripped of courage.

Ont Zejen's voice jarred him. *Why doesn't he leave me alone? I have finished my ten-hour watch for today,* Sorn thought. He replayed Zejen's voice in his mind.

"Captain! Emergency, come to the bridge!"

Emergency! Even that was better than nothing. Better than more of the something that was engulfing him. He ran to the bridge. Running felt good. He ran half the perimeter of the oval starship toward the bridge. The elevator took him the rest of the way.

He wasn't ready for anything. He wasn't ready for what he saw. A massive body of cosmic matter filled the domed view screen of the bridge. It looked like a stationary tornado of cosmic energy. Peculiar colors and strange configurations of matter swelled and faded within it. Sorn had never seen anything like this before. Nothing seemed right about it.

"This cosmic storm...or whatever it is appeared out of nowhere. The sensors had barely picked it up and we were on top of it." Zejen struggled to control his voice. He looked strangely old.

"I need data," Sorn shouted. Scanning the monitors he saw only nonsense. Matter, anti-matter, dimensional collapse, readings that went off the scale. The data was useless. Except for one fact. The gravitational pull of the mass was reaching for them.

He had to make a decision. The starship could maneuver against the gravitational pull and explore the outer layers of the mass from a safe distance. Or the ship could plunge into the clear eye of the cosmic tornado, where there was an inviting absence of gravity and matter.

The monitor flashed warnings. The gravitational strength of the mass increased by the second. *Decide, Sorn, seconds matter,* he ordered himself. Suddenly a sickness seized him. He felt dizzy, his pulse raced, his hands went cold. It was fear. He felt ashamed of his fear. He was the Captain and he had to act to save them. Every cell in his body focused on the decision before him, on the whirling threatening mass. He could not make this call. Zejen and Jenxex stood by watching him, trusting him. They thought that Sorn could do anything. Now he knew that he could not. Now he was sure he could not.

Maybe it all ends here, he thought. No, he didn't want to die. He was panicking. He had faced other crises, why couldn't he face this one? His mind went blank. Time stood still for an instant. He was without hope. His soul was barren. *I am empty inside,* Sorn thought. *Empty at the bottom.*

It was into the absolute emptiness that the angel came. She did not seem to belong here, and yet his emptiness had made a place for her. In a golden swirl of soft light she materialized beside him. She took the size and form of an average woman. Sorn's reason was brittle. His emotions were weary and confused. The angel understood at once. She looked at him with tenderness. Such fierce compassion flowed from the angel that the knot of Sorn's paralysis melted for a moment. Long enough to think.

"Go straight through the clear eye of the tornado. The eye is really a door," the angel spoke telepathically. It was a suggestion, not an order. Sorn chose to trust the angel.

It took only minutes to pass through the eye of the cosmic storm. It felt like years. The monitors and sensors flashed wildly as the crew, strapped in safety gear, felt no sensation of motion. Heard only an agonizing silence. And then the jump through hyperspace was over.

They had traveled a distance of one thousand light years in twenty minutes. It took the computer thirty more minutes to analyze the data from the event. The computer's conclusion was that the eye of the tornado had been a fold in the universe, a fold in three-dimensional space. The ship had passed through hyper-dimensional space and had come a great distance to a new place. The new place was in the boundaries of an unknown solar system. Six weeks later they reached the third planet from the sun. They discovered that its name was Earth.

II.

Sorn watched through the open screen of the bridge as his starship orbited Earth. The ship was only half a ship. But it was home for now, and it was safe.

The sight of Earth had become beautiful to the two men aboard the ship. Earth had arrived at the moment of their desperation. She had appeared out of the barren infertility of the universe, looking at first like a glowing blue star and then an oasis of life. Earth had rescued Sorn and Zejen from certain death. Her treasures included not only oxygen and water, but all the supplies they needed to restore their ship. And most astonishingly of all, there were humans on this planet.

Ont Zejen watched Sorn. Sorn was younger, taller, braver than he. Yet the stress of this voyage had left its marks on Sorn. Something between Tethra and Earth had broken him. Whatever "it" was it seemed to have deepened him, not weakened him. At least he did not wear it like weakness. Zejen did not expect Sorn to bare his heart to him. Sorn's heart was very private. And yet he shared his thinking with Zejen as if they were equals. Zejen took great pride in that.

Sorn was an aristocrat. He had fought for the right to be a starfleet officer, like everyone else. But he never lost his birth-rank. Zejen knew that Sorn never mentioned it. Perhaps he never even thought of it. But he did not need to. Everyone knew who Sorn was.

Zejen belonged to a different class, a sturdy class of manual laborers whose lives were limited by poverty. Zejen's ambition drove him to push his intellect and his body to the limit. He had become one of the finest chief engineers in the Chadran fleet. What he lacked in breeding he made up for in ingenuity. Captain Sorn valued his ingenuity and his street-fighter instincts. He had requested that Zejen serve under his command. It had been the proudest day of Zejen's life. Zejen brought great honor to the sons he left on Tethra.

Zejen had studied in silence long enough. Jenxex, the android, would never start a conversation. And lately, Sorn spoke less and less. Zejen was pleased to have learned so much about Earth in such a short time. It had been easy. The starship computer had immediately found a way to access the fragile, porous computer networks of Earth. The Tethran computer could bypass any security system to feed on the knowledge of the Earth computers. The information was disorganized, but it was accessible.

"The more we study them, the more I see the wisdom in keeping our distance from the humans of Earth. They would be terrified of us," Zejen said, hoping to stimulate some conversation.

"I agree," Sorn said. "Two-thirds of Tethran science would seem like magic to them. And yet if they look back only two hundred years ago on Earth, two-thirds of what today's humans take for granted about daily life, television, computers, space shuttles, would have looked like magic to their own ancestors."

"They are not our equals, Captain. The humans of Earth use only one-quarter of their brains. They are also primitive in other ways," Zejen said.

"They have much to teach us. They are genetically untampered. They are what we would be if we had not had our genes 'improved' forty generations ago. We would feel and think like they do." Sorn spoke softly. There was almost compassion in his voice. Yes, that is what Zejen would have called it, compassion.

"How do you think these humans came to be on this planet?" Zejen asked.

Sorn turned to Zejen and faced him. "Do you remember any of the tales of ancient Tethran mythology, Zejen? There was one tale of the Ancient Mariners, the Changelings. In it the Changelings captured a group of the children of humankind, separated them from their kinsmen and took them away to a distant planet where they could flourish."

"Do you believe in that nonsense, Captain?" Zejen asked.

"I'm not sure that belief is the issue. This is called speculation."

"I remember practically nothing of ancient mythology. Classical literature was not high on my priority list at the academy." Zejen smiled. "It surprises me that you allude to fairy tales for answers, Captain."

"Mythology is often more than fairy tales. Mythology was invented to answer very real questions. Besides, Zejen, you are a scientist and an engineer. You tell me what answers science is giving you right now about the existence of these humans one thousand light years away from Tethra, in an empty spot of the universe where there are no cosmic strings. You tell me how it is that we can be matched with these humans down to the molecular level of our DNA. Tethra has explored the galaxy for four thousand years. Why have we never found anything remotely resembling a human being until now?"

"We have only been studying Earth for a short time. It will take me and science a little longer to discover some good answers." Zejen was slightly annoyed.

Jenxex, the android, was ever watchful. "I am familiar with Orr Mythology, Captain. You were referring to the Foundation Tales."

"Go on, Jenxex." Sorn turned his face toward the android in a gesture of respect.

"The Foundation Tales were supposedly recorded 35,000 years ago. But the recorded versions were destroyed in the Great Wars of Antiquity. They were passed on by oral tradition for several generations before civilization regrouped its assets and started recording knowledge again.

"The Foundation Tales are vague about the creation of the human race. There was rivalry between the brothers of the first family. One brother killed the other. The murderer's children lived in great shame and misery. The ancient Changelings took pity on them. The Changelings were themselves exiles and sinners. They were banished from their home planet for destroying a helpless species. In order to redeem themselves they had to accomplish a good act equal to their evil act. The Changelings decided to help the murderer's children and took many of them aboard their starship. They traveled for centuries before they found another planet suitable for human life. The other planet must have been Earth.

"Before the Changelings left Tethra they gave the Tethran people the knowledge of star travel. It was left in your racial memory." Jenxex stopped briefly.

"And yet the Changelings did not give the knowledge of star travel to the humans of Earth, the murderer's children," Sorn said. "Perhaps it was a punishment."

"The ancient mythology tells us very little about the Changelings themselves," Jenxex continued. "We know only that they could take the form of human beings, animals, or inanimate objects. Mythology pictured them mostly in human forms like gods and goddesses with strange powers." Jenxex paused.

"I remember only two creatures from ancient Orr Mythology." Zejen was pleased with himself for remembering. "Everyone remembers King Xenocon who taught men weaponry and survival. And then there was the beauty, Princess Star, the epitome of erotic love."

"And truth," Sorn added. "She was the Changeling who drove men to madness with her beauty. But when she was alone with women she revealed truth to her sisters. And so women came to depend on men for protection from enemies and starvation. And men learned to depend on women for truth and love."

"I had forgotten the Plan of Harmony between men and women. I had forgotten that Princess Star was the Truth Bearer. Perhaps I did learn it long ago," Zejen said. He tapped his fingers nervously on his chair. Sorn had noticed Zejen's fidgeting while Jenxex talked.

"There is one more important fact to add to our discussion, Captain," Jenxex said. "There is one Changeling prophecy about the lost children. The Deists still hold it as an obscure part of their belief system. It states, 'When the separated brethren are reunited, the human race will be reborn. It will be the joy of the right hand finding the left hand.'" Jenxex finished abruptly. He watched Captain Sorn for a response. Sorn was pensive.

"Mythology is useless to us. I would like some solid information from Tethra. I would like to use the ansible." Zejen's eyes betrayed his anger, even though his voice did not.

Zejen unconsciously stroked the ansible panel, his link with the home world. The ansible was instantaneous communication, unaffected by distance and time; it joined all the humans in the cosmos.

"We have discussed this, Ont. If we use the ansible it will be only a matter of time before someone from Tethra traces our location here. I think it is best to keep this planet hidden for now," Sorn said. His statement was an order.

Zejen turned his back abruptly on him. He loved Sorn and would have followed him into hell. In fact, he thought he had. But he wanted to go home now. Home to Tethra.

Sorn was one of those rare men who always seemed to see the cosmic consequences of his actions. Sorn was a champion. He killed with ease when he thought it just. He probably would even die with ease if he thought it just.

After eight months alone with this man, Zejen knew that Sorn was made of steel and heart. He wished that Sorn was made of less steel and more cowardice. Cowardice would probably get them home more quickly.

Zejen glared at the Captain. He would argue with him later about not using the ansible, their only tie with Tethra. He would argue and lose. It usually happened that way. Sorn was brighter, yes. But Sorn was always right. Always kind. He would listen to Zejen's every thought as they argued. Then Sorn's logic would crash into Zejen's mind, touch his heart, and change him.

Zejen had become less a coward just being near Sorn. Zejen kicked against the heroism evolving in his own soul. Like the Captain who had been born with a noble heart, Zejen was afraid that he was earning one.

"By now they all think that we're dead," Zejen said. No one on Tethra responded to our first message four weeks ago. We have no evidence that they heard us."

"They heard us," Sorn said softly.

<h2 style="text-align:center">III.</h2>

Lieutenant Lohnarks did not expect to feel the rush of joy he felt when he heard Sorn's message. Everyone felt it. Everyone on the planetTethra and the alliance planets all heard Sorn's ansible transmission at the same moment. Lohnarks could see by the color of the light at the base of the ansible that Sorn was using the most resilient low security channel on the ansible. Sorn's message would be received by the poorest of the poor and richest of the rich on this channel. Lohnarks had to smile.

"We are well and hiding in deep space. Our quest has only begun. We will return to Tethra," Sorn said. It was unmistakably Sorn's voice, unmistakably his choice of positive, fearless, focused words. Sorn who had been classified as "Missing in Action" months ago was alive and well! Lohnarks was glad that the enemy Greole could receive this ansible channel as well. The Greole claimed to have murdered Sorn months ago. No one could refute it until now! Until the dead man spoke. Sorn denied his own death and called his desperate escape into deep space "a quest." Lohnarks laughed aloud.

Sorn's message continued. This time Lohnarks frowned. Sorn sent a coded message on the low security channel. He was required by law to send encoded messages on a closed channel reserved for military intelligence.

Lohnarks reacted immediately. He moved his fingers across the ansible and pushed the "save" key near the base of the ansible. Sorn's coded message did not record. Lohnarks was disappointed, but he was not surprised. They could not censor the message's first transmission, but they could censor its being recorded.

Lohnarks was baffled. He could think of only one reason why Sorn would send a coded message. He was in trouble and he needed help. But not from just anyone. Sorn needed help from the only two people who could decipher that code. But why did he send the message on that channel if he didn't want everyone to see it? Maybe Sorn wanted to get past the censors.

Lohnarks realized that he would have to try to get Sorn's message from secret intelligence sources. And that was not going to be easy.

What do you want with top-secret classified material, Lieutenant Lohnarks? You have limited security clearance, and you are a nobody, the high command would think. And what they would say was this.

"We will review your request for Captain Sorn's classified message. And we will get back with you."

It would take months to get back to him, months to respond to an emergency call for help from deep space. Lohnarks couldn't let that happen. He would use every ounce of influence that he could muster. For now he would simply request access to the coded message. He made his case sending an e-mail and took the landside shuttle home.

The long tubular shuttle was packed with military personnel leaving the space station for the night. Lohnarks enjoyed being in space but he hated the weightless shuttle ride between the space station and land. They claimed it was too costly to gravitize the shuttles. Fortunately the trip was brief. Lohnarks was in a pensive mood. But many people seemed talkative...even excited.

"Good news from deep space!" a tall ensign said to a non-uniformed friend. He swung into his seat and fastened his upper and lower seat belts.

"Do you think Sorn's message was the real thing or one of those simulated productions?"

"I believe it was the real thing," a third voice said.

"That's because you want to believe it."

"Crawl into a hole, cynic," a woman suddenly said. "Captain Sorn is a hero, the best we have. Sorn was talking to Chadra, to all of us and to our grandmothers. Otherwise he would have used a closed military channel."

Lohnarks listened. He couldn't believe the heated discussion. Usually the shuttles were silent. But the woman was right. Sorn knew that the nation of Chadra had suffered the loss of its beloved King this year. And the war with the Greole was in its tenth year. Spirits were low. The Chadran-led Alliance of Planets was better equipped for war than the Greole. But the Greole were a ruthless, bloodthirsty enemy and had succeeded in shocking the free worlds with their cruel tactics. Even now Sorn wanted to boost the morale of his people. Even now, wherever he was.

"I heard a rumor," an old dark-haired scientist said softly. The old man sat next to Lohnarks regularly on this shuttle and he knew all about rumors. He worked on some obscure research project but somehow he was a reliable pipeline between classified information and anyone in the solar system who would listen to him. Lohnarks bent his head toward the old man. "I heard that Sorn is so far into deep space that he did not have the use of anything but the resilient low security channel. He has lost all other communications with Starfleet...and Tethra." The scientist's voice was hoarse, but clear. His gray eyes searched Lohnarks for a response.

Lohnark's said nothing. These people knew and admired Sorn from a distance. Lohnarks knew him as a friend. He had served as Sorn's first mate for two years. And then Sorn saved his life. Lohnarks was tired of thinking. He opened the shutter to the porthole and looked out into space as the shuttle sped toward Tethra, his home, his dinner and Freepar.

Lohnarks barely had time to ponder his request for access to Sorn's coded message. He was shocked when he heard from military intelligence only three hours later. He didn't just hear from them, they came to him. With the kind of armed escort they would send to pickup a military prisoner for interrogation. He did not like the feel of this.

He kissed Freepar good-bye and handed her the passkey to his secret files. She furtively slid the passkey down her sleeve and gave him a memorable good-bye kiss. He was grateful when he looked back on that kiss. Because he was never going to see Freepar again.

IV.

Lohnarks' escort was professional and silent. He would learn nothing from them. He was relieved when they brought him to a commercial broadcasting facility. But he did not like the way they watched every flick of his wrist and never left his side. A colonel finally arrived. Maybe now there would be some answers.

"Military intelligence has selected you to present the newscast regarding Captain Sorn's escape from the cosmic strings," Colonel Veesh said.

"Why me?"

"You have the right face for the newscast. You look distinguished and trustworthy. You have a good voice. And you are an eyewitness."

"You brought me here to do a newscast? What about my request? I asked for access to Sorn's message. I am one of only two people who can decipher his code."

"You have made that clear."

"When will my request be answered?"

"Why are you in such a hurry, Lieutenant Lohnarks?" The Colonel paused. He turned toward Lohnarks, but he didn't look at him. He never looked him in the eye. It was very unsettling. "By your admission to a knowledge of the code you have put yourself in a very sensitive position, Lohnarks."

What did that mean? Did it mean that he was a pawn in some complex game? Did it mean that he would never lose his armed guard?

"Sir, does Chadran Command have any interest in decoding Captain Sorn's message?"

"You ask the wrong questions, Lohnarks."

"Stop playing games with me, and tell me what this is all about."

Colonel Veesh ignored his demand. He nodded politely and left Lohnarks alone without saying another word. Lohnarks was angry. But all he could do was wait. And follow orders.

He followed orders when they told him to change into a dress uniform. A young make-up man came in and trimmed his hair, asking Lohnarks why he had let his hair turn gray. Lohnarks didn't answer. He followed orders when they escorted him into the media cubicle and gave him a prepared statement to read.

Lieutenant Lohnarks poised himself. The Colonel had said that Lohnarks looked trustworthy and distinguished. He let the thought give him confidence. His three dimensional image was to be projected across the extended solar system in a three dimensional video hologram to the wealthy and elite. But even those who could not afford this video would receive the whole message.

He waited for his cue and then began:

"In his last battle in the high-behind of the Red Ice Quadrant, Captain Sorn was deceived by a Greole convoy. He realized that our battleship had been caught in a suicidal position. Sorn used a rare escape strategy and executed it so quickly that it worked. Our Chadran battleship, the Stealthfire, had been designed as two separate units for repair purposes. The ship had an outer horseshoe-shaped battle arm containing the weapons system. The inner, circular portion of the ship contained the living quarters. When he gave the order which he called 'Chaff,' the two hundred members of the Stealthfire crew rushed to the circular center of the ship and cloaked that portion. Sorn split the ship in two parts, separating the battle arm from the center. The central portion of the ship escaped using the cloaking device. All 200 members of the Stealthfire crew, including myself, made it safely to the Red Ice Starbase two hours later."

"Captain Sorn, chief engineer Ont Zejen, and an android stayed with the visible battle arm of the ship to distract the Greole. The Greole did not understand the 'Chaff' order. As they adjusted their controls to suck Sorn aboard their starship, Captain Sorn took his portion of the ship to its only possible escape. He stripped his starship free of all contact with the energy of the cosmic strings. The only way the Greole could pursue him would be to do the same thing with their own ships."

"Both the Greole and the Alliance Forces of Red Ice Starbase were aware of Sorn's exit from the cosmic strings. The Greole convoy did not chase Sorn as he left the strings. They stood on watch to make sure that he did not attempt to re-enter. The Greole sent out an "alert to seize" the Stealthfire to all surrounding vicinities throughout the strings." Lohnarks paused. Security would not permit him to add the next lines but he resolved to say them anyway.

"The Chadran fleet at Red Ice Starbase was too slow in taking up the challenge to defend Sorn's faltering ship. The Stealthfire failed in its only attempt to return to the strings, without back-up military support. We all watched Sorn's starship disappear from our sensors, drifting into deep space. The Greole reported Captain Sorn dead. None of us, his rescued crew members, believed that the Captain was dead." Lohnarks smiled, he felt satisfied with the words he had delivered.

Space Science Editor Sweeja Angs concluded the newscast.

"The Chadran Captain's daring exit from the strings has attracted the attention of scientists today as well. Four thousand years ago scientists proved the existence of the cosmic strings, invisible threads, thinner than an atom, which contain the intense primordial energy of the universe. Since then, all starships have been designed so that they can utilize the shadow energy of the strings to travel at .999999 the speed of light."

"There is a limitation in modern starship travel. The strings are packed in certain galaxies and unraveled in other sections of the cosmos. If a starship, empowered by a linkage with the shadow energy of the strings, disengages from the strings, it loses its light-speed capacity and nearly all of its communications systems. Captain Sorn found himself in this situation, capable only of using alternate energy sources and traveling at One-Tenth Light Speed. At this speed it would take any starship hundreds of years to reach a destination in space."

Or so everyone had thought. *Now the free worlds could celebrate,* Lohnarks thought. Now, as the Greole listened to the ansible report, they could spit in disgust. The tenacious voice from deep space had proven that man could do more than survive beyond the strings. Captain Sorn could run and hide.

The newscast ended. Lohnarks' imprisonment began. Lohnarks did not know why they were holding him. He was not a hero nor a criminal. He was only a soldier who had asked for information to help another soldier. It was rumored that Sorn was so far away that his communications were limited to only one ansible channel. Lohnarks wondered if Sorn had been able to view or hear today's newscast. He wondered if he would ever see Sorn again.

V.

Sorn splashed cold water on his raw skin. It stung. He stood in front of the mirror and looked at his newly shaven face. He had not shaved in almost a year. He had only trimmed his beard. But it was time to go to Earth now. He would need to look and act like an ordinary businessman on Earth.

His skin was pale where his beard had been. And he could not help but think that the thick beard still belonged on his face as a sign of mourning. At first he had mourned the death of his father. Later he mourned his captivity on the Stealthfire. It was difficult letting go of his mourning. But it was time.

Remind me of who I am, he thought, looking at himself in the mirror.

I am Kollann of the Sorn family. I am Captain of the Stealthfire. I am sworn to protect the people of Chadra, my people. I will always be this man. Even when I live on Earth and act like someone else. Even when I take on the name and identity of a dull man named Richard Saxon.

Sorn wanted to laugh or to cry. But neither release would come.

His heart was heavy. He had never procrastinated about anything before and he wouldn't now. Sorn walked to the bridge. Sorn gave his orders and watched as they were carried out. He severed the ship's connection with the ansible. On Tethra they might read this step as an act of rebellion. But it would probably be seen as a sign that his ship had been destroyed. And they would forget him. And their lives would go on.

But it had to be done. Because Sorn knew now that Tethra should not discover the planet Earth. Sorn knew that he needed to protect the Earth, to hide her.

Sorn had made a mistake when he sent his first message to Tethra five months ago. Sending such a message was second nature. One minute he thought he would die. The next minute Earth appeared, with all her life-sustaining resources. It was then that he had sent his message by ansible and followed it with a secret coded report. He broke the rules by sending a detailed request for a journey ship. The coded report gave mathematical and astronomical data that would lead his aides to the entry point of jump through hyperspace and to the planet Earth. The code was so complex that only two other people in Tethra should have been able to decipher it, Lohnarks and Qeeswick. These two crewmen had devised the code with Sorn and had never used it.

He now hoped that his first message had been seized by the ansible censors or misunderstood even by his own officers. But hoping was not enough. Before disconnecting the ansible today, he sent a second coded message. This message withdrew his call for a journey ship and sent contradictory coordinates about his location. He had no idea how either of his two messages had been received. Maybe he would live to find out, live to see another Spring dawn on Tethra. Maybe he would not.

But Earth was worth protecting. And Earth was vulnerable and fragile. Her most sophisticated weapons were centuries behind Tethra's.

Som's starship alone could destroy half the cities on Earth--and disappear before anyone on the planet could mount a defense.

It was one thing to protect Earth from the Greole. The Greole could annihilate Earth with minimal effort. They would probably send their predator hybrids to do the job.

But Earth needed protection from Tethra as well. He knew that the people of Earth would be unable to meet Tethrans as equals. They would see all Tethrans, with their superior technology, as threatening conquerors. In some cases, they would be right.

The discovery of a second planet inhabited by native humans would be irresistible to Tethrans. They would focus the full force of their scientific curiosity on the Earth and its people. They would find the jump through hyperspace and come in droves. Tethran scientists and explorers would vow to follow protocol and procedure as if they were meeting a new species. Every life form was considered precious. But it would be different with humans meeting humans. There would be greed and exploitation. There would be love and hate.

Som could see it all too clearly not to act. And so he acted. But at a price. A great price. He had canceled his call for the help of a journey ship. Now the only thing he and Zejen could do to survive was to modify the life-support systems of the Stealthfire and hope that when they attempted the perils of uncharted space again, they could still make it home.

Som felt a wave of resentment. *Everything right should not always be so hard,* he thought. Ont Zejen saw it in his eyes.

"I have never been disconnected from the ansible in all my forty-eight years," Zejen said.

"No one has. Are you having second thoughts?" Som asked.

"Second fears. Not second thoughts. We are doing the right thing. We are doing the only thing we can do."

"We have a good plan."

"Steal what we need from Earth. Fix our ship and go home."

"And race against time," Som said quietly.

"I have a surprise for you, sir. I can solve the problem of time," Jenxex said. He looked pleased with himself. "The return voyage to Tethra is treacherous only because it must be completed in exactly 180 days. There is no margin for delay or error because of the inadequacies of our life-support system."

"However, I found more clean veins in the system. I have checked and rechecked my discovery. I can double our life-support capacity from 180 to 360 days--if you grant me permission to work on the reconstruction of the system for an additional sixteen months."

"You told me that you could complete your work in seven months," Sorn said.

"I can reconstruct the system for 180 days in that time. If I fill the clean veins and expand the system to 360 days, it will take 16 months," Jenxex said.

Sorn hid his anguish.

"Fantastic, Jenxex! It will almost be like traveling in a journey ship," Zejen said.

"Hardly, Sir. A journey ship can carry 800 humans for 300 years."

"Just a joke, Jenxex."

Sorn was absorbed in doing calculations on his keyboard. He felt numb inside.

"Sir, do I have your permission?" Jenxex asked.

Sorn did not reply.

"What's wrong, Captain?" Zejen asked. "This is good news."

"Sixteen more months. No news about the war. About Chadra," Sorn spoke softly.

"Homesickness will only kill us if we let it," Zejen said.

Sorn nodded.

"I intend to enjoy Earth and to take everything she has to offer. Fresh food, fresh everything. And very lovely women. We will have ample time to accomplish the work of our mission and still live like men,"
Zejen said. He smiled.

"You have finally shaved your beard, Captain. I am glad. Does that mean you are ready for our trip to Earth?"

"I am ready. I think that everything is ready. You will leave in four hours. It will be 2:00 a.m. in London, England, where you are going, Zejen. I will leave later when it is 2:00 a.m. in Ann Arbor, Michigan.

"Just call me Francis Nelson," Zejen said in English and tipped an imaginary hat.

"I wish I had a touch of your enthusiasm for this mission, Zejen." Sorn also spoke in English.

"Lieutenant Zejen, you must continue to work on the pronunciation of "m's" and "n's". You have not quite mastered them."

Jenxex couldn't help but notice Zejen's forced English.

"I know, speak English as though my life depended on it," Zejen said. His eyes met Som's.

"Our lives depend on a lot of factors right now, don't they, friend," Som said in the Chadran language.

VI.

It was difficult saying good-bye to Zejen four hours later. They would not meet again for six months. They would be linked to each other and the starship through the computer systems in their Earth homes. But they would live apart in two different countries of the world, carefully hiding their true identities and living under assumed names. He and Zejen had made two other trips to the planet's surface in preparation for living on Earth. This time when they transported to Earth they would stay and live there for sixteen months.

Jenxex would remain with the ship and complete its reconstruction. Jenxex would be the master of the ship until Som returned.

When it was his time to leave the ship, Som was eager to leave. Eager to move ahead with the next stage of his mission.

Jenxex initiated the transport controls. Ten minutes later Som's cocoon craft made its buffered landing in Michigan in a wooded area full of trees beside his new home. Som used his small spade to crack open the four internal joints of his craft. The craft began to crumble into tiny pieces as it had been designed to do. But the pieces of the craft were made of an indestructible material. The only way he could hide the fragments of this transport craft was to bury them.

And so Som dug with his spade, breaking through the cold earth that had only recently thawed with the coming of Spring. He enjoyed the physical act of digging. The dirt smelled good. He could hear the calls of tiny night animals, as he buried the warm fragments. Quietly, he walked the path through the woods to his earth home. Now as he stood with his feet planted on the soil of Earth he hoped he would succeed in his mission. If he did not, he would die.

VII.

So this was Earth. Richard Saxon sat on the grass in the spotty shade of a large oak tree.

What would they do to me if they knew who I was? Richard thought. A tiny red ant crawled on his hand, walked in a circle, and left.

What would they do to me if they knew that I had never touched a red ant before? If they knew that I could order a starship orbiting Earth to do a lot of damage to their world? Sorn looked up at the golden sun in the April sky and inhaled the fresh air.

Already I have enemies on this planet who would kill me, and I have been here for barely two weeks.

Richard jumped reflexively as a squirrel scampered near him on the grass. The squirrel was more afraid than he was when it realized how close it had come to touching the human's shoe. Richard was amused.

I don't know enough right now to know what can hurt me and what cannot. But showing my fear is foolish. He talked to himself silently. There was no one else to whom he could talk.

It was fascinating sitting here in the sunlight, watching the streams of humans bustle near him. Humans of all ages and sizes. The people all seemed to be so different from each other. Technology had not altered individuality as it had on Tethra. Or almost had.

Richard wore new jeans and a cotton shirt. He held a plastic cup of lemonade and sat with a small book beside him. This was supposed to be an acceptable way to sit and watch. He sat on the lawn of Raphael Hall, an old building near the heart of campus. Central campus buildings lined the streets for four blocks in one direction. In the other directions, shops and restaurants intermingled with the buildings of the University of Ann Arbor. Ann Arbor was a sprawling little city. Only twenty-five years ago it been a college town with barely 60,000 permanent residents. Then it had grown quickly, new technology had flourished near the university. Robotics, bio-genetic studies, and Pentagon defense research had settled here. Richard had chosen this place for the new tech businesses.

Richard liked watching the cloudless sky, a sky so blue that it made his heart yearn for Tethra. But today was not about yearning for Tethra. Today was about something new. Everything was new. The trees in their Spring growth, the patches of tiny clover in the green grass, it was all new. Tethran trees were huge and lush and wild. This little Earth was populated with little things. The largest things of Earth were small in scale to Tethran vegetation. Everything here had the feel of being rustic and tame and very old.

His concentration was broken by the voice of a slender young woman who stood in front of him. She had seen him watching her.

"Your eyes tell me that you can do a lot more than look," she said. Her smile was inviting.

"Not now," Richard answered. "Now I am only watching." But he drank her in with his eyes, and he wanted her. The woman shrugged her shoulders and walked away.

Not now, Richard thought. *But my hunger to be a part of you and all this world grows with every hour. And when I am ready to join you, you will all know it.*

VIII.

Sometimes he hated sleep. Tonight the nightmare recurred. In his dream he was on the bridge of the Stealthfire. He saw the Greole's face, the perverted half-human features, the lethal cavernous eyes. Sorn heard the crackling buzz of the Greole weapon, locking its energy field on his ship. The Greole Captain meant to capture, not to kill him. He saw the Greole interrogator, ready to torture him. Ready to turn his mind inside out and shred its reality. Ready to drain him of his life. But slowly, so that the Chadran Captain could tell the Greole something before the life force was gone. The Greole had no ethical restraints. Terror was their specialty. Whatever would be left of his body, the Greole would use in some way. They would violate the body once the mind was gone.

His body. His mind. Captain Sorn saw himself, a prisoner to a hundred deaths. He acted fast. He ran away.

Saxon-Sorn forced himself awake. He took three deep breaths. He felt mildly sick and dizzy. It was the food, the bitter-tasting water, the strangeness of Earth and its smells that made him sick.

It was the dream. Why did it haunt him so? This same dream had shaken him repeatedly. How had the Greole threat reached out to him here on this serene little spot in the galaxy of the Milky Way?

He consoled himself with his father's kind of wisdom. *One day the dream will fade. And the enemy will be defeated. The Greole try to rob us of the future. But the future is not theirs to own. The future belongs to God and not to his creatures.* Sorn's father believed in such things.

Sorn's Deist father believed in God. Deists believed in the future and in the power of dreams. If he hadn't loved his father so much he would have mocked his beliefs. Instead he ignored his father's beliefs. Until recently.

In the darkness Saxon-Sorn heard the quiet rhythm of the night crickets speaking. He felt a breath of cool, moist breeze blowing in through his open window. He rubbed his eyes and saw the night fading, changing into daylight, through his mini-blinds.

Everything was alive around him. He had survived. He had trusted the angel who had led him here. She was the last angel that he had seen.

Everyone on Tethra had seen angels and demons. Richard Saxon had never seen an angel on Earth. Perhaps there were none. Perhaps the humans of earth were pathetically alone.

Tethran Deists believed that God, the Infinite Creator, loved humans. But God's infinite greatness separated humans from God. The angels were the bridge between God and man. Deists said that humans could never see God. But humans could see the angels.

Sorn respected angels. They were powerful beings, motivated by a burning love for everything human. Some were mighty warriors. Some were tender, trustworthy guides. Some were peacemakers and creative geniuses. Sorn often trusted the angels he met. But he did not believe in God.

Sorn avoided demons. Though demons were fascinating at times. They could materialize in different forms. Demons teased and taunted and gave pleasure. But they also inspired murder and destruction. Demons made hate seem palatable. And you could rarely tell whether they were lying or telling the truth. Sorn loathed demons. Yet he could not visualize the dullness of life without them.

Lying here alone in the dark, Sorn wished that he could believe like the Deists. He wanted to believe that God was loving and good like the angels and that life was as simple as choosing the ways of God. But Sorn did not believe this. He did not believe in anything.

One day the dream will fade, and the enemy will be defeated, a sweet voice said in his mind.

Today is all you have. Tomorrow belongs to the enemy, another voice taunted.

And then he knew what it was that he really wanted. He wanted the future. He wanted this lost spot in space, this planet Earth, to hand him a promise, to fill in the quaking emptiness, the dozen hungers. He wanted it. He wanted it.

Fool. Go back to sleep, and stop wanting.

But the fool saw dawn peeking its light through his mini-blinds, and he reached for it. He reached for it.

CHAPTER
TWO
MAX TRAYTUR

Max Traytur sat in a large black velvet armchair, half-naked, sniffing cocaine. His was an expensive chair, befitting a man of his wealth and stature. He had dismissed the two frightened teenage girls from his bedroom when he was through with them. Now he relaxed in the cool darkness, having temporarily satiated his lust. His mind was empty, his body tired.

Max felt a deep chill rush through his spine and then, in the dreaded reddish heat of his aura, Natas, the demon appeared to him. Max was angry that such a pleasurable evening was being interrupted. Secretly, he was horrified by the demon. In spite of all the years, the horror barely mellowed. He tried to hide his fear. The demon was even more belligerent when it sensed fear.

Max came to respectful attention and waited for the demon to speak. It projected itself larger and taller than usual, touching the ceiling and periodically altering the lengths of its arms and hands. Max could not look into the hypnotic black eyes that changed shape with every mood. Instead he focused his attention by watching the demon's tiny nose and huge mouth open and close oozing sticky, dark drool. The sentient monster spoke.

"You realize something important is happening, or I would not be here." The demon's dissonant, disembodied voice was almost a whisper. Max strained to hear, not daring to miss a syllable.

"Teach me, great one," Max said, bowing his head.

"There is a spiritual event being born, a great event of massive consequence. I have been forbidden specific foreknowledge, but we can sense it, we can smell it coming, tormenting us, driving us to action. The single thing I know is the identity of the most important human. There is a triangle of three humans being formed. At the vertex of the triangle is a woman named Selina Devon. It is crucial that we destroy her. In crushing her, the triangle will never be formed, the event prohibited. She is Christian Under Protection. But I have found two wide channels of access to her through human violence." The demon's cold discourse was interrupted by his own burst of gleeful laughter. Max respectfully joined the laughter.

"There are two humans who could destroy her, one named Pinchard, one named Beckwith. I am going to torment them until they accomplish their own goals. I have much room with which to act." Natas clapped his hands until Max's head ached with the vibrations.

"How can I serve, great one?" Max asked, hoping to end this meeting with Natas as quickly as possible.

"Keep a watch on her. Learn her weakness and her strength. Join me in destroying her," the demon said.

"Gladly, great one. You know I hate women," Max said.

"That is why we chose you, ugly albino Traytur. She lives near you, in this Ann Arbor place. And you share with us a great hatred of women. We have always hated women. Since that first woman who crushed the serpent's head beneath her feet." The demon spat a thick wad of dark phlegm at Max's feet. Then he vanished, leaving only his scent. The disgusting scent caused Max to vomit as usual.

II.

Max Traytur slept for seven hours, methodically giving his body time for the effects of cocaine and his visit with Natas to wear off. He did not awaken refreshed. His left eyelid twitched. He was anxious to begin Natas' assignment. A visit from Natas was always a mixed thrill. There was the excitement of being called and of being important. There was the terror that he might fail in doing Natas' bidding.

Max blamed himself for Natas' grotesque apparitions. Natas could take other forms. He used to come to Max as a red-haired, impeccably groomed businessman with manicured nails and a winning smile. But once Natas appeared to Max in the same form as last night's drooling gargoyle. Max made the mistake of showing fear. Natas relished Max's fear. Now he always came to Max in a gruesome form. And Max had to hide every quivering blush of disgust and emotion.

Max lay on his luxurious king-sized bed, his red satin sheets clinging to his tall, thin body. He reached, pressed the button of his intercom, and ordered breakfast. Max walked toward the bathroom adjoining his master bedroom. He glanced at the wall above his ornate desk, covered with photos of himself at different ages. He reminisced with satisfaction about his past. He had come a long way in his fifty-one years. A long way from the skinny, anemic little Max Traytur of his childhood.

The sickly albino Max was unappreciated as a child. His father was a weak, pathetic man who offered Max love. Max did not want love. He did not want to receive love or to give it. Every act of love took something away from him. Every act of greed and selfishness gave him what he wanted. His father gave up on his psychotic mother when Max was ten. She refused treatment for her illness. When his father left home, he tried to take the children with him.

Max refused to leave his mother. He saw the chance to seize power in his home with his father out of the way. His mother was just a prop. She got her checks, and Max took care of everything. Max's way. His sister Sissy was eight. She was too afraid to leave the familiarity of home. Sissy had no one but Max to take care of her. Sissy obeyed Max slavishly. He punished her freely. Sissy was not bright, but she had been able to shoplift for him and to do all the chores.

Sissy was his first victim. But she was not the last. When she became pregnant at the age of thirteen, Max ordered her to have an abortion. She refused and ran away from home. Max did not mind her leaving. By now, he had other victims. And he was learning to victimize from a master, Loe Jones.

When he was nearly thirteen, Max met Loe. Loe was a respected drug pusher, always looking for new recruits to expand his successful business. Loe gave Max special attention. Loe recognized Max's talents for cruelty and lying. Loe taught Max how, unencumbered by scruples, he could have whatever he wanted.

Loe introduced Max to Natas on his sixteenth birthday. It was a disgusting ceremony, but Max was strong enough to mask his revulsion. He had become someone important, one of the initiated. That was all that mattered. Max became both a slave and a master that day. Natas accepted him. Natas, the powerful, the King-maker, promised to make Max one of his kings. More than anything else on earth, Max wanted power. Natas was power.

Max Traytur had no regrets, not one. All his moves had been smart. All his choices had been correct. Today he was wealthy. Wealth had bought him almost everything; a subservient staff, pleasures, status, comfortable expensive things. The only thing he could not buy enough of was power. He had power, and he always wanted more. More power. More excitement. For that he needed Natas. And they used each other.

All Natas asked of Traytur was a little favor here, a little assignment there. Natas needed human disciples for his killings. The sin had to come freely through human hands.

Max's first murder was uneventful. He had been able to control everything as needed, except the twitch in his left eyelid. His second murder brought him pleasure--peculiar, delirious pleasure.

"It was not the killing but the causing of pain that you enjoyed," Natas explained to Max. "And it was not so much the causing of pain as the exhilaration of power, the total power over life and death that you experienced. God made the life. You, Max, had the power to take it."

Max finished his warm croissant and Colombian coffee in the bedroom. He threw the Sunday newspaper on the floor. It was September 5, 1999. The world was in a constant state of change. The 1990s had been good to Max. He had seized many opportunities during the recession to strengthen his financial empire. He had benefited from others' suffering.

Max walked across the spacious hallway of his mansion and went to his private den, unlocked the door, and entered. He seated himself at the computer and began an information search on Selina Devon. Ann Arbor phone book, unlisted number. Override -- seek unlisted numbers. Selina Devon's name, address, and phone number appeared on his screen. In less than an hour, Max had a profile on the woman. He had even accessed her class schedule.

A trick of excellent fortune! Selina Devon's father was a wealthy businessman, an acquaintance of Max, a former "client." He could pass this information into the capable hands of his own Private Investigation Group (PIG). They could follow a sensitive version of their usual surveillance routine. Max was not only brilliant, he was also fast. Max needed no one.

III.

Michael the Archangel stood at his vantage point in the Inbetween Spaces. He was not on Earth and not in heaven. He stood at the shining Peak of In-between where he could watch over everything on Earth and drink in the power of heaven at the same time.

Michael and his kind, the angels, had been assigned to the Earthwatch by God the Father. Assigned to serve and freely choosing it, passionately drawn to it. Michael watched, looking on the children of

Adam and Eve, watching for their moves, waiting for their decisions which would mobilize the armies of heaven. The armies over which Michael was the Prince of the heavenly hosts.

Michael cringed at the sight of Max Traytur. Traytur was one of the lost. Traytur condemned himself to torment every day. There was little left of Traytur that was human. At least his body still rebelled at the presence of Natas. At least his body and a piece of his soul still vomited at the stench of Natas. Michael ached for Traytur. And he placed his hand on the hilt of his sword, wanting to defend the tormented human. Natas and his demon kind fed on human pain, working in the darkness behind their shades of deception. Natas was devouring Traytur, one morsel at a time.

But the problem was, Traytur didn't want Michael's defense. Traytur had rejected God and the Redeemer Christ and everything good. Traytur wanted counterfeit power and counterfeit happiness. Traytur wanted Natas.

Michael looked on Selina Devon. And as he looked on her, he saw the vision of the new thing rising across the beatific horizon of the Inbetween Spaces.

Michael caught the vision as it rose. The vision that had tortured Natas. The vision formed itself like a wondrous rainbow moving against the dark, gray sky after the rain. The vision had a name, the Tethra Triangle, a triangle in the colors of the rainbow, moving in the mists of uncertainty. There were three humans joined as one; two men and the woman Selina. It was their joining and their souls that made the Tethra Triangle. Together they formed the power that was to move the universe. Power that would force darkness back from the front lines and bring the light to a million-billion souls in a place where humans dwelled away from Earth. These humans were the lost children of Cain, and through the Triangle, they were coming home.

The angels lifted their voices in a song of triumphant joy. The music matted down the hairs that stood on Natas' head. Natas and his dark spirits let out their groans and anguished cries.

And as the angels sang and the demons wailed, it depended where you stood on Earth, which it was you heard, the joy of the angels or the horror from hell. But the worse place of all that a person could be on Earth was where he heard neither. Where it was silent. Where the human groped, and in groping, heard nothing. Heaven waited for him.

And hell waited for him. Because he was empty, empty at the bottom. And standing in that place, Michael saw Richard Saxon.

CHAPTER
THREE
PRINCESS STAR

Richard's pulse raced. The car whizzing by had nearly hit him. Richard paused at the curb as the muddy water from its wheels splashed across his shoes and knees. What if his step had been a few seconds faster or the car a few seconds faster? The driver coming around the curve had not seen him, and he had not seen the car coming. In the twinkling of an eye Richard would have been killed. Then his brains would have splattered across the chrome bumper or on the road. His signet ring could not have saved him. Nor the homing device planted in his watch. He would have died.

At home on Tethra they already thought that he was dead. Swallowed up into the universe. Here on Earth no one cared that he was alive. He cared. But he didn't know why. He was living dutifully, following the instinct to go on living. But empty inside.

He was like the empty wine bottle lying on the curb near his feet. Last night someone had desperately drunk the juice of that bottle. Someone had emptied it. And now the bottle had no purpose, no function. It did not know why it felt empty now nor why it felt full at another time. And it was lying there, waiting to be crushed.

Richard reached and picked up the dirty bottle. He wanted to save it. He wanted to take it home and wash it and take care of it. A well-dressed woman in an expensive car drove past him on the street. She stared at the bottle and then at Richard in his muddy sweatpants. She shot him a look of obvious disdain. Richard felt vaguely embarrassed. He nearly threw the bottle away. But he didn't want to. The bottle deserved to be saved. Maybe someone in the universe would reach to save him. Maybe someone just had. Maybe that is why the car had not hit and killed him. It was a pleasant thought. It was a stupid thought.

Why did he always think that if he lived one more hour or one more day, that it mattered? That something would make a difference? Why did he always think that the saving answers would come tomorrow? Hope had an annoying way of sticking to him. Tonight he was going to a dinner party, and he would meet new people. And maybe

one of them would matter to him. He stuffed the bottle in his pocket.
And kept on jogging.

II.

The evening came, and the party came. Richard behaved like
the perfect gentleman and treated his date, Myrna Smith, the way she
wanted to be treated. In fact, he did everything that was expected of
him. His computer and his valet had taught him the socially correct
behavior for the evening. He followed his date's polished lead in
socializing with the guests. Dr. Myrna Smith was a tenured English
professor. Richard was a new, part-time faculty appointee. He would
not ordinarily have been included in such an event as this evening's
dinner party hosted by the university president. But Myrna was a
divorcee, and she needed an acceptable escort. Richard was lonely, and
he needed to meet people.

Myrna was in her element, lavishing intelligent praise on her
colleagues, waiting for them to return the compliments. Richard was
soft-spoken and courteous. He had been on Earth for barely six months,
and so he still listened carefully to the foreign English language as it was
spoken. He was still guarded, careful not to reveal his ignorance of the
hundreds of double meanings and idioms which he did not understand.
He thought that he had mastered the new language aboard his starship.
Until he tried to speak it among the aliens. People often said one thing
and meant another. Or there were masked meanings within irony and
sarcasm. He loved the language of Chadra, and he missed it.

Richard looked at his watch. Forty minutes of cocktail hour had
passed. He was bored. He wanted to be alone. He remembered the long
months aboard his starship when he had longed for human company.
Now he was surrounded by humans, and he wanted to be alone. None of
them reached for him. None of them tried to look beyond his earth
persona to find the well-concealed Captain Sorn. He wore his Earth
persona convincingly. No one ever seemed to question that he was
anything other than what he claimed to be: a British-born gentleman
who was a businessman and a math teacher. He should have been proud
of his success at hiding himself from the aliens.

Richard moved away from Myrna. She barely noticed as he left
her and made his way past the groupings of people and through the
dining room. He opened the white French doors leading to the outdoor

patio. A cool September breeze refreshed him. He looked up at the thick slice of moon that brightened the night sky. His home was there with the stars.

Richard walked across the patio and followed the path that wound around the garden and its manicured shrubs. When he reached the end of the path he turned around and started back toward the house.

It was then that he noticed the silhouette of a woman in the moonlight. She stood alone on the patio. She was petite and shapely, with long curls reaching past her shoulders. Her face was tilted upward toward the night sky. She was still in the shadows, gripped by silent thoughts. She did not hear Richard approach. As his foot crunched a cluster of Autumn leaves, she was briefly startled. She glanced over her shoulder at the source of the sound. Richard was stunned by the beauty of the face that turned to him.

A smile started in her large, expressive eyes and then spread across her delicate oval face. She had wordlessly welcomed him from the instant of contact. Richard saw a smile that warmed and lighted two quadrants of the galaxy. His face was stilled with admiration. Their eyes fixated on one another. She seemed to see beneath his layers, baring him in the moonlight. For an instant their souls met. The night and its stars seemed to bless them. The breezes were soft against their skins. A piece of hair blew in her eye. Richard wanted to brush aside the hair, to touch her skin.

In an instant the silent spell was broken. Myrna burst through the French doors, thoughtlessly hurrying past the young woman. She hooked her arm into Richard's arm and nestled her head on his shoulder.

"I missed you, darling," Myrna said. "I just met the most fascinating man. Richard, you must come in and say hello. He would be good for your career."

Myrna talked rapidly, and Richard missed the rest of the words. He had lost his composure. He allowed himself to be moved past the woman in the garden without saying a word. Captain Sorn would not have done such a thing.

III.

Selina Devon stood quietly on the patio. She had looked hard at him. Somehow he had moved her. She saw his bright, intelligent eyes, his noble, understanding face. But she saw more. For the first time in her life Selina had seen a knight in shining armor.

IV.

The dinner tables were elegantly set. Large centerpiece floral arrangements crowded each of the tables in the president's dining hall. The entrees were deliciously tasteful and low in fat. The conversation was titillating as the academic upper crust dined. Richard felt detached, absorbed in his thoughts. He was not like these aliens, the degreed and the distinguished. He had tried to be like them. But he did not know them or understand them. He had worked so hard at becoming the correct Earth persona that he had forgotten to be himself. Suddenly it seemed very important to be himself.

Richard watched the beautiful woman whom he had seen on the patio. She was several seats away from him, across the table. She seemed to glow somehow. He was not sure whether it was the gold in her hair, the shocking green of her eyes, or some warm light from within her. He noticed other men watching her. In the full light of the dining room, her beauty was alluring.

Richard thought that she watched him also, out of the corner of her eye. Once she looked directly at him with her deep, enchanting eyes. He did not know the rules for flirting. On Tethra he would have taken that look as an invitation. He would have left Myrna and gone to her side. Here he was uncertain how to behave. She seemed to invite him with one glance, and in the next she turned her face away from him.

Richard decided that he would meet the beautiful woman. Myrna did not know her name, had never seen her before, was annoyed that he had asked. After that, Myrna kept a possessive watch on him, occupying his attention. As dinner ended, every space in the house seemed overcrowded with half-inebriated faculty making their last marks on the evening. Richard felt irritated and impatient as he waited in line for his coat. He spotted the green-eyed woman; she had moved near him in the crowd. Richard escaped Myrna's clinging presence. He knew that if he maneuvered quickly through the small groupings he would be close enough to talk to the beautiful woman. He could reach her if he pushed himself past the bookcase, beyond the credenza, a few more feet down the hall.

He was close enough to touch her. Richard placed his hand on Selina's shoulder. He felt a tingle of emotional electricity in touching her. Touching, a beginning, but not enough. He opened his mouth to speak.

"Dr. Saxon, I have a favor to ask of you."

It was the voice of the university president. In his preoccupation with the woman, Richard had clumsily brushed past the president, ignoring him. Richard could not ignore his voice. He turned toward Dr. Adams.

"Are you aware of the International Symposium being held in January by the School of Business Administration?" Adams asked.

"Would you like me to attend?" Richard responded. He had no idea what Adams was talking about.

"I would like you to participate on one of the panels."

Richard glanced distractedly over his shoulder as he watched the green-eyed woman disappear through the front door. His heart sank with loss and disappointment.

"I... I am honored by your suggestion, sir," Richard said.

"Am I keeping you from more important business, Dr. Saxon?"

Richard understood the annoyance in the president's voice. Adams was, in Adams' mind, the most important person at this gathering. Richard turned his full attention to the conversation.

Moments later, as Richard drove home in his car, he felt the hollow echo of loss. He was not sure how much he had lost. He remembered the smile that the woman had given him in the moonlight. He remembered the touch of his hand on her shoulder. On another day, on another planet, Sorn would have battled demons to win such a woman. On this planet, there were no demons, only puzzling manners. And he had lost the woman.

V.

Richard saw the lightning in the sky and heard the thunder. Six long days passed with cold and rain and wind. He had forgotten the energy required of his body in adjusting to winter weather. The people of Michigan called this season autumn. Most others would have called it winter. Sorn had not visited a planet during its winter months in three years.

His week had been filled with variety and challenge. He had gone to Chicago for a business meeting and had taught his first week of classes. The bleak September skies threatened rain as he walked across the campus. He felt empty and numb inside. He was going home to hours of loneliness. A drizzle of icy showers began to fall. He ducked inside a small, noisy restaurant and stood near the door, bracing himself for a downpour. Thunder crashed.

It was then that he saw her. Her huge green doe eyes were more beautiful than even his memory of them, her smooth oval face and pouty lips. Her golden curls were tied tightly in a twist behind her head. She was wearing a starched striped uniform, sipping coffee with two other uniformed women. This time nothing would get in his way. He walked directly to her table.

"I'd like to introduce myself. I saw you at the faculty dinner last Saturday." Richard looked in her eyes, ignoring her companions.

"I don't think that we actually met," she said. Her voice did not disappoint. It was soft like a purr, sweet like honey.

"My name is Richard Saxon. I teach mathematics here at the university."

"I am Selina Devon. These are my friends, Susie James and Rhonda Deshaw. We're nursing students. Would you like to join us?"

"Thank you. No. But I would like a word alone with you," he said to Selina.

"You really shouldn't beat around the bush like this, professor." Susie laughed sarcastically. Rhonda joined in.

Richard stiffened. It was another one of those colloquialisms that meant something incomprehensible to him. Selina didn't laugh. She smiled warmly.

She followed him to a corner near the restaurant door. White lightning flashed outside, illuminating her face. He had not realized how young she looked until now.

"I assumed you were a faculty member since you attended the president's dinner," he said.

"No, I'm a student. I was the date of a faculty member."

"May I take you to dinner sometime soon?" he asked softly. He stood very close to her.

"You're not married or anything?" Selina asked.

Richard was puzzled. He wanted to pour his heart out to her, lavish her with gifts. Make promises to her. That would have been the Chadran way.

Instead he answered, "No."

Selina studied him. His face was fascinating, his voice captivating, his accent not quite British. She could almost see the shining armor on the knight. She was pleased that he had found her and now pursued her with a sense of urgency. Looking in his eyes, she smiled. Richard felt his heart rate increase as the rays of her smile reached him.

"My phone number is not in the book. I'll write it down for you," she said.

"I'll remember it. Just tell me."

"Do you smile... sometimes?" Selina asked. And he looked into her eyes.

Fill me. Love me, he thought. But he said nothing. Instead he gently touched her cheek with his hand. And looked away.

VI.

Richard watched the way she moved as she walked toward him. Selina looked like Princess Star, the lithesome beauty from Tethran mythology. She seemed vibrant and mystical, unearthly in soft pastels and sequins. Richard felt pleasure at the sight of her. She had asked to meet him at the restaurant. Selina had been diplomatic, but it was clear that she did not want him to know where she lived. He was secretly pleased that she had changed her plans in order to have dinner with him the night after they spoke.

Richard was fascinated with her. Each time he saw her she seemed more beautiful. He had been right in selecting the finest restaurant, the softest candlelight in which to woo her. He had been right in choosing The Emerald Moon where they could talk for hours undisturbed and then hold each other as they danced to romantic music. Richard looked forward to seducing her.

The women of Earth loved such surroundings. Richard could relax here, but it was still uncomfortably foreign to him. The edge of tension would give him an advantage over her as the night progressed. The music, the wine, the right tender words, and he would be the one to

decide when and where they would make love. She had stirred his
sexual desire by walking into the room. He would arouse and control
hers.

Richard had grown accustomed to shallow conversation. He had
learned to conceal his soul as well as his Tethran identity. He was
skilled at listening and asking the right questions so that he could learn
from others without needing to talk about himself. But tonight
something new began to happen. He had not been prepared for it. He
would not try to stop it. This woman was different. She made him talk
about himself. Her words seemed to reach for his heart, wanting to find
it. Her eyes were like gentle probes, seeing things no one else could see.
Richard felt his loneliness quaking within him, longing for the touch of
her mind, the touch of her hand. He was startled that she seemed able to
affect him so deeply, so quickly.

Selina was indeed beautiful. He knew that beautiful women
were often easy to understand, expecting to be admired and served.
Selina did not seem to know that she was beautiful. She hesitated to talk
about herself. When she did, she talked about herself in a depreciating
manner, apologizing for her intelligence, only half secure in her
opinions. He was disarmed by this and by what seemed a fragile
vulnerability in her nature. She brought out the warrior in him. He
wanted to protect her from some enemy that stalked her. But he could
not name the enemy.

She was disarming him. At the same time she seemed
defenseless, unable to strike an attack. Perhaps this was what trusting
felt like. He had forgotten how to trust. He decided to probe her, not as
the dull Richard Saxon, but as Captain Sorn.

"I have a theory about you. Men usually ignore your mind.
They cannot see past your beautiful face. Am I right?" Saxon-Sorn
asked.

Selina was genuinely caught off-guard. She glanced into his
eyes and then at her wine glass. She noticed that Richard had not
touched his wine. She did not know that he would never touch wine.

"Are men interested in women's minds?" she asked.

"I am interested in yours."

"You are evasive in answering questions about yourself,
Richard."

"Why are you interested in my mind?" Sorn asked.

"I don't separate your mind from the rest of you. I'm an artist. We see things all at once, inside and out. If I see something wonderful in the shadows, I want to grasp it and paint it." Selina's eyes sparkled in the candlelight.

"Is that how you see me, something hiding in the shadows?" Richard knew that even Captain Sorn was melting under the gaze of this woman. He reached to hold her hand. He noticed a pink blush swell in her cheeks. She swallowed hard as he touched her hand.

"Let's not talk about me just now. I want to talk about you. Let us make a pact." He lowered his voice to an intimate whisper, "Tell me all about yourself. What you think. Who you are. And I will do the same for you." His voice was rich and warm.

Selina smiled. She nodded silently. *Had she just won this pact? Or had it been his own idea?* Richard was not sure. He did not care. She had tantalized his curiosity. She had blushed at the touch of his hand.

"Your kindness puts me at ease," Selina half whispered.

He would have killed to defend her in that moment. And then she opened up like a flower, freely showing him her world and her life through her eyes. Richard was enthralled with her. There were no games. No ploys. There was only honesty. He listened as she talked. He fell in love with her.

Selina was the oldest child and the only daughter of ambitious parents. She had been born and bred into wealth and was sent to a prep school which was so exclusive that her father had registered her for it at birth. While she used restrained language in describing her father Damien, the picture emerged of a powerful, willful man who insisted on molding his daughter into the image of her mother, a perfect debutante and socialite. He persisted in stifling Selina's "useless" artistic talents. He demanded that she embrace his values.

Damien Devon viewed Selina as a piece of property, someone to mirror his stature, reputation, and fortune. Her father had plans for her to marry "just the right man" who could strengthen his position in business and his status in the social world. He was grooming her for that end.

"You don't impress me as that sort of woman," Richard said.

"I never will be that sort of woman. These are tiny ambitions for people who have souls."

Richard laughed.

"Everything changed when I was sixteen," Selina continued. "My whole life changed. I met a priest who led me into the heart of the gospel. In the gospel I met Jesus Christ. There is a thing that Jesus said, 'You will know the truth, and the truth will set you free.'[1] I came to know who God is and who I am. I was set free from my father's ambitions. That same year my father threw me out of the house. I was scared... afraid of his anger. After that, I lived with my grandfather."

"Why did he throw you out?" Richard asked.

Selina hesitated to answer.

"I was becoming socially unpopular. I wouldn't... sleep with the right boys. The friction between my father and me has been intense since then. That was nine years ago. I'm twenty-four now.

"I agreed to attend Harvard for a year to please my father. But what I really wanted was to attend a program at the San Francisco Art Institute. So I transferred there. My parents refused to come to my graduation."

"Now you're a nursing student?" Richard asked.

"I went back to school for a second bachelor's degree. I want to be able to help people in some concrete way. Art is the passion of my life. But it is also my weakness. I do it for its own sake and nothing else. Art excludes people. I want to have a heart of service and love. I want to nurture and to give, not just to paint." Selina's eyes looked unusually lovely to Richard, as if they were sweetened with some magic. He felt as if he were lost in those eyes, in those words. He kissed her hand. Selina smiled.

"Your father must be proud of you today," he said.

"My father disinherited me four years ago. My grandfather left me money for nursing school. My father and mother have nothing much to do with me anymore." Selina's eyes were sad.

"So you have lost your parents?" he asked softly.

"And I have kept my soul," Selina said.

Richard saw beyond her beautiful eyes and into her soul. Into the granite core of conviction and courage. Her strength drew him nearer to her. He found himself lost in her eyes, speaking to those eyes. He found that he was warming himself on her burning embers--like a cold man drawn to a fire. He talked for a long time. He told her lies about himself. He told her all about his earth persona, the British

---

[1]

businessman who tried to become a scholar and now taught math in the midwest.

Selina looked into his eyes. "Do you know how I would paint your face if I were painting you?" she asked with her honeyed voice. "I would paint your broad shoulders, your strong square chin, the part in your blond hair, the wrinkles near your eyes. I would take time creating your eyes, deep, dark, brown eyes that turn pale gray when you speak of certain things. Eyes that dance with mischief and seem to be filled with suffering at the same time."

He was speechless. He was ensnared.

"You seem older than you look," Selina said.

"Why do you say that?" He knew that he looked young for thirty-five.

"You see things like someone who has matured through suffering," she said.

Richard had suffered. As a starfighter he had known losses and defeats. But he could not tell her about them. Except for one.

"I suffered when my father died." He did not lie now. "He died only recently. He was very good to me, very good to everyone. I went against my father's plans also. But my father broke tradition for me, so that I could do what I wanted with my life." Richard felt the fresh grief of losing his father. In the last year he had barely had time to grieve. Tears came to his eyes, and he fought them back. He pulled his hand away from Selina and signaled the waiter for a check.

"I have talked enough about myself for one night," his voice cracked with emotion. "I would like to dance with you before this evening is over."

He did not look at Selina. He knew that she followed him with those lustrous eyes that saw everything.

The musicians played a melancholy, tender instrumental number. The haunting sounds of a solo saxophone reached into the back of their minds. Richard held Selina close to him as they danced. She looked into his face.

"It's good to cry. Tears have healing power," she whispered.

Richard didn't understand his emotions or why he felt what he felt. He only knew that someone had broken through the cold isolation that had filled his last years. He only knew that she had taken a finger and lifted the dam that held back his need and his loneliness. He pulled her by the hand and led her quickly out the rear exit of the restaurant.

He leaned her against the icy wall of the building as a cold, wet snow trickled in his hair and down his back. He kissed her, almost savagely, then earnestly, then very gently. There were tears for his father in his eyes. He didn't know if she could see them in the dark. Then she felt them, warm salty tears brushing from his cheeks onto her cheeks. She moved her hand up to her lips, separating his lips, ending their last kiss. She touched his cheek with her hand. She wiped away his tears.

Richard longed to stay near her. He could feel the chill of winter penetrating his clothes as he stood with her in the dark alley. She was the only deep warmth he had ever known. He bent to kiss her again and then stopped himself.

"It's time to end this evening. I'll walk you to your car," he said.

"It's not late. Can't you stay a little longer?"

"No," he said. "I'm sorry."

They walked to her car in silence. Richard hated the silence. They stood outside in the dark parking lot. Selina leaned her back against her car and seemed to search his face in the shadows. He knew that they had touched soul to soul.

"Did I do something wrong?" Selina asked.

"Wrong? Everything about you is perfect."

"Will you tell me the reasons why you are running away so that I can fight them."

"Selina, just let me leave you. Let me see you standing here in the snow and remember how your warmth set me on fire. You deserve someone who will give you everything. I cannot be that person. I am only visiting... this country for a short time. If we fell in love, I would have to leave you anyway." He kissed her forehead and walked away. His words had betrayed his love for her. He did not give her a chance to speak. He did not look back.

He left her quickly, fighting against his desire for her. Richard felt angry and lost. He did not want to do the noble thing. He wanted to take her and sleep with her. He wanted to take everything he could of her while he was here on Earth. He wanted to squeeze her dry. He wanted to be filled up with her beauty and her warmth. But he did the honorable thing. Empty and aching, he drove away.

VII.

Richard's muscles were tense. Fury was swelling in his joints and tendons, waiting for release. As he drove home from The Emerald Moon the slippery roads made driving difficult. Wet snow fell hard and fast, melted on the windshield, and turned to icy slush on the roads. Richard could see Selina's beautiful face in the candlelight, a bittersweet memory to be purged.

Everything felt wrong. He deserved Selina. He had given up everything for Starfleet. He had sacrificed enough for Chadra. Only once had he lived with a woman whom he could call his own. He did not love her, but he needed her. She was not a wife, but a lover. A passionate, icy lover, Xysaratar. She was all intellect and lust. But so was he in those days. She had been killed accidentally in a technical field maneuver. And he had lived.

Now he had found a woman whose sensual warmth could tame his loneliness. And he needed to run away from her. The thought of leaving her was like a stabbing pain.

Everything felt wrong. He was a Tethran warrior living like a fugitive in this remote speck in the universe. He was a starship captain exiled from his ship and his mission. Richard prided himself on his cool thinking, his skillful control. Now he behaved like some cadet, some lovesick fool.

Richard drove his car east, far outside of town into a deserted country spot. He needed to split from his earth persona. He needed to release his anger. The biting winds and the wet snow blew in his face when he left the car.

Standing still, he concentrated on his hypothalamus region. He raised his body temperature to protect himself from the cold. He removed his scarf and coat and tie so that he could move freely. He was weary of the discipline of using earth-acceptable human energy. The anger surged through his veins. He walked toward a small sapling clustered among other trees in the field. He grabbed it with both hands, planting his feet hard in the earth. He uprooted the tree from the ground with his bare hands. It felt good. He did not need to hide the neon pink glow of his skin as his body strength increased. He ran to a small tree, grasping the diameter of its trunk with his arms and hands. It was difficult to move. He felt his muscles straining, sweat rising from his glowing pores. He relished the strain. The tree's roots groaned as they ripped from the cold, hard earth. He ran and leapt across the open field in surges of power and release. He was soaked in sweat and in snow that melted on his hair, his skin, his clothes. He ran hard for twenty miles. He was guarded and alert, watching in case some passing human might catch a glimpse of him. He ran back to his abandoned car, covering another twenty miles. He began to feel the physical exhaustion that he longed to feel. He began to feel release and relief. His mind was clearing. Everything would be all right.

Sorn stumbled, then walked to the two uprooted trees. He felt a sense of humor and mischief returning to him.

"Lightning must have struck these poor trees," he said aloud. Holding his two hands together palm to palm, he stretched out his arms and aimed them at the uprooted base of the first tree. He concentrated. His skin glowed neon pink. A thick bolt of electrical power shot from his finger tips. The tree roots blackened and burnt in a quick burst of flame. The wet grass stopped the fire from spreading. He breathed deeply and rested for a minute. He repeated the electrical charge on the second tree. It almost appeared that they were both struck by lightning. The smell of electricity and burning wood filled the icy air.

Richard picked up a cold piece of tree limb and used it as a brush to erase the traces of his footprints in the melting, mushy snow. He returned to the car, wet and exhausted. His body temperature began dropping. He was too tired to adjust it again. He put his coat back on and started the car heater. His muscles relaxed.

I can live without her. I can live without anyone. I have been trained that way. Richard ignored the stab of emptiness that accompanied the thoughts.

He had no use for further thinking. *The body heals faster than the soul. Let the body heal.* He played a disc on his car stereo. Rich, dissonant tones of mood music from a distant planet. He drove away fast, skidding on patches of ice.

Loneliness used to be like an annoying insect that would buzz near an open wound. You could brush it aside with your hand. Now Richard would describe loneliness as having great weight, dimension, and a force of its own.

Danger and labor wait at the horizon. Always the same, danger and labor and being alone. Three days from now I will see Frank Nelson, the only other person who matters. Tonight I know that a Tethran still lives in this body and that running always works.

VIII.

Seven angels encircled Richard Saxon's car as it sped through the cold night. They had cast a mist around him as he leapt through the fields at Tethran speed. It was not a mist that could be seen with human eyes. It was a smoke screen to hide Richard from the demons.

"The demons must never know who he is or from where he came. He treads on hot coals and broken glass and he does not even suspect it," the angel Ryan said. His crystal wings spread wide in their protective stance.

"I am thrilled that you six have joined me in defending him. Natas and his pinworms could eat my Sorn alive just now. On Tethra, Sorn could see the demons and their dangers. Here he is blind." The great heart of Megnal spoke. Megnal was Sorn's guardian. He was one of two Tethran angels permitted on the Earth.

"We will have more reinforcements when he joins with the woman."

"*If* he joins with her. The plan could go two ways."

"If it goes the second way, are we allowed to defend him with the full force of our swords?" Megnal asked.

"The moment we unsheathe our swords, we will attract the fires of hell."

"But you have not answered my question, Ryan. Can we defend Sorn either way?"

"We can. And we will defend him either way, fighting until we can no longer raise our dimming swords. But the truth is, we will lose without the woman's reinforcements."

IX.

Michael the Archangel watched keenly, poised to defend the Tethran, Saxon-Sorn, if only Saxon would reach toward God, seeking protection. But Saxon shied away from God, fiercely agnostic and staunchly independent. He left his naked soul exposed to great risk. He barely stood a chance of surviving what lay ahead of him. Unless the woman Selina could reach into his cold soul. Unless Selina could serve as the Truth Bearer, the changeling goddess, Princess Star, in whom Saxon secretly believed. Selina did hold the truth within her. Saxon wanted the truth without knowing it. Saxon was gifted, intelligent and strong. He had refused the little lights of truth that had been offered to him. And yet at times he sought truth in the most secret places of his heart. For this reason Mercy had granted Saxon seven protectors.

Michael stood ready, sensitive to the moves and calls of the children of Adam and Eve. Waiting for the whispers and the shouts of human prayer. When he served the people of Earth, Michael worked closely with them. The humans lived on a different plane, on a parallel plane. And although there was no cause and effect between his power and the humans' power, there was a relationship. It was the humans who walked on the front lines of the battles on Earth. It was the humans who chose, who battled for God and who called down power in prayer. It was the humans who rejected God, who hated and who called down demons for destruction. The actions of the humans were always profoundly important. And the dangerous thing was that the humans didn't always know this.

The one named Saxon-Sorn did not know this. Did not know that every move he made toward God or away from God was important. Did not know that all reality moved on two planes.

And then Michael saw it. Selina Devon's prayer leapt through the clouds, in all its strength and beauty, as penetrating as a point of light. He saw her prayer as only the heaven-born could see the abstract particles of the spiritual realm. Michael heard her prayer and knew its familiar rhythms. Prayer was like a homing device, calling on and drawn toward God. Michael turned his attention on Selina. And then he saw danger roaming in the skies. Natas himself was headed for the home of Selina Devon. She was dejected and alone, exposing to Natas a deep wound in her soul, a wound that had been inflicted by men. Richard Saxon had hurt her this night, and the wound was open.

Michael knew that he could not reach Selina in time. In the matters of the people of Earth and the things of Earth, the angels were subject to the factors of time and space. Michael would instead send Natas a message and bind Natas with a display of power.

Michael summoned his angels in the Ann Arbor place. He called seven captains and seventy of their warriors, and he pulled them from their posts. Michael watched as his commands came into their minds and the seventy-seven angels sped to the destination to which they had been ordered. They flew to Selina's home, surrounded the property line of her house, and placed their hands on the hilts of their swords. They arrived only seconds before Natas.

Natas raged at the sight of them! He spread out his black wingspan to look mighty and terrifying. The angel captains faced him eye-to-eye and did not flinch and did not speak.

The angels and the demons did not touch the physical world with their forms. But the physical world could not ignore their presence and their power. A cold wind blew hard around Selina's house. It swayed the trees and rippled the waters in the river that flowed behind her house.

Natas swooped up, then down across Selina's house, to taunt the angels. But Natas knew that where there were seventy angels and seven captains, a thousand could be summoned in an instant. And he was not ready for that. Natas fled.

Michael smiled. He looked on Selina with love. Selina was not ready, either. Not ready to face Natas one-on-one. The day would come when she would be ready. It was not far away. But the Holy God would not tolerate Natas' attack on her too soon. Michael ached for Selina. For the pain that lay ahead. For the battles. For tomorrow.

CHAPTER
FOUR
ROSET

"Freddy, I tell you I am spooked by this. Last night I was at the office at 2:00 a.m. sitting next to my computer terminal. I was preparing for that God-awful budget meeting we have twice a year. I just had to stay until my numbers looked good. Anyway, I had my terminal turned off when all of a sudden the screen came on by itself. And *someone* broke into the ROSET files that Max Traytur ordered me to hide in our company system. Traytur said no one would look for anything unusual in a baby formula company's records."

"What do you mean *broke* into the secret ROSET files, Theo?" Freddy Wader asked.

"Just that--someone went into the system and searched the files right before my eyes. They knew exactly what they were looking for: updates on recent activities. Then they exited from the system without leaving a trace."

"Trouble, buddy, this sounds like trouble."

"That's what our programmer said. I asked him the next morning how someone could sneak into my private files, bypass my passwords, and leave without a trace. The programmer said it would take a high degree of skill for a hacker to do that. That whoever it was had to know everything about me." Theo talked fast.

"It happened four months ago in exactly the same way. I was here late working on the budget."

"You'd better tell Max Traytur ASAP," Wader said.

"Traytur will barbecue me on an open pit! I can hear it now. 'Someone has computer access to our secret ROSET files. But I haven't a clue who it is. And they left no trace, I can't even prove that they did it, but I saw it happen!'" Theo mocked.

"You've got to do something about it. Call Stenroos at Interpol. He's got all kinds of connections. He'll know what is going on."

"Just so Traytur doesn't find out why I called Stenroos. Just so *no one* tells him." Theo said.

"Not me, buddy. I wouldn't look good either with an apple stuck in my mouth roasting on an open fire," Wader said.

II.

Richard was beginning to relax now that he had reached his hotel and had finished registering. He was looking forward to meeting with Frank Nelson. They had not seen each other in six long months. Richard hoped that Frank was being cautious. They would check Frank at customs when he flew into Toronto from England. They would search for Frank's weapon--and hopefully not find it.

Richard double-checked himself. He patted the slim lump strapped to his chest, the narrow, flat object that fit into the palm of his hand. It would calibrate the dimensions of any room and would distort all sound leaving the room. The sound distort would jam any mechanical bugging and recording devices. Voices would sound garbled to anyone listening nearby with non-mechanical means. He checked the thick tubular lump strapped below his left elbow. It was his Tee-spray gun, a silent, fatal weapon that would stop the heart of an aggressor. On Tethra, they needed these two devices. Because of ROSET, they would probably need them here.

Richard paid little attention to the two men who got on the hotel lobby elevator with him. Until one of the men spoke to him.

"I say, old boy, is that you, Gibbings?" A thickly-built, towering man stood on Richard's left side. He was staring at Richard as he addressed him.

"I'm afraid not. You are mistaking me for someone else," Richard said.

"Come now. Let's not be daft. I haven't seen you in twelve years. At least twelve years. How have you been?" the man insisted. He moved closer to Richard and smiled broadly. "It's me, John Joe Winslow. I haven't changed that much, Gibbings."

"I don't mean to be rude, but I've never seen you before in my life," Richard said. He was becoming tense. The second man, standing on his right, also moved closer to Richard and began studying him. But the second man said nothing. *Stay cool, Richard. Don't overreact. You don't know that these two men are from ROSET.*

The elevator doors opened. And the towering man who called himself Winslow suddenly reached his strong hand and placed it on Richard's left elbow, touching his Tee-spray gun. Richard dropped his briefcase and grabbed Winslow's wrist and twisted it. Just enough force to stop the man, to gauge Winslow's strength. Not hard enough to snap the bone.

"Good God, man! What are you doing?" Winslow shouted.

The man on Richard's right grabbed Richard's right arm. Richard grabbed the other man's wrist with his left hand. Neither man was very strong. Neither man was reaching for a weapon, nor taking an aggressive stance. These two were harmless... probably.

"Let go of my wrist, you're hurting me!" the second man shouted. Richard released them both and watched them. Neither of them had any combat training, or they could have moved against him in that instant.

"Whatever are you doing, sir?" Winslow exuded indignation.

"You grabbed my arm before I grabbed yours," Richard said softly. He was confident now that he could disable both of them. Even if they moved quickly.

"So I did. Simply a friendly gesture. No reason to break both our wrists," Winslow said.

"I'm sorry. I meant no harm. Just as you meant no harm," Richard said.

"Next time you choose to annoy a stranger, Winslow, don't pick some martial arts expert," the shorter man said as he hurried off the elevator. Winslow followed him. He heard the shorter man speak in a hushed voice. "He didn't look at all like Gibbings to me. Can't quite place his accent, either."

Richard stood alone in the elevator as the doors closed. How would he recognize an aggressor from ROSET if he ever met one? How would he snap the correct neck or wrist before they injected him with some chemical drug that would cause his instantaneous death? Physical force he could fight. Guns he could fight. But the man-made drugs of Earth he could not fight. Because the drugs would kill him before his signet ring was removed.

Richard reflexively rubbed his platinum signet ring, his automatic escape device. He reminded himself that he was safe anywhere. All he had to do was remove the ring from his finger, and in five minutes a transport craft would form around his body. Five minutes later he would be aboard the *Stealthfire*. Jenxex could administer first aid. It was fail-safe. Just as his watch was fail-safe, equipped with a homing device that would summon the starship, enable the starship to find him and to assist him. It was simple enough to press the small buttons on the underside of his watch.

Richard reached his hotel room and looked out the window from the twenty-third floor. The city hid an enemy from him. But he was hiding from the enemy as well. And his starship was hiding from everyone--time-warped four minutes into the future. One surge of power hid the ship in the future. One surge of power would bring it back to the present. Only the transponder satellite was in the present. He and Frank Nelson lived secret lives. They did not even know each other's addresses. They communicated only through the starship computer.

Richard had come to know the enemy and to hate it: ROSET, the Research Organization for the Study of Extra-Terrestrials. He had not taken it seriously at first. An organization created to study clues leading to the discovery of extra-terrestrials. It was a respected, legitimate organization with members in six countries. But the ROSET enemy was the covert, illegal, underground branch of the organization. It was a group of fanatical misfits. But powerful ones. Powerful enough that they knew how to hunt people, torture them, dissect living humans, and then hide all the evidence of their crimes. They committed their tortures and murders in the belief that their victims were aliens and dangerous to the human race. It had taken the starship computer time to find ROSET's hidden files, to discover their web of deception. Every four months the starship computer searched for clues to ROSET's recent activities. Usually only completed "interrogations" or "burials" were recorded in the files.

"Never underestimate the enemy," the Rule of Battle taught Richard as a cadet. The Rule assumed that you would know the enemy. That you would know his or her face. Not here on Earth.

Richard welcomed the knock on his hotel room door. It had to be Frank. And he was tired of being alone.

CHAPTER
FIVE
BROTHERS

Loneliness rose to the surface like a wave of nausea, pressing against his facade and his breeding, almost forcing its way into an expression of tears. Richard embraced Frank Nelson, not wanting to meet his eyes.

"You're a sight for sore eyes," Frank said, his manner jovial and relaxed. "Don't I sound very American?"

"Indeed," Richard said using his most contrived British accent.

Frank Nelson looked strange in his gray suit and tie, his hair cropped short like his Earth persona, an American businessman. He carried a black leather briefcase. Frank was dark-skinned, hefty, and emotional, like many of his Bidzidularn race.

Frank studied his friend Saxon-Sorn. Richard Saxon's thick blonde hair was longer than his own. Richard's large brown eyes seemed to emphasize the whiteness of his fair skin.

"You look pale, but well, sir." Frank smiled.

"I always look pale to you." The two men laughed, a laugh of release.

Richard locked his hotel room door. He removed the sound distort from under his shirt and pressed the yellow button to activate the device.

Richard sat down, and Frank followed his lead.

"Let's discuss business later. How have you been?" Richard asked.

"No one asks that question like you, sir. I am feeling better than I've felt in years! Our visit to this planet is like extended shore leave for me. Except that here on earth I have money and power and friends. The way I spend money, Jenxex may need to confiscate a few more gold bars from the Arabian oil sheiks." Frank laughed. "Don't worry, sir, I am not drawing attention to myself. I am sure it means nothing to you. But it is a new thing for me to have unlimited funds."

"Tell me about these friends of yours," Richard asked.

"I have a lover. She has lots of friends. She is my passport to a social life," Frank said.

"I know that it's none of my business. But you are married to a loyal Chadran wife, aren't you?" Richard asked softly.

"Loyal wife?" Frank snickered. "True marriage is not for starfleet officers, you know that. Starfleet knows that. There are advantages for my family if I remain married. My wife and sons have the security and status of my starfleet salary. I have the satisfaction of knowing that my sons are being provided for and that we are legally joined. But that is what marriage means for me and my wife. We both take lovers whenever we need them. We have only seen each other twice in ten years. Right now my wife does not expect me to return to Chadra alive."

"And you. Do you believe that you will return to Chadra alive?" Richard asked.

"Yes. Absolutely." Frank responded spontaneously. He went on. "But I barely think of Chadra or of Tethra these days. I have a new motto by which I live, an expression from the wisdom of Earth--'*Carpe Diem*, Seize the Day.' It suits me. I have a home here on Earth in beautiful Great Britain. I have a lover who knows half the people in London. She works in an orphanage, so I have not only adults for friends, but a few children. I play with children in the orphanage. I rarely played with my own sons on Tethra, I was only landside for short intervals. The English have gradually accepted me. They attribute most of my 'oddities' to the fact that I am an American."

"Just as we planned."

"And what of you, Richard? Do the Americans of Michigan find you to be an odd Briton?"

"Those who notice me. Most people ignore me. In its own way it is rather pleasant being ignored," Richard said.

"That is a new experience for you, good Captain, being ordinary! The people of Chadra would be shocked to think that you could be ignored." Frank went on. "This planet is reviving me!" he said with a little too much enthusiasm. He softened his voice. "The war was deadening my insides, like an anesthetic, slowly working its way through me. All I have thought about for the last six years has been the *war*. Now I can think about *life*." Frank looked past Richard, staring out the window.

Richard understood. Frank had been in starfleet for the past twelve years in the Domestic Defense Forces surrounding Tethra. It was the hardest place to serve. With all the rigors of starfleet and none of the satisfaction of exploration. Richard had spent only four of his starfleet years aboard military starships, three of those years he had been in starbase outposts as a tactician. It had only been in the last year that Sorn had been near battle, serving in a reconnaissance ship.

"You deserve a chance at living," Richard said. Frank looked ashamed for admitting his weakness. He changed the subject.

"Does this planet have what it takes to refresh you?" Frank asked Richard.

"I don't know what I need. And so I don't know whether it is here or not."

"Will you know it when you find it?" Frank asked. It seemed a bold thing to ask his captain. It came out of his mouth too fast.

"I don't expect to find it. But yes, I will know when I find it," Richard said.

There was tension between them. Perhaps Frank liked being on Earth a little too much. Perhaps Frank's contentment with his life was emphasizing Richard's emptiness. Richard wanted to talk about life and about happiness and about how to find it. But Frank had already opened his briefcase, and now he handed Richard a report full of graphs and figures.

"Any problems with your assignment?" Richard asked.

"No problems. Who cares about an 'advanced' nutrition-extraction food processing plant outside of London. The way the world economies work, if you do not advertise, no one knows about your product. We will have double the quantity of food supplies that we will need for our return trip to Tethra, far ahead of schedule."

"That's excellent. Then, maybe you can help me with my assignment." Richard lowered his voice. "I have moved slowly these first months, learning the subtleties of maneuvering in their business world."

"Maneuvering and learning when to strike--these are definitely your strengths," Frank interjected.

"There are similarities between doing battle and doing business," Richard said. "The computer confirmed what the people of Bay Tech told me. Theirs is the only company in the world to manufacture uranium pellets with resilient coating. I visited their plant in San Diego to examine their products and methods. In terms of purity and gram weight their pellets are exactly what we need. The coating is inferior. But if I ask them to change the product I would be indicating that we will use a different technology than the rest of Earth."

"I don't think that they will conclude that the uranium will serve as vitamins for a starship," Frank said.

"No, but we are moving in a sensitive realm. Bay Tech manufactures a very specific product, custom designed for use in nuclear reactors. There is only a scattering of nuclear power plants around the world.

"I need to ask them to manufacture a huge quantity of pellets, by their usual standards. They will be happy to receive my money and my contracts. But I need a secure cover story. I am telling them that I represent a newly developed nuclear power plant in the Ukraine. This facility will account for the quantity of pellets I need to order for the ship. I can make it look believable on paper. But, in the course of the next nine months I will need to produce evidence of the physical power plant and at least one business client in the flesh, in order to validate my story. The Bay Tech people may seriously question my story if I cannot produce at least one client. This is where you come in."

"We agreed never to be seen in public together," Frank said.

"Can you think of another solution?"

"I don't like this."

"Neither do I. I am drawing too much attention to myself in this work. My 'clients' will be demanding a sizeable quantity of pellets from Bay Tech. Without intending to, I will appear to be a powerful person, responsible for contracts in the realm of hundreds of millions of dollars," Richard said.

"Sometimes I cannot help but think that we should do this in the way that is most simple for us. Seize their manufacturing plant. Enslave their workers until they produce what we need, and escape from Earth in a cloud of fog." Frank waved his arms.

"I have already looked into that possibility. Bay Tech has national security ties to the U.S. armed forces. They produce components and uranium needed in U.S. nuclear defense systems. Jenxex accessed armed forces' top-secret files to discover ties with Bay Tech. If we tampered in any way with Bay Tech, we would be tampering with the armed forces of a powerful nation."

"Everything you say makes the situation sound worse."

"If we needed to fight their armies, of course we would succeed. However, we would leave a blood bath behind us," Richard said.

"So we confine ourselves to these people's methods. We put ourselves in vulnerable positions in order to protect them from our own power." Frank was agitated.

"We try the way of peace first. As if it were the only way." Richard tried to be appeasing. He forced a smile. Frank did not speak for several minutes. He stared at his folded hands, thinking.

"I can train for this role of an Ukrainian nuclear power plant client. But please don't ask me to acquire a new accent. The use of English is enough of a challenge for me. The British are periodically tormented by my choice of words," Frank said. Richard was relieved.

"We can make this work. We need to add a few things to your personal file and resume and feed it into the computer. They will not check your background until they meet you in December," Richard said.

"December? So you have planned every detail?" Frank seemed impressed.

"Not everything. My own file is inadequate. We created my earth persona in my first two months on Earth. There were things I did not know then that I know now. But I cannot change my file in the computer. Bay Tech has scrutinized me by now."

"Thank God you are the one securing the uranium and that I came to Earth with a genius. All I have to do is manufacture nitrogen-packed nutrition sources like they used in space travel six centuries ago," Frank said. His sense of humor was returning. "Richard, I was enjoying myself until this meeting. I'm beginning to think it would have been better if we had found an oxygen-water-uranium-rich asteroid, instead of Earth. If I didn't trust and admire you so much I would never go along with this."

"Admire me? Are you still joking?"

"Of course I'm not joking. How could you not know that I admire you. Half of starfleet admires you! The other half are idiots," Frank said.

"What could I possibly have done to attract the admiration of Starfleet? No, let me ask *you*, what have I done to deserve *your* admiration?" Richard asked. He studied Frank's face for honesty.

"You really don't know, do you? I assumed that anyone with your quality of greatness would know that he was great. I'll tell you what I admire. At first, I admired you simply because you joined the working class and took on the rigors of starfleet when what you could have done was wallow in the aristocratic luxuries of your class. But since serving as part of your crew, my admiration for you has tripled. You are the kind of leader who makes every person around you feel as though he or she is valuable, some sort of priceless gem. You don't waste anything or anybody. You would probably even use a Greole on your crew if the Greole had a talent that we needed. You would find a way to reign in his twisted insanity, and you would make him valuable."

Frank surprised Richard with his enthusiasm. Richard was deeply moved. And he was embarrassed.

"I could go on," Frank said.

"Don't do that to me."

"Then I will change the subject," Frank said, looking at his watch. "There is one last thing I wanted to discuss. Something important."

Richard nodded. Then he looked directly at Frank. "You are a gem, Ont. I didn't make you into one."

II.

"Are you ready to hear some facts that will challenge your roots, your identity?" Frank asked.

"You've caught my attention," Richard said. His water glass was empty. In fact both bottles of Evian mineral water which they had ordered from room service were also empty. Their meeting had lasted for a short two hours. They were enjoying each other's company. Since coming to Earth, they rarely found themselves completely relaxed in the company of others. They always wore the masks of their Earth personas, and deep inside they were always someone else.

"We are natives of Tethra, and we have assumed that somehow, thousands of years ago, Tethran space travelers must have colonized Earth. That the original starship and records of that first colony were lost," Frank began.

"*You* have assumed that, Frank. I find it more plausible to believe that something like the Changelings brought the first human colonists to Earth. Tethra did not have the capacity for space travel thousands of years ago. There have been humans on Earth as long as their have been humans on Tethra," Richard said.

"Longer."

"Longer?"

"There is clear evidence that humans existed on Earth 36,000 years ago. Humans who used tools to make tools, and who made jewelry for themselves. The anthropologists call them Cro Magnon man. But there were humanoid primates even before Cro Magnon man. There were primates who used rudimentary tools 2,400,000 years ago." Frank's eyes grew wide with excitement as he continued talking.

"Some people on Earth believe in a theory of evolution in which man evolved from ancestral primates. And there are those who believe that even if primate species were evolving, there was a point at which human beings were created with distinct souls and abilities, different from any other primates that had ever lived.

"But either way, Richard, there are *no* close biological ancestors to man on Tethra. Not only that, but there is a unity and purity about the genetic make-up of all life on Earth--human, animal, plant. Every life form is composed of a common genetic material. Everything belongs here on Earth. On Tethra we have two strands of genetic groups. There are what we call the 'simple species', composed of a genetic material similar to man's, and the 'complex species' of plant and animal life which are genetically 'alien.'

"You, Richard, were the first to observe that Earth humans were genetically untampered. Almost nothing has been genetically altered by man on this planet. A monk named Gregor Mendel pioneered the field of genetics in 1866. Only since then have there been efforts at what they call 'genetic engineering.' But it is child's play compared with Tethran science. All Tethran human life has been influenced by genetic engineering. We have our telepathy, our physical strength, and our warrior's skills because of genetic engineering. If the Genetic Protection Wars had not been fought and won 2,000 years ago, all Tethran human life forms could be genetic monsters like..."

"...the Greole. It makes you want to shudder, doesn't it?" Richard finished Frank's thought.

Frank lost his concentration, contemplating the perversion of human nature which had developed with the Greole. Half-human monsters who could breed worse monsters. Humans who could suck blood like bats, run like cougars, secrete scents like skunks, see in the dark like owls, etc. And each time a 'genetic change' was made it altered the mind and the sanity of the human part.

"The technology of Earth has not reached the point where they can create genetic monsters. But one day soon it will. They should be warned," Richard said.

"They should be stopped," Frank blurted. He reached anxiously for an empty glass, looked inside the glass and put it down. Then he went on.

"But here's my theory. What if the humans of Tethra were natives of Earth and alien to Tethra? What if the theoretical star travelers, which mythology calls the Changelings, what if these creatures brought humans from Earth to Tethra? In that first starship they would have carried not only human beings, but also pairs of animal and plant life forms to sustain human life, just as our journey ships transport plant and animal life for long term travel."

"Like Noah's ark," Richard said.

"What is that?"

"Something I read somewhere. I didn't mean to interrupt you."

Frank continued, "Assume that the Changelings brought the humans and their native plants and animals to Tethra. But they needed to take things a step further in order for the humans to survive on Tethra. They needed to genetically alter many of the plant and animal species of Tethra so that these life forms would support human life.

"What if the Changelings did not really change themselves at all, but they were capable of changing other life forms through genetic engineering? This would explain the presence of the 'simple' DNA strands in the Tethran humans and the 'complex' strands that pervade Tethran plant and animal life. Complex because they contain alien DNA as well as native DNA. The genetic scientists, the Changelings, would have seemed like gods and goddesses to the primitive humans whom they brought to Tethra," Frank said.

"Tethrans have always been obsessed with genetic science. Somewhere back in time maybe they had the idea that it would make humans become gods and goddesses like the Changelings," Richard said.

There was a long silence in the room as the two men absorbed the gravity of these ideas. Richard broke the silence.

"The ancient Egyptians, Indians, Chinese, and Mesopotamians developed mathematics five thousand years ago at exactly the same time that we were discovering nuclear physics, robotics, and cybernetics on Tethra. It has been fascinating studying mathematics from the Earthborn perspective. But this doesn't all make sense, does it?" Richard asked.

"Only one thing makes sense. Your exasperating backward tale of the Changelings. But with one twist to the story. The Changelings brought humans from Earth to Tethra thousands of years ago. And the Changelings could not resist passing on their science to us Tethrans before they left us," Frank said.

"Why do you think they gave us their science?" Richard asked.

"So that one day we would have the science, the ability to come home to Earth," Frank answered quietly.

"Yes. Yes, I think that is what happened," Richard said. There was a smile on his face as he spoke. Frank had used science as his method and had come to the same conclusions which Richard had arrived at through intuition.

"If this is home, it is even more important that we do not bring death and destruction here," Richard said.

"If it can be avoided."

CHAPTER
SIX
OPENINGS

Richard felt the music moving inside of him, rich, victorious swells of song, reverent music exultant with courage. He sat in the front row of a cavernous cathedral. He had never been in such a place, an ancient place full of history, towering stories above him. He did not know why he was there. He only knew that he belonged. His eyes examined the intricate details of lavish architecture. And then they moved across the huge stained glass windows that lined the walls of the building. He did not understand the unfamiliar stories that the pictures in the stained glass portrayed. He liked being here.

Richard was not surprised when he saw Selina. Selina stood in front of a massive choir of red-robed singers, standing in rows like some sort of honor guard. Selina glowed, joy emanating from the core of her. She was beauty and serenity. Everything in him stirred with longing and excitement, with hunger to share in her joy. Richard felt the dream pulling away from him. He did not want to leave it. But he could not make it stay. When he awoke from his dream he lay still in bed, absorbed in the rich, evocative swells of emotion in his soul.

Dawn's light was hidden behind dreary rain clouds. But he knew that it was morning. He heard a flock of birds outside chirping loudly as they flew south for the winter. There was a strange awakening in his mind, as if he had discovered a lost sense among his senses. If this woman Selina could lead him to even a piece of this joy, even a shadow of this hope that the dream had offered him, then he could not stay away from her. He laughed at himself. Sorn had tried to practice cynicism. He had criticized the spiritualists and Deists of Tethra who claimed that dreams could hold important meanings. These people said that dreams should be valued both for their healing power and their prophetic glimpses into the future. Sorn thought that they slaughtered science with their theories. If they were wrong they could be ignored. And yet... if they were right, then this dream was a promise to be pursued.

Richard could deprive himself of the love of a woman. But he could not deprive himself of a chance at finding out the meaning of his life, to fill the emptiness. He had changed on his journey to Earth. *Have*

I become such a fool, he thought, *to pursue the promise in a dream? Yes,* he answered himself. And he thought about her eyes. And he thought about her lips.

II.

Richard sent her two roses and an elegantly simple pair of emerald earrings. A card accompanied his gift. "Forgive me for my clumsiness. When I call you again, please don't hang up. Richard Saxon."

It was not the earrings that won Selina. But he had won her. His intelligence had frightened her; his kindness had relaxed her. She had been herself with him at the restaurant. She had not held back from him. And when he abruptly ran away from her, she felt his rejection in that deep part of her that she had protected from other men.

And yet now, when he was calling her back to him, he was accepting her on a deeper level also. Selina was ready to take a risk with him--but wise enough to think about the cost.

She looked at the earrings and at his card. Then she pressed the card against her heart in the pocket of her blouse. He lost no time in calling her.

Selina felt anxious when she heard his voice on the phone. She wished that his voice did not sound so sweet and so rich.

"I would like to see you again. When will you be free?" Richard asked.

"I don't have any plans for Friday night."

"What about tomorrow night?"

"Wednesday?"

"Yes."

"I can't get together with you on Wednesday. I don't get off duty at the hospital until 7:00 p.m., and then I exercise on Wednesdays. I jog and swim at the Campus Athletic Building." Selina thought she had said no to Wednesday night. But Richard Saxon was determined, even aggressive. It was a pleasant change, to have a man pursue her. So many men blew away like feathers if a woman seemed hesitant or unsure in her response to them.

She was unsure of Richard. Even a little afraid of him. No one had been able to sweep her off her feet like he had on their first date.

Sweep her up, then drop her. Then apologize with such charm and sincerity that she wondered why she ever doubted him. He was an enigma, and maybe a dangerous one. But she couldn't resist him. And knowing that, why bother trying to run away from him? Selina thought.

So now that it was Wednesday night she braced herself as she saw him walking toward her. She stood at the pool entrance to the women's locker room. There was a collection of noises and smells in the athletic building. She heard a basketball bouncing on the hard wooden floor in the gym across the hall. The music in the aerobic class was too loud. She could already smell the chlorine coming from the pool. But all the sounds and smells seemed to fog up as she saw Richard walking closer to her. He was dressed casually in a sweater, slacks, and running shoes, and he looked younger than when she had last seen him. He was big and noble looking, attractive and kind. So kind that Selina felt all her defenses melting, and she found herself smiling at the sight of him.

"I don't deserve a greeting like that," Richard said, standing very close to her.

"Like what?"

"You have a smile like the sunrise," he said. He looked so intently in her eyes that she thought he was going to kiss her right there in front of everyone. But he didn't even touch her. Or perhaps he already had kissed her, just by looking in her eyes.

"I usually come here to exercise alone," he said softly. It was as though he was confessing to her that he did everything alone. And that he was lonely. Selina didn't know why she thought she heard all those things in his simple statement. She only knew that he was drawing compassion from her. And that she wanted to give it. She wanted to give him too much. She had to be on her guard.

Selina finished swimming her laps before Richard did. She climbed out of the pool and patted her body with a towel. She was cold, and so she slipped her long turquoise sweatshirt over her arms and zipped the zipper to the neck. The soft fabric was heavy and warm and reached to her knees.

Selina sat next to the pool and watched Richard finish swimming his laps. She had never seen a better swimmer in her life. His strokes were so powerful and swift that it only took him five or six strokes to cross the length of the pool. He swam for another forty minutes, then slowed and came to a smooth stop. For an hour he swam like an olympic master, and now he was barely winded as he lifted himself out of the pool. He was a solid block of muscle and beautiful to watch.

Richard did not bother to brush the water from his eyes. He looked directly at Selina and winked a greeting to her. But he did not smile. He did not bother to dry himself, tying his white towel around his waist and walking toward Selina.

"Did I keep you waiting long?" he asked.

"Not long. I enjoyed watching you swim." Selina restrained herself from commenting about his powerful endurance and his strokes. He was not the kind of man who wanted compliments. He was very skilled. It was only the half-skilled who wanted praise. Selina stood up from her bench. She felt small and self-conscious standing beside him.

Richard reached his wet hand toward her. He gently stroked her hair and touched her cheek ever so lightly with the palm of his hand. Then his hand moved to the top of her zipper and then his other hand was next to the zipper.

Ever so gently, he unzipped her sweatshirt all the way to her knees and looked directly at her swimsuited body. Selina did not know why she did not stop him. Somehow, it seemed the most natural thing for him to be doing. She watched his face as he looked at her. His face was still, almost stoic. She could not read his expression, because he had none.

And then he pressed his lips on her forehead and whispered one word.

"Beautiful," he said and he met her eyes with his engaging brown eyes, as if locking her in his power. Selina was afraid her knees were going to give way under her.

Then as matter-of-factly as he had said the word beautiful, he turned his back from her and picked up his white T-shirt, which was rolled up on the bench beside the pool.

"Do you get thirsty after exercising?" he asked.

"Yes," Selina answered.

"Could we go out together somewhere for a drink?"

Selina agreed, and they walked back to the locker rooms to dress. As she dressed, she chided herself for her awkwardness. She didn't like turning into jelly around a man.

It was better when she saw him fully clothed. She felt herself relaxing as they walked to the car and talked. It was raining hard, and the night air was chilling her to the bone. It had been a long day beginning at 6:00 a.m., and she wanted to go home.

"Where would you like to go for a drink?" he asked.

"I'd like to go to my house instead of a restaurant. I have several things we could drink at home." Selina said.

Selina relaxed completely when she reached her home, her haven from campus and the student life. It was a comfortable ranch house on the Huron river. She could paint and sleep here. She could be alone when she wanted to be alone. Or bring company when she wanted company. Richard seemed to be instantly at ease in her home, although it was difficult to read him, difficult to understand him. He walked through her house like an explorer, examining the most simple details and asking lots of questions. He had a way of asking questions without revealing much about himself. He stood at the door of Selina's painting studio for a long time without saying anything. Then he ran his fingers over an empty canvas and a finished canvas, and he looked at Selina with that intense gaze that she could not interpret. But there was always kindness in his eyes.

"You must see these things in your mind in order to paint them on canvas. I have never met an artist before," he said.

They talked for a long time about art and about life, standing there in the doorway to her studio. Selina forgot her tiredness. She forgot her self-consciousness. Richard asked for a snack, so she made him a four-egg cheese omelet and toast. He ate it like a starving man.

"This tastes wonderful," he said as he ate. "What spices did you use in this?"

"A pinch of garlic."

"Garlic," he repeated, as if he had never heard the word before.

She loved watching him eat. He ate with zest and speed. And yet he was refined. While he ate, he watched her, and she had the feeling that he was studying her. He seemed to notice even the flick of her wrist and the rhythm of her voice. He asked her a dozen questions, but he always deflected questions about himself. He listened with the same intensity with which he swam and ate.

When he had finished his omelet, he looked at his empty plate but said nothing. It occurred to Selina that he wanted another omelet but that he didn't want to ask. That he was self-conscious about wanting to eat eight eggs. That he was self-conscious about being different. She saw it for an instant in his eyes, a hint of pain and an awareness of being different. And her instincts told her that the most kind thing to do was to act as though he was not different, was not remarkable with his granite muscles and ravenous appetite.

"Would you like another omelet?" Selina asked.

And of course he said he would. She made him another omelet, with more toast. This time she gave him a bowl of macadamia nuts and a glass of milk for which he hadn't asked. He ate and drank everything. And when he was finished, he smiled.

"You have a beautiful smile," Selina said.

"Everything about you is beautiful," he said. He got out of his chair, leaned toward Selina and kissed her on the forehead. Selina didn't want him to kiss her. She wanted to stay relaxed and to talk.

"Let me clear these dishes away," she said. He nodded and went into the living room. Only minutes later he came back to her in the kitchen.

This time he suprised her. He approached her from the back and wrapped his arms around her and covered her hands with his hands.

"Your hands are like ice. I made a fire in the fireplace. Come and warm yourself," he said.

Selina felt the strength of his arms around her and in her mind's eye she saw his muscles cutting through the water full of speed and power. She knew she wanted those arms around her. She leaned her head to one side and rested her head against his chest.

"You have the body of a goddess and the soul of an angel. I am probably falling in love with you. It is the reason why I ran away from you the last time. I have no right to fall in love. I am only passing through your country. I can't have any attachments here." He spoke in his rich voice, the voice that stirred her every cell.

"Falling in love is a deep thing. It doesn't happen so quickly," Selina said. She knew she was fumbling. She knew she did not have the words for what she felt.

He held her quietly for a moment. And then he let her go. He walked into the living room and sat on the floor beside the fireplace and stared into the flames. He did not look at her. He did not ask her to join him, not in any words. And because he did not urge her or cojole her, she wanted all the more to go and sit near him.

And so she sat beside him on the floor. The rug was warm and the fire was warmer.

And he kissed her, a slow, long kiss, hot with budding passion. He held her face in his hands and touched her as though she were hollow crystal that would shatter with the wrong touch. And he held her in his arms, and his hands moved through her hair and across her back. And the momentum of the kissing frightened her.

Selina pulled away from him. He understood the way her body stiffened, and he released her from his arms. He sat quietly without speaking.

This sort of thing had happened many times before. Men always wanted her. They always overwhelmed her. Selina was half-angry. Or was it all fear? Because this time she wanted him, too. Selina looked at him. But he was not looking at her. He was looking at the flames.

"What are you thinking?" Selina asked.

"I am waiting for you."

"What do you mean waiting for me?"

"I want you so much that I am being clumsy. I am waiting for you to show me how I can please you. To teach me how to touch you in a way that will not frighten you or be too forceful. I have never been with a woman like you before."

"What do you mean?" Selina asked. Her heart was racing. Racing with love for him. He was seducing her with his candor and his kindness. Then, to make matters worse, he turned his face toward her and looked at her with his huge brown eyes. She was afraid that she was drowning in those eyes.

"You have a core like steel within you and a furnace that produces golden works of art, full of compassion and passion. Yet you are fragile like a rose, and if a man were to be clumsy with you, he could bruise your tender petals. I only want... to please you." He took his fingertips and brushed them across her cheek.

Selina knew her cheeks were steaming hot with blushing. And then a strange thing happened. She felt a tear roll down her cheek. She hated it. She wished that it had never shown up and wanted it to go away. Another one trickled from the other eye. And she was tongue-tied.

"So you have been hurt before. I am sorry," Richard said. He held her hand gently. And he did not try to kiss her again.

Selina wanted him. She wanted the shelter of those arms. She wanted his kindness. She wanted his understanding gentleness. She wanted to make him omelets. And she wanted the taste of his lips.

"I don't want... I cannot sleep with you tonight. I just want to kiss you and to have you stop kissing me when I say stop."

And then he kissed her. And he kissed her again. His kisses spoke to her and told her that he would not demand sex. Would not demand anything. That his hands and his lips were there to embrace and to give. That they were there to untie the knots of loneliness that also bound him. Somehow she knew from his kissing that he was a soldier and that he fought battles and won them. That he was self-assured and powerful, and yet he needed her. And she was not afraid to bare her need to him.

What seemed like only a short time later, Selina asked him to stop kissing her. And he did. When she looked at her clock, an hour had passed. And when she watched him walk away, moving quickly down the steps from her front door, she knew she had asked him to leave too soon. Or that she should never have asked him to come through her door in the first place. Because she knew that she was hopelessly ensnared, unabashedly in love.

III.

She kissed like a Tethran warrior. Like someone who was trying to steal love before it escaped her grasp. And she had everything to give. She poured everything into each kiss and then started over from the beginning. She restrained her passion but did not withhold her surrender to him. She was hungry for him and vulnerable and restless. And it was all there in every kiss, in every touch. Yet for all her intensity and her strength, she was sweet and gentle like a child.

She had trapped him and subdued him, more effectively than if she had tried. She hadn't tried. She didn't even know what had happened to her yet. What she had done to him. What he had done to her.

Richard thought about her as he drove to his own home. He memorized the look of her eyes and the curves of her body. He had challenged her, and she had met his challenge, whether she knew it or not. When he met her at the pool and saw her sitting beside it, dangling her feet in the water, something inside of him snapped. He did not want to hide from her.

She could not hide from him. It was not in her nature. And she could not hide the large, firm breasts in her modest, black swimsuit. She could not hide the perfect legs or the green eyes that made the deep color of the water look pale. She was stunning.

So he did not hold back. He did not pretend to be someone else. He swam like a Tethran and he ate like a Tethran and he kissed like a Tethran. And she had been able to handle it all. Handle it and match it.

The only other people who had watched him swim or exercise on Earth when he wasn't holding back, when he was swimming like an average Tethran, they acted amazed and impressed and questioned him about his training. But Selina didn't. She said she "enjoyed watching him." And when he ate twice what she should have expected, she didn't even comment. She accepted him without questions or conditions. And when it came time to kiss, she was honest and captivating and generous. Yet all she did was kiss.

What a soul the woman had! She did not talk like an intellectual, but she told him how much she understood through her painting. She understood too much. She missed nothing. She understood pain, and she understood triumph. And power and passion.

He wanted to stop thinking about her. He was smitten with her. To the core. This didn't fit into his plans. This had to go. She had to go. Sooner rather than later.

Richard thought about her as he turned the light out and went to bed. He thought about the lure of his dream. The dream had been the bait drawing him to see her a second time. And the bait was important, teasing him, promising him an answer to who he was and why he was. To fill the emptiness. The bait had been more important than the woman until he was with her. Then she was more important.

Richard was scheduled to see her again on Friday. He should not see her again and be with her again so soon. He should cancel their date. But as the two days passed, his hand wouldn't move to lift the phone and call her.

IV.

Friday arrived. And still he had not lifted a finger to cancel their date. Tonight he was supposed to meet her at a campus restaurant for dinner. He wanted to be alone with her in her house with the roaring fire. Chilled October winds blew against him as he walked from his car on the final block to the Back Door restaurant. He felt a dozen emotions rumbling inside of him.

He waited in a noisy, boisterous line for fifteen minutes. The line moved slowly. It was 6:15 p.m. Selina was late. The restaurant music was only noise to him. The raucous laughter mingled with smells of beer and pizza. It was offensive. Everything excluded him and made him feel alien. He was a displaced person.

Richard did not wave or smile when he saw Selina pushing her way through the people crowded in line. But he watched her, like some sweet beam of light moving among a sea of brown-gray coats. When she reached him she carried her warmth inside of her. He was hungry to be near her. Angry that he needed her. It was her own vulnerability that put him at ease.

She slid her hand into his hand. He felt the touch of her soft fingers embracing his, and he felt strangely connected to her. She looked at him with her lovely eyes.

"Sorry for being late. The last few hours at the hospital were hectic. I half-ran to get here on time."

"It's all right," he said. And he knew that it was. Her affect on him was instantaneous. Suddenly he no longer felt like an alien misfit who didn't belong among these people and their noises. Suddenly he was a young man with a bond to her race.

"Your hand is cold, Selina. Maybe I should warm you by the fire again. Maybe we should leave this place and go to your house."

He was sure that he saw her blush as she smiled. She looked away from his face. And then he felt better because he realized that she was under his power. Just as he was under hers.

"Will you invite me to your home again?" he asked.

"Yes." She did not look at him. But she squeezed his hand.

Richard watched her. He watched her remove her coat. Her yellow-green sweater matched her eyes and earrings. It was long and loose, the silky texture clinging to her curves. If all he did was watch her all night he would be content, Richard thought. He watched her hair bounce as her head moved. Most of her long golden hair was pulled back on one side and held secure by a large barrette. The brass barrette was full of tiny stars and moons that sparkled under the lights. Selina's eyes moved around the room, catching glimpses of faces and activity. *Look at me and not at them,* he thought silently. And she did. Her eyes met his, magically caressing him and soothing his loneliness.

They were seated in a large, cozy booth. The black leather seats crinkled as they sat down. Dark red brick walls surrounded them, cluttered with large and small photographs of Michigan football players. A small light hung low over their table. Background music ebbed and flowed with a tide of unpredictable rhythms.

This reminds me of starbase Dard-3, Richard thought to himself, mildly amused.

"Dard-3?" Selina asked out loud, puzzled.

She read my mind! Richard started. But before he could respond to her a gum-chewing waitress with huge teeth and even larger hooped earrings jammed large wooden menus into both of their hands.

There was almost nothing on the menu except pizza, so he ordered it. He had never eaten pizza. The music seemed to get louder. The voices and laughter in the room seemed to get louder.

"I've never been to this place before, Selina. This is an adventure for me."

"A good adventure or a bad adventure?" she asked.

"Do you like adventure, Selina?"

"I like adventure. But I'm afraid of it at the same time."

"You should not trust strange men with your fears," he said softly.

"I didn't. I told you," she said.

"Don't trust me, Selina. Don't trust anyone."

Selina looked puzzled and sad. He wanted to wipe away the sadness. And then he heard a loud, theatrical voice project itself across the room.

"Selina, darling!" A bejeweled, thin young woman dressed in an array of colors, scarves, and chains pounced herself on top of Selina.

"Nana." Selina stood up, returning the woman's hug.

"Where have you been keeping yourself the last two weeks, darling? Cooped up in that drab hospital, cleaning bedpans?" Nana's manner was exaggerated and deliberate. She wore a heavy perfume and seemed to fill the room with her presence.

Before Selina had another chance to speak, Nana went on talking. She had quickly examined Selina, her clothes, and her companion. "Well, what have we *here*?" Nana asked, peering at Richard from head to toe. In a sweep of familiarity she sat next to Richard and put an arm around him. "Perhaps I am in the wrong field. You medical types are so cute. Well, Selina is too good for you, I can see that. But I'm not. I'm not good for anyone," Nana said. Nana's perfume was too strong for him, her colors too bright. But somehow she did not offend him. Perhaps it was the cloud of dust and the laughter that she brought with her. Her small, black eyes were kind.

Selina laughed. "Richard, this is Nana O'Brien. Nana, my friend's name is Richard Saxon, he's a mathematics professor, not a medic."

"Hands off faculty!" Nana said, dramatically moving away from Richard. "Mathematics does bad things for my complexion."

"I'm a theatre major, an actress," Nana continued. She motioned to two colorful young men who followed her to the table. Without an invitation but with great finesse, the three joined Richard and Selina, pulling an extra chair next to their booth. Selina made sure that everyone was introduced. Laughing and entertaining seemed natural to Selina.

Richard felt tense at first. Selina did not know Nana's two friends. She trusted too easily. He wanted to take her away from here. And in the next minute he wanted to stay as long as she was here. Her laughter sounded like water bubbling over a brook, reminding him of his thirst. Selina had a sweetening influence on Nana. She had a way of guarding the feelings of others with a twist of warmth and affection that removed the sting of Nana's unbridled candor.

Richard found himself relaxing. Selina was the one guarding him. She was the one who understood the complexity of the humor, its power to bite, its ability to delight. She was the one who could teach him to laugh among these aliens, to understand them, and maybe even to be one of them for tonight.

The first pizza arrived. They ordered another, then ordered more drinks and a third pizza. Richard enjoyed the pizza. It tasted strange, then good. He found himself laughing as Nana sifted her opinions and realities through her unique mind and spewed them from a witty tongue.

"I'm being nice, aren't I, Selina?" Nana asked after an attempt at doctor jokes.

"I'll tell you if you're not," Selina laughed.

"She means it," Nana said, peering into Richard's face. "Sweet as honey, with a steel trap mind, that's my Selina."

Richard smiled. He had put his arm around Selina early in the evening. He felt aroused by her scent and the way her eyes followed him and the way the light sparkled in her hair. He wrapped his fingers around long strands of Selina's hair and removed her large barrette. Her golden curls cascaded into gentle streamers around her face. He had not asked her permission to remove her barrette. He just did it. Selina felt the hair fall on her face and shoulders. She turned and looked at Richard. She was the vulnerable beauty again. Not the steel-trap mind. Richard's eyes met hers. He whispered in her ear, "My love is like the morning light." He watched the goose bumps bristle across her hand and neck. Watched with satisfaction. Selina glanced down at the table.

"How long have you two lovebirds been dating?" Nana asked.

"This is our third date," Richard answered.

"Third date! Tell me you've been in love for years."

Selina looked embarrassed. Nana noticed. "But what do I know?" Nana made a joke about her own boyfriend, and everyone laughed.

Richard slipped Selina's barrette into his coat pocket. He felt a rush of desire for her. He caressed her neck with his hand.

Hours passed, but they passed quickly. Selina whispered to Richard that she needed to go home. They handed Nana some money for the bill and left the restaurant together. The others stayed and continued to laugh.

It was Friday night on campus, and Richard did not feel alone or like a misfit. It seemed important that he did not feel alone.

Richard led Selina by the hand down the dark side street where his car was parked. He unlocked the car door for her. She brushed close to him, groping in the dark for the handle. There was a gravity between them, pulling them together. Leaning against the car in the night air, they kissed. Long, sultry kisses that were rich and comfortable.

Selina gradually pulled away. "I need to go home," she said. Richard wasn't ready.

"Touch me with the dawn that is in your lips," Richard said softly. He didn't mean to say it. He was thinking it, and it came out of his mouth. It was then that he realized that he had completely dropped his guard with her.

Selina touched his lips with her fingertips and then let him kiss her again. And then he held her quietly. There were no more kisses. He was holding her gently, like one might hold his sister. But she was anything but his sister. He was afraid of these new feelings. Afraid of wanting to hold a woman as if she were his sister and wanting to sleep with her and letting down his guard with her. All at the same time.

He drove her home and walked her to the front door. As he stood on her front porch, he could see her face clearly under the porch light. Trees clustered around her house, casting shadows through the light, casting shadows all around them and near their faces. He looked into her eyes and asked, "Let me come inside with you."

And he was afraid that she would say yes. And afraid that she would say no.

"No. I have to be on duty at the hospital tomorrow. I need to go now," she said.

"What are you afraid of?" he asked gently.

"You," she said.

"Perhaps you are wise to be afraid." He stood his guard against her smile and the power of it.

Perhaps she knows intuitively how I could drain her of her beauty and her strength and all that she has to give. Perhaps she knows intuitively that I could fill her up like no man she has ever known. And she would need me always. And then I would leave her forever. Richard let her go. As he walked away he studied every detail. Her large brick house was nestled among trees on the banks of the Huron river. He could hear the river flowing softly, steadily under the trees. He could smell the water in the darkness. He drove home alone thinking of her.

I will not call Selina again for a long time, six or seven weeks. I should only be with her in measured doses. I have enough self-discipline for that. She will have to accept the scarcity of my company. If she does not, then she can end our relationship. That would be better, if she ended our relationship. It would take the chore away from me.

Her perfume lingered in the car. He reached into his pocket and touched the barrette and strands of hair that clung to it. It would probably only cause him trouble. But he had a part of her with him.

CHAPTER
SEVEN
BONDING

She stayed there in his mind, lingering with her beautiful face and honeyed voice. She laughed inside his thoughts. Richard was angry that she had such a hold on him. But now she was a part of him, and he was afraid that he might never be the same.

Nine days had passed since he had seen her at the Back Door. Each day he resolved to postpone calling her. To postpone thinking about her. It was early Sunday evening. Richard tried relaxing at what used to be a favorite pastime, reading. Tonight it was political science. He was fascinated with reading the stories of democracy, its ancient roots in Greece, its solid blossoming in America and in most of the modern world. He followed with keen interest as the fragile republics of Russia and the Eastern Block prepared for the twenty-first century. Almost nine years had passed since the overthrow of Communism in 1991. The new Russian government had stumbled through painful years of trial and error. But today in 1999 the stories were of fresh, newborn democracies. Richard could read about the living players. The lessons were priceless to him. And yet they could not hold him now. He was restless.

Richard reached into the drawer of his black hardwood desk and picked up Selina's brass barrette. He looked at the tiny stars and moons. He fingered it playfully. He picked a strand of her golden hair from the barrette and rolled it between his fingers. A strange sense of fear gripped him. Fear, then danger. As his skin cells pressed against her hair cells, he felt as if they were in some primitive mode of communication. She was calling for help in her mind. Richard had rarely experienced this sensitivity through merely rubbing DNA strands. But it did happen.

Richard had no phone in his house. He did not know where Selina was at this moment. She had told him that she was going to New York for the weekend. Was she there now or at home? He decided to drive to her house. She lived barely two blocks from his street. He was in her driveway in only a few minutes.

Selina's car was parked in her driveway. It was cold to the touch and had not been driven in hours. Her house was dark except for a dim light in the living room. If she was safely home, he could invent any excuse for dropping in. Richard moved swiftly across her yard, stopped at the front door, and listened. He rang the doorbell. He heard it resonate inside. There was no answer. Richard thought he heard a male voice. But he could not be sure. Something felt wrong. He rang it again. He heard an angry voice. Richard took his forefinger and placed it on the doorknob. A screw melted, then the door latch melted and fell off.

Richard turned the broken doorknob and entered the hall. He made a cautious entrance into the living room. What he saw enraged him.

Selina was laying on the living room floor with her hands tied over her head. A dark-haired young man had her pinned to the floor. He sat on her stomach and held a knife to her throat.

Sorn grasped the picture in a second. The attacker was stunned by his speed.

Strike injury for deterrence.   Destroy when necessary. He followed the Rule of Battle. Sorn knew all the Rules. They were ingrained in him, a part of his conditioning as surely as the physical strength in his body. It was this Rule that saved the life of Francois Pinchard. Sorn felt Pinchard's collar bone snap like a twig beneath his fingers. It was almost effortless. In obedience to Rule, Sorn dropped him. Pinchard smacked hard against the living room wall. Dazed and disoriented, Pinchard moaned beneath the pain of a double-fractured collar bone.

Sorn grabbed the gun from Pinchard's pocket and threw it across the room. He knelt next to Selina and gently untied her hands. He kicked Pinchard's knife a few feet away from Selina. She trembled and pulled herself away from Sorn as he reached to help her sit up.

Richard dropped his hands slowly to his sides and kept the distance that she needed. "Selina, you are safe. No one is going to hurt you. I can help you to stand up or I can leave you alone."

"He... he has a knife... and a gun. He has a large knife," Selina said. Pinchard had used his knife to cut three buttons from Selina's blouse. He had cut her bra straps through her blouse. He had threatened to cut her throat.

"His knife and gun are gone; I have them. He won't hurt you. No one will." Richard spoke slowly in a soothing voice.

Selina did not cry. She held her arms stiff, tightly drawn to her body, her fists clenched. She looked at Richard and then at Pinchard, her wide eyes full of unreleased pain. She nodded to Richard, acknowledging his words. Slowly, one of her hands reached to hold his hand. He let her set the pace. She sat up and began to stand.

"My God, I'm dying, someone help me!" Pinchard screamed in pain.

His voice sent terror through her. Selina jumped, clutching Richard like a frightened child. Richard bonded with her, promising her fierce protection, comfort, love. He promised in his soul, not speaking a word. She felt the promise coming through his skin, through his arms which encircled her. Selina's rigid body relaxed. Richard knew that he had offered and that she had accepted. He felt worthy, trusted, and loved in return.

Destroy when necessary. No, to kill Pinchard would frighten her, Richard thought. He phoned the police instead. Before the police arrived, Richard mended Selina's melted front door lock.

Less than an hour later, Francois Pinchard was in the hands of the police. He was arrested on charges of armed assault and attempted murder. The police were less than sympathetic toward Selina because there were no signs of forced entry. But Pinchard's weapons had impressed them.

The door closed behind Pinchard and the police. Selina sat quietly on the couch in her torn blouse with the missing buttons. She was still dazed. Distracted, courteous, she fought for control. She decided to change her clothes and make some coffee. When she left the living room Richard started a fire in the fireplace. The house was cold.

This was the second time Richard had been inside Selina's house. It felt like home. It had her touch. The spacious living room was a work of art--elegant, balanced, and comfortable. It was cozily separated from the rest of the house. A large, beige leather sectional sofa wound close to the arched stone fireplace. The walls, mini-blinds and lamps were a soft shade of peach. The only adornments were a wooden crucifix on the wall in the foyer by the front door, and a wide, richly colored tapestry hanging near the fireplace. A heavy ceramic bowl sat on the end table. Its colors matched the colors in the tapestry. One large, healthy plant was poised near the window. It reminded him of a Ytar plant.

Selina returned to the living room wearing an over-sized, long brown sweater. It made her look pale and fragile. She did not notice the warm fire and seemed to have forgotten the coffee. She sat next to Richard and started talking nervously about Pinchard. She had not seen Pinchard in over two years. She met him in Paris when she was studying art. He had been infatuated with her. But she ignored it. Friends told her that he had married someone else shortly after she left Paris. Tonight Pinchard showed up on her doorstep sitting in the rain, waiting for her when she returned home from New York. He seemed crazed. He pointed a gun at her and forced his way into her house. Pinchard had been with Selina for over an hour before Richard arrived. He had shouted at her, slapped and taunted her. Then he began his talk of raping and killing her. Selina talked rapidly, breathlessly.

"Would you like to call Nana and have her come over?" Richard asked gently.

Selina looked distracted. "I don't think so."

"Let me hold you for a minute," he said. His voice was warm and caressing.

"No. No, I should make some coffee." She walked away from him and hurried into the kitchen. Richard waited. When he entered the kitchen he found her huddled on the floor, clutching her knees with her arms. She wept quietly.

"I will leave if you would rather be alone," he said.

"Don't leave."

"I can hold you." It was a question. Selina shook her head "no" and extended her hand to touch him at the same time.

Richard sat on the floor next to her and tenderly placed one arm around her. Then his other arm. She released her sobs. She drained him of his fierce protection and comfort. She filled him up with her love and her trusting of him. They both gave what they had and took what they needed.

The fire blazed softly in the fireplace. An early snow was falling, chilling the outside world. They moved into the warm living room. Selina sat quietly on the sofa, sipping hot coffee. Richard said nothing. He just stayed near her, sitting on the floor near the fire, watching the flames.

"Why did you decide to come to my house when you did?" Selina asked.

"I was in the mood."

"You haven't called me for nine days," she said.

Silence.

"I'm not... very good company right now. I can't seem to think clearly." Selina rubbed her eyes.

"You don't need to do anything."

"Could you stay here with me tonight? I have a guest room," she said.

He would do anything for her. He would fight hell to protect her. But he didn't say any of that. He simply answered, "Yes, I will stay."

Richard sensed danger hovering in the skies. He didn't care. He was too deeply involved with her. He didn't care.

II.

Max Traytur watched from the convenient shadows of the large trees surrounding Selina's house. He did not see Pinchard enter her house. One of his detectives observed that. Max came later, and what he saw was the police escorting an injured Pinchard into their police car.

Max was disturbed. He had intended to take at least partial credit for Pinchard's success if he had murdered Selina. But he did not want to take any blame if Pinchard failed. And apparently he had failed. After all, Max's only part in this was tracking down Pinchard, arranging a chance meeting with him, and making sure that Pinchard had Selina's home address. It was not listed in the phone book, and Pinchard was rather... loosely wrapped. He would not have found Selina if it had taken any unusual intelligence.

Natas certainly could not blame Max for Pinchard's failure. How was Max to know that one of Selina's friends would come at just the right moment to rescue her? According to Max's surveillance team, Selina had a lot of friends and comings and goings. Max needed to become one of those friends. Max pointed his tiny flashlight and made his way through the trees. He walked cautiously down the road to his parked car. Max could sense the demons gathering in the woods near Selina's house. Natas must have known by now that Pinchard had failed. Natas would be angry. Very angry.

III.

Richard loved her. He was sure of it. As they sat quietly beside the fire not talking, the golden flames danced with occasional red flashes of color. He enjoyed the smell of the burning wood. And the warmth.

"Can I get you anything?" Selina asked.

"Relax. You don't need to do anything."

"Are you hungry?"

"Starving. I missed dinner," Richard said.

Selina stood up and went into the kitchen and began cooking before he realized what she was doing. She made a large plate of pasta. She threw in pieces of vegetables and peanuts and sprinkled it with cheese and butter. It tasted wonderful.

Selina sat across from Richard at the dining room table and watched him eat.

"Aren't you hungry?" he asked her.

"No. I couldn't touch anything."

"You didn't have to make me a feast. I could eat cheese and fruit."

"I wanted to... do something active." She started crying again. Richard said nothing and went on eating.

"Do you mind... if I take a shower?"

"Do whatever is best for you. Maybe you should go to bed, Selina. It's 10:00 p.m. I'll go to bed later."

"You're so... good to me," she said. And something made her cry again. She left the room.

Only forty minutes later Selina came back to him. The tips of her hair were wet. She smelled lovely, like roses. She seemed to be refreshed. Almost serene.

"Could we talk for a while?" she asked him.

And so they talked. For hours. He was starved for conversation with her. And he didn't realize it until he began to talk. Selina was a woman of bright, compassionate intelligence. She probed things with an intense curiosity and understood things like an artist, in a sweep of intuitive clarity. She always seemed to teach him something, and it excited him.

Richard was a genius who had had few teachers. His parents kept his genius a secret. Starfleet kept his secret so that they would be the best ones to exploit his mind. Many people sensed his intelligence and shied away from him. Selina did not. He wanted her to know him. He could not tell her who he was, but he could tell her what he loved. And he could tell her what he hated. At the heart of all his lies about his Earth persona, she saw his hidden self. A man who loved ideals and convictions and who hated injustice.

"Blessed are those who hunger and thirst for justice, for they will be satisfied."[*2] Selina said.

Her words shook him.

It was as if there were a force behind the words. A force capable of bringing about what the words said. He remembered the other time when he felt moved in this way. It was the time she said, "You will know the truth, and the truth will set you free." He wanted to believe the words.

Richard stood up and walked over to the fire and stirred the logs with a steel poker.

"You are dangerous, Princess Star, Truth Bearer," he whispered under his breath. And then he looked at her.

"You are too beautiful. And you understand too much," he said.

Selina laughed. She looked at Richard's face. It was sober.

"I am serious. I have never met anyone so beautifully dangerous as you. I am not sure what to do about you," he said.

"Do about me. What is there to do about me?" Selina asked.

He looked hard at her as if he were going to find the answer in her eyes or in her skin. Then he looked back at the fire and stirred the logs, trying to suffocate the hot coals and put out the fire. Each time he choked a hot spark, another spark shot up and turned into a flame. For a long time he said nothing.

"I have many important secrets, Selina. And I can never share them with you."

"I am not afraid of the things I don't know about you."

"You should be."

"I'm durable," Selina said.

Richard moved toward her. Her last statement had been like a bridge that she had just built. Flung between his loneliness of the past and the promise of love that might lay ahead for him in the future. The future might become a sweet word.

He sat next to her. He reached to hold her small hand. Then he moved his fingers inside the arm of her sweater, caressing her arm. Goosebumps rose on her skin. He saw ambivalence in her eyes. The touch of a man was still frightening to her this night. ·

"You will be safe tonight. I won't let anything hurt you. May I kiss you once before you go to bed?" he whispered.

It was then that he saw it in her eyes. Selina was in love with him. "I will give you everything," her eyes silently spoke. The kiss was like fire, warm and consuming. It burned into both of their hearts. It would never leave them alone. They kissed only once, and it was as if they had kissed forever.

"At the restaurant... you told me not to trust you."

He saw the sadness return to her eyes when she said this.

"Forget what I said then." *I love you,* he thought, and he hoped she could see it in his eyes. Selina walked away from him slowly, and closed the door of her bedroom.

Richard turned the lights out. The last hot embers in the fireplace refused to die. He decided that they were harmless. The wide room was dark except for the dim light of a small lamp.

In the space of only a second, out of the corner of his eye, Richard saw a winged creature with a human face. The angel was standing near the front door. Richard looked directly at its form, and it faded slowly. And then he sensed a still presence near him. Its goodness pierced his heart. As gently as it came, it left him. It was the first time he had seen an angel on Earth. Selina had brought the angel to him. He was at peace.

IV.

Richard did not look out the window. He did not see the other angels. There were seven captains and seventy-seven warriors. They stood tall, shoulder to shoulder in battle formation, encircling the property line of Selina's house. They stood against the demons pressing in on them on every side. The angels absorbed the vicious blows and cuts as the demons attacked. At a given command, the angels all unsheathed their fire swords. They acted as one. The demons scattered, bumping into one another shrieking. The demons withdrew. The angels had their orders. No evil would touch these humans this night. The war had begun. The battles lay ahead. The humans would need their rest.

CHAPTER
EIGHT
FAIR ONE

Michael the Archangel breathed in a sigh of deep relief and satisfaction. He could see the flickers of promise and the flames of love between Selina and Richard. Michael could see many things clearly from his vantage point in the Inbetween Spaces. He could see that Richard had made a crucial decision. Richard had decided to love Selina. And in loving her he had heard the angelic prompting to rescue Selina. He had both saved Selina's life and found safety for his soul, at least for the time being. Richard had brought himself under the protection of Selina's angel guard. Selina lived under the banner of the Christ.

Only one thing worried Michael. The plan for the Tethra Triangle was not moving as fast as it should. Michael feared that the human struggle could reach its climax at the very moment when the angels would be compelled to withdraw their action and protection. During the seven days of the Turning Point.

The Turning Point was only eleven weeks away. It happened once every century, at the turn of the century. The great days of Turning Point on Earth when the changing of the centuries brought with them the clashing of the two waves, the waves of good and evil. It would happen as the last day of 1999 ended and the first week of the year 2000 arrived. On Earth there would be a flashing and thundering as the good and bad fruits of the past 100 years met in one spot and flowed into the new century. Only one wave would dominate. The wave of good carried all the power of love, the sacrifice and the glory that had accumulated in the old century. The wave of evil carried all the force of all the sin and evil and hate that had collected.

The clashing of the tides of good and evil eclipsed the power of the angels and demons, and they could not act on Earth. Nothing could affect their power to act in heaven and hell. But on Earth they would be disabled as the humans' choices mixed in the turmoil of time.

Michael summoned the warrior angel Matthew and sent him to stay with Selina. "Hell will aim its malice at the woman. We must guard every hair of her head. Or the Tethra Triangle will be lost."

II.

Natas watched. Icy pangs of hatred tore through Natas. He had ignored the man named Richard Saxon. Richard was one of the many in Selina's life. So what if she loved him? She had loved before.

Natas had missed something. He had not expected the angel guard to be in place. He had not expected the angels to declare war by drawing their fire swords. Michael must have known something that Natas did not know--something about the timing. Something about the man named Richard. Natas would find out about Richard. Michael did not always win his wars.

III.

The sun was setting. As Selina watched the gray shadows move across her desk, she lost her concentration. She was tense. Her mind kept returning to the night before. She could see Francois Pinchard's darting, insane eyes and could remember the sting of his hand across her face. She didn't want to be alone tonight. She would go to Nana's house or ask Nana to stay here. She needed company. Just for one more night.

Her heart started pounding when she heard the doorbell.

"Who is it?" Selina asked before opening the door.

"Richard Saxon. Are you all right?"

And there he stood, tall and strong and kind. With his beautiful brown eyes fixed on her.

"My staff meeting finished early. I thought I would check on you," he said.

Selina felt safe being near him. She asked him to come in. He ended up staying for dinner, and as he ate, he seemed preoccupied and quiet. Richard would look at her for a long time and say nothing.

He moved to her fireplace and made a fire, and then he sat beside the fireplace as though he belonged there. He waited until Selina sat next to him, and then he kissed her tenderly.

"Selina, I am not really who I said I was. I do not have a business background, and I don't have a British family. That is my cover identity."

"I thought that might be the case....You can't tell me any more than that?"

"No more than that."

"Then I will not ask you," Selina said. Pause.

"No one but you must know that it is only a cover identity."

"I understand," Selina said.

"I didn't want to lie to you," he said.

Pause. His confession moved her.

"Do you still want to see me, to date me?" he asked softly.

"I will take whatever you give me, Richard. A little part of you or a lot of you." Selina felt embarrassed by her own candor, and so she added, "I'm not proud."

"Those who have reason to be proud never are," Richard said.

He seemed to relax. He talked for a long time. Sometimes he seemed like a young boy, and sometimes he seemed like an old man. He was complex and different. She could not put her finger on why he was so different.

There were unusual holes in his knowledge about places, animals, and even spices. And his language could not always keep pace with his fast mind. Many of his inconsistencies did not make sense. But Selina found that she did not care.

As he talked and as she listened it became less important to Selina to solve the mystery of who he was. It became more important to give him room to talk and to be whatever he wanted to be in front of her. He was wonderfully different, and she realized that she loved him.

It was close to midnight when Nana arrived at Selina's house to spend the night with her. Richard charmed Nana before he left. Perhaps he charmed everyone.

As Selina lay in bed that night thinking about him, she realized that another door had begun to open for Richard and Selina. Somewhere between the intense physical attraction and the spiritual passion, the two were also becoming friends.

IV.

Richard started calling Selina every day. At first it was to make certain that she was safe from Francois Pinchard.

Then the danger of Pinchard was removed. Pinchard's wealthy family was dismayed at the thought that he might drag the family name and reputation into some American courtroom. They were weary of his erratic behavior, which had cost them dearly in money and worry. He had attacked other women and had been arrested before. But this was the final blow. He had now assaulted a woman of "good family" whose wealthy lawyers had the same clout as the Pinchard family lawyers. Pinchard's family had him committed to a maximum security mental hospital close to home.

It took two weeks before Pinchard was out of the country. Richard didn't need to call Selina every day. He didn't need to see her at least three times a week. But he did it anyway. He realized that he was calling her just to hear the sound of her voice.

Richard found himself not wanting to hold anything back. He took from her and he gave to her. He took more from her than he had ever dared to take from anyone. He took all the time she would give him, and he took her meals and her conversation. He took her wisdom. He took her embraces and her beauty.

And he gave to Selina, more than he had ever dared to give to anyone. He gave her anything that she needed. Anything she wanted of him and didn't know how to ask. He taught her how to ask. He cherished her. He wanted to give her everything. And his heart ached at the fact that he could not give her everything. That he would leave her one day.

Richard decided to meet Selina after work and to drive her safely home. She was surprised to see him standing in the wide, empty corridor of the hospital at 11:15 p.m. And then he surprised her again by leaning her against the wall in the empty hospital corridor and kissing her.

At first there was the familiarity of her touch and of her body melting into the comfort of his. And then the moments when they lost themselves in each other. And then the moment when Selina pulled away. That, too, was familiar. At first he thought it was fear that stopped her from making love to him. Night after night. And he thought that he could overcome that fear.

But tonight as they walked in the dark and talked in the car driving home, Selina explained that it was not fear that stopped her from having sex with him. It was conviction. Religious conviction. And he doubted that he could overcome conviction.

He offered her the courtesy of listening. But he was angry. According to Selina, sex would never be right for her unless she were married. And once she was joined to a man in marriage, sex would be the deepening and the completing of the bond between them.

"Are you annoyed with me?" Selina asked in a timid voice.

"Maybe."

"Are you going to give up on me?"

"Have men abandoned you so easily in the past?"

"Yes," she said. There was no anger in her voice.

"Where I come from, if a man or woman refuses to have sex with their partner, it means they do not love the person," he said.

Pause.

"I love you, Richard." Selina touched his arm with her hand. Richard stopped the car. He had reached Selina's driveway. And in the dark, in the shadow of the trees, he could barely see her face.

"We should not say that to each other. We have not been given the right to love each other. I will have to leave you one day," Richard said.

"And maybe we haven't been given the right to have sex--to give and to take each other freely and completely." Selina's voice was shaky.

Silence.

"Do you love me, Richard?"

"I thought you knew. I have never loved anyone like I love you, Selina. And when I do leave you, it will be because I have to leave. Not because I want to leave. There is a mission that will take me far away from you and this place. And I will never come back. But even hell could not drive me away from you tonight."

As they kissed again, like lovers who were already saying goodbye, he couldn't help but hold onto the wish that once before he left earth she would let him undress her and take her completely. Once.

V.

Richard was three hours late. It wasn't like him to be so late and not to call and tell her where he was. Selina was worried.

There was no point in calling the airport again. She had called an hour earlier, and they told her that the flight from New York had arrived on time at Detroit Metro Airport at 4:10 p.m. The next flight would not be arriving until 8:15 p.m. Richard had told Selina that he would be home in time to see the Power Center performance of Hamlet at 8:00 p.m. Something was wrong.

Selina told herself not to worry. Richard was all right. She told
herself that he was strong and fearless and invulnerable. He acted that
way. But he was not invulnerable.

Weeks ago Selina had noticed the heavy copper bracelet on his
right wrist. She pulled it out from under his sweater and asked him about
it.

"Your medical I.D. bracelet says that you are allergic to
practically everything. This lists sedatives, pain killers, anesthetics, etc.
What kind of allergic reaction would you have to these drugs?"

"The drugs would kill me."

"But Richard... what if you were in an accident, what would they
give you?"

"Pray for me, Selina, that I won't be in an accident. You said that
you pray for me sometimes." He changed the subject.

An accident. She dreaded the thought of anything hurting him,
of anything bad even touching him. How had she gotten herself into this
situation? To be so completely in love?

She felt angry when the doorbell rang. She felt frightened. She
felt torn. And there he stood, in a navy overcoat and suit. He had come
to her house straight from the airport. His business meetings went too
late to make the earlier flight. They went too late to call her and still
catch a plane.

She listened to his voice as he talked, and she thought about how
much she loved his voice. Her anger melted. She wasn't angry at him.
She was angry at herself for caring about him so much--for knowing that
he had the ability to change her and her world.

She watched him remove his coat and tie and sit in his favorite
spot beside her fireplace. He hated flying. He told her that the early
stagecoaches were probably safer and equally as efficient as planes. He
made her laugh. And then he held her in his arms. And she was happy.
They had dated for six weeks, and it seemed as if she had always known
him. Six weeks of bliss that could continue for a time. Until he had to
leave and go away, wherever that was. A place where she could not go.
A place from which he protected her. Sadness filled her as he kissed
her. Comfort silently entered his holding of her. Sadness slid away for
now. He was here now. There would be time for sadness when he was
gone.

CHAPTER
NINE
MEETING

The tall albino watched Selina from a distance as she hurried down the busy hospital corridor. When she came near the door of his room, he jumped into bed and feigned a choking, gasping cough. Selina stopped. She entered his room, glanced quickly at his heart monitor and started to leave.

"Don't you have a kind word for a lonely man?" he asked. His voice was crusty, his diction deliberate and succinct.

"Is there anything I can do for you?" Selina asked sweetly. Their eyes met. Selina always looked directly at her patients. The albino's eyes were red. As he looked at her she experienced a chill of discomfort. His gaze was strangely hypnotic. She glanced down at the floor. The albino felt as if he had touched her by looking into her beautiful green eyes. He felt a sickening kind of lusty greed. He wanted to possess her. He let his eyes follow the curves of her body.

"I hate being in this hospital. I don't mean to feel sorry for myself. I guess I just need some encouragement." He spoke in a whiny voice.

Selina forced a smile. She walked to the foot of the bed to read his chart. "We can always find something encouraging here," she said, flipping open his chart.

The albino moved swiftly to the foot of his bed and grabbed his chart out of her hand. "I've had enough of medical science," he said. Selina was taken aback by his actions.

"I wanted to base my encouragement on reality. That's the best kind, isn't it?" she asked.

The albino made an odd face. "I'm sure you're very busy. But if you have time, could you come back later and read to me? My eyes bother me so much when I read." The albino rubbed his eyes, squinting as he spoke.

Selina said that she would try. She left him quickly. Unconsciously, she fingered the golden crucifix that she wore around her neck. He made her skin crawl.

Selina's shift was almost over when the assistant head nurse approached her. "Selina, before you leave, take some time to read to the albino patient in room 4666. He's been nagging me to send you in. He said he's rich and he'll donate a new hospital wing if you spend some extra time with him." The head nurse rolled her eyes. "They come in all shapes and sizes, don't they?"

Selina had been uncomfortably aware that the albino had been watching her throughout her eight-hour shift. He seemed to peek around corners and appear silently, never speaking.

"What is wrong with him?" Selina asked.

"He's a hypochondriac, if you ask me. He insisted that his doctor admit him for a battery of tests and a complete physical. He complains of angina and heart problems. So far he is the healthiest patient I've seen all month. His name is Max Traytur." The head nurse noticed Selina's reluctance. "Just look at him as being a learning experience." She winked at Selina and walked away.

Selina entered Traytur's room quietly. He lay on his bed with one arm covering his eyes. He knew that she had come in even though he had not uncovered his eyes. "Are you here to read to me?" his crusty voice almost whispered.

"I can come back another time if you'd rather sleep," Selina answered.

"No, I need company. I'm lonely." He sat up in bed as if the act of moving caused him pain. He pointed to his bedside table, studying Selina's every gesture. She did not see the lust in his eyes because she did not look at them. Two books lay on his bedside table, Shakespeare and a science fiction novel.

"Which one would you like me to read?" Selina asked, her eyes fixed on the books.

"Which book do *you* prefer?" Traytur asked.

"There is nothing better than Shakespeare. But it's difficult for an amateur to read aloud." Selina's throat went dry. Traytur reached for her wrist as she came near his bedside table. He gripped her wrist in a strangely hostile gesture. His skin was soft, cold, and clammy. Selina swallowed hard and gently tried to release her wrist. Traytur held it fast. If she resisted him further it might cause an uncomfortable scene.

Traytur examined her. He sensed her uneasiness like an animal smells fear. He was torn between the desire to torment her and the duty to become her friend.

"I devour all the science fiction I can find," Traytur's crusty voice stated coolly. "I'm convinced there is life on other planets. I'm convinced they visit us." Traytur watched Selina with the intensity of a cat about to pounce on its prey. Selina felt like an amoeba under a microscope. She wanted to get away from him. She did not know why. She said a mental prayer for God's protection.

Traytur grimaced. He covered his eyes with his hand. "What did you say?" His voice was loud. Traytur felt a wave of nausea.

"I didn't say anything to you," Selina said. Traytur lusted to hurt her. He dug his long, manicured fingernails into Selina's wrist. One sharp nail penetrated her flesh, ripping deep and drawing blood. Selina pulled away. He held tighter. She used her right hand for leverage and freed herself from his grip.

Suddenly Traytur's mouth hung open as he twitched and groaned. Selina pressed his call button for help.

"Get away from me," he shouted. Selina held her ground.

"Don't worry, I am going to help you. Are you epileptic?" she asked. Traytur turned away from her. He could not answer. The assistant head nurse rushed in the room. She motioned for Selina to leave since her presence was upsetting the patient.

Moments later, the albino Traytur rested alone in his hospital bed in the dark. His convulsive behavior had subsided. The doctors would run more tests to find out what had happened to him. But Traytur already knew. There were strong angels guarding Selina.

Just like that, the woman called down great power, Traytur said to himself. *I underestimated you, witch. Never again. Next time we meet you will get a taste of the kind of power I can call on.* Traytur clenched his fist. Selina's blood had dried under his finger nail. He scraped the dried blood into a clean white handkerchief and saved it. Just as he saved his hatred.

II.

Selina leaned against the wall of the lady's room. The Traytur patient had badly shaken her. But why? It was then that she noticed the wide scratch bleeding on her left wrist. Traytur had accidentally hurt her! She was surprised at the size and depth of the wound. It was actually more like a cut than a scratch. She washed and medicated it.

But the strange wound quickly became infected. Only twenty-six hours later, a tell-tale red thread of blood poisoning was moving up her arm from the wound. A staff doctor at the hospital gave her an antibiotic injection when she showed him the wound. The infection healed, but the cut did not.

Infection Control regulations required that a medical person with broken skin needed to wear rubber gloves. Wearing rubber gloves every day only irritated the wound further. The gloves closed off the cut from fresh air, irritated and sometimes tore the scab as the gloves went on and off. The bending of her wrist reopened the wound repeatedly since it was located at the wrist joint. Occasionally she noticed the pain. It was strange how the cut did not seem to get smaller. Selina tried to forget about the eerie Traytur patient. After all, she would never see him again.

CHAPTER
TEN
NANA'S PARTY

Richard wished that they had not come here. He stood at the jammed doorway to Nana's living room. The party was in full swing, and he was late. As always, Nana had crowded a fascinating collection of people into her home for one of her "little happenings." Nana was a walking party, a perpetual hostess. Her tiny rented apartment had only one large room - always full of guests and music. Selina had not seen much of her friends for the past six weeks. Richard was the only one she saw. But tonight they had agreed to attend Nana's birthday party.

Richard was tired and tense. He had arrived late from a business trip. Now as he pushed his way into the party he saw Selina standing in a corner against a wall. A small, muscular, handsome man seemed to have pinned her in the corner, leaning one of his arms against the wall. He was talking quietly to her, looking into her eyes. Selina laughed. She looked at him in a way that inflamed Richard's jealousy. On Chadra he would have beaten a man for coming near Selina. But then on Chadra he would have married her by now. Or at least claimed her as his own, and no other man would dare to come near her. Then he stopped himself. This was not Chadra. He could not claim her as his own. He would leave Earth and someone else would give her children. Give her children! Richard felt the hot anger burn its way to the surface. He turned around and left the room. His pain was deep. His skin would begin to glow any second now. Richard hurried past Nana's porch and down the front steps. Nana saw him leaving.

She had seen his entrance and his exit. Nana was impressed. His hot anger, jealousy, possessiveness--it was all there in his face. He was just the perfect man for Selina, and Nana would tell him so. And she would tell him why. Nana had already formed her own theory about Richard and Selina and what needed to be done. Nana followed Richard quickly, hurrying out the front porch and down the steps.

"Richard, before you trot off, how about a word with the birthday girl?" Nana shouted.

"I need to get some air, Nana. I'll talk to you later." Richard continued walking away.

"If you want Selina, you must be willing to fight for her," Nana said, hurrying after him.

Richard paused and looked back at her, surprised.

"It's obvious to me what's going on. I never saw jealousy until I saw it in your face. You are the man who can fight for Selina." Nana felt triumphant. Richard had even stopped running away from her.

"I don't understand what you're saying," he said softly.

"I don't mean fight the little guy at the party. He's nobody. Selina is madly in love with you. I've never seen her so in love before. But there is a sense of loss mixed with her feelings about you. As though she already thinks that she's lost you. And she's never had you."

"What has she told you about me?"

"Nothing," Nana said. "That's what worries me the most. You are some sacred, taboo subject. But I've figured it all out. She is deeply in love with you. She's afraid she'll lose you. Afraid that her father will chase you off like all the rest."

"All the rest?" He was curious.

"Her old man is a real S.O.B. He thinks he has the power and money to rule the whole world. Selina has never let him run her. So he chases away her men, even some of her friends. Two years ago Selina was almost--maybe in love with this precious law student. He was full of ideals, smart, and poor. Her father cornered him one time at a party and told him if he ever wanted to practice law in the English-speaking world, he'd better leave Selina alone. He never came back. The wimp deserted her. Selina was heartbroken. It happened one other time also. And in high school... forget those days. But not with you, Richard Saxon. You've got what it takes. When you meet the old man during the holidays, put a fist between his teeth and tell him that his daughter and you are free from his threats.

"No one deserves Selina unless they are willing to fight off the dragon: her father. Deep in her heart Selina thinks no one will ever love her for herself. Stand up to Mr. Power and Money." Nana had finished her discourse. She was pleased with herself until she looked at Richard's face.

Richard's heart felt like lead. New emotions piled on top of old ones. A great ache inside of him seemed to crowd out his reason.

"Nana, I know you mean well. I just need to be alone." Richard's voice cracked. He walked away. Nana's heart sank. Nothing

witty came to her mind. Standing on the sidewalk in front of her house
she watched him walking down the street. She realized that she had said
the wrong thing at the wrong time.

Richard walked for a long time, hard, fast strides. He was
grateful for the darkness that seemed to hide him in the busy little town
full of Friday night noises. Each new thought brought with it a new
pain. Selina needed him. The very energy of a fighter and a rescuer,
which came so naturally to him would have, could have served her so
well. He ached to rescue her from her father. He ached to keep her with
him always. But that could never be. He had raised her hopes only to
dash them to the ground. He had taken her love because he needed it so,
only to turn her away and leave her. It was time to put the whole thing
to rest.

He headed back toward his car, parked in front of Nana's house.
He would call Selina later. He would write her a letter to say goodbye.

When he reached his car, he saw Selina sitting on the steps of
Nana's house waiting for him. Nana had told Selina everything about
their conversation. Selina stood up and walked toward him.

Go away, Richard said in his mind. *I cannot look at you. I
cannot touch you.* Selina saw his face in the shadows, a sad, tormented
face.

"Nana was wrong to--" she began.

"I have been wrong. Wrong to take what I needed from you.
Wrong to allow you to be hurt by me. I have known from the beginning
that our relationship could never be the thing you need. You need one of
those men in there." Richard pointed to Nana's living room. He choked
back a deep emotion.

"We have both known. I am not a victim." She reached to hold
his hand. His hand was hot. He pulled it away.

"We are too attached to each other. I... we need to distance
ourselves from each other for a while," Richard said.

"You mean we need to break up," Selina asked.

"I owe you so much, Selina. I don't know what is best for you. I
think that you need to spend more time with your friends. It will be
easier for you when I go." Richard struggled to express his thoughts.

"I'm not ready for this. I'm not ready for you to go now," Selina
said.

"You will never be ready. I will never be ready to leave you. I understand separation better than you. I have lived longer."

Richard's voice was unsteady. Selina said nothing.

"Sometimes I wish that you would get angry. Demand an explanation," he said.

"I told you in the beginning that I would never demand explanations. That I would accept your secrets and the mission that would take you away from me." Selina seemed calm. Her voice was gentle. Richard reached for her and held her in his arms. The night seemed unusually dark around them. He could see no stars or moon. He could only feel her near him.

"I can't go on like this," he said. "Let's spend some time apart. I will call you one more time before I leave... Michigan. This is the first goodbye. There will be another. Knowing there is one more goodbye will make it easier." Richard stroked her hair as Selina cried.

CHAPTER
ELEVEN
BROKEN

Selina trembled with emotion as she watched Richard drive away from her house. She doubted that she would ever see him again. She could still feel the warmth of his arms holding her. And then the tears began as the loss tore through her. Maybe Richard no longer loved her. Maybe no one could love her.

Selina flung herself on her bed sobbing. She was almost too weak to stand as the force of the emotion rushed through her. For weeks now she had prayed for God's guidance. She had not gone into this thing with Richard alone. Each time that she had prayed and asked for God's guidance she felt sure that God wanted her to love Richard unconditionally and to pray for Richard's soul. She had done both. Selina had abandoned all caution, had abandoned her distrust. She loved Richard as she had never loved before. How could the Lord ask this of her? Or maybe God had never heard her prayers. Never guided her. A new pain gripped her. How could the Lord not have been in this love?

She cried as she talked to God. "Lord of the Universe, you know I love you. You know that I accept your will in all things. But not this time. Not in this." Selina pounded her fist on her pillow.

The angel Clare stood near her by the bed. Clare knew Selina well and had guarded her since birth. Clare spoke to Matthew, the warrior angel who watched over Selina always during these days.

"I have never seen her like this before."

"Don't you wish that we could comfort them in all their pain?" Matthew said.

"Sometimes we can."

"But not now."

Suddenly the angels were horrified to see Natas enter Selina's bedroom. Michael had not warned them!

"What does a demon of your class want with my Selina?" Clare asked Natas. Clare placed herself between Selina and the demon.

The demon did not answer. He had ten times the strength of Clare and tossed her across the room. He did the same with Matthew, who reached for his fire sword. The angels were paralyzed.

Natas leaned against Selina's sobbing face. His hot breath spoke to her in thoughts that sounded as if they were her own.

I hate Richard, how could he do this to me? He treats me like a queen, then thrusts me aside. All he ever wanted was sex. Since I wouldn't give it to him, he's tired of me. Just like all the rest. I will never love him or anyone again.

Natas spoke the thoughts, and Selina listened. She sobbed again and this time threw her pillow against the wall. Anger opened the door to hate.

Richard doesn't know and wouldn't even care to know how I have prayed and sacrificed for his soul. I have fasted from my greatest passion, painting, for six weeks now. I attend Mass twice a week as my living prayer for Richard. There is nothing I would not do for him. But no more! No more! He is just like my father!

They all end up being like my father, with hatred in their souls.

Selina accepted every thought as her own. And now a cold resolve was entering her, a cold resolve to hate. She pulled herself off the bed.

No man is worthy of my tears, Natas spoke. Selina walked into her painting studio and picked up a charcoal to sketch. Selina looked around the room for the right kind of sketch pad. And then she saw it, a crucifix hung on her wall centered between the two large windows of the room. Windows that streamed with sunlight during the day. The crucifix turned her thoughts to Christ. His love beckoning to her from the cross. His sacrifice, obvious and eternal.

What does He know of love? He was a man, Natas shouted in her mind. The thought was not her own, and Selina knew it.

"I reject that thought. Forgive me, Lamb of God, you who take away the sins of the world. You know all things about love, Jesus. And I know nothing. Forgive me for the hatred which I allowed to creep into my heart. Wash me clean with your blood, Jesus. Wash and protect me by your sacrifice on the cross." Selina sat in a crying heap on the chair by her window. Natas had been silenced, but he was not helpless. He took one set of claws and pressed them in her mind. The other set of claws he dug into her heart.

Selina's mind was filled with confusion and condemnation. Her heart ached with self pity. She felt overwhelmed and abandoned. And yet Jesus hung there on the cross.

"Have mercy on me, a sinner," she prayed. Her tears burned in her eyes. Her prayer unleashed power.

Archangel Gregory ripped through the ceiling with his fire sword drawn. Natas fought back. Three other warrior angels joined him, dragging Natas away from Selina's home. Matthew and Clare fought the smaller demons until Selina was free.

Selina's eyes had not been made to see the battle of the angels. But she knew that God had answered her prayer. She felt a heaviness lift with the self pity. She felt exhausted.

"Great Christ, upon your cross, help me to love. I need two things right now. Help me to give and not to count the cost. Help me to accept your will in all things," Selina prayed, sitting next to her easel. And then she started getting dressed for bed. As she ran her bathwater, she began to cry again.

One thing is necessary. Let go. Let go, the gentle thought said.

Selina pondered the command as she bathed and dressed for sleep. *Let go*, she thought as she knelt in prayer beside her bed.

And then she understood. She could not let go of Richard Saxon. She could not let go of her secret desire, to marry him and to be a part of his world for the rest of her life. She had done everything with this dream in mind. She had always believed that she would marry him. And have her own way. The Lord had never shown her that she would marry him. Richard had always told her that he would leave her. It was she who held on, not only to the present, but to the future. It was she who had to let go.

I don't want to let go of Richard Saxon. I don't want to let go of my dream, to marry him and to be a part of his world for the rest of my life. I have never wanted anything so much. You alone see my heart, Lord. You know me. How am I to let go of the prize that I carry in the center of my heart? She could not hold back the tears.

"By your grace, O God and in the name of Jesus, I will let go. Make it so, O God. That you may be served in this life and that I may be one with you in heaven someday." Selina felt the letting go rip through her. She resisted as it tore, and then surrendered. She fell asleep, too exhausted to cry any more.

II.

Pulsing, pulsing like a heartbeat, pushing life's blood into human veins, the power of God was being released. While Selina slept, power was being poured out. New armies of angels were being commissioned to uphold the humans.

"You must feel great joy in her," Archangel Gregory said to Clare.

"Remember the boy by the Sea of Galilee, the one in the Gospel who was the only person who remembered to pack his lunch? He had five barley loaves and two fishes," Clare said. "And Jesus asked the boy to offer his little treasure to Him. Once the boy did so, Jesus was able to take his small sacrifice and multiply it, by His power and mercy. Jesus multiplied it to feed the thousands."

The seven angels standing in Selina's bedroom remembered that moment in Galilee 2,000 years ago. Today they saw it happening again in the new space of Selina's life. Selina had made her sacrifice, she had given up her love for Richard Saxon. And now that love was in God's hands.

"Whether Selina lives or dies in the warfare of these next weeks, she has done well," Archangel Gregory said.

And the angels sang a victory song.

III.

Selina awoke just after dawn. She felt broken and at peace. She felt loss and sadness. Muted sunlight poured in her windows in warm rays of color. She went to her studio in her nightdress, and sketched and painted. Painting was her final release. It went beyond emotion, beyond thought. It joined somewhere between prayer and the physical world. The sketch took form, and then the watercolors flew. Her hands seemed to know what they were doing. The final product was a haunting scene-- a cool, early morning sky showed two silhouettes standing near a small hill. They were a man and a woman, serene and still. The two figures' heads were turned toward the sky, watching the fading traces of the full moon. *Draw two moons.* A quiet voice inside Selina spoke. She had learned to trust that quiet voice when she painted. And so she added a second moon, a smaller moon, separate but slightly tugging toward the larger moon. It just seemed right. Drained, renewed, empty of her dreams, Selina felt nearer to God.

Then as she dressed for work she noticed the tiny microphone hidden in her bedroom. She searched and found the other two in her living room, near the fireplace. Selina was angry.

IV.

The more she thought about it, the more her anger grew. Who and why was someone bugging her house? She didn't feel that she could deal with one more thing. She had lost Richard. She was less than a month away from taking her final comprehensive nursing exam. And now this.

She needed either Richard's advice or her father's advice about the bugging. She decided not to act until she was sure what action to take.

Selina reported to work at the hospital as usual on Wednesday. She had only been there for an hour when she was called into the head nurse's private office. Ms. Ursil, the head nurse, introduced Selina to a distinguished-looking man in a gray business suit named Mr. Adams. She left Selina alone in her office with him. "When Mr. Adams leaves, wait in my office. I'd like to talk to you," Ms. Ursil said. Selina felt slightly anxious as Ms. Ursil closed the door behind her.

"Ms. Devon, Mr. Max Traytur sent me here to talk to you. He wanted me to personally extend his apologies to you for the unfortunate incident in the hospital a week ago. He was quite embarrassed by his behavior toward you. He was ill and when he had a seizure in front of you--well, he's very sorry." Mr. Adams' manner was warm.

"You can tell Mr. Traytur that there is no need for apologies. Hospitals often bring out the worst in people," Selina said.

"Nevertheless, he asks you to accept this little gift as a token of his appreciation for your nursing care." Adams presented Selina with a large box of expensive gourmet chocolates wrapped in an elegant golden box.

"Really, I did nothing. I should give the candy to the rest of the nursing staff," Selina said.

"I presented a box to your head nurse for the rest of the staff. This box is for you. Mr. Traytur thinks that you have a special gift for helping people."

Selina listened uncomfortably.

"Which brings me to my next point of business." Adams handed Selina a large white envelope addressed to "Miss Selina Devon and guest." It was a formal invitation to a black tie Holiday Party at Traytur's home on December 23. Selina quickly prepared an answer.

"I am honored by Mr. Traytur's invitation and thoughtfulness. But I will not be able to attend. Unfortunately I will be out of town on the day of his party." Selina tried to sound charming.

Adams frowned at her answer, nodded politely, and excused himself. Selina waited for the head nurse to return to her office. What seemed like a long time later, the head nurse returned with a second woman. The other woman introduced herself as Barbara Bartell, assistant director for Hospital Fund Raising. Ms. Bartell was a slender African-American woman, stunningly attractive and well dressed. The two women sat down to talk. The head nurse let Ms. Bartell speak first.

"We understand that you rejected Mr. Traytur's Holiday Party invitation, Selina," Bartell began.

Selina was confused that these two professionals were interested in the invitation. She answered, "Yes."

"Selina, Mr. Traytur is very wealthy, and he is considering making a *major* donation to the hospital. He has shown no interest in meeting with anyone from the fund-raising office. You are the only member of the medical staff to whom he has shown personal attention. It would be a special favor to the hospital and its patients if you would join his party and bring the needs of the hospital to his attention. I would think you would view this as an incredible opportunity to help the hospital--one rarely offered to student nurses." Ms. Bartell looked at Ms. Ursil, the head nurse.

"Why can't you go, Devon?" Ms. Ursil asked.

Selina felt cornered.

"I am flying to New York on the day of his party to spend time with my family at Christmas," Selina said.

"Christmas is a month from now. Can't you change your plane reservation?" Ms. Bartell was indignant.

"I am not comfortable with Mr. Traytur's attention. Why did he invite me rather than the Chief of Staff to discuss the hospital's needs?" Selina asked.

"He also invited Dr. Fujama to his party," Ms. Bartell answered.

The head nurse looked directly at Selina. "It works this way sometimes, Selina. As nurses we are functioning in our routine, but something that we do reaches a patient and makes a difference for him. You are the one who represents us in his mind." The head nurse paused. "We're not asking you to prostitute yourself for the hospital. If you cannot accept the man's invitation, forget it." The head nurse smiled.

Selina agreed to go if she could change her plane reservation. Secretly, she counted on the fact that she could not. She noticed that her palms were sweaty. Traytur's cut on her sore wrist began to bleed.

CHAPTER
TWELVE
A BUD UNOPENED

Richard sat in a small booth near the window in the quiet restaurant. It was 7:00 a.m. and pitch black outside. He did not have class until 9:00 a.m., but he had been unable to sleep these past five nights. He left his house as early as possible to escape the loneliness. It was Thursday and he had not talked to Selina nor seen her in five days. He could not believe the hole that had been created in his life.

Her presence had been the warmth, the sanity, the joy, the light, and the beauty that had filled his days.

The waitress brought his eggs, toast, and coffee, then hurried away. The food grew stone cold as Richard doodled in a notebook on the table. He watched outside the window waiting for the sunlight, waiting for the campus to awaken, waiting for life to stir around him. Something had to change.

It was better being alone and self-sufficient. Perhaps he could decide to forget Selina completely. He knew how to do it. He knew how to forcibly bury something in his unconscious. He had been trained to do it for self-defense. *That which weakens you must be destroyed, whether it is physical or mental, The Rule of Battle counseled.* In battle school they trained you how to forget. You needed injections to make the forgetting total. But there were steps you could take without injections.

He wasn't ready for forgetting, not this morning. As deep as the pain ran, so too did the love he felt for the woman. He wasn't ready to let go of her, not this morning. He wanted to keep everything that she had taught him. He wanted to keep the part of himself that she had changed. *I am deliberately holding on. I have no one to blame but myself.*

"You look like the young Hamlet just before he did himself in," Sam Steinberg spoke suddenly, then slid himself into the booth across from Richard. Sam was the assistant chairman of the mathematics department, a distinguished-looking man of sixty. He was short, almost bald, and soft-spoken. He was a tenured, respected teacher and a good listener. Sam liked Richard. Sam liked everyone.

"I was going to leave you a note telling you that I couldn't meet you for dinner tonight. But now that I've bumped into you, maybe we can have breakfast together anyway," Sam said. His cheerful countenance shook Richard loose from his dark mood. "So, did you lose your best friend?" Sam asked.

"Do I look that bad?"

"Let's just say that I can see your own personal rain cloud hanging over our table here. But listen, son, I don't mean to pry." Sam thought of everyone under the age of fifty as being someone's son.

"Or maybe I do," Sam continued. "Do you want to talk?"

"I'm not sure I know how."

"It's easy. First, you make sure that the person you're talking to wants to listen. Which I do. Then you make sure he is discreet and won't gossip your secrets all over campus. Which I won't. The next move is yours."

Richard forced a smile. Sam was not only lovable, but trustworthy. He was perhaps Richard's only friend.

"I made a serious mistake. I fell deeply in love with a woman and let her fall in love with me. Then I ended the relationship, and now there is only pain."

"If you two were so deeply in love, why did you end the relationship?" Sam pushed his glasses up on his nose and frowned.

"There is a major obstacle that prohibits me from marrying her. I can't explain my situation to you."

"Maybe you just need to love her for today and not worry about tomorrow. Not worry about marrying and all those complex, awful things."

"Is that how you approached dating your wife?" Richard asked. Sam paused thoughtfully, love and memory stirring behind his eyes. Sam ordered breakfast from the waitress and asked her to bring Richard fresh coffee.

"My wife, I always felt I wasn't good enough for her. She deserved the best. What shocked me the most was that she thought I was the best." Sam chuckled. "If you're already thinking about this woman of yours as a wife, then you're in trouble, Richard."

"I know I am. Just tell me how to get past the pain of losing her. Someone has to know."

"I know about *my* grief, son. But I may not know about yours. Esther died two years ago. We had been married for thirty-five years, married and in love. I can still hear her voice sometimes, smell her pies baking, feel her next to me in bed. Sometimes I wish that she could have died slowly so that I would have had time to get used to her leaving me. But she didn't. She died suddenly of a heart attack. In the middle of the afternoon."

Sam's eyes began to mist with tears. "I wasn't even with her. I was at school. She died alone. I wasn't even there to help her." Sam's voice choked. The waitress shoved his breakfast in front of him.

"Now you've got *me* losing *my* appetite. See if I have breakfast with you again," Sam continued.

"But what I'm grieving is different than what you're grieving, Richard. I'm grieving the woman who shared my life for all those years. I have four children that we shared. I have memories, I have everything that she gave me. You have lost hopes, lost dreams of things that never happened. You have a bud that never blossomed."

"I have no choice." Richard's eyes flashed with anger, but his voice was soft and controlled. He had watched Sam's face as he talked. Now he looked away.

"You always have choice. At this point, Richard, I'm pretty darn curious to know more about this obstacle thing. But you're not going to tell me any more about it, are you?"

Richard shook his head. He bit a corner of greasy cold toast.

"So she rejected you because of the obstacle?" Sam persisted.

"No, she doesn't even know what it is." Richard felt annoyed. "Let's change the subject."

"Let's not. Call me a matchmaker, but I'm taking this a few steps further," Sam said. There was nothing but kindness in Sam's eyes.

"I never gave Selina a choice about me. I always laid out the terms and forced her to accept them. I talked in riddles, and she accepted them, accepted me. She loves me unconditionally." Richard had lowered his voice.

"So give her a choice, son. But before you go offering her a choice, be sure that you have made yours. You have to know that you not only love her, but that you want to marry her."

Richard knew. He knew the first time that he spent a night alone with Selina. He knew the first time and the second and all the times he spent with her after that. He knew more certainly than ever at Nana's party that this was the woman he loved enough to marry. Sorn's father had once confided in him how he knew that he should marry his mother. "I knew I wanted to marry your mother when I visualized another man giving her children. Her children belonged to me, I knew, on some level deeper than rational knowing." Richard had shocked himself at Nana's party when the same reality struck him. He felt a flame of desire not only for Selina but for the children she could give him.

"I struck a nerve, didn't I?" Sam said, pleased with himself.

"I can't offer her a choice," Richard said. "It's not something I can do." But even as he said the words he doubted them.

"You sure know how to frustrate a guy, Richard. I'll throw out my final ace in this hand. Do you believe in God?"

Richard was surprised at this turn in the conversation. "No," he replied. "Do you?"

"I'm an old Jew. Of course I believe in God. When I was a young Jew I believed in a Creator who started the universe expanding and then took his hands away. But now, after all I've lived through, I have seen the Creator's hand creating good for us, over and over again."

Richard looked hard at Sam. "And so?"

"Ask Him, and God will reach out His hand and create good for you one more time." Richard felt uncomfortable.

"You've been a good friend to listen to me. Thank you." Richard smiled. He glanced across the aisle of the restaurant and caught the eye of a red-headed girl who flirted with him. Richard quickly turned his eyes away from her. *Never again,* he thought. *I'll have nothing to do with women again.*

CHAPTER
THIRTEEN
REVELATIONS

Selina was running away. Running and running, she was all alone. He knew he could never reach her on time!

The alarm woke him. Its sound rang through his dream and jarred him. His head ached. The awareness of loss and emptiness told him he was conscious. He showered and dressed for class mechanically. Today was Monday, his longest day on campus. Today he had three hours of lectures and a two-hour staff meeting at 4:00 p.m. It would be a long day.

Richard cursed the November cold as he drove to campus. He felt irritation at the clumsy traffic. He made it through his 9:00 a.m. lecture with no problems. Then as he was leaving his classroom, a small brunette teaching assistant almost chased him down the hall.

"Professor Steinberg sent me to find you. He said he has an important message for you and hasn't been able to reach you all weekend."

"I'll see him at 4:00 p.m. today."

"He said you should come to his office as soon as possible this morning."

"Is he all right?"

"He seemed fine to me."

Richard went to Sam's office immediately. Sam was not there. His secretary had no idea where he was. She said there was nothing written on his calendar until 4:00 p.m. that day.

Richard jotted a note for Sam detailing where he could be reached for the rest of the day. He tried calling Sam at home, only to reach an answering machine.

The afternoon passed slowly. Richard was vaguely apprehensive about Sam and his message. Shortly before 4:00 p.m. Richard again went to Sam's office. He found the old man absorbed in reading at his desk.

"Richard, good to see you. I missed you this morning and got tied up all afternoon. Where were you Friday? Your friend Selina was looking for you on Friday morning. I was at your office looking for a journal article when I saw her."

"Was she... all right?"

"She was beautiful, if you ask me. Fine woman. But she did act a little mysterious. Must be why you two get along so well." Sam chuckled to himself.

"What do you mean mysterious?"

"Well, she asked me to show her my driver's license, to prove that I was who I said I was, your dean and your friend. Then she gave me this letter and told me to hand it to you *in person*." Sam handed Richard a peach-colored envelope. The letter read:

"Richard,

I need to ask your advice. Two days ago I found
bugs planted in my house. Then I noticed someone following
me on campus, at home, everywhere. I thought I should ask
you about this before calling my father or someone else.
Please come instead of calling.

Selina."   -Friday A.M.

Richard folded up the letter and slipped it in his jacket pocket. "Sam, I need to be excused from the staff meeting. I don't think this matter should wait. Can you cover for me?"

"Get going, Richard." Sam shook his head. "You two worry the heck out of me." Then Sam's face became earnest. He looked at Richard over his glasses. "Your father would like her, Richard."

II.

Richard's adrenaline was flowing. He was grateful for the way it sharpened his senses and invigorated him. He had dreaded the day when he would have to encounter ROSET. He had planned for it. But the plan did not involve another person, not Selina, not anyone. He cringed at the thought of fanatical ROSET witch hunters holding Selina. He visualized her helpless and alone. He forced himself to put the picture out of his head.

But his anxiety increased when he reached her home and she did not answer the doorbell. He still had her front door key. He went in. The house was cold with only one light on in the living room. Selina was nowhere to be found. Her refrigerator was empty. Her text books were gone. There were no signs of violence. But she was gone and had been for some time. She had written her letter to him four days ago. *Selina, helpless and alone*, he thought.

Ask Him, and God will reach out His hand and create good for you one more time. The thought rang clearly in his mind. Richard looked in Selina's bedroom and guest room. There were no clues.

Ask Me, the words nudged.

I never believed in You, so why should You help me now? Richard answered the thought. But his heart moved toward God as he said his first prayer. "If You ever cared about me or Selina, show me now. If You give signs, give me a sign. If You do not, then I will know that I have always been alone." Richard spoke out loud to God. Nothing happened.

Richard's heart pounded with emotional intensity. There was only one more room to search. He turned the light on in her painting studio. His heart stopped for a minute at what he saw. On her easel stood a new painting. An astonishing painting of a man and woman standing together in a muted light beneath the two moons of Tethra.

And then it struck him, faster than thought, deeper than emotion--his soul was pierced to the core with the presence of God. God had given him a sign. And now he saw and now he knew that the same God who was with him here on tiny Earth had been with him on Tethra. The same God who had been with him as he crossed light years of galaxies beneath a thousand thousand moons.

Richard walked out to his car and watched the sky. Dark violet shadows cast themselves in the background of the peach and yellow sky. The golden ball of winter sun stood center stage and near the ground. Indeed there was a Creator. And Richard wept.

                                III.

Richard moved with the pace of his anxiety as he drove to Nana's house. Nana might know where Selina was. The sounds of music and raucous laughter boomed through Nana's front door, reassuring him that Nana was home.

"Well, what to my wondering eyes should appear!" Nana greeted him. "Welcome to the party." Nana clutched his arm and

shuffled him quickly in the door. She bolted the door behind him.
Before Richard had a chance to speak Nana whispered softly. "She's in
the back room. I presume you're here for my Leena." Richard's obvious
expression of relief and delight pleased Nana. She hustled like a
successful cupid accomplishing an important task. He followed her to a
tiny study across from Nana's bedroom.

IV.

        Selina sat on the floor next to two textbooks, pharmaceutical
chemistry and gross anatomy. She had given up on her chemistry and
sat with her sketch pad in her lap, drawing sketch after sketch of human
hands. She heard Nana coming near her door and did not bother to look
up. Nana's house was full of people coming and going. And then she
saw his feet. Looking up at him from the floor she saw Richard standing
next to Nana. He wore his heavy lambskin coat which added inches to
his broad shoulders. He looked unusually big standing in the doorway,
filling it. Nana looked thin and frail beside him. He was glad to see her,
his dark eyes penetrating her with a dozen emotions. He was beautiful,
Selina thought. Selina steadied herself. *He is not mine anymore, I must
hide my eagerness to see him.* And then his arms encircled her and she
felt like crying.
        "I came as soon as I could. I only received your letter an hour
and a half ago from Sam."
        Selina felt relief. She wondered if he had tried to stay away. He
had ended their relationship. She fought back tears as he looked at her.
She had missed him so.
        "Will you come and talk with me in my car where we can be
alone?" he asked. He kept his hands on Selina's shoulders. "Bring all
your things."
        "I've been staying here with Nana for the past few days. Let me
explain to her that I am leaving with you." Richard carried Selina's
small suitcase of clothes and large backpack of books and placed them
in the back seat of his car. Selina followed him a few minutes later.
Richard locked the car doors and pulled a small black box out of his coat
pocket, pressed a yellow button and turned to Selina. She felt his hands

caressing her hair, his fingers gently stroking her cheek. Selina avoided looking into his eyes. She found it hard to speak.

"I knew that you wanted some distance, some time apart. But this seemed important. I didn't know if the bugs in my apartment and the men following me were somehow related to your secret mission," she said.

"You contacted me rather than your father in order to protect me, didn't you?"

"Yes," Selina said. Richard looked at her with a look that she could not interpret. It may have been gratitude, it may have been love.

"And you waited four days for me to respond?"

Selina nodded, trying to conceal the pain of missing him.

"I was out of town. I would have come to you on Friday if I had received your letter. You did the right thing in coming to me about this. You and I may be in a lot of trouble." Richard spoke gently in the voice she loved.

"I feel safe now that I am with you," Selina said.

"That is because you know me better than anyone else knows me. You know that I would kill to protect you."

"Kill! That is awfully strong language." Selina did not try to hide the surprise in her voice.

"I would flatten a city to protect one hair of your head."

"You sound dangerous."

"I am dangerous." His dark eyes were intense.

"Richard, I don't like having you talk like this. It's... sort of odd."

"It would be odd to talk like this if I were not dangerous. But I am dangerous. I think you know that about me, and yet you trust me. You are not afraid." Richard's voice sounded different to Selina.

"You sound as if you're challenging me."

"I am trying to be truthful."

"Do you want to scare me? Do you want me to run away, run out of your life?" Selina asked.

"I don't want you to leave me. I want you with me. But I don't want there to be anything false between us anymore. I am dangerous, and if you accept me, that is part of what you accept about me." Richard's voice was cool and authoritative.

"Is this fair, to tell me only this much about yourself? To say that you are dangerous and to keep all your other secrets from me?"

"I will keep no more secrets from you. I will tell you everything tonight--if you want to know."

There was silence between them. Selina was shaken. He always sounded so confident. He always knew exactly what he was going to say and why. Tonight she did not know what she thought.

"What has changed? Ten days ago you ended our relationship. You could tell me nothing then."

"I am ready to tell you now, Selina. I am sorry for hurting you."

Richard did not look at her when he spoke. Selina felt one tear trickle from her eye. She could not seem to hold it back. Another tear followed the first one.

"Are you afraid of danger?" Richard asked. He put his arm around her and pulled her close to him.

"Yes, I am. But I am more afraid of losing you than of anything else."

"Good." Richard's voice was calm and self-assured. "Then you won't lose me. No one will take you away from me. And no one will hurt you." Richard paused to let his words sink in.

"I want you to tell me everything now," Selina said.

"We may both be in danger as we talk. It would be better if we took steps to define our danger and uncover our enemy. After that we can talk. We can take our time. I have things to tell you that will be hard for you. I want to do it gently, in a good way. Will you trust me one step farther?" Richard spoke like a lover, a soldier, and a friend. All his complexity came through in his words and in the eyes that Selina studied.

"Who is the enemy?" she asked.

"I don't know. I know who it might be, a group of fanatics who are murderers. They could try to harm both of us."

Selina felt a wave of real fear.

"I have the power to protect you." And then to answer the question in her eyes he said, "I am one of the good guys."

"I have always known that you are good. But who are you?"

"Let me take my time answering that."

"But you will answer it tonight?"

"Yes."

There was a smile on Richard's face as he looked in Selina's eyes. She had begun to relax under his protection. The sense of oneness between them was tangible. He kissed her. For a moment nothing else mattered.

V.

Richard lifted a metal box that was hidden under the driver's side of his car. He opened the box by pressing his thumb on the lid. A blue spark shot up. He pulled out a thick cylinder the size of a small tube of toothpaste. "This is a gun. It is called a Tee-spray. I want you to keep it. If you are in trouble, use it." He showed Selina how to use it.

"When was the last time that you saw someone following you?" Richard asked Selina. The cool, authoritative voice had returned.

"This afternoon when I left the hospital and came to Nana's house. The same man has followed me since Thursday. Nana and I switched clothes and classes on Friday when I brought the letter to your office. He followed Nana. Nana noticed him too and screamed. He stayed away for a day or so, and then a second man followed me on Sunday. I thought it would be better staying with Nana. There are always a dozen people at her house."

"Is Nana discreet?"

"She can be discreet for brief intervals. By tomorrow morning she will need a full explanation from me or she might panic."

Richard started the engine of his car. "I'm going to choose a deserted road and lead our pursuers to it. They have seen us together by now. I want to know who they are."

Richard accelerated his car to 80 mph, driving west far outside of the city to an empty country road. Then he parked on the side of the road. He pulled a small black remote-control device from his pocket and pushed a red button. A neon-green light flashed through the car.

"I just hid our car. We are cloaked out of their sight. But we can see them." A gray Buick came speeding down the street. It passed them, then turned around and drove slowly back down the road. Richard watched.

"PTL 624, gray Buick." Richard turned his car around, uncloaked it, and accelerated until he passed the gray Buick. Then he slowed down so that the Buick could follow him and drove for ten more minutes back toward town. Richard stopped at a tiny, dilapidated diner. "Let's go inside and watch who follows us. Try to act natural, no matter what I say or do," he said.

Selina and Richard seated themselves in a booth near the rear of the restaurant. The tables had red and white plastic tablecloths, and the leather seats creaked when they moved. They waited. They ordered coffee, and they waited some more.

Richard studied every person in the room. No one new entered the restaurant. The coffee arrived. Richard hated the waiting.

Just then a wrinkled, thin woman wearing heavy lipstick walked into the restaurant. She chose an empty booth within earshot of Richard and Selina.

Richard put his arm around Selina and pretended to be necking. "We are leaving quickly, as soon as I get one of her fingerprints," he whispered. Richard watched as the waitress brought the wrinkled woman a drink. He exited the rear of the restaurant next to the men's room. A small red Mercury was parked next to his. He memorized the license plate. It had not been here when he arrived. The gray Buick was not in the parking lot.

Richard came back in the restaurant from the rear entrance. As he passed the thin woman's table he knocked her purse off the table. Apologetically he picked it up and returned it to her.

Richard and Selina made a quick exit from the restaurant to their car. Richard turned the engine on.

"That woman was following us. She knew my name in her thoughts. Sometimes if I try, I can read people's thoughts," Selina said.

Richard nodded. In his rearview mirror he saw the gray Buick parked on the other side of the street. There was no one in it. Richard drove in a circle and parked behind the Buick. Like lightning he jumped out of his car, melted the Buick's front door lock and pressed a metallic sheet of paper on the steering wheel. He folded the metallic paper, returned to his own car and watched. A stocky gray-haired man in a trench coat ran out of the shadows of the restaurant toward his Buick as its burglar alarm system shot noise into the night.

"Give me the gun," Richard ordered Selina.

"You don't need to hurt anyone tonight, do you? You just need answers." Selina's voice was gentle.

Richard turned and looked at her. He was angry. Selina had never seen him angry before. He looked frightening.

"You're right. I don't need to kill him." Richard said. He had wanted to fight. He had wanted to end the fear.

"I could annihilate them all," he said.

"You're one of the good guys," Selina responded quickly.

Richard smiled in spite of his anger. Selina reached affectionately to touch him.

"You're burning up with fever." She pulled her hand away from his hot hand.

"No. My bio-kinetic body energy is gearing up for a fight."

Richard drove away so fast that the wheels of the car squealed. He speeded for several miles into the country and checked his rearview mirror. No one was following them. He parked and cloaked the car once more. He activated the sound distort.

The car was almost black inside. There was a sliver of moon in the sky. But the distance from the city meant that there was little artificial light anywhere. Richard felt himself calming.

"You need to come to my house with me tonight. It is the safest place for both of us."

"I have never been to your house. I asked you why one time and you didn't answer me."

"I'll answer you now. I have a very expensive computer system that needs to be protected. No one has ever been to my house, no one knows my address. Before I take you there I want to talk. So that you don't feel trapped or frightened when you get to my house."

"I don't feel trapped or frightened by you," Selina said.

"You may be frightened by the truth." Richard caressed Selina's hand with his warm hand. "I will tell you who I am. I am a military captain in an army that is fighting an evil dictatorship," Richard articulated slowly. "I have been temporarily disabled here in your country. Once my ship is secure and ready to travel, I need to return home where I am needed."

"What kind of army? What country are you from?"

"Selina, tell me about the painting on your easel, the painting with the two moons."

"Please don't change the subject. I'll talk about my art another time."

"Humor me, darling. Why did you paint it that way? Have you ever been on a planet with two moons?"

"Of course not, no one has."

"I have. The country I am from is called Chadra; the planet is Tethra. Tethra has two moons."

There was silence in the dark. Selina did not move her hand from his. More silence.

"Ask me something, darling," he said.

Selina withdrew the hand that Richard was holding. She fingered the golden crucifix on her neck chain. Her head spun. All the fears and the pieces of the puzzle moved quickly together at one time. Selina knew he was different. She had seen him through the eyes of love and she told herself that he was only somewhat different. But he was very different. He was at times incredibly learned, at other times strangely naive. He knew facts of science that no one on Earth had yet discovered. Sometimes his knowledge slipped out. Yet he had never seen a mosquito. He marveled as he watched his first mosquito, let it bite him, and then put it in a jar. He seasoned everything he ate with mint. The list went on. *Why is it so easy for me to believe something so incredible about him? Because all the pieces fit*, Selina thought.

"You're not trying to make a joke or to tease me?" Selina finally spoke.

"No, I'm telling you the truth."

"Can you prove it?" she whispered.

"Yes, I can."

"I thought you would say that. You are fully... human?"

"I am fully human."

Richard could feel her anxious energy in the darkness. She fidgeted nervously. But he could not see her face. He did not like the prolonged silence. Richard reached up and turned the ceiling light on in the car. They looked into each other's eyes. Selina moved her hand to touch his face. He kissed her fingers. Richard watched a wave of relief pass through her.

"It is only me, the man who loves you," he said.

VI.

Selina asked a hundred questions. Richard answered most of them. He did not tell her everything. There was knowledge that could endanger her, himself, or Frank Nelson. These things he kept from her. Her emotions fluctuated from minute to minute. When he felt she was ready to go with him, he uncloaked the car and drove it to his house. He had work to do there.

As they drove they talked. Richard told her about ROSET.

"ROSET is the major threat. But they are not the only ones. There are many on your planet who would harass me if they knew who I was. I could not lead a life here if anyone knew my secrets."

"I would die before betraying you or your secrets."

"Don't talk of dying, Selina," Richard said. He swallowed hard.

"Why did you decide to tell me everything tonight?" Selina asked. She watched his face move in and out of the shadows of the passing street lights. He turned and looked intently at her. "I'll tell you why another time. This is enough for now."

"Selina, do you love me?" His voice was quiet.

"I have always loved you."

"Do you love me *now*?" His voice was almost a whisper.

"I love you even more now."

"It hardly seems possible that I could love you more," he said. He did not take his eyes off the road.

Selina was surprised to discover that Richard's house was only two blocks away from her own. Richard cloaked his car as he drove near Selina's home, passed it, and turned down a winding dirt road that headed deep into a thick woods. Hidden amidst the trees was his brick ranch house. In the dark, Selina could not see the large cable that protruded from the side of the house and continued underground.

Selina half expected the stark mystique, the black decor of his home. The living room and dining room furnishings were black and glass. There were black wool couches and chairs in the living room. Black leather chairs fit snugly in the dining room with a glass table. The only decorations in the living room were heavy Egyptian sculptures.

Richard led Selina to his small bedroom, placing her suitcase and books on his bed. The room was simple and unadorned except for a geometric print purple bedspread. Richard left her there and went to the kitchen to prepare some food and drink. Selina's artist's eyes began to examine the angles and shapes of everything. She walked quietly through the house.

The only room that he had not shown her was his den. The door was closed, so she reached to open it. As she touched the door knob, an electric shock threw her to the floor. A strange sound shot through her head and knocked her unconscious.

When she awoke she was on the couch, shaking. Richard gingerly placed a tiny blue pill under her tongue and held her. Selina felt the spinning stop. She relaxed and then smiled. Selina felt euphoric and sensual. Richard had stretched her out on the couch and elevated her feet to improve her circulation. He knelt beside her on the couch. Selina felt sexually aroused. The smell of his hair excited her. She reached to kiss him, pulling his face toward hers.

Richard was startled by her kiss but was relieved that she had revived. Selina began to laugh and cry almost at the same time.

"Relax, darling. I gave you a pill, which may have been a mistake. Your hormones and energy system are all mixed up," he said.

"Never a dull moment," Selina laughed.

"You tried to enter my computer room. It is not programmed for your touch. The security device could have killed you. I gave you a proton-stabilizer drug. But I am afraid it's wrong for you," Richard said. He took her pulse. It was fast.

Selina laughed at his anxious concern. She was not capable of full rationality. "This is not drunk. This is released. Released from the nonsense of worry and inhibition. This is euphoria." Selina covered her mouth with her hand. "I can't help it if I'm in love with a star man."

Richard was worried as to how severe her reaction would be. He picked Selina up and carried her into the computer room with him. He asked the computer for help. The computer found Selina's medical history in the records of the University Nursing School. It analyzed the drug and gave its advice. "No damage to brain functions or other organs is expected. Administer quantities of water and protein. The drug reaction could last six to eight hours. Side effects currently being experienced are release of inhibitions and failure to withhold truth if questioned."

Selina was quiet as Richard forced her to drink glasses of water. She did not want to eat the chunks of cheese that he kept feeding her.

She looked intently into his eyes and spoke with a drunkenly serious quality, "I could become a soldier, too. Would you let me travel to the stars with you?" Richard did not answer.

Selina was afraid to talk for fear of what would come out of her mouth. Finally, she fell into an exhausted sleep after crying about her relationship with her father and his unpredictable cruelty toward her.

Richard carried Selina into his bedroom. He removed her shoes and placed her under the covers of his bed. He checked her vital signs. As he watched her breathing change to deep sleep, he marveled at her. He had placed his life in her hands tonight by revealing his identity to her. Today he had surprised himself. He had dared to trust both God and Selina. Neither of them had disappointed him.

VII.

It was close to midnight when Richard returned to his computer room, confident that Selina was sleeping well. He took the folded sheets of metallic paper from his coat pocket, and laid them flat on pieces of paper. Rubbing the metallic paper against the blank paper with a ruler, he made impressions of several fingerprints. He fed the fingerprints into his fax machine, keyed in a message to central FBI files and waited. Ten minutes later the fax machine returned a message to him in the form of two separate sheets of paper, police profiles on the two people who were fingerprinted.

The man in the gray Buick and the woman in the restaurant both had criminal records. The woman had been convicted on six counts of felony fraud. She had only recently been released from prison and placed on parole. The man, Andrew Rock, had served prison time for fraud, embezzlement, and assault.

Richard gave the computer their social security numbers and the license plate numbers of their cars. Within half an hour the computer told him what it knew. Andrew Rock was a private investigator from New York City who had a failing business. The gray Buick was rented from a local rental agency. There was practically no current information about the woman except a home address in New York and her parole officer's name. The information led Richard nowhere. In the morning he would track the private investigator who had been following Selina. The car rental agency could lead him to Andrew Rock.

Richard moved to a second computer screen. The symbols on these keys were in the alphabet of Eetan. When he activated the computer, a three-dimensional hologram of Jenxex appeared, hovering above the computer terminal. "Prepare micro circuitry for an Automatic Escape System to be placed in a third ring, identical to mine and Zejen's. Also prepare micro circuitry for a homing device for implantation in a watch. I will send the watch and ring to you within twelve hours for customization. My explanation will follow. Peace to you, Jenxex." Richard turned the computer off. For now he needed sleep. He had no idea what tomorrow would bring.

VIII.

Richard awoke suddenly at the sound of footsteps in the dark. His body was ready for combat before his mind had awakened. It was the way to stay alive. He sprang to his feet and assumed the posture for attack. Selina switched a small light on in the living room. She jumped at the sight of Richard poised in a stance like a Ninja warrior, his fingers pointed, his knees bent ready to pounce like a cat. His taut body relaxed quickly, and he lowered his hands. In his half-sleep he had forgotten that Selina was in his house. He was shaken. No one had come near him in the middle of the night, no one in years. In a few more seconds he would have killed her. He would have aimed his first two blows at the source of the footsteps. Selina was small and would have put up no defense. In only a matter of seconds she would have been dead.

"Why did you sneak up on me like that?" he asked.

Selina was upset by the tone of anger in his voice. "I'm sorry. I didn't mean to scare you. I felt cold in the bedroom and thought I would look for a blanket or the thermostat." Selina's voice was hoarse, her eyes were heavy with sleep, her hair was tousled. She looked fragile. Richard cursed under his breath.

"It's not your fault. There is so much you don't know about me." He concentrated on removing the anger and fear from his voice. "One thing you *do not do* is to catch me off guard, night or day."

Richard's mind flashed back to his training in battle school. He was only eight when he was badly beaten for the first time. All of the lectures had exhausted him, and he slept too deeply. He was groggy and slow to respond when an attacker nudged him in the middle of the night. The attacker defeated him with two kicks and one blow to the jaw. It was his worst score. The fact that he was eight and had been in bed sleeping was not taken into consideration by his trainers. It took him months to win back the combat points that he had lost.

Richard asked Selina to sit with him on the couch.

"My body is a trained weapon. Each part of my body knows how to go on fighting independently if another part is injured or disabled. My training began when I was seven. If you were not the best fighter, you were always sore," he said. Selina placed her hand on his arm and gently caressed him. His muscles tensed at her touch, and then he consciously relaxed them.

"Be patient with me, darling. Only two nights ago when I went to bed I knew that I needed to understand the complexities of my world. Now my world is two worlds, two planets, and everything I need to know has doubled." Her voice was honey.

"Teach me patience, Selina." Richard placed his arm around her. They both slept for two more hours. As dawn broke, Selina taught Richard how to watch the sunrise. She felt the colors and the textures as only an artist could feel them. And as he listened to her talk, Richard began to feel the sunrise too.

And yet, he knew there was a storm on the horizon.

CHAPTER
FOURTEEN
CAPTURE

Nana strode briskly down the halls of the Math and Science building. She had a mission. She had not heard from Selina in seventeen hours, and she was worried. *Didn't Saxon have a phone? What kind of games was he playing with Selina? First to break up with her, then to pop back mysteriously into her life and take her away from Nana without an explanation. And who were the dredges of society that had been tailing Nana and Selina?*

Nana postured herself indignantly as only she could. She was dressed in what she considered to be "underplayed conservative attire" today in preparation for a part for which she would be reading. Her thin, black hair was tied in a knot behind her head. She stood outside of Dr. Saxon's office and knocked. The door was locked. She grew increasingly annoyed, when she found that not only Richard but everyone in this wing of the building seemed to be away from their offices. Finally she strolled into the office of an older, baldish looking professor sitting alone at his desk, talking on the phone. His desk plate read "Dr. Sam Steinberg."

Nana waved to him and stood obtrusively in front of him so that he could not ignore her. The professor acknowledged her with a nod and continued his phone conversation. Nana studied every detail of his office with wide, dramatic eyes as if she were viewing some new cage at the zoo. *How could a person devote his life to numbers?* Nana wondered. Nana extended her hand in greeting the instant Sam hung up the phone.

"Dr. Steinberg, I do hope that you can help me."

"You know my name, but I don't know yours," he said.

"Nana, Amanda O'Brien. I need to talk with Dr. Saxon today. It's quite urgent. Would you know where I could find him?"

Sam checked Richard's course schedule sheets and explained that Richard had no classes on campus on Tuesdays. Sam was not at liberty to give a home address or phone number to Nana.

"If I left him a little note, could you be sure to give it to him in person? I wouldn't want it to fly off his desk or something."

"Do you want to see my driver's license, too?" Sam asked.

"I could, if you're quite proud of it." Nana's transparent face always revealed exactly what she was thinking. "Very strange person," her face read.

Sam chuckled at Nana's expression. He found her to be tantalizing.

"You're the second beautiful lady in a week who has given me a note for Dr. Saxon. I'd like to know how he does it."

The word beautiful seized Nana's attention for an instant. She did not think of herself as beautiful. Dr. Steinberg suddenly seemed attractive in an odd sort of way, she thought.

"Was the first beauty named Selina?" Nana asked with a worried expression.

"I don't think I should be answering personal questions, Ms. O'Brien."

"My dear friend Selina and Dr. Saxon could be in some type of trouble. I'm trying to find out where they are today," Nana blurted out.

"Maybe you shouldn't be telling people that sort of thing. That could start trouble all by itself," Sam said.

"Of course, of course." Nana looked flustered and embarrassed.

"Ms. O'Brien, why don't you wait to hear from your friend? If I can be of any help, you call me. If I see either of them today, I'll call you." Sam handed Nana one of his business cards. "What's your number?" he asked Nana.

Nana looked anxiously over her shoulder as though she was afraid of being overheard. Could she trust this Steinberg person? He had such a trustworthy feeling about him. Nana forgot about the note, scooped up Sam's card, and backed away quickly.

"I'll call you later today, professor. Meanwhile, forget what I said. We like a bit of drama and mystery in *my* crowd of friends." Nana used her eyes flirtatiously; her technique was calculated to distract Sam from her own anxiety. She didn't know whether or not it had worked.

                                II.

Selina saw Richard through new eyes this morning. He was an alien. The air he breathed, the food he ate, the language in which he thought and spoke, it was all foreign to him. He had adapted to an uncomfortable, strange world. Now an enemy stalked him. Who the enemy was, how and when it would strike, he did not know. His cool demeanor did not reveal the anxiety that must have been there. He was unusually silent and deliberate in his actions. He seemed unmoved when Selina encouraged him. She touched him, and yet he did not seem to feel her touch. Perhaps his stony veneer was part of his protection.

It would have helped Selina if he could have been gentle with her this morning, if he could have spoken to her in his sweet, delicious tone of voice. But she had to let go of that wish. Richard had become someone distant and reserved for now.

"Today I will take the offensive. I will find out who is following you and what they want." Richard had used his officer's voice. It was deliberate and determined. If he had tried to soften his voice for Selina, he had not succeeded. "You need to stay with me until I am sure that we are both safe. I don't want you out of my sight." He did not look at Selina. He watched the road in front of him.

Rain and sleet poured from the sky. Sleet cold enough to chill them to the bone, but too warm to change into snow. The sky had grown dark in the last half hour. It had an eerie dusk-like quality. Richard waited on the dirt road until the main road was free of traffic. He uncloaked the car and drove toward town.

Their first stop was at a pay phone. Richard did not have a phone at his house. Selina called the hospital and said that she was sick and could not work her eight-hour shift. Richard called his business answering service. Selina decided to call Nana later. Nana would not be home in the morning.

Selina stayed in the car when they reached the rental car agency. Only a few minutes later Richard returned to the car.

"The man who followed us last night is named Andrew Rock. This morning he traded his gray Buick for a white Ford. Perhaps he thought it would make him anonymous if he continued to follow us in a different car. We have no local address for Rock, only the license plate of his rented car and his New York home address. It will not help us much," Richard said.

"How did you get that information from the car rental agent?" Selina asked.

"I paid him well."

The weather seemed to be getting worse. Selina moved closer to Richard for warmth. She put her hand on his arm. But he did not respond to her. He was cool and preoccupied even as he drove to a jewelry store and bought her two expensive gifts. He bought her a platinum signet ring and an expensive watch. He waited quietly while the jeweler engraved Selina's initials in the ring. Selina was confused. It seemed a strange time to buy gifts.

When they were safely in the car Richard told her that the purpose of the ring was to be an escape device, and the watch was to carry a homing device. Selina's eyes grew wide. She was to be linked to the starship and placed under its protection. She did not like this. It was too much, too fast. But she said nothing. Richard started the car again and concentrated on his driving. He did not look at Selina when he spoke.

"I will keep you under my protection for as long as you need it. But you are free to leave me at any time."

"I'm not really free to leave you. I love you."

"I will never leave you unless you send me away, Selina."

"Until it is time for you to return to Tethra and your people," Selina said softly, and she touched his hand.

Richard said nothing more for a long time. The rain changed into heavy sleet, and the skies grew darker. The roads became slick as the temperature continued to drop. The sleet turned to snow.

"Where are we going?" Selina asked.

"To all the places where Andrew Rock expects you to go."

They drove to Selina's house and found no trace of Rock's white Ford. They parked and looked inside her house. Nothing had been touched. Selina silently showed Richard the bugs which she had not removed from their hiding places. Richard crushed them with his fingers.

The icy roads grew increasingly slippery, and the snowfall became heavy as they drove to Nana's house. A block away from Nana's street, Richard spotted Andrew Rock's white car. Rock was nowhere in sight.

Richard parked his car directly in front of Nana's house.

"Rock is somewhere nearby, and I am going to find him. Selina, you walk slowly onto Nana's front porch. Stay clearly in view and act as though you are leaving a note for Nana. Then walk back to my car."

Selina knew that she was the bait. She did not let her fear show. She followed her part of the plan. Snow melted in her hair as she walked. She could feel her heart pounding. She did not see what happened next.

III.

Richard saw Rock before anyone saw Richard. He chased Rock behind Nana's house. Rock held a pistol with a silencer on it. He fired it at Richard and missed. Rock slipped on the icy ground. Before Rock knew what had hit him, Richard grabbed his wrist, snapped the bone, and snatched his gun. Richard looked Rock in the eye and spoke softly. "You have two choices. One is to walk quietly with me to my car and talk. The other is for me to kill you here and now." Nana's house was on a side street, not in clear view of the main road. The two men were hidden in the shadow of Nana's house. No one could see them. Rock must have believed what he saw in Richard's eyes. Rock knew that this man who had snapped his wrist as if it had been a twig could snap his neck as easily. Rock responded to Richard's shove and moved toward the car.

Richard grasped Selina's situation immediately as he reached the front of Nana's house. Rock's female accomplice, the tall woman from the restaurant, had also been hiding in the shadows of Nana's house. The female had acted fast. She had jumped Selina, probably injected her with a drug, and had quickly shoved Selina into her own car. She had almost made it safely to the driver's side of her own car. Her back was facing Richard.

Richard was not aware of the flood of his emotions as he lifted Rock's pistol and aimed it at the woman. For a few seconds he had a choice. He could hit the back of her head and kill her or he could hit her shoulder and stop her. His aim was perfect. The force of the bullet threw the woman against the car.

Richard shoved Rock in the back seat of his own car. "If you try to escape, you are a dead man." His voice was breathless and angry. Richard ran to the woman's car, lifted the unconscious Selina from the front seat and carried her to his car. He glanced at the female attacker. Her hands trembled as she reached for her own gun. Her face was pale. Blood oozed from her shoulder wound. The woman caught Richard's expression and ducked away from him on the opposite side of the car. He barely looked over his shoulder to check the woman's next move. He expected her to drive away, to escape as quickly as possible. The pistol shot had been quiet. The heavy snow fall had provided a blanket of covering. Richard doubted that anyone had seen Selina's attempted kidnapping.

As he placed Selina in the front seat of his car he could feel his pulse racing and his adrenaline flowing. Richard wanted to kill and kill until Selina was safe--until there was nothing left that could hurt her. His hand shook as he placed the key in the ignition. He wanted to kill, and yet he had chosen only to wound the female kidnapper. Why? He would kill Andrew Rock unless Selina woke up quickly and looked at him with her perfect eyes and said once more, "There is another way."

IV.

Forty minutes later Nana arrived at her house. The heavy snowfall had ended, burying most of the morning's footsteps. The little note that was folded and stuck in Nana's front door had been written in haste. Selina had torn a piece out of her purse calendar and scribbled on it. "Nana, I'm fine. Selina." Nana did not believe the note or its message. It was written in Selina's handwriting. But Selina had ended it too quickly. She would have said more. Deep in her gut Nana knew that something was very wrong. Later that evening Nana locked the doors of her house and called Selina's father.

V.

Richard hated Rock. He had no tolerance for Rock's belligerent refusal to answer his questions. He did not waste patience on him. Richard placed the tiny blue pill under the tongue of an angry Andrew Rock. The pill would do its work as truth serum. Rock made a lewd remark about Selina. Richard struck him in the face. It was a controlled strike, intended only to stun him and not to break bones or cause deep pain. Richard wanted Selina to leave the room while he interrogated Rock, but she would not leave. She fought the effects of the drug she had been given. She sat drowsily on the couch behind him.

Richard towered above the disheveled, lumpy private investigator even when Rock was standing. Now the middle-aged Rock was sitting in a chair in Selina's living room. Richard must have looked like a giant to him. Rock was an unappealing person with small deep-set eyes and weather-worn skin. He became repulsive under the effects of the drug, whimpering at his helplessness before Richard, cursing at the miseries and disappointments of his life. Rock studied Selina, peering at her from head to toe. Then his eyes darted nervously to Richard.

"You'd probably kill me for what I'd like to do to the babe here," Rock laughed.

"Not probably. I would." Richard bent down and leaned his face close to Rock's face, almost touching him. Rock saw Richard's anger, dark and powerful. But the drug had loosed Rock's tongue, and his inhibitions seemed to have dissolved. Even the restraint of his fear could not force his mouth to behave. As a sense of helplessness seized him, he remembered everything bad that had ever happened to him. He began to pour out tales of personal hardships in a rain of obscenities. Richard listened and began to understand the thought patterns.

"Tell me who you work for and why you have been following Selina."

"Howard T. Beckwith hired me and two others to kidnap Damien Devon's daughter, Selina here. It was a good plan. She was supposed to be an easy target, unsuspecting, lived alone. Something got screwed up though, 'cause here I am."

"Who is Howard T. Beckwith?" Richard asked.

"He's the S.O.B. I embezzled from ten years ago. He tells me some sob story about how Damien Devon is the worst S.O.B. on the planet. Devon cheated him, weaseled him out of a fortune. Beckwith said everyone hates Devon. No one would weep for Devon if he lost five million dollars ransoming his daughter. That is, if the bastard decided to pay it. We were supposed to kill the daughter either way. Revenge, teach Devon a lesson, you know?"

Richard felt his rage flare. Rock was a murderer and would have killed Selina for money! The skin on Richard's face and hands began to glow with its neon pink light. He knew that if he struck Rock, the blow would do real damage.

"What is happening to you, Richard?" Selina's voice was a frightened shout. She had never seen his skin glow before.

"This creature does not deserve to live." Richard raised a glowing hand and then changed his mind. He struggled with the rage that wanted to kill and the self-control that wanted to wait. Perhaps Selina did not know what would happen next. And then she prayed aloud.

"Dear God, help us. Send us your power." The words were simple.

Richard's body responded to the prayer in an instant. His body relaxed; the pink glow faded. He inhaled deeply as a calm descended on him. For a moment he realized that the anger had controlled him. In the next minute he knew that he did not want it to control him.

Selina moved toward him, and he motioned her away. "Are you all right?" she asked Richard.

"You should die," Richard said to Rock. His voice was calm. "Try to save yourself. Answer every question that I give you, instantly and completely."

Rock stammered in his fear and eagerness to please the glowing giant. Rock detailed the kidnapping plan, his own part and the roles of two other kidnappers, a man and a woman.

The three were experienced kidnappers and extortionists. They had not anticipated any difficulty in capturing Selina. But for some reason, Selina became aware of their surveillance. When she moved in with Nana, it became complicated. They changed their plan to include drugging or killing Nana and anyone else who got in the way of Selina's abduction. And then Richard showed up.

"Who are you, anyway?" Rock dared to ask Richard.

"Someone who nearly killed you. Give me the names and addresses of the other kidnappers and Howard Beckwith." Richard taped the whole interrogation.

Then he switched the tape recorder off and activated his sound distort. He questioned Rock about ROSET. He asked the questions in different ways. Rock had never heard of ROSET and did not know what Richard was talking about. Rock grew pale and anxious. He could not even invent anything about ROSET in order to please Richard. Rock and his partners had not planted the bugs in Selina's house. He wished that they had. Rock seemed numb with fear. He began to cry like a frightened child as Richard pressured him. Finally Richard was satisfied. Rock could not lie, and he could not sustain his resistance while drugged. Richard was finished with him.

Rock ate and drank and passed out from exhaustion as Selina had done the night before. Richard tied a triple knot on the kidnapper's feet. Rock's right wrist was broken. Selina placed a temporary splint on the arm. Richard asked Selina to follow him to her studio. He activated the sound distort.

"We must call the police immediately." Selina spoke first, urgently.

"No, we cannot call the police. I cannot be pushed into the limelight of the legal system."

"We have no choice."

"We always have choices. The most simple way to stop these murderers from their crimes is for me to have them killed. I have their addresses. I can send orders to my ship. We will not be involved in any investigations."

"You can order people to be killed from your starship!" Selina was incredulous.

"It's simple."

"No, Richard. No, we cannot do that. We have no right to kill them. They are criminals, and they need to be punished--but by the law, not by us."

"Your laws are written for different situations than this. My only responsibility is to protect you and myself."

"The law is the law. We cannot pick and choose when to follow it."

"Selina, think for a minute. You are asking me to become embroiled in your legal system and to endanger my own safety. Your legal system is a clumsy set of social norms." Richard could feel his anger rising.

"Not social norms, God's law. You shall not kill."

"*They* nearly killed *you*." Richard reached for Selina's hand and held it too tightly. Selina heard her own voice crack with emotion. Only now was it beginning to hit her that she had been in danger. Still, she spoke the words.

"Love your enemies," Selina said softly. "I've never had an enemy before. But that is Jesus' command."

"Jesus, your God, right?" Richard loosened his grip on Selina's hand. He tried to control his exasperation and listen to her. Listen, so that he could hear and understand. Not listen so that he could control.

"It was this God who gave you power for me tonight. Why does He give power when you ask for it?"

"Because He is merciful. Because I serve Him." Selina seemed unprepared for his question.

"You have put yourself in the service of this God, and so you must follow His commands. Is that how it works?" Richard asked.

"Yes," Selina answered. "That is a good way to put it, I am in the service of Jesus, the King."

Richard thought for a long time. He barely moved. There was a supernatural strength within Selina that he had not fully studied. A quiet power came from her, came from her God. It had swept in gently and saved Rock's life when Richard's rage would have killed him. Quiet power, but greater than his own anger. Richard, who was a man who had known power all his life, knew power when he saw it. And he respected it.

"We will follow the command of your God. Not because I serve Him, but because you do. If I don't have these murderers killed, there is another way to handle them. It is more complex, and there is more risk. I will need to make a deal with your father."

"My father! Richard, he doesn't make deals. He will try to crush you just because you care about me." Selina had been sitting down. Now, suddenly, she jumped to her feet. "I don't want my father to hurt you."

"I'm glad that you love me as well as your enemies." He smiled. "Your father will not crush me. And for your sake, I will not crush him."

"It will put you in more danger if you meet my father than if you go to the police. I'm afraid for you."

"I am not afraid of your father." Richard moved close to Selina. He put his hands on her waist. She turned her face toward his. Tears had formed in her eyes. Her beauty washed over him. The sweetness mellowed him. Richard's voice was gentle.

"Listen to me. I may need to kill in order to save us both. I will try to obey your Jesus' commands. But I may need to kill in order to save us both. And you will need to follow me and trust me." He waited for Selina's answer. Her eyes said "Yes," and then she nodded in agreement.

CHAPTER
FIFTEEN
LOVE

Richard hated waiting. And he hated not knowing who the enemy was. He still did not know who was bugging Selina's house. Or why. He had been trained to seek and find and destroy enemies. But in order to do that he had to know who the enemy was.

Richard told Selina that she should spend one more night in the safety of his house. He wanted to customize her protective devices before she returned to her home. Selina trusted him. She had never complained about any of her danger or fear. Richard suggested that she take her time getting her things together for another night away from home.

There was no need to hurry at the moment. Andrew Rock slept in a drug-induced state in Selina's living room. Rock slept so soundly that he barely seemed to breathe. Richard would not get rid of Rock until nightfall, two hours from now.

Richard rummaged through Selina's kitchen for a snack. He found another microphone hidden under the counter near her phone. He ripped it out and placed it in his pocket to examine later. It reminded him that he was angry and that Selina may still have been in danger. Richard found a can of nuts, opened them, and decided to bring some to Selina.

He knocked on the door of her bedroom and asked if he could come in. He closed the door behind him.

Richard had seen Selina's bedroom from the hall on other occasions, but he had never been inside. Now he felt the warmth and intimacy of her sleeping place. The room was ivory-white, decorated with green vines and yellow roses. It was comfortable and beautiful like Selina. It was unpretentious and elegant. It was a good place for her to rest. A good place for her to be just now.

Selina sat on her bed fumbling with a few of her things. Her eyes were swollen, and her clear porcelain skin was blotchy from crying. She pulled a long strand of her golden hair with her left hand and twirled it around her finger. Richard understood the gesture. It was saying, "I am pondering something important." Richard knew this woman. He knew that words did not always come easily to Selina. She expressed her deepest thoughts and feelings through her sketching and painting. She sculpted clay to speak for her. She was learning nursing skills so that she could nurture with her hands. Now Selina struggled to express something important using only words.

She looked at Richard standing by the door. *I am in pain*, her eyes said to him. And then her words were more specific.

"Andrew Rock was going to kill me. Twice... twice in the last two months people have wanted to kill me. Why is all of this happening?"

Selina did not expect an answer from Richard. He moved toward her and sat next to her on the bed. He had briefly forgotten that some people lead lives free of violence and danger--that these intrigues seemed more commonplace in military life, but that they were not normal for her. He had taken her courage for granted.

Richard wanted to comfort her. "I would like to tell you that everything is going to be all right. But I cannot promise you that. I can promise you that I will protect you." Richard's voice was kind and full of love. Selina reached to touch his large hand. She held his fingers tightly. The source of her deeper pain pushed its way to the surface.

"What is going to happen to us?" Selina asked. Richard put his finger to his lips and shook his head. He reached into his pocket and activated the sound distort.

"Go on," he said.

"You honored me with your trust, when you told me who you really were. I wanted to know the real *you* and not your mask. But it is painful to think that there is no future for us... no chance for us."

"There is a chance," Richard said. He hesitated to go on. It did not seem to be the right time and place for this discussion. And yet, she had a right to choose the time.

"Selina, if you love me, I have put you in an impossible position."

"I do love you."

"I told you my true identity so that you would be able to make a choice about me. I want you to be my wife and to come with me to my world. I want it with all my heart."

Selina was stunned. It was clear by the look on her face that she had no idea that Richard was going to say this. He lifted Selina's chin in his hand so that he could look in her eyes. Her beautiful eyes glistened with tears.

"I know that you will need to think long and hard about this before you answer me. There is so much for you to consider. The first question is, do you want to be my wife? But it is not the only question. What I am asking you to do is to become involved in space travel and war. And are you going to be able to leave everyone and everything behind you?"

There was pain in Richard's eyes, and Selina saw it. She started to speak, but he put his finger on her lips, signaling her to be silent a minute longer.

"Tethra's war is desperate. You have not had such war on Earth. I am a member of the governing class of the most powerful nation on Tethra. As my wife you would have to share my responsibilities. If my nation wins the war, we will have a good life together. I will give you everything that you want. But if we lose the war, you will die with me.

"This war has nothing to do with you and your people, and you should not have to fight or die for it. Do you see how unfair it is for me to ask you to marry me?" Richard paused. Selina watched him with a look of wonder on her face.

"Selina, I want to woo you like a lover and a husband. What I sound like is a commander selecting a recruit. I hate doing things this way." He brushed her hair away from her eyes. He wished that she would say something.

"I have wanted to marry you for a long time. I don't have to think about that. I do have to think about the other things, though." Selina's face almost seemed to glow. She smiled.

Richard dug his hands into her sweater and drew her close to him. Slowly, he kissed her cheeks.

"What else is it that you need to ask me? I can see the questions in your eyes," he said, and he kissed both of her eyes. Selina opened them again.

"The questions I have are all for myself. When I feel rested I need to look inside and ask God to show me what I am made of," Selina said.

"Has the thought occurred to you to ask me to stay on Earth with you, to give up my mission?" Richard asked.

"It is not an option," Selina answered.

"Why?"

"Because I love you. Because I understand what you are. We have a name for you on Earth, Richard. A knight in shining armor."

Richard was silent for a moment. *Thank you for not tearing me in half, Selina,* he thought. He knew she could have done it in that moment, torn in half the man who belonged to Tethra from the man who belonged to her.

"You understand so much. Your God must teach you certain things. No one else could know them," Richard said.

"God is love. Love understands."

Selina caught a look in Richard's eyes. And then it was in both of their eyes. A look of pure, untainted joy. It was the joy of the right half that had found its left half. Gently the joy reached out for its embrace, and the lovers kissed. They knew each other's lips and arms and hands and thoughts. For an instant. And then Richard ended the kiss. He wanted to lay with her there on the soft white bed and satisfy his physical hunger for her. But instead he stood up and walked to the door of the bedroom. *I will not tear you in half, Selina,* he thought. *I will not tear the half of you that obeys your God and chastity from the half of you that would respond to my body. At least, not now.*

Selina looked at him standing by the door. There may have been a thousand things she wanted to say. But only one came to her lips. "I'll be ready to leave in one more minute." She smiled. Richard nodded and left. *God is teaching me, also,* he thought. God was beginning to seem real.

II.

Natas panicked. It was the sheer agonizing pain of helplessness and fear. The panic tore through his being, throwing him into a thrashing heap. It tortured him. It ate him from the inside, swallowed him, and spat him out. And when all that panic and all that pain had destroyed him, still he went on living. Living in an agony that could not be soothed.

Natas could not stay near them when they were together like this, Selina and Richard, both loving each other. The power of God that glared up at him was more than Natas could bear. Their love was more than he could bear. It was sacrificial love. It had to be extinguished at any cost.

Natas woke Traytur from a sound sleep. He dug his claw into Traytur's groin. Traytur moaned, grasping his right side as the sharp spasm seized him. Traytur curled up in a ball of pain.

"How would you like to have an appendicitis attack tonight? I could give you excruciating pain for perhaps an hour and then just as your body exhausts itself, I would take your soul." Natas sensed an instant of relief as he shared his panic and helplessness.

"B-but, great one, you promised me fifty more years. You promised I would live to be a hundred." Traytur could barely form the words. The pain increased when he inhaled.

"Promise, you gnat's behind!" Natas laughed. The laugh itself shot through Traytur in a new wave of pain. "If you fail me in this Selina issue you will not live to see next month." Natas tormented Traytur a little longer. The sharp pain in his groin throbbed, ceased, jabbed once more, then stopped. The pain forced its way up through his body, and Traytur leaned over the side of his bed and vomited. He was covered with sweat. Natas gave him only seconds to recover.

"Your stupid microphone bugs are useless against the woman. And yet you stumbled across a way to reach at the man. This Richard Saxon person must be stopped. Go after Richard. Track him down." Natas twisted Traytur's arm.

Traytur grimaced, groping to regain his senses and his strength now that the appendicitis pain had passed.

"Who is Richard, great one? I beg your mercy for my ignorance, but I do not know him." Traytur tried to sound steady.

"He is the second member of the Triangle. He is the man who comes to her for love and for the gospel. Have you understood nothing of the conversations that you have heard with your bugs?" Natas pulled Traytur by the hair and whacked his head against the brass headboard. Traytur muffled his scream. He had, in fact, heard almost nothing of Selina's conversations with Richard.

"Leave me my senses, great one. I shall be a better servant for you if you do not handicap me." Traytur was nauseated, weak, and dizzy.

Natas leapt away from Traytur.

"I called you against this Triangle for one purpose, to destroy them. I can come against their souls. But in order to kill their bodies I must follow the lead of a human. Pinchard and Beckwith both failed to kill the woman. You must find a way to kill her and Richard as well. Fail me, ugly one, and you will die an excruciating death--and then I will drag your soul into hell."

"Where does Richard live?" Traytur asked meekly.

"Find out, sewer scum. Are you not supposed to be some kind of private investigator?"

"Do you... have you... worked on Richard yourself, great one?" Traytur was desperate for some knowledge about Richard.

Natas flew into a rage. He whirled around in a circle, thrashing about, breaking things in Traytur's room.

"I have been forbidden to touch him until Christmas! I know only snatches about him, because I cannot bear to stay and listen for long when he and the woman are together." Natas threw some sort of pain in Traytur's eyes. Traytur screamed. One of his bodyguards heard the scream and ran to Traytur's bedroom. Natas vanished, leaving his scent. The bodyguard caught the foul scent as he opened the door to Traytur's room. Both the bodyguard and Traytur vomited.

When he recovered, Traytur's purpose was set. His own life was to be spared in exchange for Selina's and Richard's deaths. Traytur had not even been given a chance to tell Natas about his brilliant plan. Selina was to walk into Traytur's own home on December the twenty-third. Now the plan must be perfect.

CHAPTER
SIXTEEN
CRIMES

Why did he feel a tinge of sympathy, a tinge of softness in his heart for this Andrew Rock, a slime of a character, who would kill an innocent woman for money? And yet Richard knew that he felt it. That something like sympathy had grown in his heart for Rock in only a few hours. Richard knew that he was changing.

It was dark now, and the light snowfall would hopefully be an aid in covering new footsteps on the ground. Andrew Rock leaned drowsily against Richard's arm as he walked through the almost-black alley. Richard planted Rock's half-sleeping body against the rear door of an exclusive jewelry store. Richard used a tiny flashlight to find his own footprints in the snow leading to the entrance. He backtracked and carefully messed each of his own footprints, trying to erase them while leaving a clear, readable set of footprints that matched Rock's shoes. Richard moved back toward Rock in the mushy patches of his old footprints. With gloved hands, Richard wiped fingerprints from Rock's weapons and returned them to their owner. He placed the screwdriver in Rock's hand, the gun in the other hand, and Rock's knife in his back pocket. Richard thrust a strong twist of Rock's screwdriver into the rear door lock. The force broke the lock and set off a screeching alarm system.

Richard ran quickly through the blurred patches of his footprints to the end of the alley where Selina waited for him in the car. The two drove away in seconds, traveling at a normal speed. They stopped the car two blocks away in the busy center of town. Richard waited for a few minutes until he saw police cars heading for the jewelry store.

Richard and Selina heard shots fired near the jewelry store. Richard made a fair guess at what had happened. The screaming burglar alarm had aroused Rock's fear. In his blurry, drugged condition, Rock had probably fired shots at the police. He would be charged with armed robbery and resisting arrest. The police would note Rock's criminal record.

Selina drove the car a few blocks farther and parked it on a main street in town near a phone booth. She looked pale and anxious.

"I'm sorry that you had to be a part of all this business," Richard said. Now that his task was done, he was relaxed.

"My last hurdle for this day is probably my hardest," Selina said.

"That is saying a lot, considering what kind of day you have just been through," Richard said.

Richard stood outside of the phone booth and watched Selina as she picked up the phone. Her neck and facial muscles tensed. She dialed her father's work number in New York. Selina waited while a secretary put her through to an assistant. It was 7:00 p.m. at night, and as usual, her father and his staff were still at work. Selina waited for three minutes. She had rehearsed her introduction.

"Dad, this is Selina. I have an emergency that I need to discuss with you."

"What kind of emergency?" Damien Devon barked.

"I need to ask you to come to Ann Arbor and talk with me in person," Selina said.

"Why don't you come here to New York? All you have to do is skip a few classes. You know how busy I am. My time is valuable. What kind of trouble did you get yourself into?"

"My life is in danger," Selina stated calmly. "I need you to come here."

"What do you mean, your life is in danger? Tell me what the hell is going on, and tell me now." Damien raised his voice.

"I don't want to explain things on the phone," Selina answered.

"You're not going to drop some bombshell on me like that and keep the details to yourself," Damien said.

"That's how I need to do it for now. I'm sorry, Dad."

"You'd better have a stunningly good story when I get there. I can't cancel the morning. I'll be there around 3:00 or 4:00 p.m.--at your house, I presume. Or should I meet you at your jail cell?"

"I'll be at my house at 3:00 p.m. Thank you. I need your help." Tears formed in Selina's eyes. Her father could hear them in her voice. Selina had never clearly asked for his help before.

"That dingbat Nana called be about two hours ago and told me that you were in some sort of trouble, that someone had been following you. I sent one of my men to your house. He should be there within the hour," Damien said.

"No! I don't need a bodyguard. I don't want one of your 'men' here. My... boyfriend is taking care of things."

"Your boyfriend?" Damien articulated the words sarcastically. "Does this boyfriend have a black belt?"

"Something like that," Selina answered. "He's the best."

Selina could mentally see her father's mocking expression. He would roll a paperwad into a hard knot and throw it across the room.

"If you have a boyfriend's help, you don't need mine," Damien said.

"I do."

"You ask for my help, you do things my way. My man will be at your house tonight, whether you like it or not." Damien started to hang up. "I'll see you tomorrow."

"Dad... Dad. You can send your bodyguard to my house if you want to, but I won't be there."

"Where will you be?" Damien shouted this time.

"Safe," Selina answered. "Somewhere safe."

"Girl, I'm not going to argue with you..."

Selina interrupted him.

"Thank you for coming, Dad. I'll see you tomorrow at 3:00 p.m." She hung up the phone before he could shout again. Her hand was shaking.

Selina sat in the car in silence as they drove away. They picked up a Chinese dinner at a carryout restaurant and then went on to Richard's house. When they were safely inside his home, Selina still seemed tense.

Richard wanted to make everything better for her, to take away her enemies and to fill her with joy. But all he could do was to try to comfort her. And try to understand.

"You are seriously afraid of seeing your father tomorrow, aren't you? You showed less fear when I told you that fanatical ROSET murderers could be after you and when you found out that Beckwith's kidnappers intended to kill you. What has your father done to you?"

Selina thought before she answered.

"He fought me. He fought everything I was from the time I was tiny. I was dependent on him, and he tried to use that dependency to thwart what was good in me. He has always had powerful adult tools to use against me. I had to learn to defend myself. My self. I had to find tools of my own. I became very hard and very strong."

"There is nothing hard about you. You are the most warm, vulnerable woman I have ever known," Richard said.

"That is the me I fought to save, the me that is capable of loving and giving and taking. I couldn't have saved myself. Jesus was my Savior," Selina said.

"I don't understand religion. How could mere ideas save you, Selina?"

"Not ideas. The person of Christ was with me and stronger than my father."

"You must hate men," Richard said.

"No. Hatred is something to be avoided. It is one of my father's things. I went through a phase when I realized that my father didn't love me. He did not love anyone. I felt angry and hateful toward him. But before the hatred had a chance to harden into cement, the gospel started changing me. I heard the gospel, accepted it, loved it. Loved Jesus. He set me free to forgive... even my father."

"But you still tremble at the thought of seeing your father," Richard said.

"One day I will not," Selina said.

Richard heard and understood. Damien Devon was Selina's father and her enemy. Selina had learned to love her enemies through her gospel. But Richard Saxon did not love his enemies. He would be prepared for his meeting tomorrow with Damien. He would be prepared to beat him.

II.

Richard did not know whether Selina heard him working alone in his den late into the night. He knew that she had gone to bed and turned out the light. But perhaps she had stayed awake listening to him, half-hearing him as he spoke to Jenxex, the computer, and his starship.

Perhaps she heard the strange sounds as the starship took her ring and watch to implant protective devices in them. But Richard knew that he did not want Selina to hear traces of the information that was pouring into his computer terminal now.

He pressed the "print out" key so that he could read the words. He needed to study these facts and then to burn them. Richard needed to know Damien Devon's secrets. He did not want Selina to know the information about her own father that the computer was giving him.

Joseph Devon, Selina's grandfather, had left the bulk of his fortune to Selina and not to his son Damien. Joseph died when Selina was twenty years old. Damien had taken Selina to court to contest the will. Damien lost. Selina had never mentioned her grandfather's inheritance to Richard. Perhaps one day she would feel that she could tell him.

The computer continued its search. It culled information from several data base sources. It fed the results to Richard, uncovering both hidden and easily known facts about Damien Devon. Damien was a well-educated Manhattan businessman. He had committed small crimes and big ones.

He had paid a large sum of money to a law enforcement agent to hide the facts of one particular heinous crime. Damien Devon was one enemy who needed to meet justice. One day, on the right day, Richard Saxon would find a way to bring him to justice. Damien did not know that he was about to meet a challenger who could match him.

CHAPTER
SEVENTEEN
DAMIEN DEVON

Selina looked at her watch for the third time as the car pulled into the driveway of her house. It was exactly 3:00 p.m. on the cold, sunless November afternoon. She hurried out of the car and into the house, turned on her coffeemaker and went to the bedroom to comb her hair.

Richard watched her hurrying and her anxiety. He sat down in the living room to wait. Richard was calm and prepared to meet Damien. He had dressed in a severe dark business suit for this meeting. With his broad shoulders and 6 ft. 2 in. build he was a commanding figure. That was his intent.

By 3:30 Selina paced nervously in the living room. There was still no sign of her father. Selina had been on duty at the hospital since 11:00 a.m. Her nursing supervisor had permitted an exception in allowing her to leave for an hour to meet with her visiting father. But there was no acceptable excuse for missing grand rounds at 4:00 p.m. She had to be back at the hospital by 4:00 p.m. And yet it was crucial that she introduce Richard and her father before she leave. She thought that her father would have Richard arrested as a kidnapper if she did not present herself as healthy and Richard as her protector.

At 3:35 a large, black limosine pulled into Selina's driveway. Three suited men emerged from the vehicle. Richard watched them march toward Selina's door.

Damien Devon was the second man to burst through the door, flanked by his bodyguards. He glanced up at Selina as he removed his overcoat. He did not even look at Richard as he stamped his snow-covered feet on Selina's doormat.

Damien Devon glared at Selina with keen, steely gray eyes. They were the kind of eyes that noticed everything around them and revealed nothing about the man inside. His small bulging eyes protruded slightly from his round face. Damien was meticulously well-groomed in an expensive gray European business suit. The color of the suit blended with his gray hair. He was short with narrow shoulders, yet he exuded a sense of self-importance and power.

"So you're alive, I see," Damien said coldly. This was how he greeted the daughter he had not seen in six months. Selina walked toward him and gave him an awkward hug. The two bodyguards stood by silently, like stone statues. They did not seem to see or hear anything.

"Who and what is this?" Damien asked sharply as he pointed to Richard.

Selina walked back to Richard and put her arm through his arm. There was no mistaking the affection in her gesture.

"Richard, let me introduce you to my father, Damien Devon. Father, this is my... boyfriend, Richard Saxon." Selina had intentionally offered the greater respect to Richard by introducing him first, a rule of etiquette that Richard knew would not escape Damien's notice. Neither man extended his hand for a handshake.

Richard looked Damien in the eye. Damien did not expect that, and he quickly looked away. Perhaps Damien did not expect any of what he saw in Richard Saxon. He had expected Selina's boyfriend to be a young, timid student, easy to frighten, eager to please her powerful father.

"What is *he* doing here?" Damien asked Selina curtly. He still refused to address Richard.

"Dad, Richard and I would like to talk to you *alone*, without your bodyguards. Could we go into my studio?" Selina asked.

"These are my business associates. Why should they leave and Richard stay?" Damien barked.

"This is personal business. We want to talk to you *alone*," Selina insisted.

"*We*," her father mocked her. Selina ignored it.

Damien signaled to his bodyguards to stay in the living room as he followed Selina and Richard into her studio.

"I'm grateful to you for coming to see me, Dad. I know it's hard for you to get away. Richard agreed to talk to you and explain everything, because I have a time conflict at work. I have to leave right now for an important nursing meeting at 4:00, and I won't be back here until after 7:00 p.m. I tried to be excused from work, but I couldn't. Student nurses are at the bottom of the pecking order in hospitals," Selina said.

"They are at the bottom of everyone's pecking order," her father said.

Selina ignored his insult and continued. "Richard and I have been dating since September. We are very close. He knows everything... about the danger I've been in. Richard saved my life."

"Am I supposed to be impressed?" Damien quipped.

"You're supposed to listen to him." Selina was losing her patience. "I need to leave immediately." She reached up to kiss Richard on the cheek.

"One of my men is going with you," her father ordered. He shouted "Akram!" and a hefty dark-haired bodyguard appeared at the door of the study. "Akram, take my girl to the hospital, and bring her home safely," Damien ordered.

Selina glanced nervously at Richard. Richard nodded a silent agreement, accepting the bodyguard.

"Since when do you need *his* permission to do what *I* tell you?" Damien snapped.

"I *trust* Richard," Selina said.

"Make me a scotch and water before you leave," Damien said. Selina contained her exasperation and did as he asked. She knew that her father was playing control games with her. But the important issue was that he negotiate with Richard. Selina could surrender to his small demands as long as she won the big ones. Richard knew how she thought.

Richard stood by silently, poised and controlled. He had not spoken one word since Damien's arrival. He waited until Selina was gone, then he quietly activated the sound distort in his coat pocket. He did not wait for Damien Devon to speak first.

"One of your enemies named Beckwith hired three criminals to kidnap Selina, hold her for ransom, and then murder her, whether or not you paid the five-million-dollar ransom. I interrogated one of the kidnappers and have all the details of their plan on tape."

Damien was clearly shocked. But only for an instant. Then his cold mask was back in place, and he glared at Richard. Richard had taken the initiative and had pulled the rug out from under him.

"What do *you* get out of this, besides the fact that you are screwing my daughter?" Damien asked.

This time Richard was shocked. But Damien had failed to make him angry. This was a battle, and he knew how to keep his head clear in battle.

"I'll tell you specifically what I want to get out of this. I want Selina's safety. I want the criminals stopped and sent to jail," Richard said. "The man is your enemy, not Selina's."

"So call the police," Damien said.

"I don't want to be involved in a police investigation. For a number of personal and professional reasons, I do not want to be the central figure in uncovering a kidnapping. I will give you all the information about the crime. You can present it to the police as if one of your own private investigators succeeded in getting the information."

"Well, this *is* interesting.... So you'd like to avoid the police. You have a criminal record, then?" Damien asked.

"No. I have a reputation to protect. Mr. Devon, I don't want to offend you. But frankly, I come from a good family. One day soon, I would like to introduce Selina to my family. One could assume that she came from a family of mobsters or something unsavory like that, with a kidnapping plot generated from a family enemy. This simply is *not* the kind of thing people in my family do. I behaved like some sort of private investigator for your daughter. I am not fond of the role. I am fond of Selina." Richard had been convincing in his snobbish stance.

"Listen to me, you S.O.B. Don't trot in here telling me that Selina and the Devon name are not good enough for you. Selina is my prize possession, and I'm not ready to give her away to you." Damien was red-faced with anger. Richard had obviously hit the right nerve. He thought Damien was going to slap him.

"Mr. Devon, I had no intention of insulting you. It's just that you forced my hand. You insisted on prying into my motives," Richard said.

"I know plenty of British upperclass types who are involved in sleazy deals! I'm holding all the cards, buddy. All I have to do is call the police, tell them what you told me. If you don't get involved, they'll charge you with suppressing evidence related to a crime. If that doesn't work, I'll find another way to get you. I'm putting you away."

Damien took a large gulp of his scotch.

"Mr. Devon, I don't want to be your enemy. But you have been hostile toward me since we met."

"I don't have anything else to say to you." Damien headed for the door. Richard stopped him. He put his tall frame in front of Damien and looked down at him.

"I will blackmail you if you don't handle this kidnapping investigation as I asked you. I prefer to put it another way. If you protect your daughter from her kidnappers and leave me out of this, I will withhold information about you. Information that you have tried to conceal," Richard spoke quietly.

Damien stopped in his tracks. He cooly collected his thoughts.

"What do you do for a living, Richard? Selina has told me nothing about you."

"I have some business investments. And I teach math at the University," Richard said.

Damien turned and faced Richard. Until now he had deliberately avoided looking at Richard. Now he focused his cold, analytical stare and examined Richard from head to toe. Damien took a large cigar from his breast pocket and lit it. The prolonged silence was intended to unnerve Richard. It did not.

"I doubt that you have operated in the big time, math teacher. You are playing a dangerous game when you start talking to a man like me about blackmail." Damien spoke calmly. He inhaled the smoke.

"You have asked me nothing about Selina, about how she is doing, about how this kidnapping may have affected her, about how close the kidnapping came to succeeding. Would you like to know any of those things?" Richard asked.

"No," Damien replied flatly.

"Why does my request to remain out of this public investigation seem so unreasonable to you?" Richard asked. Damien ignored his question.

"What secrets do you think you have on me?" Damien asked, looking at his cigar. Richard was frustrated. He began to think that he hated this Devon.

"I know, through a friend of a friend that you have paid numerous expensive bills for a young woman named Christine Carns. Most believe she is your mistress." Damien looked out the window. Richard might see the anger peeking through his eyes otherwise.

"Most people of my stature have a mistress. So you think you will shock my wife with this?" Damien asked.

"It may shock some of your business associates to know that your mistress has been giving you insider trading information. That you regularly benefit from her illegal advice in building your stock investments. There are things that can be proven." Richard said each sentence slowly and deliberately.

Damien turned his face toward Richard's. This time he did not hide the flashing look of hatred. This time he blew a thick puff of cigar smoke in Richard's face. Richard coughed at the noxious fumes.

"I guess we have a deal. My silence for your silence." Damien said coldly. "But there is still one thing I don't like about this deal. What about the next time you want something from me?" Damien fixed his icy gray eyes on Richard.

"I will never mention this again." Richard stared back at Damien.

"Of course, of course. This will be our little secret," Damien said sarcastically.

"You can go now." Damien dismissed Richard. He turned and walked away from Richard and did not bother closing the door of the study.

Richard followed Damien. He handed him the audio-tape of his interview with Andy Rock. Damien accepted the tape without looking at him.

"Selina and I had planned on taking you out to dinner this evening. If you prefer to go with her alone, I will back out," Richard offered.

"I won't be here when she gets home. My business is finished here. The bodyguard stays until I have these kidnappers out of the way. You can take the bodyguard out to dinner." Damien spoke in a monotone.

Then he looked out the window as he watched Richard get into his car and drive away.

II.

Damien was impressed. He knew that Richard Saxon had come prepared to do business with him. Damien had not come prepared. If and when he ever met this Richard Saxon again, he would be prepared to subdue and control the man. Richard would never live to see the day when he would take possession of Selina Devon.

III.

Damien Devon rested his feet on the top of his huge walnut desk. He enjoyed looking down at New York City from his spacious office. He liked the feeling of having the city under his feet, as he peered down from the eighty-ninth floor of the building. The city, black and loud and smoggy, dazzling in its nighttime glow, was hiding all of its dark secrets. Damien had summoned his chief aide and confidant, Brendan Stills. Stills was younger and brighter than Damien, a highly paid attorney of various talents and connections. Stills stood almost at attention, receiving his latest confidential orders.

"I want good professional hit men to do a job for us. Pay them to break both legs of each of the three kidnappers. One of them is in jail in Michigan, don't forget him. Destroy the tape once the job is done." Damien nudged the tape on his desk with his hand and went on talking. "The hit men are to tell their victims that Damien Devon is going to be watching them. If they misbehave again, they're dead."

Damien paused and licked the tip of his unlit cigar. He smiled. "I want Howard T. Beckwith killed. It must look like an accident, of course. I want him dead by the end of this week," Damien said.

Brendan Stills nodded. "Will there be anything else, Damien?"

"One other thing. I want a thorough background check done on this Richard Saxon guy, my daughter's latest 'companion.' She sinks lower every day." Damien laughed an ugly laugh. "I want to see what the computer and the FBI say about him. Just a paper check, no private investigators yet. And I want the information before Christmas." Brendan left quietly, closing the door behind him.

The important things were done for the day. Damien placed his long cigar back in this coat pocket. Damien had completed the matter of Selina's kidnapping in his own way. He had never intended to involve Richard Saxon or the police in an investigation. He had only intended to control Saxon. This too, was his own way.

"Richard Saxon feels sorry for you. He thinks that you are comical and that he has beaten you at your own game," Natas spoke into the mind and heart of Damien Devon. Damien was accustomed to negative thoughts about manipulation and deceit. He never questioned where the thoughts came from.

"Ask yourself, Damien, how does Saxon know so much about you?" Natas prodded silently, resting in the invisible shadows of

Damien's office. Natas was comfortable in Damien's office. "He's smart, and he's got a lot of powerful connections," Natas said. "You can get rid of Howard T. Beckwith with a flick of your cigar. Why don't you get rid of Saxon?" Natas spoke forcefully into Damien's mind.

"Timing is everything. I want to find out who this Saxon is and what he wants," Damien said aloud.

"He is probably using Selina to get to Damien," Natas said. And then Natas quickly placed a mental picture in Damien's imagination. It was a picture of Saxon sitting in Damien's office with his feet on Damien's desk. Saxon was laughing. Saxon had won everything--Selina, her fortune, and her father's financial empire.

The picture disturbed Damien. He stood up abruptly and looked around the room. This office represented everything that was important to him. Damien felt anger and fear bubbling inside of him. Stronger men than Saxon had tried to overthrow Damien and failed.

Saxon was young and tall and handsome and he looked so much better than Damien sitting in the Devon Inc. Executive Offices. Damien nervously lit his cigar and inhaled as he paced across his office. *No way,* Damien told himself.

Natas clutched two chunky demons, one under each arm. Their names were Fear and Jealousy. They knew how to lie and tease and conjure pictures in the imagination. Natas pressed the demons inside Damien Devon's soul. They fit easily, attaching themselves with leech-like mouths in the pores of Damien's soul. And the demons stayed.

Natas grinned, then hurried away. There was nothing else that he needed to do with Damien Devon.

CHAPTER
EIGHTEEN
DECEMBER

Akram Kasab did not need anyone's help in being a pest. If Damien Devon wanted him to bodyguard and to stay close to Selina all day and night, wherever she was, then he would do it. If Mr. Devon wanted him to jump off a cliff, then he would do it. Mr. Devon owned him. He paid him better than Akram could have imagined being paid. Akram did not need to speak fancy English or learn all the complex things about this culture in order to earn a good living here. All Akram had to do was to be big and mean and strong and follow Mr. Devon's orders. And Akram could send nice checks home to Mama in Iraq. And he could buy nice suits.

Selina didn't like having Akram around. He could see that she was embarrassed when he followed her everywhere, especially to the hospital where she had to work as a nurse. Akram hated hospitals, they made him nervous. He had had most of his ear cut off in a fight one time, and they brought him to a hospital to fix it. The hospital was full of smells and pain and people who bossed you around.

Akram sat quietly in the nurse's lounge and stayed put like Selina asked him to sit. He read some magazines and watched all the nurses coming and going. Sometimes they laughed at him.

Selina didn't laugh, though, and she was the prettiest of them all. She was so sweet and polite to Akram. She treated him like a person, even though she didn't want him around. After his second night in Michigan Selina had asked him,

"Akram, would you like to go to an Arab restaurant for dinner tonight? I know of a restaurant that is owned by Chaldeans."

"Akram is Chaldean," he had said.

"I thought so, with a name like Akram Kasab," Selina had said.

After that Akram loved Selina. White Americans thought all Arabs were alike. Selina had recognized Akram's proud Chaldean heritage from his family name.

"It is not for Akram to pick da restaurant. It is for Ms. Devon to do," he had said respectfully.

And so Selina chose the Arabian Knight, and Akram had some of the most delicious Chaldean food he had tasted since coming to the U.S.

Selina had been quiet during dinner. Her Saxon boyfriend was not with her, and she seemed lonely. But maybe Selina was thinking about her kidnappers or the hospital or something. Then she surprised Akram in the middle of dinner by asking him about himself.

"Akram, what kinds of things do you do in working for my father?" Akram felt anxious.

"It is not Ms. Devon's business what kind of work I do for Mr. Devon," he had said.

"You're right, it's none of my business what you do for my father. What you do with your life is between you and God," Selina had said, looking at him with those green eyes. Her words had a bite to them, but he didn't know why. Her tone of voice had been gentle.

But for a minute it was just as if God Himself had spoken to Akram. As if God could see through Akram's heart. Akram pushed away from the table and was angry. He walked out the rear entrance of the restaurant and kicked a can on the ground. He kicked it hard. He wanted to punch Selina, but he knew he couldn't do that. And then Akram saw in his mind the badly beaten body of a businessman, laying in a dark alley like this one. And then he saw the bruised face and broken arm of another man whom Mr. Devon had paid him to hurt. And he thought about a lot of other ugly things he had done for money, and it made him want to cry.

Akram felt nervous around Selina for the next few days. But he felt as if she liked him. Like she didn't see him as a piece of dirt or something. Although maybe he was that.

And then after being in Michigan for only six days, Mr. Devon called Akram back to New York. Akram heard Richard Saxon talking on Selina's phone the day he left, ordering some new kind of security system for Selina's house. Akram knew that Richard would take care of Selina, even better than Akram could. Mr. Devon would want Akram to tell him everything about Richard. He knew that Mr. Devon would want to hear all the bad things about Richard. But Akram couldn't think of any. Richard was nice to him. Kind of bossy, like Mr. Devon. But nice.

Akram did not want to go back to Mr. Devon and New York where everything seemed dirty. He wanted to stay here, where everything felt clean.

II.

Richard Saxon hurried home. It was Friday evening after a long and hectic week. As the sun set on the cold winter's day, he was excited to be going home. Selina was his home, and her living place welcomed him. Richard had learned that coming home was not just leaving work. Coming home was being embraced and accepted and cherished. Coming home was having your needs met and being refreshed. Coming home was finding the best of yourself and meeting the best of the ones you loved. Selina was home.

Richard walked up the icy steps in the dark. It was already nearly pitch black at 5:30 p.m. He de-activated Selina's alarm system and walked inside the cold house. Selina would not finish her shift at the hospital until 7:00 p.m. He would shower and relax and make a huge fire in her fireplace before she got home. Tonight they would be alone for the first time in a week. And there would be lots of fire.

Tonight Richard wanted to talk to her about Tethra and his real family and the Greole War. He wanted to fill her head with wondrous images of a Journeyship, soaring through space like a massive city. He wanted her to set foot on a starship and to travel 1,000 light years with him. There was no reason to hold anything back from her now. And the more she knew about Tethra, the easier it would be for her to decide--to decide if she would marry him and leave with him. He wanted that more than anything now. He had never thought he could want something so much.

Richard removed his coat and tie and shoes. He sat beside the fire sipping cranberry juice and lime. What if Selina would not come with him? He would only be on Earth for another seven months. What would happen to them when he had to leave? Then he would have to keep Selina forever in his mind, the way in which one preserves the memory of an angel. One knows that he is forever changed by the visit of an angel. But the angel does not stay forever. His coming is gentle and perfect. His leaving is the same. Richard could cherish Selina like that in his mind.

But his heart was a different matter. It would be torn to pieces. It would be wounded and broken. Selina's fingers had encircled his heart, touching him, loving him forever. When it would be time to leave her, he knew that she would leave her fingerprints, all ten of them, on his heart. And he would do his best to survive.

III.

Selina parked her car in the garage. She saw Richard's car in the driveway and the warm glow of light from the living room. She stopped for a minute on the front porch to de-activate her alarm system. Richard would have locked it again after entering. She paused and did not want to go inside just yet. Richard's car belonged there next to hers. The warmth in the living room belonged to him. How could she live without him?

Selina looked at his footprints in the snow; large, confident footprints leading to her front door. She thought about how he had entered her life, stepping past the cold that had surrounded her, moving toward her, closer, closer, ignoring all the walls that fear had built. She had distrusted all men. But not him. And once he had come into her life he protected her in her danger. And respected her in her strength. What kind of hole would he leave in her life if he left for Tethra and she stayed here? What would this planet hold for Selina without Richard Saxon?

And yet the doubt was there, deeply rooted: Selina Devon, an astronaut? Richard called them star travelers. He said that humans who travel between the stars are the star-keepers. They keep the universe and its children whole. It sounded beautiful when he said it. But it frightened her. Selina Devon, the only Christian in the solar system of Tethra and its neighbor planets. How could she single-handedly bring the gospel of Christ to a galaxy? She doubted that God was asking this of her. And then the cycle of anxious thoughts began, and she had to stop them. She had not had a minute alone in the long, strange week since Richard had proposed marriage to her. She had had no time to think. And what was worse, no time to pray. Maybe that was why she was standing here for so long on the icy cold front porch, because she needed time alone.

But Richard was waiting for her, and he opened the front door to greet her. Her heart leapt with joy to see him. It was those eyes that were like no other eyes in the universe. And those large arms encircling her. And a smile like the sunrise moving across his face. She felt such love for him that she knew she must be expanding inside in order to contain it. And they kissed.

IV.

David Stenroos of Interpol received the phone call from George Theopholus at his home office. He was furious. No one from ROSET was ever supposed to call him at home. It would have been worse at work. No one from ROSET was permitted to contact him except Max Traytur who had a respectable cover identity. Stenroos closed and locked the door of his den.

"If you think that SOMEONE is seeking your... files in the U.S., why did you call me? This is Max Traytur's business," Stenroos said.

"You are a law enforcement agent. I... didn't know what Mr. Traytur could do," Theo said.

"What do you expect me to do?"

"I just hoped you might have some idea what was going on. Can't Interpol trace something like this?" Theo asked anxiously.

"From what your own computer expert says, it cannot be traced. Do you think I have some magical powers?"

"But whoever did it has to be like the CIA or the Justice Department or something. They knew just what they were looking for, most recent activities..."

"Shut up, you idiot," Stenroos interrupted him. Theo tried to collect himself so that he would say just the right thing in just the right way. He had confided his mystery in a powerful ROSET leader. If he could not persuade Stenroos to believe him, he would look like the worst fool.

"I suppose I could have someone stand by twenty-four hours a day and watch our European network's records. Then if SOMEONE searches our files, we won't miss it," Stenroos mocked.

"It happens once every six months at 2:00 a.m." Theo said.

"You moron, you've only been at your computer twice at 2:00 a.m. Perhaps it happens weekly."

"I never thought of that," Theo said softly.

"There is a lot you never thought about. Crawl back into your hole and never, ever call me at home again!" Stenroos hung up the phone with a bang. But he was too paranoid to ignore the possibility that Theo could have been warning him about something important.

Stenroos did exactly what he had made fun of doing in his conversation with Theo. He selected a watchdog from the ROSET secret police and put him to work. He stationed the watcher at the computer terminal that hid most of his important European ROSET records. Late at night, when the terminal was not in use, the watcher stayed and waited. He posed as a security guard, sitting alone in the medical offices of young Dr. Alan Stenroos.

Stenroos had chosen to hide his secret files within the computer system of his son's medical practice. He hated to involve his family. But he had to have access to computer files that belonged to someone totally innocent, totally reliable, and very close to home.

It was early December when it happened. Exactly as Theo from Detroit had described to Interpol Officer Stenroos in Germany, the computer terminal turned itself on. It scanned straight for the hidden ROSET files, seeking "most recent activities," and then it turned itself off.

Stenroos felt the blood rush from his head. This was big trouble! Only someone with a high degree of skill, someone with an international organization, could have the computer expertise to do this. Someone who had to know that ROSET was not only a secret underground but who knew two of the most hidden sources of buried information. If "they" knew this, "they" might know everything. And "they" were not on Stenroos' side. Stenroos was professionally dead. Perhaps personally dead.

Within a week the leaders of the underground ROSET around the world were on alert. The leaders kept their panic to themselves for the time being. They were afraid to contact each other and afraid not to. ROSET's masters of secrecy were being watched by a greater master.

A very secret meeting was scheduled for December. Paranoia complicated the planning of the meeting. No one could be too careful about the meeting place and time. ROSET leaders must never travel together. They must arrive at different times.

There was a railroad strike in France that seemed to interfere with the European leaders' traveling plans. There were weather problems at the airports. Finally, it was December 15 before they could accomplish the meeting, arriving at the rarely-used English country home of Stenroos' sister-in-law. They all waited an extra day for Max Traytur to arrive from the U.S. No one felt comfortable meeting without Mr. Traytur.

The tension was palpable in the drafty, poorly lit, old English mansion. Traytur felt it in the warm, musty, indoor air when he arrived.

The mansion crawled with trusted armed bodyguards. The few servants were also bodyguards.

The twelve assembled leaders met for hours. Who was ROSET's enemy--someone who had known their most intimate secrets for months and who had made no move against them? What were they to do? Max Traytur had one plan.

"Attack is the best defense. We will smoke them out if they will not come after us," Traytur said.

"We have no idea who they are. How will we smoke them out?" Stenroos asked. He bit his fingernails as he talked.

"They don't know that we have discovered them and their prying into our computer records," Traytur said in his crusty voice. "Computers can lie. We will plan one set of activities through the computers. And while they read our plans we will do the opposite," Traytur explained.

"I like it," the Belgian general said.

"Let 'them' chase after our phony ROSET activities, while we change our records and our identity and disappear once more into the computer files," Traytur said.

"They found us once, they could find us again." The fear grew among the ROSET leaders as the meeting lasted loud and late into the night. Panic took its logical course.

"It is not enough for me just to find a new hiding place in the computer system. I want to find ROSET's enemies. I want to know who they are and how strong they are," Stenroos insisted.

Traytur felt that his hiding plan was adequate. *But no, they want to draw a little blood,* he thought.

"Then we need a witch hunt," Traytur said. His left eyelid twitched.
They all agreed.

And we need a scapegoat, Traytur thought.

V.

Richard thought about purple velvet insignias etched into formal family clothing. And there would be golden threads woven into the purple fabric. And rich, warm music everywhere. He thought about the fountain in the east dining hall and of talks there with his father. The flashback only lasted for an instant as he stood at Selina's dining room table. She had set the table in purple linens and napkins and flowers for this evening's dinner. It was deep Chadran purple. He had told her that purple was his favorite color. And she had responded a week later by decorating this room in purple.

Tonight her eyes glistened in the soft candlelight. Tonight she wore a black dress, because he wanted her to wear black. She seemed, at least on the surface, to belong totally to him. But there was that free-flowing artist's spirit in her that would never be tamed or understood. He didn't really hope to own her, just to share her. Just to love her. But sometimes he knew, he wanted to control her.

Lately, she had been pushing him away. She always needed more time to herself. She shortened the evenings they did spend together. She said she needed more time to study. He wanted to believe her. He wanted to believe that the pressure of her pending exam was really the thing that was draining her. He didn't want to believe that she loved him less. That she was struggling with the need to leave Earth in order to marry him. He did not want to see ambivalence within her. Even if it was there.

He watched her move in her black velour dress, so graceful, so alluring. He couldn't wait to touch the velour. He watched her eat, and he listened as she talked. And when he felt it was the right moment he asked her his important question. He did not like Selina's response.

"Of course I would love to go with you, darling. But December 22 would be impossible! That's the date of my oral comprehensive exam. Without that exam I cannot complete my nursing degree in December."

"Could you schedule it a few days earlier and then join me in San Diego on my business trip?" Richard asked.

"I haven't studied enough to move up the date, even if my instructors agreed to change it. My exam is only nine days away from today, and I need every available minute left for study time," Selina said.

"Is that why you are kicking me out immediately after dinner tonight?" Richard tried a touch of levity.

"Darling, you know that I'm under a lot of pressure. I have lost so much study time in these last eight weeks. Things have hardly been uneventful!"

"You could do with one less star man."

"I could do with less threats on my life," Selina said. She smiled now, trying to see humor in her situation.

Richard stood up from the dining room table. He moved next to Selina and bent to kiss her. She melted at his touch. And he loved it.

"There is more to this San Diego trip than usual business," he said, looking intently into her eyes. "I need your help. I need you to improve the credibility of my shallow business persona. I need to use you," Richard said.

"Use me?"

"I must cement a very important business deal with these San Diego clients who are not sure whether they trust me. I need to have you sit at my side when I have dinner with these people. I need you to be Damien Devon's daughter, someone with a real past on Earth."

Selina frowned.

"Selina, if this business trip fails, it will affect my journey... home."

"Why?"

"The less you know, the safer you are."

"You said there wouldn't be any more secrets," Selina spoke quietly.

"I'll tell you everything later. Trust me that it is better that you know very little about the details of these things right now." Richard kissed her forehead and returned to his seat. He could see that Selina was thinking hard. She twisted a golden strand of hair around her left forefinger.

He wanted to tell Selina to forget the San Diego trip. He wanted to make everything better for her. But he couldn't do it this time. Frank Nelson would be in San Diego, and Richard would tell him about Selina. Frank would need to meet the woman who might be sharing his oxygen supply for the return trip to Tethra. It was crucial. He had some idea what Frank's reaction would be. It would help Frank to meet Selina. But Richard could tell Selina none of this right now. The less she knew, the better. Frank's secret identity needed to remain hidden from her.

Selina seemed to wait for Richard to tell her to forget the San Diego trip, to ease the pressure for her. But he did not. She pushed a piece of food on her dinner plate. Then looked up at him.

"Nothing in my life is more important than you. My exam is in the morning on the twenty-second. I'll fly to San Diego right after my exam and be there in time for your business dinner," Selina said. She had to see the wave of relief that passed through Richard.

"Thank you. Then we'll celebrate the end of nursing school!" he said, smiling.

"No, I'll have to leave the next morning to be back in Ann Arbor for that Mr. Traytur's party on the twenty-third."

"Selina, you'll be exhausted! Forget that party! You know that I don't want you to attend it without me. And I cannot cut my business trip short in order to be there."

"I am going to go without you. I'll be fine." Selina rubbed the unhealed cut on her left wrist as she thought of Traytur.

"I have a bad feeling about that party," Richard said.

"I know how you feel about it, darling. We are taking all kinds of precautions about everything since we still don't know who tried to bug my house. It's just that I have to go on living my life. I cannot suspect every new person whom I meet and think that the whole world is out to get me. The fund-raising people at the hospital say that this Mr. Traytur is a well-known, legitimate businessman. And they really, really want his financial support. I can play my little part, pop into his house for an hour or so, and then leave. It may benefit the hospital. If I want a nursing job later, their recommendation could be important."

Richard spoke warmly. "You are caught between two worlds right now. If you stay here on Earth you will need to do well on your exam. You will need to help raise money for the hospital. If you choose me, you can forget those things and relax with me in San Diego."

"I need to finish what I started," Selina said. "I have had to work and sweat for every step of this nursing degree. It did not come easily to me like art did. I don't want to fail now." Selina had that vulnerable, fragile quality in her voice. It always broke Richard's heart.

"I would do exactly the same thing if I were in your place. You wear your perseverance beautifully," he said. Richard had said the right words. He had said them in order to encourage her. But he struggled with himself.

Richard picked up his coffee cup and quickly drank a hot gulp. He looked up at Selina and then at the purple of her dining room table. He wanted to dress her in purple and to make her a Sorn. He wanted to take her with him and forget all the things that could pull them apart. He was feeling impatient and possesive tonight. He was feeling as though Earth was too small. And he wanted to leave. He wanted to command a starship and to forget Richard Saxon.

Discipline yourself, Richard thought. *You have miles to go before you rest.* All these emotions coming to the surface just because of purple. Or just because of pressure. Maybe even fear.

CHAPTER
NINETEEN
TIMING

Fear. It was a splendid way to control people. Generally Max Traytur preferred using fear to control people rather than giving them positive rewards. But for the more involved, complex affairs one needed a different way of controlling people.

That is why Max Traytur decided to use hypnosis against Selina Devon. He did not have the skill of a master hypnotist. But he knew someone who did. Dr. Jules Fray was the unquestioned authority on complex hypnotic technique. He was well-known and respected and had the good sense not to write books or too many journal articles describing the specialities of his methods. It put him more in demand than if he had been freely sharing his knowledge. In fact, there were only three others in the United States who knew how to hypnotize and program minds like Dr. Fray. It had taken Max a while to learn what Dr. Fray's price was. Dr. Fray was already wealthy. What could Max offer him?

Max could offer him more wealth. And a confidential haven for those times when Dr. Fray wanted to engage in his... vices. Men of his psychiatric profession needed to be very private about their own vices. Max understood and was such a good friend to Dr. Fray. Now when Max needed Dr. Fray, the skilled hypnotist was quite ready to return a favor.

"I want this woman completely under my control. I want to be able to snap my fingers and have her grovel at my feet. That kind of thing. But I also want all her intellect intact because I want her to be part of a rather intricate plot. She needs to remember detailed instructions and to carry them out for me," Max told Dr. Fray. They sipped sherry near the warm fireplace of Max's private study. Max knew that he was talking fast and seeming too eager. But he couldn't quite help himself.

"She must be intelligent to begin with, to understand your instructions," Dr. Fray said.

"She is. I checked her I.Q."

"Is she also strong-willed?" Fray asked.

"I assume so. I can't say for sure."

"But she will be unwilling to... follow your instructions unless you hypnotize her. Correct."

"Absolutely. I'm going to order her to deceive her lover and lead him into a death trap. Of course, she musn't be told that it's a death trap," Max said.

"Don't tell me either. This is sounding more and more unsavory. I have a few scruples of my own, you realize," Dr. Fray said.

"Very few, Jules. Don't act like some virginal prince Galahad on me." Max's eyes changed for a minute as he looked pointedly at Fray. It always frightened Fray when he looked like that.

"Besides, this is all just a game. A cat and mouse game. The woman is a pawn. You know what fun these things can be," Max said.

Fray did not exactly know what Traytur meant. But he didn't want to know. He just wanted to do his little job for Max and not ruffle too many feathers.

"My point is this, Max. If the woman puts up any resistance to you or to the hypnosis or to the thing that you want her to do it could negatively affect the results.

"She needs to be relaxed and to trust me in order for the hypnosis to be most effective. Does she have a trusting relationship with you? Since it is you who intend to enter her subconscious once I have hypnotized her," Fray asked.

"She knows very little about me."

"That will help," Fray said under his breath.

"Will drugging her beforehand help to subdue her?" Max asked.

"It might."

"Why don't you hypnotize her the first time and order her to trust me. Tell her she is bonded to me, that I'm like her brother or something," Max said, groping to understand something about trust.

"Then the second time you hypnotize her, I'll step in and take over with her. Would that work?" Max asked.

"A two-step process would be better... I suppose."

"Can you do it twice in one night?" Max asked.

"That's pushing it."

"I want you to push it. I'm going to have her in my home for the party on December 23. Before she leaves here, I want her thoroughly programmed, under my control and ready to do my bidding.... And I want to... mess with her a little before she leaves." Max again had that look in his eyes that Fray hated.

"It would be better not to overdue things, Max. This is a sensitive process," Fray said.

"Are you saying that my demands are beyond your skills?"

"I'm saying that you don't want to cause serious psychological trauma to this woman."

Max burst out laughing. "No, we wouldn't want that." He laughed some more. "You let me worry about her trauma, and you do what I tell you to do... ask you to do. You'll be well paid for your part in my game," Max said.

"How well?"

"Name your price. I'm good to my friends," Max said, smiling.

And then, true to his word, Max served Dr. Fray a sumptuous dinner, complete with a most expensive wine. Max showed Dr. Fray every courtesy and even escorted him to his front door when dinner was over. Dr. Fray enjoyed being treated like a dignitary.

After Dr. Fray left, Max went upstairs, high into the crevices of his mansion where he had a special little room. It was in this room that Max kept some of his most important things. It was in this secluded little attic that Max completed his rituals to conjure spirits.

Max double-checked the steel safe in the attic. The capsule was there, safe and sound and waiting for Selina. The capsule which, when swallowed, would attach itself to the inside wall of Selina's esophagus. It would only irritate her a little. Then it would take thirty days for the capsule to dissolve in her system, and once dissolved, it would instantly kill her.

If for some unforeseen reason Max's first plan failed to lead Selina and Saxon into a death trap, Selina would still die. It would happen on January 22. No one could possibly trace her sudden death to Mr. Traytur or to the evening of December 23. One couldn't be too careful.

Max closed the safe. He lit six candles in the attic and watched as the dark shadows danced across the walls of the closed room. He did his rituals to conjure spirits, and a few spirits came. But Natas did not come.

Natas has written me off, Max thought. *He is ignoring me.* The demons laughed to read Max's thoughts of failure and insecurity.

"Tell Natas that I need his help on December 23 with Selina Devon. She will undoubtedly come here with an armed guard."

"We don't need to tell Natas anything, you human fool. We don't do anyone's errands."

"Natas will punish you if you do not give him my message."

"Aren't *you* important!" the demons mocked. Then they tormented Max by starting a fire in the dry attic. They left when Max doused the flames with a fire extinguisher. Max was only a little shaken. Max knew that this was just their way. But they would deliver his message to Natas. Everything was going according to plan.

II.

The temperature dropped to below zero before Richard reached the Detroit Metro airport. He did not let Selina drive him to the airport for his 7:30 a.m. flight. The cold was so intense that his leather gloves stuck to the icy door handle of the taxi. The taxi dropped him off at the departure terminal only minutes before he had to board his plane. The terminal was not crowded this early in the morning. And Richard thought that he noticed someone following him. He was not sure. But he was in too much of a hurry to double check.

Once he had boarded his plane and was settled in his window seat, he began to relax a little. He watched as the plane lifted him above the snow clouds clinging to the frozen Earth. He watched as the sun beamed warmly above the dark clouds, lifting him higher and higher into the sky. Into the sky where he belonged. The sun and its roaring colors soothed him, and he relaxed more deeply.

The plane trip to San Diego would last almost five hours. He could use the time to clear his thoughts and to review his upcoming business meetings. It was December 21, and he would be in San Diego until noon of the twenty-third. He was not looking forward to the trip.

This last week had been one of his worst weeks on Earth. Everything seemed to go wrong. The San Diego meetings had been difficult to arrange. The computer told him that two separate sources had done a background check on his personal file. One source was in San Diego, and one was in New York. So Damien Devon was already on his case.

And things had been very tense with Selina. He wanted her to marry him yesterday, right away. He wanted her promise never to leave him. Always to be his. But he had to restrain his wanting. Because he understood that she needed time to consider marrying him. And she needed space. He was tired of being understanding.

And there was the sexual tension. Her beauty excited him too much, too quickly. Sometimes all she had to do was to sit near him. He had argued with her for the first time. He had not meant to hurt her feelings. But he had never loved a woman so intensely and tasted so little of her physically. Something had to change. He didn't know what nor how.

The flight attendant wore heavy make-up, and she looked harsh and oldish. But that was because he compared her to Selina. When he stopped comparing her to Selina, she was an attractive woman with shapely legs. He enjoyed watching her.

But Selina was not the worst source of his frustration. She was simply the easiest to understand. The emptiness inside of him was impossible to understand.

Emptiness had been seeping back into his conciousness. He could feel the annoying dripping. Like a drip from a leaking faucet that was not supposed to be leaking. And then before he knew it, the leak had soaked him, seeping with its cold wetness deep into his loins. Emptiness like he had known aboard the *Stealthfire*, penetrating him, draining him of too much of his energy. Except it made no sense. Now there was hope, solid hope that he could leave Earth and return to Tethra. Now there was Selina. She was everywhere in his life, filling him. Still, he was empty.

The hours dragged on. The loud hum of the archaic engine irritated him. Richard opened his briefcase and took out the small leather book that Selina had given him. The pages were edged in gold. The print was small. He opened it to the Book of John. And then he felt odd stirrings in his soul. This book seemed to reach into all his questions and his longings. It was full of mysteries and puzzles and beautiful, moving dreams. This book was full of pain and of the soothing of pain. And longing and the soothing of longing. It seemed to call him with a voice of its own. This book was frightening, and he closed it.

What if the answers really were in this book? What if the quaking emptiness could be stilled? Selina thought that it could. She wanted to talk to him about her God and her answers. But he always stopped her. He did not want to ask her questions. He did not want anyone to touch his questions. He knew that the worst tragedy of all would be this: if he finally asked his questions and found that the answers disappointed him. No one, not even Selina, was permitted to touch on the ground of his questions. And as he realized this, a wave of desolation swept through him.

The plane was beginning to descend. *Thank God*, he thought. *I need to keep busy.* God, he thought. And he remembered being touched by God in Selina's studio. He remembered being embraced by the God of Tethra's two moons.

He didn't have time to think about this. He needed his energy to deal with Donald Cantril of Bay Tech and with Frank Nelson. And with the unknown.

III.

Even the San Diego sunshine seemed to annoy Richard. California was too bright and too warm. The golden-tanned Bay Tech Executive who met Richard at the airport was too exuberant and too energetic. His first meal, a late morning brunch with Donald Cantril, was too rich and too elegant.

And then finally, after a three-hour meeting with Donald Cantril and two members of his staff, Richard had had enough. But it wasn't enough. Donald Cantril had arranged a tour of the new Bay Tech laboratory which Richard had not seen on his last trip to San Diego. Cantril insisted on the tour, as new evidence of Bay Tech's forward-moving technology.

By the time evening came, Richard was tense and restless. He looked forward to seeing Frank Nelson later that evening. Frank was scheduled to arrive in three hours. When Richard returned to his hotel room, there was a telegram waiting for him from Frank. Frank had been caught in a snow storm when he reached the U.S. He was grounded in an airport in Chicago and did not know whether he would be arriving in California for another twelve to twenty-four hours.

Most of tomorrow's meetings would have to be rescheduled for the twenty-third so that Frank could attend. Too many meetings and too many decisions would have to be crammed into that day. There was no way that Richard could leave California by noon on the twenty-third and attend Traytur's Holiday party with Selina that night. She would have to go alone. And tonight, Richard would miss Frank's company.

He had done too much sitting and too much thinking for one day. He had to exercise or he would explode. Richard found his way to the hotel swimming pool and began swimming vigorous laps. He lost track of counting the laps. He contined until his muscles ached with exhaustion. He did not notice the sun setting or the artificial lights rising in the pool room. When he had finished, he felt better.

He pulled himself out of the pool and dried himself with a soft towel. A young petite woman with long, straight, raven-black hair walked slowly and seductively toward him.

"Are you some sort of olympic athlete?" she asked in a deep voice.

Richard shook his head no. The woman was comely. Her red bikini was tiny. Everything seemed very simple.

That night Richard slept with her. It was a delicious experience. He felt relieved and released. He let his mind go blank and stay blank. The woman returned quietly to her own hotel room when it was over. He could not remember her last name.

Richard slept soundly and deeply. Until the morning. He woke up suddenly and sat up in bed. It was 6:00 a.m. He did not need to get up for another hour. His sheets still smelled of the woman's perfume. It sickened him. He took a shower to remove every trace of her from his body. And then he knew that what he felt was shame. Shame, burning like a pain in his chest.

He had slept with many women before. Why should he feel shame? Because now there was Selina. He had not slept with anyone since he met Selina. Selina held sex as something special, a physical union to add to a spiritual union. He had come to believe this without meaning to believe it.

And there was another reason for his shame. There in the overcast light of the morning he knew that he had slept with the raven-haired woman as an act of defiance. It was between Richard and God. God could hold Selina back from him, but God could not hold every woman back from him.

Richard sat at the edge of his bed and looked out the window. So now he was arguing with God, instead of denying that God existed. Now Selina's values were inside of him; they had gotten to him. And Richard did not know where to go from here. *Does God lead you to a desert where you can taste your thirst and then hold back the water?*

Does He allow you to feel your pain, only to abandon you? Richard thought.

An hour and a half later, he passed the raven-haired woman in the lobby. He felt the sense of shame return, and he was cold toward her.

He decided to take a walk on the beach and absorb the sunshine. The sun was hidden behind large white clouds. The Pacific Ocean looked wild and gray and heavy with white waves beating at the shore. The waves reminded him of his own turmoil. Shame had been added to the emptiness. The waves reminded him that water could wash a person clean. And he wanted to be washed clean.

A large seagull flew low and swooped near Richard, as if to taunt him with its freedom. "Today is all you have. Tomorrow belongs to the enemy," the voice inside of him seemed to say. He hated believing that voice. But he did not hear another.

IV.

Natas felt the ticking and the tapping against his skin. It came from Max Traytur's conjuring. It annoyed Natas. "Let the toad wait," he thought.

Natas paced restlessly within the Inbetween Spaces. He was not on Earth and not in hell. He stood at the colorless Peak of Inbetween where he could watch everything on Earth and draw his power from hell at the same time. He hated time. He was always subject to it when he dealt with the things of Earth, subject to time, a concept of order. He hated order.

Natas raised his voice and summoned Deceiver. Deceiver was at his feet instantly. He rarely knew where she was. She had the power to deceive with her form as well as with her words. Deceiver was indeed one of the greatest of the demons. She was cunning and brilliant. Deceiver slithered her black worm-like form next to Natas, then shot it out proudly so that Natas could see her full majestic length. She was bloated with pride. Natas needed to remind Deceiver that Natas was the stronger of the two, even if Deceiver did possess perfected talent. He pulled a hot whip from his waist and slashed it viciously across Deceiver's clammy hide. Deceiver groaned at the seering pain, then curled her body into a knot. When she recovered from the pain,

Deceiver flattened her form into a subservient posture, showing that she bowed to Natas.

"I know that you are the stronger. I submit my awesome talents to you for your use. I have a gift for you, mighty Natas, but only if you withhold your pain from me. For in the matter about which you have called me, I know much. I know more than you. I can either tell you some or I can tell you all of what I know. If you withhold your pain, you can be certain that you will know it all. If you weary me with more pain, you will never be sure of what it is that you lost."

Deceiver spoke respectfully and did not lift her head. She waited in her slavish posture for Natas' response.

Natas paused. He crept slowly toward Deceiver's form. Then even more slowly and deliberately he flipped Deceiver upside down so that Deceiver's naked, vulnerable soft side was exposed. The skin was pinkish gray and sensitive. Natas raised his poisonous claw above Deceiver's soft pink. The waiting was misery for Deceiver. Gooey sweat began to drip from the twenty hairy tentacles around her wormlike form.

"How do you know what it is that concerns me?" Natas hated it when Deceiver was ahead of him in thought or deed. Natas touched his claw on Deceiver's soft spot. The claw did not penetrate.

"You need me, Natas. Not that you do not know how to deceive yourself. You are the father of lies, who even now hide your true name from those around you. You call yourself Natas, the backward name of Satan, your true name. But I am skilled, great one, I am the mother of lies." Deceiver spoke boldly.

Natas dug the claw to make a scratch. In this way he reminded Deceiver of the pain in his power. He reminded Deceiver how much worse the pain could get. Deceiver shrieked. Natas released Deceiver from his grip, as he watched the fluid ooze from Deceiver's wound.

Natas watched Deceiver writhe with fear for just an instant. Deceiver was indeed the mother of lies. She could not be matched in intellect. Natas was the enemy of love, and in his blazing hatred he could not be matched. But Deceiver was the enemy of truth, and in her brilliant deception she could not be matched.

Deceiver dared not move from her subservient posture. She lay very still at Natas' feet. She focused her two red eyes from the indistinguishable head-end of her wormy body. She waited, tense and frightened.

"You have not answered my question. How do you know what it is that concerns me?" Natas let his voice boom forth in its impressive power.

"Do not try to destroy the Tethra Triangle without me. Why do you not come against the priest?" Deceiver asked. She knew she had but seconds to impress Natas with her worth.

"Which priest? Do not speak in riddles," Natas snapped. He raised his claw again.

"I know which of the priests is destined to be the third member of the Triangle."

"How do you know?"

"I spend most of my time among the clergy. They are the keepers of truth," Deceiver answered.

"If you know so much, prove it. You still have told me nothing."

"There is one named John Fisk. The angelic protection around him is thick. His soul is ripe to do the bidding of God. And pure and strong. And then I found the key. This Fisk priest knows the Selina woman. This Fisk priest harvested her soul." Deceiver's eyes were keen and sharp as she spoke. She had given Natas a worthy prize, and she knew it.

Natas lowered both claws to his sides to show her that the pain would stop for a time.

"What else do you know?"

"Give me reward first, great one."

"What reward do you want?" Natas asked. He craved her knowledge now, and the service that would go with it.

"I want sovereignty over Europe for ten years," Deceiver said.

"Five years," Natas decreed. And Deceiver knew not to argue.

"Fisk will meet with Selina and the Saxon man on December 24. He plans a visit with her on that evening," Deceiver said coyly.

Natas' face became enlarged and distorted and he roared in anger. "Too soon! That is too soon! Come fly with me. You are to help me with the woman while she is vulnerable. Come observe her while I work on her for a time."

"We are an invincible team, Natas, you and I. It is wise for us to go against the strong ones together, because they are grounded both in love and in truth."

Natas grabbed Deceiver near her face. "Do not babble at me. Obey me." He tossed her down. When she could speak again, Deceiver held back her speech. She did not remind him of the Fisk priest and of the priest's vulnerability to the demons at this moment. She held back her knowledge because he gave her pain.

CHAPTER
TWENTY
TO FACE THE LIONS

"Natas prepares to attack her. And yet you say this is the time to withdraw?" The angel Clare asked. Archangel Gregory's face beamed as he looked at Selina. He stood shoulder to shoulder with the eleven other warrior angels who were residing in and around Selina's house.

"We love Selina also," Archangel Gregory said.

"How many are to withdraw?"

"All except for you, Clare."

"I cannot hold back Natas' hand. His very shadow bruises me," Clare said.

"We move when the Holy God orders us to move."

"Selina is vulnerable. She could easily lose in a direct attack from Natas."

"We cannot change that."

"It is hard to watch her suffer."

"The Holy One is with Selina. He never withdraws His Spirit from her, nor His power, nor His love," Gregory said. "When He sends us to Selina, we will come again."

"Selina has not prayed in six days," Clare said.

"Natas knows that also."

The angels raised their arms in prayer, covering the sleeping Selina, her bedroom, and her house with their great wings. Their beauty intensified as they began to pray.

"May God grant you, Selina woman, the heart and soul and skills of a warrior. May He give you true wisdom to know His voice, courage to persevere. And healing. Healing deep like a fountain of water, flowing through you and over you, in you and out of you."

They prayed in unison. They prayed in joy. And then the twelve warriors opened their wings and were gone.

And Natas came.

II.

Selina was sleeping soundly, basking in the peace that had settled over her as the angels prayed. But she woke up coughing.

Natas dug his black claw through her flesh, and sickness entered her. The microscopic burning flames suppressed her immune system. She felt weak and dizzy. She looked at her clock. It was 3:00 a.m. on December 21.

Her throat was acutely sore. Each new cough felt like sandpaper scraping against raw flesh.

I can't get sick today. My oral comp exam is tomorrow. My trip to California is tomorrow. I can't get sick, Selina told herself. And yet she was sick. Her joints ached, and she felt a weakness in her arms and legs when she tossed and turned in her bed.

Richard is so selfish, demanding that I fly to California on the same day as my exam. Natas interjected his thoughts as if they were her own.

But he would never ask me to do it unless it were very important. I know he loves me, Selina thought.

He doesn't care if I'm sick and exhausted and under pressure from school. He doesn't mind using me, just like my father. Like a pawn in a game of chess, Natas said. The thought hit its target, poking deeply at Selina's oldest wound. Natas poured his power into the wound.

Men have always treated women like worthless pawns. Men are fickle and loveless. They only pretend to show respect to women. Do you think Richard is so different than all the rest? Richard is a master manipulator; he was able to manipulate even your father. Don't you think it was odd that he wouldn't tell you why your father agreed to keep him out of an investigation? Richard knows how to get his way.

Selina sat up in bed. She felt an ache in her chest and a wave of disappointment.

We... love each other. I want to help Richard when he needs me.

Get used to it. Get used to jumping when he snaps his fingers. That is what he expects of his woman, Natas snapped.

I can't let myself think this way. Richard would do anything for me, Selina thought. Natas could not read her thoughts. But he pressed his own thoughts into her tired mind.

You only believe what you want to. He is a powerful, strong-willed man. Richard does what he wants to do when he wants to do it. Can you deny this? Natas accused.

The accusation was frightening. Selina couldn't deny it. She wanted to cry.

What does he want with someone like you? Natas' words struck another old hurt--the pain of feeling worthless.

Natas placed a burning finger on Selina's skull. She felt the pain shoot through her in the form of a throbbing headache.

Selina lay alone in the dark, beseiged by pounding painful thoughts, sickness creeping through her body, and an ache in her throat. She was acutely aware of being alone. She felt defenseless and exposed. Defenseless against the sickness working its way through her body. Defenseless against the doubts and fears wracking her soul. Selina sat up in bed.

"I cannot deal with this negative thinking. I am going to ignore anything that comes into my mind until the morning when I'm feeling better," Selina said aloud.

That's a wise decision. Don't face the truth until you think you're strong enough to face it. But you know that you cannot deny how you are feeling. And right now you are feeling insecure about Richard. You know that he could have any woman he wants. What does a man like him want with a woman like you? Natas asked.

Selina couldn't deny her feelings. Richard was intelligent and handsome and strong. She was inadequate. A tear trickled down her face.

But don't think about how you have nothing to offer him. You won't even give him sex. Don't worry about facing the truth tonight. Natas had secured himself in her mind. She was listening to his every whisper. He watched as the gray phlegm of his power seeped into her. That power that was invisible to Selina, but not to Natas.

"Help me, Jesus, Son of the living God!" Selina prayed suddenly. She felt nothing.

Why does the Lord not show His face to me right now, reach out a hand of comfort? He has the power to do so. But He isn't doing it, Natas shouted quickly into Selina's mind. His grip was loosening with the turning of her heart to God.

God claims to come to His people when they need Him. But this time He won't, Natas said.

"Yes, He will," Selina answered aloud. "He is here now because He can never abandon His children. I cannot feel His presence. I do not understand His ways. But I know that He is here," Selina spoke to her own doubt. But she felt nothing. No relief. No sense of God's presence. Nothing. And she knew that she also felt abandoned. Alone in the night.

Selina pulled herself out of bed. She seemed to feel the pressure of the covers as they moved across her aching body. She went to the medicine cabinet. In the mirror she saw her glazed eyes and her flushed cheeks. She swallowed two vitamin C and two aspirin tablets with a cold gulp of water, then climbed back under the covers.

Natas pushed against the shield of Selina's faith in God. The shield that was invisible to Selina but not to Natas. Natas cursed. He could not penetrate her mind as long as the shield was there.

In her artist's imagination, Selina saw a group of ancient Romans walking together into the coliseum. She was one of them. She was a Christian, and she was walking to meet her martyrdom in the arena. She smelled the lions before she saw them. She knew the lions were about to eat her alive. God had been with her before, and He would be with her again. But she did not sense His presence now. God did not seem to be there in the space between making her decision to face the lions and the meeting of the lions.

It was a long walk toward the lions' den. She could hear the lions roaring and the bloodthirsty crowds cheering for her death. She was terrified. She had to face the lions, and no one could walk this walk for her.

Now she saw the lions coming. At first they did not run. They were cats, and they were cautious. But they were hungry, and they smelled her fear. Now Selina wanted to run and run and run. Now she was utterly alone. In the next instant the lions would sink their teeth into her flesh and eat her alive. But on the other side of death she would be greeted by the perfect Savior.

Selina sweated from her rising fever. But she had to smile, in spite of her tiredness and sore throat, in spite of the mental pain and the pressure she was under. Her artist's imagination had not failed her. It had shown her the right picture at the right time. It had given her the picture while the Holy Spirit taught her truth.

The Lord God wanted her to face the lions, wherever they were. Face her exam. Face her sickness. Face the illogic of loving Richard. Selina did not know what it was that sought her in the darkness, in the future. She only knew that God wanted her to face it. And in the facing of it she would also find the courage.

Selina wanted to pray, but her tired mind had ceased to work well. She had not gone to Mass today, but she had gone to Mass three times a week during most of her adult life. And now the Mass was in her. When other things failed her, some prayer was always available. "Lamb of God, you who take away the sins of the world, have mercy on us. Lamb of God, you who take away the sins of the world, grant us peace."[*3] And He did. And she fell into a deep sleep.

Natas crouched in a corner of her bedroom. He did not know what had happened. He had been silenced and weakened by Selina's sudden change of heart. But he did not leave. He regrouped for another attack. Her defenses would be down again soon, once the sickness did its work in her body. Once the circumstances again began to weigh on her. Natas was cautious, and he could wait. For like the lions, he too was hungry for her blood.

III.

Natas was on top of Selina before sunrise. He spat hot lies into her brain. He prodded her to anxiety about her exam. He scrutinized her motives. He criticized her, using the voice of her father. Selina was on the verge of tears all morning. She found it impossible to concentrate or study.

I must be having a nervous breakdown, Natas spoke for Selina.

As the long morning dragged on Selina's sore throat worsened. She knew that this was no ordinary cold. She suspected that it was strep throat and that it would not improve without an antibiotic. But she was cramming hard for her exam and she didn't want to waste time waiting at the student health center or a doctor's office.

The fastest way to get a prescription was to ask Todd Weako, a good friend who was a second-year resident at the hospital. She dialed his number.

"Hello, you've reached Todd and Leo's answering machine. Obviously, we're not home right now. Leave a message and one of us will call you back soon. Whenever that is."

[*3]

"Todd, this is Selina Devon. It's Tuesday, December 21. I have a final exam tomorrow, and I'm leaving town on the same day. I think I have strep throat. Could you do me a huge favor and give me a prescription for an antibiotic, probably penicillin?"

Selina struggled through the tedious afternoon. She sat on the floor drinking hot coffee, hot tea, hot cocoa, anything to relieve her sore throat. She poured over her notes, with the words often blurring before her eyes. The room was beginning to grow dark, and she realized it was 5:00 p.m. Todd Weako had not returned her call.

The health center would only be open for another hour. Selina decided that she could not avoid taking the time going to the doctor for a prescription.

She drove to the health center and walked through the biting cold winds to the entrance. Everything ached. After a forty-minute wait, a throat culture, and an exam, the doctor declared that she did have strep throat. He jotted a prescription for her. Selina stuck it in her purse.

"Your throat looks bad, and your left ear is infected. Get that prescription filled right away. And stay in bed for a couple of days," the doctor said.

"My final oral comprehensive exam is tomorrow morning," Selina told the doctor.

"Reschedule it," the doctor ordered.

Selina moaned inside. It was dark by the time she left the health center. Dark and very cold. She thought it was the wind that blew her purse out of her hand and knocked some things in the mushy snow by her car. Natas snatched the prescription from her open purse and pushed it deep into the snow.

Selina collected her things from the ground and pushed them back into her purse. It was not until she had driven to the pharmacy and waited in line for twenty minutes that she realized that she had lost the prescription. The pharmacist felt sorry for Selina. But he could not dispense medication without the prescription. And the health center was closed by now, so it could not be reissued.

Selina burst into tears as she drove home in the dark. It was 7:30 p.m. when she reached her house. Todd Weako still was not home.

Selina took a warm bath and aspirin. She ate hot chicken soup for dinner. She tried to collect her thoughts. Natas pecked away at her reason and her resolve.

You'll fail tomorrow. You're no Einstein. You've bitten off more than you can chew. Give up, Natas said.

It was the words "give up" that prodded Selina. It was her grandfather's words that gave her courage. "It is not the size of a man in a fight, it is the size of the fight in the man. Or woman, whichever the case made be." It was the gospel of Jesus that gave Selina power. "In all these things we are more than conquerors,"[*4] Scripture said. St. Paul knew about days like this. He knew that the small things can kill you. Not just the big ones. Selina realized that a collection of small things were draining and defeating her. And now that she saw them as small things, she knew that she could beat them. She would face one thing at a time. And she would win.

I'll study tonight. I'll take my exam in the morning, and then I'll go to California. I'll get a new prescription. I'll get better. Selina felt a new resolve. She only needed encouragement. She called Richard in California. Her heart sank. He wasn't in his room. She didn't bother to leave a message.

The circumstances had not changed just because she felt different inside. She was still sick, still alone. No one was going to walk to the lions' den for her. No one was even going to pat her on the back as she went.

She thought about calling Nana to talk, but she changed her mind. She could hear Nana's words. "Lighten up, Selina! You don't need nursing. You have Richard and money and your art and money." Nana never studied. She thought that people who had to study were in the wrong field. Maybe Nana was right. Maybe Selina was in the wrong field.

Selina realized that her mind was wandering. She made herself a cup of hot tea and poured over her review notes. She had covered everything in the last nine days. But her weak areas glared up at her, pharmacology and pathophysiology.

Natas flashed a mental picture from her memory into Selina's mind. It was Mrs. Alexander, the most relentless of her teachers.

"I don't like you, Devon, and I don't like mistakes. Nurses don't make mistakes. They catch mistakes that other people make."

Selina wished that she hadn't remembered that particular incident with Mrs. Alexander. Mrs. Alexander had blatant favorites in

---

*4

her classes and obvious scapegoats. Selina had never been a scapegoat before. She pushed the picture of Mrs. Alexander out of her head and tried to concentrate. The picture popped back into her conciousness. This time her father was standing next to Mrs. Alexander, peering down at Selina's clumsy lab work.

"You don't have what it takes, Devon," Mrs. Alexander said. And her father nodded.

Selina felt the pressure of the tears behind her eyes. She was determined not to cry.

Sleep and study. I'll catch a few snatches of sleep then study more. I'll do it all night, She told herself. Her decision took her through another forty minutes. And then the chemical formulas in her notebook began to blur and run together. Her eyes drooped. Selina fell into a sickness-induced sleep. A heavy, feverish sleep.

And as she slept she dreamed of a disgusting dark creature with huge, hot claws. It drooled red phlegm from its massive mouth. It picked at Selina's body like a vulture tormenting a dying carcass. She could not get away from it. In her dream, Selina reached her trembling hand to touch the foot of Jesus' cross. And as her fingers touched the cross, instead of feeling wood, she felt a hand reach out to her.

Natas hovered over the sleeping woman, yes, like a tormenting vulture, chewing on tiny pieces of its victim. The vulture was on top of its prey. It was not allowed to kill her. But it could inflict deep injury. Spinal meningitis was the right touch. The thought pleased Natas. And he had the power. He opened his mouth and his left fang dripped with injury and disease. He leaned to bite Selina's spine with the dripping fang.

Natas was absorbed in his pleasure. He did not anticipate the force that suddenly grabbed his throat. Archangel Gregory seized Natas, reaching his left arm around Natas' neck. He placed his right arm around Natas' head. Gregory relished his task. He did not mind the burning sting of Natas' hide against his skin. Natas screamed in rage. But before Natas' scream filled the air, the angels knew how they could fight and win. Robert and ten other warrior angels surrounded Natas. Robert seized Natas' arms, and another seized his legs. Six of Natas' warrior demons leapt at the angels' faces with their claws. The angels were silent. They synchronized each motion and each gesture. They fought as one. The angels bound Natas and dragged him, screaming and vomiting, from Selina's house.

A calm began to settle in Selina's bedroom. Two sentry angels, Beth and Jane, stood with their fire swords ready, waiting for the aftershock. It came, suddenly and with great noise, but with little force. A second wave of angry demons flew at Selina. Clare's wings covered the sleeping woman, Beth and Jane were swift as lightening, waving their blazing swords. The huge Deceiver demon stood very still as she watched the failed attack. Deceiver lifted her wormlike head and hissed an order of retreat to the other demons. And the demons fled.

Clare held Selina's head and comforted her. She prayed a peaceful sleep on Selina. And then at 6:00 a.m. Clare woke her.

IV.

Selina woke with a jolt. She had forgotten to set her alarm, but something had awakened her. She had forgotten everything last night and had slept soundly through those last precious study hours. Selina shook with fever and chills. Each new cough felt like a whip cracking at the flesh on the back of her throat. Even her skin hurt. Her head spun when she moved too quickly. *Just get to class. Get to California. Someone in California can give me a prescription. Get moving. Think later. The cold will wake me up. Exam at 8:00 a.m. San Deigo flight at 11:45 a.m.* It all made sense in the fog of her fever.

Selina made it to the right classroom. The building felt moist and drafty. She pulled her sweater down to cover her icy hands. And then Selina's heart sank as she entered the classroom for her oral exam and saw the three-member panel of instructors from the Nursing School. It was headed by Mrs. Alexander. She watched Mrs. Alexander grin as she pushed her black-rimmed glasses down on her nose and stared at Selina with her blue-gray eyes. Mrs. Alexander's eyebrows were white, but her hair was dyed red and her plump face held the acid tongue.

Selina knew that she looked disheveled and flushed with fever. She wore her hair long today because it made her head and face feel warmer. She tried to act confident and composed. She tried to hide her anxiety. And then Selina felt a rush of adrenaline and grace, and her mind was sharp.

The panel listened to Selina's raspy, hoarse voice when she spoke. They pulled their heads back and turned away whenever one of

Selina's coughing spasms hit. After seventy-five minutes of testing, Mrs. Alexander addressed Selina.

"Ms. Devon, if it was your intention to impress us with your spunky spirit and determination today, you did it. To be perfectly honest with you, I have never thought that you would make a good nurse. I had judged you by your paperwork. I had prejudged you as being a priveleged rich girl, a pampered artist who didn't belong in nursing school. But I was wrong.

"Your reviews from your in-service training as a student nurse at the hospital sparkle with praise. Your patients think that you would die for any of them. And your supervisors say that you are conscientious.

"Today, dear, you came coughing in here with a fever. If you had been anyone else I would have told you to go home and reschedule after Christmas. But since it was you, I said to myself, *don't make it easy on her*. Nursing isn't easy on any of us. Selina, you pass this test. You've passed all our tests. Now go home and get healthy. And I'd better not catch your cold."

It is finally over, Selina thought as she drove home. But she had trouble concentrating on her driving. Chills shook her. Chills and self-doubt.

V.

The phone was ringing when Selina reached her house. She hurried to answer it.

"Selina? Hey, this is Todd Weako. I'm glad I caught you before you left town. I've been working insane residency hours, but I did get your message. Did you find the medication taped to your front door?"

"Yes, I did, thank you sooo much...."

"I don't make house calls for just anyone," Todd said.

"I wouldn't have had time to get a prescription filled before leaving town. I've only got a few minutes before I have to leave for the airport. You're such a dear, good friend."

"Ahhh, still...just a friend. My luck. So what's all the rush about? You're not leaving town before your oral comp are you?"

"No, I just had my oral comp exam this morning."

"You aced it, right?"

"No, I didn't ace it. But I passed it. I'm so relieved that it's over -- the exam, nursing school, nursing. All of it finished."

"Why did you study nursing if you hated it so much?" Todd asked.

"I didn't really hate it. But I didn't like it either. It was just something that I had to do. I had to learn some practical skills for helping other people. I had to get past my artistic narcissism. But the truth is, now that I have a nursing degree, I'll never use it. All I really care about is art. Science cluttered my brain. It drained by energies away from my art. Art is my passion and my weakness."

"Some weakness, you actually sell your paintings for money, Selina."

"I would paint even if I never sold a thing. Nothing matters, nothing has ever mattered to me other than painting and sculpting. When I was little I spent so much time drawing and coloring that my mother was afraid I was going to be warped. She forced me into playing sports every now and then, so that I would be more well rounded."

"I know what you mean, Selina. I've wanted to be a doctor ever since I was six years old. I used to operate on my sister's dolls and my sister when she would let me. Don't tell anyone this, Selina, but the truth is, I would practice medicine even if no one paid me. Now that I'm killing myself in medical school, I couldn't be happier."

Selina laughed aloud. She could picture Todd on the other end of the phone. He would be disheveled as always, his red hair falling in his eyes. His face playing tricks on anyone who tried to figure out what he was really thinking.

"I need to go, Todd." Selina spoke softly.

"Be sure to take your meds and call Dr. Todd if you have any more ailments."

Selina promised yes on both counts.

Todd's phone call had lifted her spirits. Now she had only one thing on her mind. She was free to vacation with the man she loved. She and Richard planned on going to New York for Christmas Eve and visiting there for two days. Then they would fly to Sanibel Island and have a week in the sun.

Aunt Nancy owned a beautiful beach house on Sanibel. Her yard was filled with tropical plants and extended all the way to the sandy shore of the ocean. During the winter Aunt Nancy refused to go north to her Connecticut home. But she loved company. Especially family.

Aunt Nancy would be a gracious, generous hostess and a subtle chaperone for Richard and Selina.

Selina ached for this vacation with Richard. Nothing could touch them, nothing could shake them when they were together. She would sketch and paint Richard in the sunlight. Richard, as he walked along the seashore, his beautiful strong body moving against the wind and the ocean waves. His beautiful body resting in the sand. She would sketch his hundred facial expressions and his muscular hands. She would save him and his youth on her canvases. And she would save the sunrise and be joined with the Lord in all her painting.

Selina hurried to her studio and began collecting pencils and charcoals and sketch pads to take with her. But she had to stop for a moment and look.

Rich daylight was pouring in through the long wall of windows in the studio. Selina had bought this house because of this room and its light. The house was angled pointing toward the river and the northwest sun. And the point was in this room, the room Selina had converted into her studio.

She found her voice recorder in a drawer with some of her favorite charcoals and decided to take it with her. Suddenly she had to stop for a moment and look.

Selina turned on her voice journal, wanting to remember this moment. Wanting to remember the patterns of light that she saw. She began speaking.

"The late morning light is beautiful as always. And it is always different."

"If I half-close my eyes and look at it in one way, the light looks surreal with pinks and grays and random streaks of violet moving across the porous empty canvas on my easel. If I look at it like an Impressionist I can see the shadows moving in and out of a dozen colors. Living colors. And the shadows are full of meaning, and the shapes move in and out of the shadows. I know I am an Impressionist at heart. I understand Van Gogh, half-mad with love for the light and tormented by the dark. But half in love with the dark and with everything that can move a shadow. I understood Van Gogh's insanity at times. And it frightens me. Because I know that I am half-mad with love for art--and that, if I let myself, I could be ruled by my passion for it and its embracing of my soul. My passion and my need for art frightens me.

Yet even as I fear it, all I want is to delve into the colors and the light. I think that God understands. I hope that he approves."

Selina's thoughts were interrupted by the angry honk of the taxi in her driveway. She grabbed another sketch pad and a handful of pencils from her drawing table and stuffed them in her large brown leather tote. The taxi driver was knocking at her front door. She had lost track of the time again. She flew in a flurry out toward the car. The driver carried her luggage, and Selina carried her purse and tote and scarf and gloves and locked the door behind her.

As she sat in the cold back seat of the taxi, a wave of fever and chills passed through her. She was glad that she had called a taxi instead of trying to drive herself to the airport. She was aware that the sickness was draining her.

Selina fell into a sick sleep aboard the American Airlines flight to San Diego. Her last thoughts soothed her. She had only two more chores to complete--a dinner in San Diego and a party at Mr. Traytur's house the next evening. Then she could enjoy Christmas and the Florida sunshine and forget about facing lions for a while.

VI.

Deceiver dared not twitch a muscle so as to taunt the angel guard around Selina. Deceiver was not ready to act now. She only wanted to watch and to listen. Deceiver had seen others like this Selina over the thousands of years. But there was always something slightly different about each human. Unlike Natas, Deceiver did not stereotype the humans. Deceiver had learned over the centuries never to underestimate their complexity, their stupidity, and their occasional brilliance. Deceiver watched Selina act and listened to Selina's words and heard everything and forgot nothing. And Deceiver learned.

CHAPTER
TWENTY-ONE
CALIFORNIA

Frank Nelson hated the plane trip to California from Chicago. He hated the way the plane bumped through air pockets and smelled of diesel fuel. When he arrived in California he was wearing a warm woolen suit and carrying an overcoat. He asked to go to his hotel room to change into lighter clothing. When he finally arrived at the Bay Tech offices, he was tired and anxious.

This whole affair made him nervous. He and Richard working together publicly, trying to pull off a phony business deal. Pretending to own and operate a nuclear power plant that was nonexistent. There was no margin for error in this affair. If they left any loose ends, it would draw attention to their false credentials. If this business deal failed, they would need to resort to force, starship warfare scale force, to secure the uranium pellets they needed from Bay Tech.

Frank didn't like any of this. A seventeen-hour layover in frozen Chicago only made matters worse. When he arrived in San Diego what he wanted was to exercise, shower, and rest.

Instead what he found was a conference room full of fast-talking, fast-thinking Americans and Richard Saxon. He had learned American-style English from the starship computer. But he had spent almost his entire Earth-life among the English. He tried adjusting his hearing to this new style of American business talk, and it was taking extra effort.

Richard understood Frank's awkwardness immediately and started fending for him. He gave Frank extra minutes to read written reports and graphs. He repeated complex phrases with his own British accent. And it was Richard who called an end to the Bay Tech meeting after two hours.

Donald Cantril, president of Bay Tech Industries, supposedly ran the meeting. But Richard acted like a captain in this setting. His leadership power was obvious to Frank, if not to anyone else. Richard said that he wanted to end the meeting so that he could check on his "lady friend" who had flown in this afternoon to join them for this evening's dinner.

Richard had a lady friend who had flown to California to be with him? Richard ignored the look of amazement on Frank's face as they filed out of the conference room. Frank was sure that Richard had seen it.

Frank was aware that Donald Cantril had moved close to him. Frank had watched Cantril during the meeting. The man was squeaky clean, both in his appearance and his language. His courteous manner seemed almost too thick, and his words were always too well-chosen and calculated. Frank wasn't looking forward to talking with Cantril one-on-one. But the time for that had arrived.

"Frank, could you spare me a few more minutes before you return to your hotel? My office is just down the hall," Cantril asked, but it was not a question. There was no room to say no.

Frank and Richard looked at each other.

"I'd like to meet with you alone, Frank. Richard and I have had several opportunities to talk together." Cantril smiled a cold smile.

Frank agreed. He followed Cantril into his long, wide office, impeccably decorated in mauves and purples. The surroundings were almost too well done, just like Cantril.

Cantril had a perfectly proportioned face and a medium-sized body. He had a fast mind and a soft-spoken leadership style that made Frank feel uneasy. As he sat down, Frank reached his hand inside the pocket of his suit coat and pressed the yellow button of his sound distort while Cantril was fumbling with something in his top desk drawer. Cantril sat down, attempting to look relaxed.

"I need to be blunt with you, Frank, and I hope that you will not take offense at my questions. This is a significant business deal that we are working on bringing to closure. And there seem to be a few... irregularities."

"I'm listening," Frank said.

"My questions do not concern you. Your assets and investment background are very impressive. You have maintained a solid financial stability throughout the turbulent nineties. We are thrilled to be doing business with you. But I have a few... minor reservations about Saxon, your middle-man financier."

"I wouldn't be sitting here talking to you now if Richard Saxon had not done his homework well. *He* chose *you* to work with, and I chose to follow his judgment. He has no problem with you. What is your problem with him?" Frank asked coldly. His posture became very stiff.

"Please, don't take offense."

"What is it that you want to know?"

"A man with your financial resources would ordinarily have someone with a... different background handling such a major contract as this. This Saxon has minor business experience with an extended academic history and a part-time teaching appointment. Something doesn't check out here."

"It's not supposed to," Nelson said coyly.

"I'm not following you."

"Richard's most important credentials are not on paper. He has a rather, shall we say, discreet clientele. His clients are among the very private old rich. Richard researches and purchases things like islands and $10 million works of art for anonymous clients. Richard is very well connected and very, very competent. I was fortunate enough to meet him during my year at Oxford. If I had not associated with the right people I would never have met such a man.

"My investment in the rebuilding of the ChevKar nuclear power plant in the Ukraine has involved several stages of sensitive negotiations, some of it political. Richard knows a lot of people. And he knows money. If you don't want to do business with him, you don't want to do it with me."

Frank was almost finished when Cantril interrupted him.

"I've handled this whole thing very badly, Frank. Forgive me. We want your business, and we enjoy working with Richard. It's just standard procedure to be very careful about... *all* the details in my business."

"Can you satisfy my timetable? You seemed to avoid giving us an answer in today's meeting." Frank changed the subject.

"We have every intention of meeting your deadlines," Cantril answered. He began doodling something on a notepad at his desk.

Frank lifted himself from his chair. "I need to shower and change before dinner." Frank looked at his watch. And then he moved close to Cantril's desk, leaned both hands on its surface and spoke very softly to Cantril. "I may have told you a little more than Richard would want you to know about his background. And I appreciate your keeping it in the strictest confidence."

"Of course," Cantril said.

They exchanged a few polite courtesies before Frank hurried into the men's room. The room was empty when he reached it.

Frank leaned against the wall and inhaled deeply. *It went exactly like Richard said it would. And I played my part well. Thank God it's over.* Frank did his relaxation breathing exercizes for a few minutes. His pulse rate began to slow down. *This should have been the worst hurdle for me. The rest is up to Richard.*

Donald Cantril doodled nervously on his scratch pad. He looked thoughtfully at the intertwined geometric figures on the pad as he doodled. The tape recorder in his top desk drawer had failed to pick up any of his conversation with Frank Nelson. It was a sensitive, expensive piece of technology. It should not have malfunctioned. The recorder had played during the span of the conversation, but it had failed to record a sound. He was irritated.

Nelson had overreacted to his questions about Richard's credentials. But his answer was plausible. If there was something shady about Nelson and Saxon, he could not put his finger on what it was. Nor could he prove it. The preliminary Justice Department reports on the two men were unrevealing.

Cantril put his pencil down and stood up. He was satisfied. Theirs was to be a long-term relationship. This first installment of uranium cargo was an $80 million contract. After the first installment, Nelson's Prometheus Inc. would need regular replacements of uranium. Cantril would ask the Pentagon to dig a little deeper into Nelson and Saxon's background to make sure that the uranium was not being used for nuclear weapons production. But Cantril would leave well enough alone for now. He wanted the profits from the first $80 million.

II.

Frank knew that his body would not fully relax again until he was alone with Richard. He was relieved to find Richard waiting for him, holding the car keys to drive the two of them back to the Cielo Azul Hotel. Richard had convinced Cantril's eager assistant that he could drive himself back to the hotel without getting lost.

Neither Frank nor Richard bothered to activate the sound distort once they entered the car. They each thought the other would do it, if there were a need.

"Cantril says that your business background stinks," Frank said.

"It does," Richard responded. The two men laughed. It had been a long, tense afternoon. They were glad to be in each other's company.

"I enjoy watching the way the shadows move on this planet. A hairsbreadth difference in the distance between the planet and the sun, and everything is different. The shadows of Tethra are sharper and more distinct than here," Richard said, looking out the window.

"I haven't forgotten," Frank responded.

There was a long pause as they wove in and out of the busy lanes of traffic.

"I'm ready to go home, Richard. When I saw you four months ago, I was afraid that I would never want to leave this exhilarating little planet. But I'm fickle. I've had my vacation and my share of adventures, and I'm ready to leave."

"We have seven more months left before we can go home."

"I know," Frank spoke wistfully. "I'm ready to step back on the starship, though."

"Cantril deliberately avoided making a commitment to deliver our first installment of pellets in January, with a promise for the second cargo in May. I don't like that," Richard said.

"In his private meeting with me, he said he could meet our deadlines. He told *me* since he thinks *I'm* the boss." Frank smiled.

"Tell me about your adventures. Have they been fun?" Richard asked.

"Fun? I didn't know you were a big one for fun," Frank said. "I expected you to ask me if I kept good scientific journal notes of my adventures. And then I would impress you by saying 'yes.'

"I paid a small fortune to participate in an archaeological dig in Egypt. And I took a one-week safari to Africa with a group who, fortunately, knew what they were doing. My next adventure is a trip that I have planned to China, India, and Mongolia."

"Sounds great! What have you learned?" Richard asked. He pressed too hard on the accelerator, and the car jerked.

"Tell me about *your* adventures first, old boy," Frank said.

"I have been adventuring through the minds of my students. We Chadrans know five times more about math than they have discovered here. My students love what I can teach them. They can't get enough of it."

"Surely, you're not teaching them *our* math." Frank was aghast.

"I couldn't begin to do that. All I am doing is feeding them clues about the discoveries they will make in the coming centuries.

"At first only the most intelligent ones understood what I was doing. Then I created study teams, mixing the smart ones with the slower ones. Now they all understand what I'm doing.

"There is a long waiting list to get into my classes next term. I had to tell administration that I didn't have time to teach additional classes.

"But it has been very satisfying. I started this teaching thing because I knew I could learn so much from my students, about how their minds work, about how Earth education works. But it has been a mutual giving. Because I found that I had something I could give them also." Richard spoke with such enthusiasm that Frank almost envied him.

"Sometimes we see things backward, Richard. I am surprised that the students had something to teach you, not vice versa."

"You wouldn't be if you met them. Earth's children have such original, unique minds. There is a thirsty flexibility in their thinking. Whatever the Tethran scientists have done with our genes over the centuries, they have taken something from us that these students still have."

"Richard, the moment we arrived on Earth, you saw good in these humans. And I saw primitive barbarians."

"And now?" Richard asked.

"Original-thinking barbarians."

The two men laughed as they pulled into the parking lot of their hotel.

Nine stories away from the hotel parking lot, Stan and Bobo listened intently to their headphones. They had listened to Saxon's conversations in the Cantril auto for two days.

"I don't think I understand what these two guys are talking about. Do you, Stan?"

"No way. Sounds like they're from another country, I mean *really* far away. Maybe they're like spies or something. We'd better save this tape for Mr. Traytur. He'll know what it all means," Stan said.

"At least we got something for Mr. Traytur. Our mikes don't pick up nothing when this Saxon guy is in his hotel room."

"Uh-huh," Bobo said. And he took a large bite of his raisin bagel.

III.

Richard followed Frank into his hotel room and sat down as though he had something specific to say. But he kept him in suspense and said nothing. Frank watched as Richard activated his sound distort.

"I'm finally beginning to unwind a bit. I hope that I didn't act like some sort of fumbling idiot in those meetings this afternoon. I was just so tense," Frank said, plopping himself into an uncomfortable chair. The chair was an artistic addition to the luxurious hotel room, but it felt like he was sitting on a bicycle seat. He jerked himself off the chair and sat on the bed.

"You did seem tense. But not like a fumbling idiot. Everyone knew that you had just flown from London to Chicago, had a long layover in Chicago and arrived in San Diego only hours ago. Donald Cantril should have canceled the meeting this afternoon. But he's eager to wrap up all our business today and tomorrow. He wants to spend Christmas Eve with his family," Richard said.

"A jolly good idea if you ask me," Frank said.

"You're sounding awfully British these days. Maybe you'll have to work on your American accent," Richard teased.

"I may *sound* British, but you surely don't *look* very British any more. Is some yankee woman picking out your clothes for you now?" Frank asked.

"As a matter of fact, yes. She is also responsible for my new haircut. She sent me to some artistic 'stylist' who serves teas with his hair cuts." There was laughter behind Richard's eyes. Maybe joy.

Frank smacked his hands together as he laughed. "I can't believe it, the Captain has fallen for one of the Earthborn!"

"Yes, I have." Richard's face became very still when he said this. And he did not laugh. He was too still and his look was too serious.

"Well, that's fine... it's really none of my... business." Frank didn't like the look in Richard's eyes.

"It is your business, Frank. It's very much your business."

"I don't understand. Why is it my business if you're having a fling with some woman?"

"Because I'm not having a fling with her. Frank, there is no easy way to talk about this. I am completely in love."

If Frank thought he had been tense before, he had been wrong. Now he was beyond tense. Now he felt as though he was something like a small knot tied inside of a large knot. That is how he would have described his internal organs at this minute.

"I'm not following you," Frank said. But he was following him. He just wanted Richard to spell out every detail.

"I want to marry an American woman. I want her to return to Tethra with us when we leave."

Frank said nothing. The two internal knots drew together tighter. He began to tap his left hand on the bed, and then he tapped it faster and faster. And then he sprang to his feet and moved very close to Richard.

"Tell me that I just misunderstood you. Tell me that you do not intend to bring a civilian woman, an alien, aboard a starship which is ill-equipped for its homebound journey. Tell me that you don't intend to increase our oxygen-risk factor. Tell me that I'm wrong." Frank had forgotten his manners. He had forgotten that he was talking to his Captain, to a noble-born son of Chadra. Or maybe he didn't care.

"I would do nothing to interfere with the successful completion of our mission. But sometimes... a man has to be true to himself first. He has to feed his own soul before anything else makes sense, before he can get anything else to work...." Richard spoke softly and slowly. He remained in his sitting position, looking up into Frank's face.

"Taking a woman is feeding your soul?" Frank asked, incredulous.

"Taking a wife. Not taking a woman. The reason I asked her to fly here on the same day as her final exam was for your benefit. So that you could meet her."

"You didn't tell her about me?"

"Of course not. As far as she knows I am the only Tethran on Earth..."

"Then you told her about you--about Tethra and the starship?" Frank interrupted.

Richard nodded.

"I can't believe this... I can't believe this. You're breaking all the rules!"

Frank began to pace across the room in his anger.

"What is so unbelievable about falling in love, about trusting someone with your whole life?" Richard's tone of voice had changed. He was meeting Frank's anger with anger.

The two men argued for almost an hour, and then they ended their discussion on an uncomfortable note. It was getting close to the dinner hour.

IV.

Richard Saxon had gone off the deep end, and Frank Nelson was supposed to accept it. Frank almost refused to go to dinner as an act of protest. But it would not have worked. The people who would have been most offended would have been the Cantrils. Richard would have trapped him later anyway and forced him to meet the Earthwoman. So he held on tight to his ice-cold anger and braced himself for a miserable evening.

Richard introduced them at the door of Frank's hotel room. He was cautious about being polite to the woman. Richard would not tolerate his showing her anything but respect. Cold respect. He did not have to look at her, and he could hate her if he wanted to.

Frank watched her get into the front seat of the car. She looked shapely, even top-heavy in her sleek black dress. It was fitted but not too tight. It was short but not too short. The woman had chosen this outfit carefully, even calculating the tiny little curls that fell on her face from the hair piled on top of her head. Frank intended to sit silently in the back seat of the car all the way to the La Jolla restaurant. But the woman drew him into the conversation. She turned her back sideways so that she was half-facing Frank and Richard at the same time. She had a lovely face. She talked with her hands. They were agile, graceful hands that spoke a language of their own. Her hands reminded him of the people of Ytar. They were healers and empaths. They were peacemakers. The association of Selina with the people of Ytar put him at ease with her. And he had to fight to hold on to his hatred for her.

The Salvage restaurant was exquisite. It had too much of everything in all the right ways. The golden napkins and flatware, the long-stemmed crystal glasses, the flowers and curling candlesticks. It was lavish, and it didn't need to be. Because a stunning view of the ocean wrapped around the restaurant and was beautiful enough in its own right.But Frank understood that rich people like too much of things.

Selina charmed the Cantrils. She was warm and gracious. There was nothing false or pretentious about Richard's woman. Frank had hoped that she would be a cold, ruthless amazon of a woman. But Selina would have tamed an amazon.

The Cantrils led them to a choice table right next to the window. Frank wished that they had not placed Selina next to him, with Richard on her other side. The sun was at its final stage of disappearing for the night, and Selina could not resist watching it. She had to bend her neck toward Frank to catch the full view.

Frank watched her face as she watched the sun setting in the ocean waters. It almost took his breath away. For a minute Selina's soul was lost out there in the ocean, seeing something that only she could see. Everyone else at the table was making labored small talk. And then Selina caught herself and forced her attention back into the conversation. Her absent-mindedness was appealing.

Frank felt self-conscious here. The Cantrils exuded class and style. They had gone to the right schools, lived in the best neighborhoods, traveled to the best places. Mrs. Cantril's jewels were huge but still tasteful. And Selina fit in with these people. She was comfortable with opulence. She knew the places and names that Mrs. Cantril was throwing around. Enough so that Selina was making her own quiet impression on Mr. Cantril. And Richard, he had been born into a wealth to which these California people would have bowed. It was only Frank who did not belong here.

If this were Tethra, Frank would never be socializing with the aristocratic Sorns or the wealthy Cantrils. When he returned to Tethra, he would be respected because he was a starfighter and a friend to Sorn. But the upperclass would notice his table manners and his accent, his posture and his Bidzidularn surname. And he would never, could never, be an equal.

Frank devoured the succulent lobster dripping with golden butter. He tried to savor it politely and slowly like the others did. But it tasted so delicious, it was hard to be nonchalant. Frank felt a deep resentment well up inside of him. He wanted to be an equal.

Frank dared to sip the wine with its forbidden alcoholic content, so alien and so dangerous to one of Tethran chemistry. But he was feeling angry and estranged. Richard had noticed the touch of the wine glass on Frank's lips. Richard raised a concerned eyebrow. Frank ignored it and looked away.

Selina saw something also. She leaned toward Frank to say something, but he missed the words. The waiter fumbled and spilled an entire glass of white wine across Selina's lap. Frank noticed her grimace at the touch of the cold wetness on her lap. He saw beads of sweat break out on her forehead, and her graceful small hands shook as she excused herself from the table.

When she returned a few minutes later Selina seemed poised and collected. She ignored the large wet stain on her dress and returned to the conversation. The Maitre d' waited for Selina's return. He came to the table, bowed toward her, and addressed Selina quietly.

"I am most apologetic, Ms. Devon. The restaurant will handle your cleaning bill. Your waiter has been thoroughly reprimanded for his clumsy behavior."

"Then he should also be complimented for his excellent service. I have been impressed with our waiter's skill. He is one of the best I have seen. You must do a good job training your staff." Selina spoke it like a queen. The Maitre d' glowed at her praise. He thanked her.

Frank let himself see Selina for the first time. She had treated the servant like a brother. The sister, covering up for his mistakes. Frank knew nothing about Selina's past. But he knew now that she had been mistreated by someone. And he knew that she had a heart of gold.

"Why do you care what happens to the waiter?" Frank whispered to Selina.

"I just do," she said softly. And then, putting her face very close to his, "You care about him, too, don't you?"

Frank looked her directly in the eyes and for the first time he let her meet him, soul-to-soul. Yes, he nodded, yes. And then he knew that she understood everything about him. About how he was just a clumsy Bidzidulam sitting here with the upperclass people. About how hard life can be. Frank reached and squeezed her hand. He wasn't going to hate her any more. Frank smiled.

Frank let his eyes see what he had been avoiding all night. Richard was distracted by Selina's presence. Every hair on his body was aware of her, distracted by her. Richard had taken on the Chadran stance of stoicism. The other people at this table would not recognize it, or understand it. But Frank, the other Chadran, understood. Richard wore the stoic mask of self-control, the thing a Chadran did when he was too angry, too frightened, or too overjoyed. It was supposed to hide the intensity of the emotion, the possible leaking of self-revelation. Richard barely looked at Selina, barely talked to her or touched her. His concentration focused on his business associates, on fulfilling his Earth persona. But underneath, in his Chadran soul, Sorn could smell Selina's perfume, was aware of the bare skin exposed by the black dress, was concerned about her every feeling and need. And was utterly in love with her.

Selina was the opposite of Richard. There was no stoic veneer. She was bent toward him like a flower toward the sun, maleable to his wishes and his touch. Vulnerable, wanting to please him. And yet she was the conqueror. It was she who held him with the grip of her distracting power. And she didn't even know it.

Or maybe she did. And maybe knowing it and not trying to be the conqueror were all part of what she was. Innocently, the conqueror.

Richard looked like a tame lion sitting next to her, holding back his violence and his power for her. And Frank watched how Selina looked at Richard with those beautiful green eyes of hers. There was enough love in those eyes to last Richard a lifetime. Frank remembered years and long distances ago when Yangar, his wife, had looked at him that way. Or maybe she never had. But he liked to think that someone had loved him like that once.

Maybe Richard was an arrogant aristocrat writing his own rules. Or maybe he was just like every other man, capable of falling in love, needing to take a risk.

V.

The three of them were relieved that the night had ended. They were all relieved for different reasons. Selina looked flushed and had not stopped coughing all night. Frank and Richard walked her to her hotel room, and then Richard left her so that Selina could go to bed and he could talk with Frank.

The door to Frank's room was barely closed when he heard the faint crackling noise of the sound distort.

"Everything seemed to go smoothly tonight, don't you think? The Cantrils enjoyed themselves--" Richard began.

"Selina is beautiful, inside and out. I still think that you are making a big mistake in bringing an alien with us aboard the *Stealthfire*. But... if you had to bring someone, it might as well be her."

"She's hardly an alien. She is a human being just like us."

"She is an alien and not just like us. This is how you have changed, Richard. You don't see her and your math students as aliens anymore. I still do. So will everyone on Tethra. Do you think it will be pleasant for someone as sensitive as she is, to be regarded as some kind of a freak by all the rest of the human beings she meets for the rest of her life?"

"How can a man who has served on galaxy-class starships be so closed-minded and small in his thinking? There are a dozen brands of aliens in the galaxy, from the colonies and the distant planets," Richard said.

"There is only one brand of human. And all have biokinetic body weapons, and some are telepaths and empaths."

"Selina is a telepath. She doesn't call it that, and she is self-concious about it. She reads my mind, at times. She has had no training. But with proper training, she will be a full-blown telepath."

"That will help," Frank said. He knew that there were telepaths genetically scattered on Earth. Telepaths who had no idea what to do with their innate skill.

Richard was standing, leaning against the wall of Frank's room. He didn't look up at Frank when he spoke.

"I didn't want to fight you on this. But I am prepared to fight even you, Frank." Richard was heartsick.

"You don't have to fight me. I think that you deserve Selina. I'll back you on this."

Frank said the words. They seemed inadequate in trying to express what he felt.

Richard's tense body relaxed. He sat down and removed his wristwatch. He seemed to be studying it. Then he looked up at Frank.

"Six months ago I had a disturbing dream. My older brother Jarn and I were vacationing in the mountains of Efthab. We were staying in one of those beautiful houses built into the stony mountainside. The side of the house opening to the mountain view was made of clear acrystill so that you could see every blade of blue grass, every bird and flower and tree within hundreds of miles." Richard paused.

"I have never been inside a Glass House, but I have seen them in travel logs," Frank said.

"The sky was silver-blue, and the sunlight was warm and intense, glittering in the mountain waterfall flowing near the house. My father used to take the four of us to this house in the autumn." Richard's eyes were wide and sad with remembering.

"In the dream, Jarn and I were on the roof adjusting the telescope for night watch Jarn tripped awkwardly on the slanted edge of the roof and fell. No one could reach him to help him. I watched him tumbling down the mountainside, falling slowly, falling. And I knew when he reached the bottom he was dead."

Richard looked down at his watch.

"What if Jarn has been killed? What if many are dead?" Sorn asked softly.

Sorn had shared a piece of his heart with Ont. Something he would not have done six months ago. Ont was touched to see his weakness, to see the core of doubt and pessimism in the soul of one he considered to be invulnerably brave. Ont wanted to say something brilliantly reassuring. But nothing brilliant came to his mind.

"Your brother Jarn is heavily guarded. And so is all of Tethra. Few of us will die," Ont said.

Sorn smiled. Ont had said the right thing.

"If anything happens to me, will you protect Selina for me?" Richard asked.

"Nothing is going to happen to you."

"But if it did?" Richard's eyes were focused intensely on Frank's face.

"I will defend her."

"If Selina decides to stay on Earth when we leave, we must eliminate ROSET. We can root them out like the lice that they are. We can pick them off, one at a time," Richard said.

"We have pledged to leave the people of the Earth untouched, unharmed," Frank said.

"Except in defense. We agreed not to hurt them except in defending ourselves. To hurt her is the same as hurting me. I cannot leave her defenseless and alone." There was too much emotion, and Richard looked away.

"I understand," Frank said. He had just gained a sister. And he didn't really want her.

"I will defend Selina with my life."

CHAPTER
TWENTY-TWO
DECEMBER 23

The binding of Natas was slipping away. Archangel Gregory and his band of nine warrior angels dragged Natas to the Inbetween Spaces and held him there with their iron grip of might and determination. Dozens upon dozens of demons were descending on them. The angels fought hard. But Archangel Michael did not call them to retreat. There was no order to retreat, and so they followed their nature and continued to fight. Still no help came.

This meant that something had gone wrong. There was a delicate balance between good and evil in the Inbetween Spaces and throughout the war-torn Earth. The balance was being tipped toward evil now. The reason was usually a mystery. Too many humans had turned away from prayer for this instant in eternity. Or there were too many battles to be fought at one time on the Earth.

Michael's order came into their minds. "Stay and fight, hold the line," the order said. And so the angels fought. They would stand and fight until the fire in their swords dimmed, until there was no energy left in every pore of their beings. Until Natas and his demons bound and drained them. Demons descended from everywhere, viciously clawing, gruesomely ugly and insane, tearing at the perfection of the angels. And the angels kept their stand until they fell, exhausted, useless for the moment.

Gregory and his guard of nine rested. They would recover soon. They had won one battle and lost another. They had rescued Selina and had bought her time with their fighting. Somehow Michael had decided that it was worth the angels' pain to buy some time for Selina and the others. And Michael could be trusted. The holy God could be trusted.

Natas screeched a blood-curdling squeal throughout the Inbetween Spaces. With outspread wings, he swooped gleefully at having been set free from his bondage. He mocked the angels and flew away like a flash of black into the daylight. He flew toward Earth and toward Selina and the beautiful hotel beside the sea in California.

II.

Deceiver was waiting for him. She felt power coming into her as Natas and his band of warriors came closer and closer. Deceiver had stayed within range of Selina. There she could listen and learn. Deceiver chose not to challenge the two sentries and the guardian angel who watched over Selina. But the three angels would be no match for Natas and his forces.

Deceiver curled herself comfortably on the roof of the Cielo Azul Hotel as she watched Natas tear through the building and bind Selina's sentry angels and guardian. Deceiver waited attentively for Natas to summon her. And then she hurried to his side and bowed to him.

"What have you learned?" Natas asked. He was breathless with eagerness. Deceiver knew that she needed a worthy answer for him, or he would give her pain.

"Selina has a talent worth twenty talents. She creates beauty inside her soul and uses her hands to put it on canvas and into clay. The power of the twenty talents drives her. It can be used to destroy her."

"Selina already uses it to destroy my power. She fasts from the art. Her longing for it is the sacrifice of prayer. The prayer moves against me. I have seen the soul of Saxon grow ready, hungering for the presence of God. I hate the woman and her twenty talents!"

Natas contorted his face as he spoke of his defeat. Deceiver braced herself for the pain he would inflict on her as he suffered from his own pain.

"She is flawed, great one. We can turn her talent against her. Grant me your wondrous permission, and I will proceed to destroy her."

"You think that you can accomplish what I have failed to do! I have hated this one since her baptism. She found her talent at the age of four. I used her father and was grinding her into dust until she turned sixteen and turned toward God. When she was sixteen she gave her ten talents to God, and he turned them into twenty!" Natas moved his claws in and out as he spoke, like a cat sharpening its claws on a tree. Deceiver tensed in dread as she watched his claws move. Gooey sweat revealed her concealed fear.

"I could never match you in skill, great one. No one can. It is just that I have a specialty. Is that not why you called me?" Deceiver sweated profusely. She saw Natas raise his hand toward her. She leapt away from him before his blow came.   Natas whirled around and grabbed a warrior demon by the throat.   He bashed its face with his fist. Natas moved toward Deceiver and cut her with his claw.   Deceiver writhed in pain.   As she bled she held in her thoughts.

I will hold back my best from him.   I will earn my reward but hold back my best.   Because he gives me pain, Deceiver thought.

"You, Deceiver, can imitate the voice of God to those humans who do not know God.   And to those who do know God but who are lonely, sick, confused, distressed.   Enter the wounds of Selina and imitate the voice of God.   Convince this Selina that yours is the voice of God and that the Holy One has taken from her the gift of His artistic talents.   Convince her that God is cruel like her father Damien.   Turn her away from her God by striking at her passion for art."

"I will obey, great one," Deceiver said meekly.

"Take this Selina.   Twist her mind.   Tear at her heart and distract her from the God she serves.   Do it now.   Do it quickly.   While she sleeps.   Before her prayer or someone else's prayer stops us, thwarts us, torments us."   Natas' anguished panic was visible to Deceiver.   Deceiver let out a high-pitched groan of pain, and all the surrounding demons joined her in a howl.   Deceiver wrapped her wormlike form next to Selina and gave Selina a dream.

III.

Selina sat beneath a huge autumn tree.   Its branches were heavy with leaves of vibrant gold and red and orange.   The colors were rich in the warm sunlight.   As she looked up through the tall branches of the tree, the sky was stunning in the clarity of its blue.   Selina's easel was perched securely in the ground, her palette and colors ready, waiting for her hand to fill the canvas with color and meaning.   Selina paused and took it in.

"Give up your art and walk away from this.   All of it.   Did you not promise that you would sacrifice your painting as a prayer?   Give it up.   Not just for a few weeks here and there.   Give it up for the rest of your life."   Deceiver's voice imitated the voice of God.

"Lord, it was you who gave me my talent. Did you give it to me once, only to take it away?"   Selina asked.

"The Lord gives, and the Lord takes away," Deceiver said in the most gentle tone.

Suddenly Selina's canvas caught on fire. The paints spilled on the ground, with the colors mixing in a garish mess on the grass. The tree caught the fire of the canvas and burned in a frightening blast of hot light. Selina stood too close, and she felt the fire brush against her. She coughed as the choking smoke blew into her face and into the sky above her. Black smoke, a charred tree trunk, heat everywhere. Selina backed away, tripped, and fell. Nausea seized her.

Richard sat next to Selina on her bed. He wiped the lukewarm washcloth on Selina's burning forehead, then her face and neck. Selina jerked as she woke from her dream. Her fever had reached 103 degrees before Richard came into her room. His room was next to hers. When he heard her scream in her sleep, he did not wait for a second scream before coming to her.

Selina looked up at Richard. Her lips were tight and sore as she tried to talk.

For a minute she didn't know where she was. "Your fever is breaking. You'll be all right soon. I'll stay with you," Richard said. Selina looked into his eyes and reached for the strength in them. Her heart burned with love for him. She could give up art, give up anything to help his soul, she resolved. But the light bothered her eyes, and she closed them. And then the room was spinning and she was dizzy, and it felt as though she was on a starship. The fever made her delirious. Everything was mixed up. Then Selina saw two hideous red eyes staring at her. She screamed again. This time Richard called the hotel manager for medical assistance. He wasn't sure what Selina needed. Richard said a prayer.

IV.

Selina woke up exhausted. It had been a long night. Her fever had finally broken after what seemed like hours of delirium and sweating and chills. Richard must have stayed with her all night. He was there in all her blurred memories. There had been voices, and a woman had been in her room for part of the time.

Richard's note was the first thing that Selina saw, taped on her nightstand next to the clock. It was already 11:00 in the morning! Richard had gone to his Bay Tech meetings. He left her a phone number where he could be reached. Richard had canceled her 12:00 flight to Detroit. Selina couldn't possibly make the flight. She was too sick to go to Traytur's party. Or anywhere for that matter.

Selina felt weak and dizzy when she walked into the bathroom. She was wearing one of Richard's long loose white T-shirts and nothing else. Her own flannel nightdress was damp with sweat and was hanging in the bathroom. Selina didn't remember Richard undressing her. She combed her hair and washed her face. She decided that she needed to go back to bed a little longer. The thought of breakfast sickened her. And then another thought sickened her. She remembered the dream and the vivid horror of the flames burning up her canvas.

It was the clearest thing about the long night that she could remember. Selina pondered the dream. *The Lord does not speak to His people that way,* Selina decided. Deceiver studied Selina intently, hungering to read her mind. Unable to read it, only to feed it thoughts.

"You are young, my child, and you have much to learn," Deceiver spoke clearly, imitating the voice of God in Selina's mind.

"Give up art for the rest of your life. It is my will for you," Deceiver said.

Selina's heart pounded with anxiety. Was it really the Lord speaking to her? Her heart felt sick, and her body felt sick, and she pulled the covers tightly over her and slept for another hour.

When she woke up suddenly, she felt her strength returning to her. And she felt obsessed with the desire to sketch. Selina opened the curtains to let the warm California sunshine into her room. She ordered lunch from room service and settled herself and her charcoals and sketch pad on the table near the window.

"I am starting my Christmas holiday. No more fasting from art," Selina said out loud.

Deceiver moved against her. Deceiver dug her invisible sharp tentacle into the wound of Traytur on Selina's left wrist. It was an excellent pressure point at the bend in her wrist where dozens of tiny bones gathered at the joint and muscle. Deceiver was limited, she could only give the symptoms of arthritis, not the actual disease. But Selina wouldn't know that. The mock pain would feel like real pain. Deceiver's arthritic pain traveled instantly into the small bones of the hand and fingers. And then it traveled out from the other side of the wrist wound right into Selina's elbow. Deceiver was pleased with the assistance of Traytur's malice.

Selina gripped her charcoal pencil in her left hand. Her hand trembled. A sharp arthritic pain shot through her hand and wrist. Selina dropped her charcoal when she felt the pain. She picked it up once more and tried to sketch. The pain increased. It was punishment to hold the pencil. Selina went ahead anyway. Her hand did not follow her commands. It trembled and scribbled awkwardly. "This doesn't make any sense. Arthritis does not have such a sudden onset as this," Selina consoled herself aloud.

"It did in your grandmother's case. She too could have been an artist." Deceiver's voice was tender.

Selina remembered her grandmother, kind and sweet to everyone, helpless and crippled. The phone rang on her bedside table.

"Will a man like Richard want you when you are crippled and useless?" Deceiver spoke in Damien Devon's voice this time.

Selina swallowed hard. She got up to answer the phone. Fear was taking root in her heart. Disappointment's seeds were planted. Because she did not question nor confront them, the seeds began to grow.

V.

The phone call from Selina came first. And then the visit from Natas came ten seconds after Max Traytur hung up the phone. Max was alone in his den when Natas cornered him.

"It is not my fault! I did not make her too sick to attend my party. I had the perfect plan! And I tried to conjure you and seek your help, great one! I would have done it all alone, but I needed your help with the angel guard! It is *not* my fault!" Traytur was in a state of sheer panic. He had forgotten to address Natas respectfully. He knew that Natas was going to punish him even though Traytur had not done anything wrong.

Natas stood eerily still. Heat was coming from him, as if he were a blazing fireplace. He said nothing. Natas raised one arm. Traytur burst into tears. Traytur's weeping was disgusting, but Natas savored the human's helplessness.

"I am going to strike you impotent. You will regain your sexual power each time you offer me a killing. I want Selina dead. I want Saxon dead. I want a priest named Fisk dead. I want everyone who helps the three of them, dead. I want it done by your hands. Not your paid killers." Natas ordered. He threw pain into Traytur's groin. Traytur fell into a heap on the floor. He did not even see Natas vanish. Traytur pounded his fist on the ground. He vomited and cried.

Two hours later Traytur met briefly with his detectives, Stan and Bobo. Their surveillance in California had not been a total waste. They had one conversation on tape, a conversation between Richard Saxon and someone named Frank. Traytur listened to the tape twice. He was euphoric as he listened. "Saxon is an alien, I can't believe it! Saxon is a bloody alien! This makes everything perfect. I don't even have to lie to ROSET! I'll have the whole blasted organization behind me!" Traytur spewed a dozen obscenities in his glee. This tape was worth its weight in diamonds! Traytur couldn't wait to share the tape with his ROSET colleagues throughout the world. Traytur would definitely satisfy Natas' demands for blood. And at the same time Traytur would be a hero! He was about to save the world from an alien invasion.

CHAPTER
TWENTY-THREE
THE DAY BEFORE

Aleece Devon was awake before anyone else. She had a dozen things to do before this evening's Christmas Eve party. She was excited for only one reason: Mickey and Selina would both be home today. Her two children only came to visit her twice a year in her New York home. They always came home for Aleece's July birthday and for Christmas.

Damien sat down at his usual spot at the dining room table and ate his usual hard-boiled egg and yogurt breakfast. Aleece drank coffee and sat quietly with him at the table.

"You haven't really told me anything about this Richard Saxon person," Aleece said.

"What's to tell?"

"He must be very special to Selina... if she's bringing him home for Christmas," Aleece continued.

"You don't need to sound so honored," Damien scowled disapprovingly at Aleece.

"I... I was just curious," Aleece apologized.

"I've got to run. I'll be home by 4:00 p.m. I trust you have everything in good order for the party tonight." Damien didn't wait for an answer. He picked up his briefcase and bustled out of the dining room.

Aleece looked inside her coffee cup. A wave of loneliness passed through her. Damien knew that he could count on Aleece to plan and host a tastefully lavish party tonight. He knew that he could count on her to look perfect, to behave graciously, to remember everyone's names, and to add all those special touches which only the "old rich" knew how to add. Aleece knew that Damien had married her only because she was "old rich" and graced with the education and the breeding of that class. Damien knew how to make lots of money, but he had no sense of style or taste, no upperclass breeding. And he needed a wife who did. Aleece's family had run out of money and had little to offer but breeding.

Aleece was nothing special to Damien. They were not friends. He never talked to her. He gave her orders. And since she was slightly afraid of him, she followed them. After twenty-five years of marriage, she expected very little of Damien. But she still felt lonely at times. Aleece resented Damien because she needed the lifestyle that he could give her. And she hated Damien because he had separated her from her children. He tried to control Mickey and Selina with an iron fist. Damien had made Mickey into a timid, dependent wimp. Damien had tried to crush Selina time and time again because she wouldn't bend to him, wouldn't break. Aleece hated herself because she couldn't help her children.

Aleece swallowed a lump in her throat and decided to keep busy. She went upstairs to her bedroom and checked her To-Do list for the party. An hour later she heard Mickey and his wife Felicia coming down the stairs for breakfast.

Cook had set a tiny corner of the long dining room table for breakfast. The dining room, like every other elegant corner of the Devon Park Avenue apartment, was embellished with red and white roses and tasteful Christmas decorations. The rich interior was exquisite. Aleece had a talent for bringing the holiday spirit to life in her apartment when the children were home.

"I was hoping that Selina would be here by now," Aleece said, touching her grapefruit lightly with a spoon.

"I'm not picking her up at the airport until 3:00 p.m. today. She loses three hours traveling from California to New York," Mickey said.

"Whatever was she doing in California?" Felicia asked.

"She went to a business dinner with her new boyfriend. She was too sick to fly back until today because she came down with a bad case of strep throat," Mickey said, looking apologetic. Mickey was round-faced like his father, of medium build, and 23 years old.

"Thank God, her boyfriend at least has business to which he must attend. At least he is not some starving artist or missionary type." Felicia sipped her coffee breakfast, claiming as always not to be hungry. Felicia lived her own code, which was that no one could be too rich or too thin. She knew she was the perfect wife for Mickey, she knew she could push him to "make something" of himself.

"Richard flew to Detroit to pick up Selina's luggage. Then he's coming on to New York. So he won't be getting here until about 4:30 p.m. I'm bringing Selina back here then picking him up." Mickey looked nervously at his wife.

"Why didn't they travel together?" Felicia asked Mickey.

"Richard didn't want Selina to have to stop off in Detroit. Apparently she left her New York luggage at home because she meant to fly back there before coming to New York. But she was too sick."

"How gallant of him! But I don't see why you have to be everyone's chauffeur today. Have Harrison pick them both up at the airport." Felicia glared at Mickey. The expression said, "You idiot, do what I tell you to do."

"I... I want to do it! I want to spend a little time with each of them." Mickey knew that it was a difficult thing to oppose Felicia's will. But where Selina was concerned, everything could wait. Even Felicia.

Aleece excused herself from the table as Felicia started an argument with Mickey. She didn't like Felicia. Aleece didn't like to think about anything hurting her children. Usually she could avoid thinking about them. But when her children were home, Aleece was aware of all these uncomfortable emotions.

Aleece continued her party preparations. Tonight would have to be perfect to please Damien and his sixty "close friends." These sixty were either people Damien "wanted to be seen with" or people whom Damien was rewarding for services rendered throughout the year.

Aleece would have preferred to have only close family with her on Christmas Eve. Her own relatives would drive in from Connecticut, and she would have her two children near her. That was as close as she could come to having her own way. Aleece had learned to live with Damien's way.

II.

Selina's mother followed her up the stairs to the same lavender guest room her mother always prepared for her. Selina badly needed a nap before the long evening's festivities. But her mother badly needed to talk to Selina. It always went that way.

Aleece hurried down the hall to get a gift she had for Selina. She came back carrying a long garment bag.

"I bought you a new dress for Christmas Eve. It's green velvet, and you look so pretty in green... I just couldn't resist it."

"That was sweet of you, Mom. But I have lots of clothes."

"I wanted you to have the *right* kind of outfit for tonight. When you're attending... an important social function like this."

Selina felt the irritation rising in her. Looking good was not enough. Her mother always had to look perfect and correct.

There was a hidden message here. Aleece did not want Selina to look like some dowdy nurse from a midwestern university, not around *their* friends. Selina had fought this battle repeatedly since she was sixteen. But she would not fight it now. The loving thing to do would be to give her mother what she wanted. Selina could choose more important battles to fight than this one.

"Thanks, Mom. I know that you have excellent taste in clothes." Selina accepted the garment bag. She did not bother to look inside it.

"Selina, this young man whom you are bringing home, he... has a tuxedo for tonight, doesn't he?"

"Yes," Selina smiled. "He's very presentable and from a good family."

"He is... financially secure?"

"Yes, Mom. But these aren't the most important questions to ask, are they?"

Selina's smile was gone. She searched her mother's blank expression, trying to read her face. Aleece did not sit next to Selina on the guest bed. She paced nervously. Then looked directly in Selina's face.

"Does he... make you happy, dear?" Aleece asked.

"He makes me *very* happy. I have never met anyone like him, so strong and so good."

"Good... in what way?" Aleece asked.

They were not speaking the same language. There was love between them, but they had never understood each other. Selina decided to plunge ahead with the conversation. She knew that both she and her mother *wanted* to understand each other.

"What made you decide to marry Dad?" Selina asked.

Her mother's face stiffened, and her eyes darted nervously from Selina to the wall.

"Lots of things. He was just the right man... for me."

Selina felt a surge of compassion for her mother. Aleece's will had been swallowed into the bowels of Damien's will. Aleece never openly disagreed with Damien.

There had only been a few times when Aleece had gone behind her husband's back. It was always on behalf of her children. It was Aleece who had searched to find a nanny with artistic talents to nurture

Selina's abilities. And it was Aleece who had congratulated Selina for her art degree by sending her an expensive gift. Her mother had called Selina and said, "If your father finds out about this gift, I will deny it to his face and yours."

Selina learned the lesson. Oppose Damien, and you are in big trouble. But Selina learned another lesson also. There are many adaptations to evil. It never occurred to Selina that her mother was a coward. It only occurred to Selina how hard her mother's life must have been.

Selina pondered her deepest fear about marrying Richard. It was that one day she would become like her mother, dominated by a powerful man. Richard was powerful and strong-willed and assertive. He always treated Selina as an equal, and yet....

"Was Dad different before you were married? Did he listen to you and ask you your opinions of things?" Selina asked.

Selina's mother laughed. "Damien has never listened to me. He has never thought that my opinion mattered. What about this Richard? Does he listen to you? Or does he just tell you what to do?"

"He listens with his whole heart. He even thinks that I'm intelligent."

"I was in love with a man like that once, Selina." Her mother blurted it out as though she wouldn't say it unless she said it quickly. "I was deeply in love with a kind, gentle man who liked to listen to me talk. He thought I was intelligent, too. He was an artist, very talented and adventurous. But very poor. You don't marry someone like my artist, you just love him.

"People like us, we have to marry people of the same class. I met Damien when I was... dating the artist. Damien was wealthy and ambitious and all the things I had been taught to respect in a man."

"And you loved him, too?" Selina asked.

Her mother didn't answer. Didn't pretend to answer.

"Damien has always been afraid that you would marry a man like my artist. And I have... always been afraid that you would marry someone like Damien." Selina's mother bit her lip. She seemed ashamed. Selina sat quietly and accepted her mother's honesty as a gift. She reached across the bed to hold her mother's hand. The hand was icy cold.

"Selina, you have an adventurous streak in you. Don't be afraid of it, and don't settle for..." her mother didn't finish the sentence. The two women sat very still for a minute, each absorbed in thought.

III.

Richard half-expected what he found when he walked into the Devon Park Avenue apartment. But he was also half-surprised. Damien Devon obviously held back no expense in trying to create a stunning home. By New York standards, the apartment had a huge living room and dining area. The study, entrance hall, and staircase were smaller, but impressive. The kitchen was designed for industrial sized cooking as well as family cooking. It was clear that the Devons did lots of entertaining. The decor was impeccable, the furnishings rich. One of Selina's paintings graced the entrance hall. Richard knew her strokes. Then he saw her tiny name etched in the corner of the painting.

"Dad didn't want any of Selina's paintings in the house. But the interior decorater said you would have to search seven continents to find anything more perfect for that spot in the house," Mickey said proudly, when he saw that Richard had stopped to look at Selina's painting. Richard liked Mickey. At first Mickey looked a little too much like his father to be agreeable. But Mickey was kind and sheepish and nothing like his father. And Mickey and Selina loved each other. That put Mickey in a special category.

Mickey carried half the luggage, and Richard carried the other half up the winding staircase to the four bedrooms on the upper floor. Selina heard them coming and hurried out to greet them. Mickey did not look away when Richard and Selina kissed.

Richard was tired from a day of travel, airports, and automobiles. He needed a few minutes alone, and so he took them. After his shower, there was a knock on his door. He answered it in his bathrobe. It was Aleece Devon. Richard immediately saw some of Selina in her. She was petite and well-proportioned, feminine, and soft-spoken. But Aleece had dark brown hair and brown eyes. And the eyes were lifeless.

"I wasn't here to greet you when you arrived. I just wanted to welcome you and to see if you needed anything."

Aleece seemed timid and anxious. Richard wasn't sure why.

"You must be Mrs. Devon, Selina's mother," Richard said with a smile.

"I'm... sorry. I didn't introduce myself. Call me Aleece."

"Thank you for your hospitality, Aleece. I'm honored to be in your home." Richard found himself talking to her as if she were Selina, with that same warmth and respect he reserved for his woman.

Damien Devon suddenly appeared behind his wife, staring at Richard over her shoulder.

"When you're *dressed*, I'd like a word with you in my study," Damien said coldly.

"Richard really needs a rest, dear, he's done hours of traveling today," Aleece said softly.

Damien ignored her comment, as if it had not been said. Aleece looked at the floor.

"I'll meet you in your study in half an hour," Richard said. "What time do your dinner guests arrive?"

Damien ignored his question and walked away.

"In about two hours, Richard," Aleece answered quickly. Richard thanked her and then stood by his door as she left. Devon treated his wife like a servant, Richard thought. He looked down the hall at the thick gray carpet, at the sterling sconces perched on the walls next to the expensive art works. All this luxury and finery, and Damien still had the soul of a Greole. Richard wasn't in the mood for Damien. Not at all.

IV.

As he walked down the staircase of the Devon apartment, Richard reminded himself that he was doing this all for Selina. He would rather be alone with her now on the Island of Sanibel. But Selina wanted to be here. She only came home twice a year, for her mother's sake. And this was one of them. If Selina left with him to go to Tethra, this would be her last Christmas with her mother and Mickey. He owed her this. As he knocked at the door of Damien's study, Richard reminded himself that he loved Selina. More than life.

Damien wasn't in his study, so Richard decided to wait for him there. It was probably Damien's way of feeling important, to make someone wait for him. Richard looked around the room. It was a monument erected to Damien Devon's ego. The walls were loaded with ornantely framed degrees, plaques for achievements, recognitions for community service. Damien was apparently a philanthropist of some sort. He gave money to the arts and to the homeless. The hypocrisy was striking. This room, like the rest of the apartment, exuded wealth and status and style. The fireplace was blazing a beautiful real fire. It flickered soft light on the heavy burgundy leather furniture. The fire was the only genuine thing in the room.

Damien entered the room quietly. He closed the door, walked to his desk, and picked up a long cigar from a gold box. He did not sit down nor offer Richard a chair.

"Do you and Selina consider yourselves to be engaged?" Damien asked.

"Shouldn't you ask your daughter about our relationship?" Richard answered.

"Where I come from, a gentleman speaks to the girl's father first, and asks his permission to marry the girl."

"I'm not ready to do that," Richard said. *I'll never be ready to ask you for anything*, he thought.

"Are you after Selina's money?" Devon fingered his cigar and looked at his desk.

"Selina has much more to offer than money. Perhaps you've never noticed that," Richard answered. *Keep cool*, he reminded himself.

"I'll be candid with you, Richard. I had you checked out. You have a puzzling and not too impressive set of financial assets. You have one living relative in England and you are a... math teacher." Devon said the last two words with articulated disdain. "In short, you don't have a damned thing to offer Selina or this family. I want you out of her life. If you try to fight me, you will lose." Devon lit his cigar and inhaled a few puffs of cigar smoke.

Richard collected his thoughts.

"Is that all you have to say to me?" Richard asked. His voice was ice.

"That's about it."

"I see. Well, I have no response for you at this time." Richard showed no anger. He showed no emotion. "I will see you at the Christmas celebration," Richard said politely. Then he left Damien standing in his study.

Richard found his coat and saw Mickey standing in between the front door and Damien's study. He told Mickey that he was going for a short walk.

Richard walked quickly in the winter air, through the noisy streets, through the energy and excitement of the city, thinking, thinking. Hopefully, Richard had confused Damien. Damien wouldn't know whether he had won his battle or lost it. Maybe this would postpone Damien's actions against him. Maybe it would push Damien farther. Richard just kept walking.

V.

Richard looked at his watch. He wanted time alone with Selina before the guests arrived at the Devon apartment. He had taken too much time walking. Richard avoided Damien and Mickey when he returned to the apartment. He walked quickly up the winding staircase and knocked on Selina's door.

Selina looked ravishing with her long hair worn loose and curly around her face and pulled back on one side. Her dress was starkly simple and deep velvet green.

"That dress needs a little jewelry," Richard said.

"I didn't know that you noticed things like that! My mom is going to lend me some rhinestones." Selina smiled.

"Why don't you try these on for size? Merry Christmas!" Richard handed Selina a large velvet box with a golden bow. The box contained a three-carat emerald solitaire necklace, adorned by two carats of diamonds. There were matching earrings. Richard wasn't sure when he saw the jewelry on Selina who was more delighted, Selina or himself.

"This jewelry is exquisite!" Selina bubbled.

"Only when *you* wear it."

The moment was deflated. Damien Devon opened Selina's bedroom door. He hadn't knocked. He didn't seem to think he needed to knock.

Richard searched Damien's face, trying to anticipate Damien's next move.

"Your mother wants you to come and help her with something," Damien said to Selina. "Well, what have we here!" Damien came close to Selina and touched the emerald necklace.

"Isn't it beautiful?" Selina said, trying to act natural. She felt the tension hanging thick in the air.

"Is this a payment for services rendered?" Damien asked softly.

"I... I don't understand what you mean, Dad," Selina said.

Damien turned his gaze toward Richard. "Selina is a whore who held out for the highest bidder. That must be you. I would have thought that a man like you would want some puppy he could kick around. But maybe she lets you do that to her." Damien's voice was mellow.

"Dad, what is the *matter* with you?" Selina raised her voice.

Damien shot Selina such a look of anger that Richard thought her father was going to hit her.

"That's enough, Devon!" Richard said.

Damien had struck the right nerve. If his plan had been to enrage Richard, it was working. Richard struggled to control himself. And he knew that Damien could see the struggle.

"You're a slut, Selina," Damien said coldly.

Richard saw a look of pain pass over Selina's face. It seemed to say, "My father has always seen me as being worthless. And now Richard sees it also." It was too much for him to take.

Richard grabbed Damien by his collar and shoved him through the open door of Selina's bedroom. Selina said something to him, but Richard did not hear it. Richard half-carried Damien into the next room, rammed him against the wall of the empty bedroom, and slammed the door shut.

"You moron, take your hands off me! Do you think you can beat me up in my own house and live to tell about it?" Damien shouted.

"Lower your voice, Damien. I am simply setting one ground rule. You will not insult Selina. You will not hurt her. Do you understand?" Richard's voice was a husky whisper. He did not loosen his grip on Damien's collar.

"I only gave her a taste of what I have in store for her, if you stay around her. I will grind Selina into mincemeat... in front of everyone. You know better than anyone else that she is a whore!" Devon shouted the last sentence. He wanted Selina to hear him in the next room.

Something inside of Richard snapped. He felt his skin warming. He covered Damien's mouth with one hand and moved his other hand around Damien's throat. It would have been so easy to break his neck.

Damien grabbed Richard's hand with both his hands and pulled it from his mouth. "Do you want to bring a bastard into your fine family? Selina is not my daughter. She is a bastard," he whispered. Richard looked in Damien's flashing eyes, and he suddenly saw the hatred of a murderer. Murder that sent a chill down his spine. And Richard knew in that moment that what the computer had told him was true.

"If you dare--*dare* to hurt Selina, I will see to it that you pay. I know who you are and what you have done." Richard's voice was slow, succinct, and a whisper.

"I know that you murdered your own father, Joseph Devon. I know that you paid to hide the evidence. I can only assume that you murdered your father because he told you that he would change his will and leave his money to someone other than you. But your murder was too late, because Joseph Devon had already changed his will. And you, Damien, did not receive a penny from him."

Damien was shocked into speechlessness. He turned his face away from Richard to conceal his fear. Richard's grip had tightened harder and harder around Damien's throat.

"For Selina's sake, I will keep your secret. But if you ever hurt Selina or come after her again, I will see that you pay for your crime."

Richard loosened his grip on Damien's neck. Damien did not move. Richard slammed the door and then stormed into Selina's bedroom. He closed her bedroom door behind him. His skin began to glow, hot, neon pink. And he needed to break something. He saw a family portrait on Selina's chest of drawers. He picked it up and smashed it on the floor, smashed Damien's face and the murder in his eyes.

Selina watched him. Large tears trickled down her face. Richard turned and looked at her with his hot, glowing skin. "I'm all right now. I lost my temper, and I shouldn't have. But I'm all right now." Selina came near him, and he put his hot arms around her.

Richard knew that he had made a mistake. He should not have said that to Damien. He should have said something else to frighten Damien. But in the heat of his anger, the hideous awareness that Damien had murdered his own father, it was too much for him. Richard thought of his own father. And he could think of no worse crime.

VI.

Natas hovered above the Devon home. There were a dozen demons inside and a dozen hovering outside with him. Natas addressed the demon, Murder.

"Well done. You pushed the humans too far. It was clever of you, to show your colors to Saxon." Natas liked Murder.

Murder had a family with thousands of cousins. And Natas liked them all.

Natas was excited. And his energy began to draw a crowd of demons. Gradually a dark vortex formed. Thousands of demons began to gather at Natas' side. At midnight on Christmas Eve, Natas would at last be permitted to strike at Richard Saxon. Saxon, the unbaptized, the alien, the unaware. He would become Natas' plaything. And through Saxon Natas would have special access to Selina. And even before the hour of midnight, Natas could strike the Fisk priest. The Tethra Triangle, before it even formed, it would be crushed.

CHAPTER
TWENTY-FOUR
CHRISTMAS EVE

Even the servants knew that something frightening had taken place upstairs. They hadn't heard much. Only a few doors slammed, only some muffled shouting. But they could feel something moving in the air, a kind of tension, a dreadful sort of excitement. They watched Aleece Devon as she hurried up the stairs. Aleece wouldn't know which way to go when she reached the top of the stairs. Should she side with her husband or with one of the children? Of course, she headed straight for Damien's bedroom.

"I don't know if I can pretend to be civil to your father for the rest of the evening," Richard said to Selina, sitting on the edge of her bed. "How can you bear to stay in the same house with him?"

"I have tried to sidestep him... much of my life." Selina hadn't collected her thoughts.

"Does he always treat you like this?" Richard asked.

"Tonight was worse. Tonight he was vicious. I don't understand what was going on." Selina fingered a long strand of hair. "What I do know is that if we run away now, my father wins." Her point was well taken, and Richard knew it.

"I offended him... in a way that I should not have. I cannot take back what I said." Richard looked at Selina.

"What did you say?"

"I don't want to talk about it right now."

"All you did, darling, was to defend me, something no one has ever done. No one inside and no one outside of my family." Selina caressed Richard's shoulder. He looked unusually downcast.

They both jumped slightly when they heard a knock on Selina's bedroom door. Aleece Devon identified herself, and asked to come in. Aleece stood in the hall by the door looking confident and poised.

"Richard, I need to apologize for my husband. He has quite a temper, and he has no manners." Aleece spoke in a clear, loud voice. Damien overheard her, grabbed his wife by the shoulder, and spun her around.

"Who do you think you are, apologizing for *me* to that... that animal?" Damien said to Aleece. She looked him in the eye.

"Shut up, Damien!" Aleece shouted. She turned her head toward Richard and gave him a warm smile.

Selina heard it. Mickey, standing anxiously at the top of the stairs, heard it. And even two of the servants heard it. Aleece Devon had told Damien to shut up! They restrained their heartfelt applause. Even Damien was dumbfounded for a moment at the mouse that roared.

"I want to talk with you *alone* in our bedroom," Damien shouted to Aleece.

Aleece brushed past her red-faced husband. "I haven't time for you right now. I have a party to attend to. Selina darling, come help your mother."

No one had ever seen Aleece behave this way. No one. It gave everyone some strange kind of courage. Mickey walked past his father and spoke boldly, "Richard, uh... I could use your help with something, too."

Richard and Selina had been welcomed in. Damien had been left out. Richard and Selina looked at each other for a minute.

"You deserve a Christmas with your family," Richard whispered. "I think the angels are with us."

"I think so, too," Selina said. And she left him to join her mother. Richard went toward Mickey. Already they could hear the first guests arriving.

II.

Richard stood next to Selina like a sentry. This was probably her last Christmas on Earth, and he did not want anything to ruin it for her. Damien had tried. For the moment Damien had failed.

Richard watched Selina as she moved among the guests. She radiated beauty and serenity. He knew that she was memorizing every moment, so that she could keep the good things with her if she never had a Christmas Eve like this one again.

The house sparkled with glitter and festive glamour. There were two harpists and a pianist who played Christmas carols and classical music. There were lighted Christmas trees in every room. There were candles everywhere. And a lavish layout of food and drink and flowers and champagne.

And yet, everyone seemed uneasy. Everyone seemed tense. People bumped into one another, and the servants spilled things. There was almost a sense of foreboding in the air. Or was it only Richard's imagination?

Richard couldn't put his finger on it. But something was troubling everyone. It was as if the shadows were concealing enemies. Gossip flowed freely. Did there seem to be a bite to the gossip? Selina wanted to get away from the lean white-haired woman with the bony fingers. She had a tongue that cut like a knife.

Perhaps it was because he was the only stranger here. Most people seemed to know most people in the room. Damien was like a king among his courtiers. He was basking in the luxury of everyone's admiration. Damien treated Richard with obvious indifference. Selina avoided Damien. Mickey sat quietly in a corner with the Connecticut relatives. And Aleece was ever the gracious hostess, staying near the door, welcoming each person as if that person were the only guest in the room.

Richard felt starved for a soul mate--someone who would talk to him about the things that mattered. The party was barely an hour old, and already he was bored. Perhaps that is why he felt glad when the priest arrived. Selina had told Richard that Father John Fisk was coming strictly for the purpose of meeting him. Still he did not hurry to the door when the priest arrived. Only Selina did.

III.

He was someone you might overlook in a crowd. Until he smiled. And then the life of his smile would infect you, and you would want to seek him out and listen to him. That is what Selina had said about Father John Fisk. And now Richard saw him for the first time and was secretly amused that he had to agree with Selina. Richard was standing only a few yards from the entrance of the Devon home. He watched Selina as she greeted the priest. Father Fisk was conspicuous in his Roman collar. Selina's mother cooly ignored him, a strange departure from her usual behavior. Selina showed more enthusiasm toward the priest than she had shown toward any other guest. This priest was Selina's spiritual champion, her teacher, and her friend. Richard was intrigued.

He made no effort to approach the priest and waited until Selina brought Father John to him. She introduced the two men, then led them through the crowded rooms to the privacy of her father's study.

John Fisk exuded warmth as if a fire burned within him. He had a young face for someone with so much gray hair. Thick, long gray hair, with several black strands blended in it. And John Fisk had deep blue, penetrating eyes, surrounded by tiny smile lines.

Selina watched Richard's face. She recognized the meaning of his stiffened jaw. Selina could read Richard's every mood. She knew that Richard was encountering John as an adversary. That Richard was poised to make a challenge. Selina looked worried. She pulled gently at Richard's sleeve to whisper to him. He pretended to ignore her. Aleece Devon hurried into the study and asked Selina to return to the party to greet the other arriving guests. Selina did not want to leave her two beloved men alone just now. But her mother's insistence became an embarrassment, and Selina succumbed. She left the study.

The two men met eye-to-eye. They were the same height. Richard was taken aback by the blue of John Fisk's eyes.

"What is a priest?" Richard asked, without polite preliminaries.

"A servant of Christ."

"Selina says that she is a servant of Christ. How are you different?"

John Fisk shifted uncomfortably from foot to foot. He spoke softly. "I have been ordained in a special way to represent Christ."

"Isn't that a rather arrogant thing to say, that you represent the Son of God?"

"It would be arrogant if I claimed to have anything to do with it. God is sovereign. Because he chose to ordain me I can neither be proud nor ashamed."

Richard liked the answer. But he did not permit himself to smile.

John lifted a heavy silver chain that he wore under his shirt. A large silver crucifix hung on the chain. The priest pointed to the crucifix. "Let me tell you about Jesus Christ, the Son of God, who sacrificed everything and gave His life on this cross for you."

Richard was stonefaced.

"Will you give me that cross?" Richard asked.

"I will get you one like it. This particular cross was given to me to commemorate my ordination. I have never taken it off in seventeen years."

"I want that one," Richard insisted. He thought that he read disappointment in John's face. Perhaps even sadness. And then after only a brief pause, the priest lifted the chain over his head and handed it to Richard. The cross that he had not parted with in seventeen years.

"May it remind you always of God's love for you, as it has me," John said.

Richard felt something inside of him thawing. Something very private that he did not want this stranger to see. He controlled his facial expression and challenged John once more.

"I want your watch, too." Richard's tone of voice was cold.

"Do you need a watch?" The priest was puzzled.

"I need *your* watch."

"It is not a very good one. But I like it." John looked down at his watch. Without pausing he removed the watch from his wrist. He held it out to Richard. Richard took it.

"You just gave me two of your prized possessions. Are you not going to ask me for anything?" Richard stared in the priest's eyes.

"I'm going to ask everything of you. I'm going to ask you to bare your soul to me. I'm going to ask you to let me touch your questions. You don't want anyone to touch your questions. But I want to."

John seemed to look at him and through him. His words had caught Richard completely by surprise. Was this man a telepath? Richard put his guard on tight.

"Questions about what?" Richard asked.

"Perhaps about God."

"And you think you have all the answers?" Richard's voice came out sounding a little too sharp.

"I think the answers are available to us. I think that we are the sons and daughters of God and that we were made for the truth. And that we starve for the truth. Until we find it."

Richard felt the deep thaw continue inside of him as the blue-eyed priest spoke.

"How old are you, John?"

"Forty-four."

"How much traveling have you done?"

"Some," the priest answered. "And I'm not a brilliant scholar. I'm nothing special."

Richard was disarmed by the priest's humility. Richard had only seen humility one other time in his life, in his father.

"I don't mean to be offensive, John. I don't know anything about religion or priests. I don't know how anyone can claim to have answers about God and the meaning of life."

"God made the answers very clear. He sent his Son, Jesus, to show us the nature of God, the realities to live by, the Way, the Life, the Truth. God did not want us to grovel for the truth. We were born for the truth."

Father John paused. Something was moving deep inside of Richard, thawing, thawing.

"Why did God send His Son to this backward little planet? Why not... somewhere else?" Richard asked.

"I don't know why. I only know that He did. So that every human being, wherever they are, could have the full revelation of truth, could know who they are, could know who He is." John conveyed love as he spoke. The love was in his eyes. "You will know the truth, and the truth will set you free," John said. "It is a promise."

Richard wanted it. He knew it in a flash that was white like lightning, in a roar that was like thunder. And with a hurt that ached like a nail driven through his hand. He wanted to know the truth. This John-priest had grabbed him by the spine and had shattered every silence that he had built. There was a momentum in this conversation. It was actually going somewhere.

Richard bristled when Damien Devon burst into the study. Damien was not alone, he had a business associate with him. Damien's face was red with anger the instant he saw the face of the priest.

"What are *you* doing here, Fisk?" Damien's eyes moved to Richard. "I should have known. What a fine pair!" Damien rolled his eyes. "Richard, I need to use my study. And you, priest, I want you out of my house, *now*." Damien raised his voice.

"I'm not leaving until Selina or Richard asks me to leave," John responded quietly.

"You're a fool, priest." Damien moved close to John.

"God chose what is foolish in the world to shame the wise; God chose what is weak in the world to shame the strong,"[5, 6] John said.

Damien's fist flew toward the priest's face. John stopped Damien's arm in mid-air. The priest had the reflexes of a trained fighter. It happened instantaneously.

"You're supposed to turn the other cheek, hypocrite," Damien shouted at John.

"Not tonight, Mr. Devon. Merry Christmas. Richard, let's leave the man to his study."

The priest released Devon's arm from his iron grip. Damien looked small beside him.

Richard glanced over his shoulder after they left Damien's study. "Damien hates you, I see. I'm beginning to like you," Richard said.

"Damien thinks that I'm the big bad wolf. He thinks that I can blow his house down. Just because his children like to talk to me about their lives." John smiled as he spoke. There was no anger in his voice. Maybe the priest *could* blow Damien's house down, Richard thought. Maybe the priest was the father Damien could never be. Maybe this John had a power that Damien feared--that Damien lacked. It was becoming clear to Richard that John Fisk had power, knew power, and used power.

Richard and John tried to be inconspicuous and to find a vacant spot in the living room that was farthest away from the front door.

"Richard, I don't want to waste any time. I have to leave to catch a plane in twenty minutes."

"You can't answer my questions in twenty minutes, John," Richard laughed softly.

"No, we need at least an hour. I don't mean to impose on you, but could you drive with me to the airport? Then we would have more time."

Richard said nothing for a minute, marveling at the man who thought he could answer a lifetime of questions in an hour. And then it suddenly struck him. He was not afraid--not afraid to have this man touch his questions. Richard looked up and saw Mickey making a bee-line across the room toward him. Mickey was almost breathless when he reached the priest.

---

*5, *6

"D... does my father know that you're here, Father John?" Mickey blurted out. He glanced nervously over his shoulder.

"Yes. We've greeted one another," John answered.

"You shouldn't be here. You know he threatened to--"

John interrupted Mickey. "He won't kill me, throw me out, or have me beaten up during one of his parties. Not with all these important people here. I'm safe in a crowd, Mickey. You worry too much."

"But you--"

"Just give me a few more minutes here with Richard. I'll be going soon," John said. Mickey was not reassured. He had to find Selina.

"What is the problem, John?" Richard asked.

"Damien and I have a history together. Let's not waste time talking about him. The love and miracle of Jesus Christ is reaching out to all of us tonight. Do you know what Christmas is about, Richard?"

Richard did not answer. He only watched as the priest talked. John had the kind of face that glowed when he talked, glowed with life and energy.

"'God so loved the world that He gave His only Son, so that whoever believes in Him would not perish but would have eternal life.'[7] God's Son was born as a baby in Bethlehem."

"John, don't you think it is rather incredible to say that the Creator of the Universe would reproduce himself as a human being merely to be some sort of messenger?" Richard asked.

"Jesus was not a messenger. He was the Message, the Word made Flesh. He did not speak about Truth. He was the Truth. You cannot grasp truth with your mind. You apprehend truth, intuitively, completely, in your soul. You seize onto truth, onto Jesus."

John paused. "I'm excited. I'm going too fast. And I see Selina headed for me with that serious little look on her face. I'm about to lose my last fifteen minutes with you. And I want you to have it all, Richard. More importantly, God wants you to have it all. To meet Him tonight. Because there is something important about you and something important about tonight." Richard felt the yearning in his soul. He wanted the priest to be right.

_____

*7

John was right at least about Selina. She looked entreatingly at John with her wide green eyes.

"Mickey told me that things have gotten worse between you and my dad, John--that dad was furious when Mickey flew to Rome last month to visit you. Why didn't you tell me? I would never have asked you to meet us here tonight."

"There was no other way that I could fit in a visit to see Richard. My schedule has been so tight during this trip to New York."

"We could have met you at a restaurant!" Selina said.

"I was afraid that Richard might not come," John said.

"So you came after me." Richard smiled.

"You could say that. Anyway, I have to leave now to catch my plane. I'll get out of everyone's way." John began to walk toward the door.

"I want to drive to the airport with John so that we can talk more. Will you be all right... with your father on the loose?" Richard asked Selina.

"He is too absorbed in himself and his guests to bother with me tonight," Selina whispered to Richard. She reached toward John and kissed him on the cheek. "We love you, Father John." When Selina looked at someone with love, they knew they had been showered in it. John almost blushed. He reached in his coat pocket and pulled out a large white envelope.

"This is an invitation to my ordination as a bishop, Selina. I don't expect you to come all the way to Rome for it. But I want you to think of me and to keep me in your prayers that day."

"Mickey told me you were being made a bishop. This time the church really knows what it is doing," Selina said.

Richard and John waited for a taxi. And waited. Finally they were on their way through the frantic holiday traffic, jerking and bouncing their way to the airport.

"Suppose, John, just suppose that you can't answer all my questions tonight. What does a skeptic like me do when he gets a bite of truth. And then he never finds the rest?"

"You will find the rest."

"I had someone slip what they call a 'tract' in my hand at the street corner this afternoon when I went for a walk. It had all these enticing phrases about finding God and His Son, Jesus. But the tract-carrier went away. He didn't stay and tell me any more," Richard said.

"Is that what you think I'm doing? Telling you that you can find the truth and then dropping out of your life?" John asked.

Richard said nothing.

"I'll see you through your questions. I'll contact a priest in Ann Arbor to talk with you whenever you need to talk."

"I don't trust many people. Maybe I trust you."

"I'll write to you. I'll give you whatever you ask for," John said. And Richard believed him. He knew it was odd to believe this stranger. But he knew that he did.

"Can I visit you?" Richard asked.

"I'll be in Cincinnati visiting my brother and his family for the next nine days. Then I'm returning to Rome. That's where my job is."

"Then maybe Selina and I will come and visit you in Cincinnati. Will that be all right?"

John nodded "yes," and then he looked intently at Richard as though he was hearing or seeing something unusual, as though he could see something that Richard did not know was there.

"I have something that belongs to you, John." Richard reached into his pocket and removed the priest's crucifix and watch. He placed them in John's hand.

"You knew that you had to relinquish your treasures to me. You knew that I was challenging you. If you refused to give me your crucifix, I would have said, 'How do you expect me to listen and to believe that your Christ gave His life for me, if you, a priest, will not even give me your piece of metal?'" Richard said.

"I can't take credit for having known all that," John said sheepishly.

"Then why did you give me your crucifix?"

"Because you asked me for it. Because when I was on my way to see you tonight, I sensed the Lord guiding me and telling me to give you anything that you wanted."

"God *speaks* to you?"

"Yes, He does," John said, looking at his crucifix. "I would be lost without Him. Some days I can barely put two and two together without His help." John spoke matter-of-factly. He was an enigma. The things he said were no less astonishing than the way he said them. John took for granted the power of God. And he lived with an easy acceptance of his own powerlessness.

Richard looked out the window of the taxi. Perhaps he could collect his thoughts better if he looked away from John's face. It was all so very odd, to meet a man who said that God spoke to him--to meet a man who *lived* as if God spoke to him. Either the priest was crazy, or God did speak to him.

"Why did you risk the 'wrath of Damien' in order to talk to me tonight? Was it for Selina's sake?"

"It was for your sake. Selina already knew that God loved her. But you didn't."

"I don't believe in God," Richard said flatly.

"I see," John said.

"Why don't you challenge me about that statement? Tell me that I'm wrong."

"I already did that. Everything I have said, everything I believe, everything that I am, is telling you that you are wrong--that there is a God. But it is still your choice to believe otherwise."

"Will God speak to you again? Or has He given up on me?" Richard asked. He felt uncomfortable. He felt pain. What if God did give up on him? What if God hated skeptics and starship captains? What if God hated people who threw questions at His priests?

John said nothing. He only seemed to study Richard.

"I didn't mean to offend you, John. I didn't mean to sound bitter."

"You didn't offend me, Richard. You are honoring me by being honest. So I will be honest with you. The truth is that I don't always hear God speaking to me. Sometimes I am deaf to His wisdom, numb to His urgings. I felt that God said something specific to me for you, but it didn't make a lot of sense to me. And so I've been trying to figure it out." John fumbled with the buttons on his coat.

"When did God speak to you for me?" Richard felt an excitement stir in him. Then he stifled the excitement.

"A few minutes ago, when you returned the crucifix to me, I felt that God was saying, 'Tell him that the future belongs to God and not to His creatures.'" John did not look up from his buttons when he spoke.

Richard's heart began racing with excitement. He heard the words, and he heard John's voice. But he knew it was not John's voice. It was the voice of God. Unmistakably piercing. Unmistakably real.

"That has a special meaning for me," Richard said in almost a whisper. But he didn't want to say anymore.

"We are the children of the future. We are Easter's children," John said. "God's Kingdom will come on Earth as it is in heaven."

Richard was silent. Why was he choking with emotion? Why did he almost begin to cry? He turned his head away from John to look out the windows once more.

John put his hand on Richard's shoulder. For a few minutes they rode through the New York streets in silence.

"Was I hearing God for you?" John asked quietly.

"Yes, you were."

"That's a relief," John said.

"Will God help me if I have trouble believing?" Richard asked softly.

"Every step of the way. You only have to take one step at a time."

"I am impatient with slow learners."

"God is not. Everyone is a slow learner compared to Him."

"How can you be so certain of everything?" Richard was slightly envious.

"Let your hunger show, Richard. Don't be ashamed of it. Let your emptiness be filled. If ever I met a man in a moment of hunger for God, it is you." John's blue eyes saw right through him. Anointed eyes. Loving eyes. That saw right into his soul.

Richard did not look away from him. Richard was eager now. He was trusting. He was open. He was hungry, like the hungry people in Selina's Bible. The ones who stood next to Jesus in the open fields and waited for Him to feed them. Feed them with His truth. Feed them with the loaves and fishes.

"What is the most important thing for me to know tonight?" Richard asked.

"Know that God will never fail you. People will fail you. I had a stomachache tonight, and I almost didn't come. But if I hadn't come, God would have sent someone else to you. Know that God will feed your hunger. That hunger is a blessing. The more you ask Him to fill you, the more He will fill you. But He won't force Himself on you. If you run away from Him, He will respect your freedom to run."

John kept his hand on Richard's shoulder. He spoke like a father to him. He was barely nine years older than Richard, but he used the heart of God for his fathering.

"I don't know where to begin. I don't know how to pray," Richard said.

"Most of us think that we don't know how to pray. But it is as simple as breathing. Say, 'God, have mercy on me.' The best that God can ever give us is mercy. Mercy in the miracle of a perfect virgin and in her giving birth to the perfect Son. Mercy in Christ's life and death and resurrection. An old priest told me once, 'Mercy is fresh every morning.' I count on that, Richard. Because I don't deserve a thing."

John's voice sounded like music moving through the air. But it was thunderous in its power. Richard didn't know why, but he understood every word. It was complex and yet so simple.

Mercy was the thing a valiant captain gave to a vanquished enemy when the enemy deserved nothing and the captain had everything to give. One wave of the captain's hand, and a thousand lives could be spared. Of course it had to be that way between God and man. Only more so. And every breath we took was an act of mercy.

IV.

The taxi came to a full stop as it pulled up to the curb of the Delta departure terminal. Richard decided to treat this priest like a brother and escort John to his departure gate.

They had to hurry to reach John's gate in time. The traffic had moved slowly through the crowded streets, and now the airport itself was one mass of bustling bodies. John needed to stop in the men's room before boarding his plane. Richard waited outside.

Richard felt uneasy. And then suddenly he saw two boys and a man burst out of the men's room. "Some guy is getting mugged in there," the man said, and they ran away. Richard charged through the door of the men's room. Three men were beating John Fisk. One man had pinned John's arms behind his back. A second man delivered a brutal punch in the priest's stomach. The third man had already stabbed John in the shoulder with a knife. He drew out the knife quickly and raised it again.

Richard did not think. He reacted. In seconds he was at full speed and full power. He moved almost close enough to touch the two armed attackers whose backs were facing him. He stretched out both hands and aimed directly for the attacker's spines. There was no time for minor injuries. These attackers were killers. Richard shot two electrical bolts from his glowing fingertips. The electric charges traveled through the two men's spines, throwing them on the floor in cold convulsions.

The third attacker was facing Richard, holding John's arms behind his back. A look of terror struck him and he released the priest's arms and reached for a gun in his breast pocket. Dizzy and bleeding, John tried to push the gun aside. The attacker threw John to the ground. Richard did not have time to struggle for the gun. He shot an electric current from his left hand into a pressure point above the man's shoulder. It was a vulnerable point, too close to the brain. But Richard could not worry about his enemy. The attacker fell unconscious to the ground.

John Fisk was too weak to lift himself from the floor. Richard helped him to the sink and began washing blood from his bleeding shoulder.

"Are those men dead?" John asked.

"I don't think so," Richard answered.

John leaned against the sink. He looked at his wounds in the mirror. His Roman collar had been torn off. His left shoulder was bleeding profusely. Richard was already cleaning his shoulder wound with hot water and paper towels. John wiped blood from a cut above his right eye. Already the bruise around the eye was swelling and forcing the eye shut. Richard's skin still glowed a neon pink.

"What did I just see back there, Richard?" John asked weakly.

"I learned to fight in the military." Richard mumbled his words.

"You learned to shoot electric bolts from your fingers in the Marines, right?" John half-smiled.

Richard did not answer.

"I don't need to know anything you don't want to tell me," John said. He paused to catch his breath. "Damien Devon sent those goons to remind me to stay away from his house and his children. They said they were not going to kill me. But they were going to *almost* kill me. You need to know this, Richard. Be careful of Damien; he can be ruthless. Be careful if he ever comes after you. He has a history of driving men away from Selina." John seemed to swoon for a minute. He turned very white. Beads of perspiration forced themselves to the surface of his forehead. He leaned into Richard's strength as his knees gave way. Richard held him up. "Don't tell Selina or Mickey about this." John's voice was shaky.

"Maybe they should know what kind of man their father is."

"I don't want them to be afraid to come to me when they need me." John leaned on Richard, and his strength seemed to return to him.

"Your left shoulder is badly cut. I will take you to the hospital," Richard said.

"No. No. I want to catch my plane. It's Christmas Eve. If I don't catch my flight to Cincinnati, I won't get another flight for hours. The airlines are booked solid tonight. I don't want to spend Christmas Eve at Big Apple General Hospital. If I can just get to Cincinnati, my brother will take care of me. I can stay with the family then. My condition will just confirm the fears of all my Cincinnati relatives who think that every visitor to New York gets mugged." John laughed nervously, and as he did he split open the cut on his lower lip.

"All I need to do is to look good enough to get past the flight attendants and get seated on the plane. Then they'll give me a little first aid. But if I look like a mess, they won't even let me on the plane." John looked at himself in the mirror. His left arm was covered in blood. His right eye was almost swollen shut. His right hand was bloody from touching his shoulder. "Doesn't look good, does it?" he said. He looked dejected and defeated.

"I've handled worse," Richard said calmly.

And then he handled it all.

"How long is the flight to Cincinnati?" Richard asked.

"About an hour. I'd wait that long in the Emergency Room at Big Apple General." John's laugh changed to a cough.

"You'll lose a lot of blood. Force yourself to drink lots of fruit juice on the plane. Loosen the bandage that I'm wrapping on your shoulder in twenty minutes." He used his long black woolen scarf to make a tight shoulder bandage on John's arm. He finished cleaning the blood off John's face and hands. Richard removed John's bloody overcoat and replaced it with his own. John looked much better when the two men faced the flight attendant at the boarding gate.

Richard bribed the attendant with three one-hundred-dollar bills. And when he was sure that John was cleared to board his plane, Richard took a tiny blue pill from his wallet. He bit the pill in half and placed the large half under John's tongue.

"This pill will make you feel drunk. But it will also help to coagulate your blood," he whispered.

"I owe you, Richard. May God have mercy on us all tonight. Will you go back and help the three muggers now?" John asked. His one blue eye was swollen shut, but the other eye still smiled.

Richard did not answer his question. He watched John walk unaided, slowly, carefully down the ramp toward the door to his plane.

Richard half-ran to find a taxi. It appeared that God was granting him his two requests. John had made it to his plane, and Richard had made it past the police. Richard had prayed that the police would be slow to respond to John's mugging and that he could escape through the crowded airport in a blood-stained shirt with a limping priest. Richard could not explain the attackers' wounds to the police. He could not explain the weapon he had used. And God had heard his prayer and had answered it.

When Richard reached the Devon apartment, he paid the taxi driver and then asked the doorman's help in concealing the blood-stained shirt. He borrowed the doorman's overcoat and made it upstairs to his bedroom without drawing attention to himself. Except from Selina. She had watched the front door for the last hour waiting for him to return. Richard heard her knock and her whisper at his bedroom door.

He asked Selina to wait while he changed his bloody shirt and replaced it with a clean one. He straightened his tie, then opened the door for Selina.

Selina noticed one blood stain on his coat sleeve, then helped him to rinse it out with cold water.

"This isn't my blood. I'm fine. There was a mugging at the airport. I was slightly involved," Richard said. He combed his hair. Selina watched him.

She said nothing. But her wide eyes studied him, and he knew that her powers of telepathy were at work.

"You were gone for a long time. I felt danger. I got worried," Selina said.

"You know that I'm stronger than any of them. And I can take care of us," Richard whispered. He wrapped his arms around Selina and kissed her before she could ask any more questions. There was a hint of delight in his face, and he thought that Selina could see it.

"Did someone try to hurt John Fisk?" Selina asked.

"Stop reading my mind and listen to my voice. John will be fine at home with his brother tonight." Richard tried to distract her again with a kiss, but she turned her face away from his lips.

"Will you come to Midnight Mass with me and Mickey? We have to leave in half an hour." Selina looked up at him.

Richard hesitated.

"Christmas means that God is with us. Doesn't it?" he asked.

Selina's face lit up. "He is always with us."

"Then why do we need to go to Mass to find Him?" Richard asked.

"To worship Him. Because He's God." Selina always sounded matter-of-fact when she spoke of God.

Richard laughed a deep laugh. He did not know where the joy came from. It didn't make sense. This night had been a harrowing collection of experiences, and it wasn't over yet.

"Let's go and pay our respects to your family before we go to Mass. Don't mention the mugging or the change of clothes to your parents. I need to have my secrets, Princess Star."

He stopped and kissed her.

What next? he thought.

V.

Damien Devon hated Richard, and his face showed it. Just for an instant, Richard caught Damien's look out of the corner of his eye. Damien was watching Richard with seething hate. And when it was time for Richard, Selina, and Mickey to make a discreet exit from the party to slip away to Midnight Mass, Damien was angry. All the cold anger he was feeling toward Richard and dared not express to Selina, Damien lashed out at Mickey.

Mickey had seen Damien's anger before. But he didn't expect it now. And not here. Mickey looked as if someone had punched him in the stomach. The twenty-five remaining guests heard Damien call Mickey "a foolish wimp" for leaving the party early to go to "some church." They winced at the stream of obscenities mixed with insults about Mickey's character that followed. The guests watched with cold curiosity. Mickey hung his head. He told his father that he wouldn't go to church if Damien thought it would disrupt the party. Richard wanted to fight. John Fisk's blood was still drying on his hands. But he held his peace, stoically, as he had been trained in battle school. It was Selina who shocked everyone.

"How can you tell Mickey not to attend Mass? What is wrong with you? What kind of a white-washed tomb are you anyway, Father? If you cared about your guests, you wouldn't disrupt their evening with your temper. And if you cared about your son, you wouldn't shout at him in front of your guests. Mickey is worth ten of you."

You could have heard a pin drop on the carpet. And its echo would have shattered several nerves. Even the music stopped. Damien took two steps closer to Selina and raised his hand. Richard did not move a muscle. Until he saw Damien's hand moving toward Selina's face. And then he stopped Damien's hand with his hand. Damien pressed his angry palm against the force of Richard's palm. But only for a few seconds. And then Damien dropped his hand to his side. Damien glared at Selina, and Richard saw the murder in his eyes again. Selina must have seen it too. She looked away quickly as if she had glanced directly at the sun, and then started to walk away.

"I'm sorry, Mom, to have upset your party," Selina said softly, and headed toward the front door. And then Mickey followed her. Richard held his place until they were both standing at the front door waiting for him. He was stonefaced and very still. And then Richard nodded politely toward Aleece Devon and toward Damien.

"Goodnight, Aleece... Damien."

They heard the music begin again as they stood outside the door of the Devon apartment. Mickey was almost shaking with anxiety. His face was flushed. And then he smiled.

"Little tiger-tongue, that's my sister! You haven't done that well mouthing off at Dad since you were sixteen. Nobody talks that way to *Damien*! And Richard, God, I didn't even see Dad's hand move, and you had already stopped it! Superman!" Mickey laughed nervously. The tension needed release.

Richard put his arm around Selina. She was shaken, but he couldn't read her expression.

"I blew a fuse," Selina said softly. "It's as if there is something in the air tonight."

They drove to Midnight Mass in silence. The Devon limo was far more comfortable than a taxi. Richard kept his arm around Selina. She leaned her face close to his ear. Her whisper excited him.

"You are my knight in shining armor. Tonight we slew the dragon." Richard kissed her forehead. He knew better. The dragon was in chains. But only for this evening. Richard knew that danger hung heavily in the air. But for tonight, he didn't care.

CHAPTER
TWENTY-FIVE
ANGEL FIRE

Natas was livid! Sorn was not supposed to have recovered from his anger toward Damien. Sorn was not supposed to lap up the crumbs of Scripture that the priest threw at him. He was not supposed to save the priest's life. The bonding of the Tethra Triangle was not supposed to happen. But it was happening. Sorn and the priest had bonded. And the depth of their bonding was strong, so strong that even they did not understand it yet. Natas raged as he looked on Sorn, the agnostic kneeling in a cathedral before the cross of Christ, growing in his love for the woman Selina. Natas lusted to destroy them.

He would satisfy his lust in ten more minutes. He watched the stupid clock tick away its seconds toward the hour of Midnight on Christmas Eve. At that moment Natas would pounce on Saxon-Sorn, the choice meat of his hatred. Deceiver was poised at Natas' right side. And one of the great anger demons was ready on his left. Selina would soon crumble under the powerful arm of Saxon's anger. Even now Selina weakened, doubting things she had never doubted before. The arthritic pain in her left wrist was numbing her resolve to believe in God's love for her. Pain that came with a curse that she would never paint again. And she was slowly believing the curse. The seeds were planted.

Natas' sense of excitement intensified to manic heights. Thousands of his darkest, most fierce and mighty demons left their posts and flew to Natas' side to enjoy the thrill of the kill.

And then there was a stillness in the sky. And then a silent ripple of white light. White light full of gold and radiant color. Light coming on all sides, from every angle. Moving silently, coming too close to Natas. Natas froze.

"Who dares to blind me and to bind me?" Natas screeched.

"I, Michael, bind you, Satan, in the name of Jesus Christ, the King, and by the power of His cross which has vanquished you," the white voice boomed. Blindingly beautiful, Archangel Michael stood tall in his aura of radiant light. The light spread as far as the demon's eyes could see.

And then a sound began, a sound deep and resonant as a drum roll, but as soft as a kitten's purr, as sweet as the morning dew, a rumbling, harmonious sound. Michael was awesome even as he stood alone. Everything looked small beside him. But this time when Natas squinted to look up, hundreds of thousands of angels joined Michael. The angels stood quietly in disciplined columns. Clean, controlled, fierce they stood behind their champion, Michael.

"In ten minutes, eight minutes, you are to stand aside, Michael. I am to pick the bones and spit out the soul of the unbaptized Saxon whose second name is Sorn," Natas shouted. He blew up his form so that he could reach the size of Michael. And he ached with the memory that once, long ago, he too had been beautiful like Michael. Then he squinted before Michael's brilliance.

And Michael spoke: "Mercy has granted Saxon-Sorn more time. He will have the twenty-four hours past midnight to make his choice. And I am here to defend him for that time. To defend Saxon-Sorn and all the rest who kneel to God this holy night."

Natas cursed a string of violent obscenities which roared and quaked, no more disgusting in their sound than was their stench. Thousands of demons took up the wail of Natas' curses and echoed each word, senselessly, aimlessly, echoing hatred and frustration.

Michael did not flinch. He stood erect and calm. He had endured the stench, the noise, the sight of the demons as an act of love. He could bear anything out of love. This and more.

"He is mine. He is mine!" Natas screamed.

"We wait on the human and his choice," Michael said.

There was a hush.

"Why are there so many of you?" Natas raised his voice louder.

"There are as many of us as the Holy God willed there to be," Michael said.

"Are a few worthless humans needy of such forces as these? Why so *many*?" Natas' desperation tore through him.

"We do not give you reasons. And we do not need reasons to obey," Michael said. His face was too bright for Natas to see his expression. Power rippled throught Michael's limbs. His sword was unsheathed and still.

A blind fit of panic seized Natas and sent a wave of desperation out from his bowels. Instantly, a thousand angels swooped together in battle formation and formed an arc. Their arc absorbed the wave of desperation, shielding the people of Earth below them from the groan from hell.

One million angels' eyes focused on the grotesque body of evil in front of them, focused through the keen and perfect eyesight of Michael, who was leader for them all. For they were all completely one, as completely as the ocean and its waves are one. And they were all completely different. Each angel as different as a horse is from a rose. So many kinds and types of power concentrated for the Good, stationed in strength against the sewer of evil parts facing them. Natas stood and faced the angels. He faced them now as he had countless times before. But still it struck him each time as new horror, fresh pain, fresh misery, facing the armies of God like this.

Natas knew that all he would have to do was to twitch his little finger and Michael would see it and would order the crushing of Natas into a cinder. Michael would not even have to say it to his angel warriors. He would only have to think it, and they would all understand him. For at times like this they did not need speech or even thought, united in their might, united in their purpose, united in their obedience to the Almighty One. And there they stood, their love for God a fire burning bright before Natas' eyes. Their obedience and love were an excruciating pain.

"You are all fools! I serve no one!" Natas screamed.

The piercing cry of his hatred reached the angels, and they raised their shields to deflect the agony. It bounced back and was absorbed by Natas own demons who writhed in pain. They writhed silently, for at this moment, any sound would be punished by the ruthless claw of Natas himself.

Natas would not take the humiliation silently. Yet he dared not move a muscle, except for his massive mouth.

"You do not know everything, Michael. You do not know who will triumph in the battle at hand. I will have the lives of the woman, the man, and the priest. The world belongs to me!" Natas cried. "Mine. All mine. The hatred. The ugliness. The lies. The rape. The murder. The drugs. And all the lords and all the victims of these idols. It is all mine!" Natas' voice bellowed, even as he agonized to remain still.

And Michael spoke. His words were thunder.

"Today is all you have. The future belongs to God the Father and to the Christ, the Lamb who was slain for all their sakes. And for all their souls. And He shall reign forever."

At the sound of the truth, Natas could not speak. His rage drove him to insanity for the moment. He was helplessly bound. There was no vent, no outlet for his agony. There was only more agony, building like a terrible steam in his gut, releasing itself inside of him.

Natas and his forces were paralyzed. It was Christmas Eve in the year 1999. And he could not stop it from happening. There was peace on Earth.

II.

Richard had never been inside a church before. It was not one of the structures that interested him on Earth. But he felt that he had seen this place before. Perhaps he had seen it in a video. No, he felt that he had *been* here, not seen it. He looked up at the towering pillars, the massive brass-plated lanterns hanging everywhere. Multi-colored Christmas lights and sweet-pine smelling green wreaths decorated every corner of the building. Strings of light wound around the pillars and the walls. There was a tangible sense of awe. There was an expectancy in the air. Richard felt it. Richard tasted it. Perhaps it was in the music. A well-trained choir of red-robed singers stood on the right side of the altar facing the congregation. There were forty of them, young and old, men and women. Their voices blended in three and four-part harmony. Their faces were beautiful when they sang.

Richard seated himself next to Selina, so close that he was touching her. He looked at her. A part of Selina left him when they entered this place. She was absorbed in her unseen God. He looked in her beautiful face. And he wanted to see the face of God.

Well, John, I took one step, Richard thought. *I have taken one step to try to believe in God. John said that God would help me every step of the way. Wouldn't it be nice if He really did? If such things were true?*

The music was moving in his soul. Richard was impressed. Such longing, such exposed need, such faith in the words of these songs.

And then he felt as if some intangible force had seized him. Almost too gentle a force to be called a force. But it was compelling, reaching for him. It drew his eyes toward the altar. And toward the manger scene. It led his eyes to study every detail, every inch of each porcelain figurine in the creche. The statues were frozen in their joy as they beheld the infant Jesus in the manger. "He is the message, not the messenger. He is the Way, the Truth, and the Life," John had said. The statues looked at the Jesus statue as though they believed John's words. Selina looked toward the altar as though she believed those words.

Richard looked a little higher, toward the focal point of the manger scene. There was a large four-pointed star above the stable. His heart started racing with excitement. Every Christmas card, every crib he had ever seen in this last month on Earth, they always showed a star. He felt a chill move along his spine.

Why had it never struck him before? The choir chimed in with its evocative music as if to emphasize the realization forming in Richard's mind;

"Oh-Oh-Star of wonder,
Star of light,
Star with royal beauty bright...
Westward leading, still proceeding
Guide us to thy perfect light."

The words rang in his consciousness. Richard leaned toward Selina with a question. He did not take his eyes away from the manger's star.

"Why do they always show a star over the stable?" he asked.

"The night Jesus was born, 2,000 years ago, a brilliant star appeared in the sky. Astronomers from surrounding countries saw the star and followed it to Bethlehem, where Jesus was."

"Did they ever name the star?" Richard asked. Goosebumps formed on his arms.

"I don't know," Selina whispered.

Someone in Tethra had named the star, Richard remembered it all clearly now. The star may have appeared slightly larger on Tethra, or perhaps smaller than it appeared on Earth. But it had appeared. It appeared about 2,000 years ago, and its presence coincided with the rebirth in Tethran space travel. They named the star Angel Fire. They said the star looked as if a thousand angels crossed their swords in the sky. It had marveled the scientists with its beauty, its configuration, its strange lifecycle. Why had Richard never made the connection before? Every cadet at the starfleet academy had studied the Angel Fire.

Thoughts began to explode like fireworks in Richard's mind. God had given them the star of Bethlehem, their own Angel Fire. It was a sign that this baby Jesus belonged to Richard Saxon as well as to all the people of Tethra.

"Yes, I am for you and for all of Tethra," a voice spoke in his heart. A holy voice. He knew it was the voice of God. It thundered through all his being. Richard began to sob, quiet sobs that were drowned by the voices of the reverent choir. Heaving silent tears, Richard reached for Selina's hand. She held his hand tightly. She clutched his arm and held it snugly. She asked no questions. She knew he was in God's hands.

Richard could not control his weeping. It gradually subsided as the prayers of the Mass proceeded. He listened intently to every word of every prayer. Astonishing words. The mystical quality of the evening made everything seem unreal. And then it was more real than any reality he had ever known.

"Is that what John Fisk does?" Richard asked, pointing to the priest on the altar. The priest raised a white host above his head.

"Yes," she said. "John says the Mass prayers every day of his life. His hands have been consecrated to change ordinary bread and wine into the body and blood of Christ."

Richard's mind flashed to the priest he saw beaten in the airport men's room. A priest with a stab wound and a bloody face would be at the hospital tonight. Because he wanted to deliver his message to Richard. "I came for your sake, Richard. Selina knows that God loves her. You don't know that God loves you." Richard felt a lump in his throat. "I pray for mercy, because I don't deserve a thing." Richard's eyes moved slowly to the crucifix of Christ above the altar. "He is the perfect sacrifice who won atonement for our sins, so that once again humans could see God face-to-face." Father John's words fell into crevices that had been empty throughout Richard's entire life. The desperation was being drenched with mercy. Richard felt a large tear trickle down his face.

And he knew in that instant that he had just been forgiven all his sins. All the mistakes, all the killings that could have been avoided, all the unclean sex, all the unkindness, all the arrogance. All forgiven. He began to weep as the jagged crevices of pain and emptiness were filled in. The night air swelled with joy everywhere, surrounding and caressing him. He rested for a moment, and then he felt light, he felt joy.

Richard's eyes were swollen and red-rimmed, but he wasn't embarrassed. He watched his beautiful Selina and her brother Mickey walk to the front of the church to receive communion. Night of miracles, the body and the blood of Christ! He would taste that one day when they told him he was ready. He watched his woman as she walked to the chalice of the priest. And then Selina paused in front of the choir. She glanced up thoughtfully for a moment.

It was in that split-second that Richard remembered his dream. The September dream, when he was first attracted to Selina. In his dream she stood in front of a choir of red-robed singers in a towering structure with stained-glass windows--in this structure, with these singers.

God had planned this night for Richard. It had all been designed for him by his Creator.

"O, Little Town of Bethlehem
How still we see thee lie
Above thy deep and dreamless sleep
The silent stars go by..."

Richard began to weep again as he was filled with wordless wonder. He walked to the back of the church as others filed to the front. He went outside where no one could see him, as he released the sobs that wracked his body. He sobbed so hard that he fell to his knees on the cold snow that was beginning to cake itself on the ground. He could still hear the choir. Its music traveled in the night air, bringing its power and its meanings across the snow to him.

"The hopes and fears of all the years
Are met in thee tonight."

Richard's body shook with sobs and still he sobbed some more. The midnight church bells began to chime. He looked up at the stars in the sky.

"Yes, I am for you and for all of Tethra," God's voice had said to Saxon-Sorn.

"Yes, Lord God, and I belong to you. Take all myself, all that I have held back and all that I will ever be." Saxon-Sorn knelt in the snow. And then he laughed. He was finished with crying.

III.

Selina watched Richard in the soft light of her bedroom. He looked vulnerable. He had never looked vulnerable before. His hair was damp from the snow, and his hands were cold. Richard's deep brown eyes were red-rimmed from crying. He looked like a man who had been shaken by the fierce mercy of God. He looked like a new man whose head was poking from its newborn shell. He seemed unsure of himself and of how the world looked. But it must have looked wondrous and exciting, to see everything old with new eyes. *He was empty*, Selina thought, *but now he is full.*

Selina didn't know what to say. Or if he wanted her to say anything. But she knew that he had asked to come to her room after Midnight Mass. She and Richard had sneaked past the handful of guests remaining in the house. Richard did not want to have anything to do with them. But he did not want to be alone. Not just yet. Perhaps he wanted Selina to reassure him that this new life in Christ was not an illusion, but that it was real. Selina guessed what she could from the look in his eyes, from the uncertainty in his posture, from the tenderness in his hands.

Richard was acting so tenderly toward her. As though he thought she might break from the pressure of his touch or vanish if the light changed. Or maybe in the new light of God's life in his soul, he saw her as being precious and worthy of such tenderness.

Selina removed her coat and sat on Richard's lap. She put her arms around his neck and rested her head on his shoulder. She caressed the back of his head with her hand. At first she said nothing, and he said nothing. And then the right words seemed to come to her, so she offered them to him.

" 'In the beginning was the Word, and the Word was with God. He was in the beginning with God. All things were made through Him, and without Him was made nothing that has been made...'[*8]

Jesus was the Word. He came to His own, and His own received Him not. But to those who did receive Him... who were born of God... He gave the power to become sons and daughters of God." Selina spoke softly, confidently. Richard held her tighter than before.

"Sons of God," he whispered. "It is too astonishing."

"Yes it is," Selina said.

They sat in silence, almost not moving. Selina felt Richard's fingers delicately touch the velvet on her back. It was wonderful, talking with him this night. Talking against the darkness.

---

*8

"Life will only get better and better every day," Selina said. "At first you will worry that knowing God is just an emotional high and that it will end. The emotional high will end. But the day-to-day living with God will never end. Each year, you will learn new things about His amazing power, about the breadth and depth and height of the ways of God. Sometimes, when you are not looking, He will transform you. And you will realize that you did not work at it yourself, but that His power is bearing fruit inside of you. Sometimes He is a warm candle in your soul. And sometimes He is a blazing furnace."

"Sometimes He is the Angel Fire, come to light the world with promise and with power and with the beginning," Richard said. "And the Word was made flesh and dwelt among us." His voice was new.

Selina felt goosebumps on her arms and Richard touched them gently. They sat in silence. Rich and wondrous silence.

They had become brother and sister tonight. Not only lovers who had met in the delight of their passion. Not only friends who had tried to erase the loneliness of being separate. They were brother and sister in Christ. And Selina knew in this moment that she would marry him if he still wanted her. That this was the unity that had been missing, and that now that it was here, she could not leave him. She would marry him, and leaving Earth and everything that she had known or loved would not matter. For as she held him this night, with Jesus holding both of them as the third partner, it was all complete.

God had given her a guideline in planning for the future. "There are but three things that last; faith, hope and love. And the greatest of these is love." Loving Richard would last. Loving Jesus would last. And being loved by them. Loving everyone else whom God would send them, it would last. Earth and Tethra would pass away. But she would be a part of the things that would last.

IV.

Richard felt no urgency to kiss her. Just to hold her. He was gentle with her and with her painful left wrist. He had understood so little, and she had understood so much for so long. How patient she had been to wait for him to understand. How wise she had been not to force him before he was ready to embrace the truth. How hard it must have been to hold the fire in her soul and to contain it. Or maybe she was just trusting. Trusting her God that her God would reach Richard. Trusting Richard that he would reach for God. He did not want to live without her.

"Selina, will you marry me?" he whispered.

"Yes. Yes, I will never leave you," she answered.

They sat in silence for a long time, holding one another. *Then it is sealed,* Richard thought. *We will take our love and Christ's gospel to the solar system of Tethra. Or die trying.*

CHAPTER
TWENTY-SIX
CHRISTMAS DAY

$\mathbf{R}$ichard enjoyed the feeling of Selina's gloved hand in his. He enjoyed being near her. And the tantalizing chill of the cold winter air. They stood in the middle of Central Park and watched the bright noon sunlight create thousands of tiny points of light on the white snow.

Everything looked new and alive on this Christmas Day. Even the frozen, barren trees were guarding the hibernating life within them. A new powdery layer of clean snow had fallen in the morning on top of the thick gray layer of old hard snow. The city towered over the treetops. And the sun shined on it all. It was easy to forget the bad things--to forget the painfully awkward Christmas brunch with Damien, Aleece, Mickey, and Felicia. Felicia's superficiality had been the saving grace. Her bubbling nonsensical conversation was capable of distracting everyone else from their emotions.

Richard inhaled once more. Nothing could dampen his soaring spirits on this glorious morning. He had been "born again," just as Jesus had explained to someone named Nicodemus that such a thing could happen. Richard hungered to be baptized with water and to find his way to John Fisk.

Selina freed herself from Richard's arm, walked a few yards away from him, scooped up snow, and made a huge snowball. She aimed the snowball at his face, but missed and hit his shoulder.

"What are you doing, Selina?" Richard was startled. A second snowball hit him in the face, melted quickly, and dripped down his neck.

"This isn't fair. I can't hit you back. My throw would be too hard and I'd hurt you." He wasn't sure he liked this.

"Too bad," Selina said. She laughed with the ease of a child and then quickly pummeled him with a third snowball. Then she ran away, running off the sidewalk path into a field of untouched snow. Richard chased her, caught her, and gently knocked her down in the snow. She tried to scoot away and pulled him with her. He fell only because he wanted to fall. They both laughed as they rolled in the snow.

"Let me show you something," Richard whispered into Selina's ear. He glanced around the park, noticing where other people were standing. No one was close to them.

Richard unzipped his coat and held one side of it next to Selina, cloaking a small patch of snow between them. Richard stuck his forefinger in the snow and concentrated. His hand glowed slightly and then the heat of his forefinger melted the snow, melting deeply through its layers until it touched the grass five inches below.

He printed the letters S-O-R-N with his finger. "This is my true name," he said.

Selina's large eyes grew larger.

"Are you showing off?" she asked, laughing. "Will you teach me to do that with my finger?"

"You can't do it, Selina. Your genes have not been altered. But I'll teach you other things. When I take you home with me, someone there will teach you to read people's minds. I think that you have the right genes for that." Richard spoke so softly that he wasn't sure Selina heard him. He quickly erased his name and covered the burnt hole with piles of snow.

Selina stood up unexpectedly and leaned near his ear. "I love you... Sorn," she whispered and then ran away from him. He chased her, caught her, and kissed her.

Richard wanted to take her to the *Stealthfire* at that moment. All he had to do to make it happen was to remove the signet rings on their fingers. The thought was consoling. If only it were all that simple.

"I'm ready to face the lions," Selina said, smiling, looking in his eyes.

He knew that what she meant was that she was ready to go back to the Devon apartment. It was a cold day in spite of the sunshine. Selina was feeling the cold. But her words reminded him of the lions who would have to be fought, defeated, or avoided before they could go safely home to Tethra. And then Richard realized, in a wave of joy, that there was a change in him. For the first time since coming to Earth, perhaps for the first time since he had been born, he knew that he was not afraid to face the future. And that feeling, he knew, was power.

II.

Traytur hated Christmas Day. He hated most of the holidays, but this one was the worst. Everyone had somewhere to go on this day. Everyone but him. Even the servants begged for the day off to be with friends and family.

He didn't get up until noon. He had partied feverishly the night before. It had been a frustrating evening filled with all the usual pleasures. But one pleasure eluded him, drove him to obsessive behavior--he was sexually impotent. The man who had never been able to control himself with any woman was now a Eunuch. And so this morning he woke up with one more obsessive desire: to begin his killing.

He had to kill in such a way as to go undetected. He would never risk his reputation and fortune with a sloppy kill. Everything had to be perfect. And so he fantasized how he could commit the perfect murders of Selina, Saxon, and the priest. Selina's would be first, the comely virgin, putty in his hands. That murder would be a slow one, filled with pleasure. He needed to know more about whoever the Fisk priest was. Surely there had to be extra points for Max in killing a priest. And then there was Saxon. What a challenge, what a fabulous challenge! An alien who had to possess incredible powers and hidden weaknesses.

Max noticed the blood rushing to his head as he looked in the bathroom mirror. He ran his shower water hot so that it was painful on his skin. Sometimes pain felt good.

In an hour Max would meet with one of his private investigators. He would try to finish the job that Stan and Bobo had failed to do. Max remembered yesterday's conversation with Stan.

"Saxon took a different flight out of California than Selina. So I decided to meet Saxon's flight at Detroit Metro. I followed him all the way to Ann Arbor. He picked up his own car at Selina's house on Huron River Drive, then all of a sudden the wierdest thing happened! His car disappeared."

Stan told his stupid tale.

"You mean you lost him, you fool," Max said.

"No, I mean it, like his car vanished into thin air. I drove my car into a driveway next to her house, acting like I was visiting there. I didn't want to follow him too closely, so I kept my eye on his car and waited until he drove about a block or so away. I backed out of the driveway and kept watching his car. But his car just vanished into thin air! So I don't know where he went."

"He's an alien, you donkey's hoof! He is capable of anything! So you lost him?"

Stan nodded.

"I trust you recorded the exact spot where his car disappeared on the road?" Max had asked.

"Of course, Mr. Traytur."

"Take me to the identical spot in the road where his car disappeared. I have a party tonight, but we'll go tomorrow."

"Mr. Traytur, tomorrow is Christmas Day!"

"I don't care, you whimpering sloth, I don't pay you to take holidays."

Max wished that everyone was as competent as Max was. Fat chance! Stan showed up at Traytur's home at 1:00 p.m. He drove Max to the spot where Saxon's car had disappeared. There was no burnt hole in the ground, no trace of an explosion.

Max explored three hidden driveways close to "the spot." Two of the driveways led into dirt roads and large homes inhabited by families. The third home was buried deep in the trees at the end of the dirt road. No one appeared to be home.

Max took detailed pictures of every inch of the outside of the house. When Stan tried to fumble with the security system, a shock wave blew him across the porch and onto the lawn. Max finished taking his pictures and then drove Stan to the emergency room of a nearby hospital. Stan's hands needed to be bandaged from the electrical burns. He lost two fingers. They treated him for shock and released him later. Or so Max heard. He didn't have time to hang around the hospital.

It was Christmas Day, and Max had things to do. He knew he had discovered Richard Saxon's house.

III.

There had been an ambulance waiting for John Fisk at the Cincinnati airport. Although he couldn't remember all the details, somewhere before he landed on the ground, John started fading in and out of consciousness. He remembered feeling very cold and nauseous. He remembered seeing his brother Larry standing next to the stretcher. He remembered feeling vaguely embarrassed.

And then John woke up in the hospital an hour after surgery. The doctor said that the stab wound had been deep and that whoever knew enough to wrap the scarf bandage on his shoulder should have known enough to take him to the hospital in New York. John didn't say anything. He didn't feel like talking. He was just glad to be with Larry and close to home.

The doctors discharged John from the hospital only because it was Christmas morning. John's vital signs had improved after they fed him two pints of blood and IV antibiotics. His shoulder wound was their main concern, although he had also needed thirteen stitches for the cut above his eye and he had three broken ribs. One of the ribs should have punctured a lung, but it didn't.

When Larry's children saw John hobble in through the front door, three-year-old Aimee said he looked like a monster with his big swollen black eye and swollen lip. John felt stronger as the morning passed. He drank in the pleasure of being with his whole family; his brother Larry and his sisters, Peggy and Pat and their spouses and children. The "children" ranged in ages from sixteen to two. There were eight in all.

He loved Larry's cozy, crowded home full of children and cooking smells and polished early American furniture. They had saved the Christmas festivities until "Uncle-Father John" could join them. And now he was here.

John was quiet this morning. He was not the clowning uncle who let the younger children climb on him. He was not the big sweet-eater that he normally would have been. The antibiotics made him nauseous, and the pain killers made him fuzzy and drowsy. But he was glad to be alive and to be here.

"Can I get you something to drink, John?" Peggy asked gently.

"No, sweetie."

Peggy moved close to John and sat on the floor next to his chair. She reached to hold his hand.

"I had our whole parish pray for you at Midnight Mass last night. I felt like we were praying against a wall of darkness--and that we were going to win."

"Nice going, Peggy," John said. Peggy was two years older than John. She had always been the steadfast older sister, the rock of faith in his family. And then John began to remember all of the other faith-warriors he had known throughout his life. He began to see a pattern of mercy unfold in the plan that was his life.

He should have been focused on the huge pine tree adorned with lights and bulbs. He should have heard the music and the laughter and the nieces and nephews unwrapping their Christmas presents. But something powerful was going on inside his mind, and it absorbed his attention. It was as if his life was flashing in front of him.

John stood up with awkward effort and excused himself for a minute. He went into the downstairs guest room which was his. He closed the door and sat on the bed. He turned his mind to God. And then he felt an overpowering sense of gratitude. And he knew and he understood in his spirit that he could have died last night, *would* have died if Richard hadn't been there and hadn't known how to stop three attackers at once.

Damien's men had barely started on him when Richard intervened. They told him that they weren't supposed to kill him. They were supposed to "almost kill him." But would they have known when to stop? It would only have taken a couple more knife wounds in the right places. He remembered the trauma of seeing the knife go in and the dizzying pain of feeling it ripped out. He saw the knife heading this time for his groin, and then he saw Richard. Richard's eyes became fierce and focused, and then his skin glowed. In seconds it was all over.

John felt a wave of emotion. He couldn't identify what it was, probably it was many emotions all coming together. And then he had a renewed flood of memories. Memories of struggle and triumph. He remembered his ordination. He was twenty-seven, and he had completed his Master's in Theology in the same year. He felt self-confident, wise, and educated. Until he prostrated himself at the foot of the altar with the other priests who were being ordained. And then he felt tiny before the power of God, and he felt humbled, and he felt loved.

He remembered his tearful exit from La Senora de Guadalupe parish in Peru. He spent three years there, assisting a brave old priest who cared for a huge congregation of 36,000 Catholics spread throughout the impoverished villages and towns. Everything that he really knew he learned in Peru.

But his bishop had other plans for John Fisk. They were preparing him for "special things." They sent him to teach at Sacred Heart Seminary in Connecticut. A year later they made him assistant director of the Seminary. It was here in Connecticut that he met Selina when she was sixteen years old. She was a lonely little Catholic at the secular Rothbury Academy. And she and those like her were spiritually starved, like the peasants in Peru. He liked the spiritually hungry.

He spent four years teaching at that seminary and then five more years as the Rector of the Seminary that he had requested, Santa Cruz seminary in New Mexico. Here once again, he was among the poor; young Indians, Chicanos, Mexicans, and a handful of Anglos who all wanted to be priests. But these men were not spiritually poor. John loved Santa Cruz.

Then there were the last five years. The dry, grueling years in Rome. Somehow, John had impressed the hierarchy through his work at Santa Cruz. They liked what he did with his seminary and his seminarians. Enough so that they brought him to Rome for further studies and gave him an assignment at the Vatican. It was an honor, but it was not a joy. He did not like administrative work. It was that simple. But his superiors said that it was not that simple. They told John that he could do a lot of good--more good than anywhere else. And every time John talked about wanting to go back to the mission fields, they gave him additional responsibilities, what might have been called "promotions." And then a year ago they gave him his present assignment. He was to become secretary to the cardinal who served as head of the Congregation for Evangelization of Peoples. He knew that he had been given power in this latest assignment, power to influence decisions that could change thousands of lives.

And in that same week when he received news of that assignment, he received the letter calling him to be a bishop. John remembered the day, the hour and where he was standing when he read the letter. It was a Thursday, and the sun was shining. He read the letter several times, and then he went alone and prayed. His whole life had prepared him for that day.

John remembered that day in Rome, as he sat here in his brother's house on Christmas afternoon. *God must have some more plans for my life,* John thought. Because the Lord had sent the agnostic Richard to save John from death on Christmas Eve, John knew that the Lord had saved his life for a purpose. And he sensed that God would show him what that purpose was. John felt tiny inside and grateful. Just like that day when he had been ordained a priest.

IV.

The Lord didn't wait long to speak to him. John was taking a much-needed afternoon nap after the Christmas brunch. The warm bed was comfortable, and he slept for three hours. Peggy had apparently come into the room, closed the curtains, and placed a comforter on him after he fell asleep. When he woke up, the room was dark. The little clock beside the bed told him that it was only 5:15 p.m. But night came early in December.

The house was unusually quiet. Maybe all the children had gone somewhere until dinnertime. John knew he could get by with a longer nap. He was the wounded uncle. No one would ask him to stir until dinnertime, probably an hour away. He felt the soreness in his limbs from the beating. And he just wanted to sleep.

But he felt the Holy Spirit moving in him, so he lay on the bed and prayed. Richard Saxon was on his mind, so he prayed for Richard. As he prayed for Richard, he was filled with joy. He found himself speculating as to what kind of power a man would need in order to be able to electrocute people with his bare hands. But John controlled his speculations. Richard was entitled to privacy and even secrecy. John prayed that God would curb his curiosity and let him serve Richard in whatever way he should.

And then an odd thing happened. A beam of yellow light streamed in through a crack in the closed curtain and shone above John's head. He was too curious not to chase the light, so he pulled his stiff body out of bed and looked out the window. As he opened the curtain, the light disappeared. It was dark outside. He could not find the source of the light.

"You are the light of the world."[*9] Always go where I lead you," a voice said in his mind. John turned the bedside lamp on and began to pray seriously, wide awake prayer, heartfelt prayer. It came easily. And he sensed a growing conviction that Richard Saxon's life was about to touch his own life in such a way that it would never be the same. John felt frightened and overwhelmed. He rubbed his shoulder wound. He didn't want any more beatings. On the other hand, he had agreed a long time ago to carry the same cross Jesus had, to die on it if necessary. Maybe none of the martyrs set out to be martyrs. Maybe it just happened because they said yes. And with that thought, instead of fear, John felt joy.

---

*9

V.

Larry waited until after dinner to tell John that someone named Richard Saxon had tried to reach him on the phone. Richard had not left a number where he could be reached, but he said he would call again that day.

At 8:00 p.m. the phone rang. John was half-excited to talk to Richard.

"Your brother told me that you were doing all right," Richard said. John could hear the restaurant noises in the background of Richard's phone call.

"Thanks to you, I'm fine, Richard. I have to return your overcoat to you sometime soon."

"How about this week? Could Selina and I come to visit you in Cincinnati? I don't want to impose on you. But it is important that I speak with you."

"What's up, Richard?"

"Selina said that I need Christian instruction, teaching."

"There's plenty of time for that," John said. He enjoyed the eagerness in Richard's voice.

"No. There isn't plenty of time. I need to leave the country soon. Besides..." There was a long pause before Richard continued. "I have waited my whole life to find the truth. And then I found Him, last night at Mass."

"Glory to God!" John said into the phone, and he waved a triumphant fist in the air. "Richard, I can't promise to be the perfect teacher, or even the best one that you will find. But you're welcome to come here and stay for as long as you like. My brother doesn't have any room in his house for more guests. But I can arrange for you and Selina to stay at a monastery retreat house in town. It's not far from my brother's house." John paused. "It would be better if you kept your visit here a secret from Damien..." he said.

"That goes without saying. *No one* will know that we are visiting you," Richard said. "And I don't want you to go to any trouble for us. Selina and I can stay in a hotel."

"No, you'll be better off at a monastery. You can go to Mass every day. And pray and think. As long as you intend to set aside time for God, let's do it all the way," John said.

"That's why I want to see you," Richard said.

"Why?"

"Because you do it all the way."

Larry saw the look on John's face when he hung up the phone. John was elated and encouraged. Richard had inspired him. "Who needs you now?" Larry asked.

"This is my vacation, Larry. I won't get embroiled in anything heavy."

"Does a snake have legs?" Larry asked playfully. "Does my brother John know how to say no?"

John didn't laugh as Larry had hoped he would.

"You don't stop being a priest just because you're on vacation," John said. And he didn't like the weariness in his own voice. John knew that he looked forward to seeing Selina and Richard tomorrow. He would have someone else pick them up at the airport. And he wouldn't spend *all* his time with them.

But late that night after everyone else had gone to bed, John struggled with himself. It was his vacation; Larry had been right to remind him not to overextend himself. He was tired and wounded, and he needed extra rest.

The tired part of him longed for a break from being a priest. Wherever he went he was always a priest, and someone always needed him. His superiors had sent him to America to rest. They had sent him here where he could be an uncle and not a father. Where he could sleep in late and visit with his family. Where he could watch TV and play pool. Where he could be like everyone else.

John tossed and turned in bed. And then he remembered who he was. He was one of those who was the light of the world. He had given his life away when he gave his life to Christ. And the servant part of John reached to serve God and to know God's heart and to hear God's will.

As he prayed alone in his room that night, an unsettling idea formed itself in John's mind. Richard Saxon was not only going to be a passing acquaintance, someone who would be a part of John's service to God. Richard's needs were to consume John's service to Christ. Nothing would ever be the same after this week.

John clutched at the present, at what he liked and understood about the familiar. His weary flesh was dragging him down and holding him back from the Lord's next adventure for him. But the priest in him rose up and spoke. And what it said was yes to God. "Yes, Father, yes, and always yes," John prayed. And the heavens thundered.

CHAPTER
TWENTY-SEVEN
ENEMIES

Michael, the Archangel, knew that he needed to withdraw most of his army at midnight on Christmas Day. The armies were needed throughout the globe in hundreds of battles. He had a plan that he hoped would work. He began dismissing his forces early, very gradually, very quietly. As he stood before Natas he did not alter his own posture an inch. Nor the postures of his main guard who stood near him. He knew that their light blinded Natas, and that Natas would not know that the forces were leaving, obediently following the orders that sent them far and wide. If they could leave early, the angels could reach their battle posts before Natas' even knew that they had gone.

Michael kept his eyes on Natas. But he was absorbed in his mental commands. Absorbed in the strategies going on behind his back. And he wasn't ready for Natas' one move at the stroke of midnight.

In a burst of black fury, Natas threw a hot spear toward the heart of Archangel Michael. Archangel Gregory did not wait for a command. He intercepted the spear with his own body. And fell silently on the ground in front of his commander.

In that split second the fiery battle began.

Michael was left with only a third of his original force. Natas had every demon that he could gather from the winds. The battle lasted for two days.

Michael caught his first blow in the face. Natas was escaping his binding. As he felt his power building, Natas' vicious blows increased, his vehement thunder, his crashing vengeance all intensified.

The thick black cloud of dreadful forms was everywhere! The major demons masked the great escape of their sworn leader. And Natas fled. He fled like fire, burning a path of hate and destruction wherever he went. There was no pattern to his fleeing, only mindless desperation.

Michael paused. The balance between good and evil had tipped against him. He caught the scent of Natas' fleeing trail and watched him. Then, in a burst of power Michael shot out after Natas, pursuing him through the fire and smoke and the gaseous fumes of sin. Pursuing Natas, but not catching him.

II.

December 28! It was not too late to destroy the Tethra Triangle! Natas flew in his rage. He flew to the heart of the cities, and he entered their wounds. Wherever there was malice and despair, wherever there was apathy and where minds were open to his lies, Natas sent his legions of demons. They searched for hatred, pride, and injury, the conditions of the heart that opened doors for Natas' evil. He took his time and he took his power and he did his work.

Natas lived in the wounds and worked in the wounds. Once he entered a wound there were only two courses the destruction could take. Either the wound would worsen and the soul would die, or the person with the wound would fight Natas and his lethal gaming. If the fighter fought at all, he had a good chance of winning. If he fought well, he might save both himself and others from their wounds. The weapons that the fighters used were love of God and one another, Scripture, prayer, and the sacraments. Natas avoided all these things. He could always flee to other places where there were no weapons set against him. There were countless victims, countless wounds. And Natas rarely tired.

Deceiver stayed at a distance--stayed hidden from her master, Natas. She did not want to be near him to deliver her news to him. Deceiver sent him a mental message from her hiding place.

"The three of the Tethra Triangle, they have joined and have taken refuge in a fortress. While we battled Michael, the three found a place of safety,"

"Stop your imbecilic analysis! Tell me the place," Natas said.

"The Monastery of Our Lady of Peace, in the city of Cincinnati. It is impenetrable, built almost one hundred years ago to train priests."

"Nothing is impenetrable to me, you weak-livered slug!" Natas spat at a nearby demon.

"I will not go in there," Deceiver said.

"You will go where I order you to go," Natas snapped.

"I wait for the priest at the entrance to the monastery. I attack him in the evenings at his brother's house. It is the best I can do for now. They cannot stay at the fortress forever."

"You are a coward, Deceiver. I am not. I will attack them wherever they are," Natas boasted. And then he took his hot energy and he flew.

Deceiver hated Natas for calling her a coward. She would find her vengeance somewhere in the battles of the future. But for today, Deceiver was driven to attack the Fisk priest. He and his kind were her compulsion, her addiction. They caused her misery with their gleaming purity of heart. But she longed to bite them, to chew on them, to hurt them at any cost to herself.

It was Natas who was the true coward. Deceiver could take pain as a part of her work. Natas always ran from pain. He would do little harm in a place like the monastery where righteous faith had settled guardian angels in positions of power for a century. Natas would do something trivial like start a fire in the kitchen or cause the heating system of the monastery to fail.

Besides, Deceiver thought, and she heaved a heavy sigh. *The Turning Point is near. Only three days away.* And during the Turning Point of a century, neither Deceiver, nor Natas, nor Archangel Michael himself--none of them would have enough power to blow a fig leaf across a meadow.

III.

Damien Devon sat in his New York City office, watching the cold snow clouds hanging in the late afternoon sky. In only minutes they would dump white inches of snow everywhere. His feet rested on his leather desktop. He exhaled measured puffs of gray cigar smoke. His eyes darted nervously as he thought. And thought. Brendan Stills was familiar with this posture and the waiting. Brendan would wait as long as Damien wanted and would jump when he heard Damien's fingers snap. Right now, that knowledge gave Damien a special sense of satisfaction.

"I have a new enemy, Brendan. You met him two nights ago at my Christmas Eve party: Selina's boyfriend, Richard Saxon."

"The big British guy with the soulful eyes? He made an instant impression on my wife," Brendan commented.

"He is one slick operator! He must have been the one who stopped our men from finishing the priest. He had to be there, at least to witness the beating. But then he walked right back into my home on Christmas Eve. Cool as a cucumber, poised, clean, and pressed. And he didn't say a word about anything, just sipped eggnog and pawed Selina!" Damien's blood boiled at the memory.

"I doubt that this Saxon could have taken all three of them without so much as breaking a hangnail," Brendan said. Damien did not interrupt him, so he went on. "Two of the hit men had their backs to the 'vigilantes.' They have no idea what happened. Louie was the only one of the three who faced the priest's defenders, and he's blind now, so he couldn't identify anyone. Whoever they were, they packed a mean kind of weapon. The doctors said that the paralysis, burned tissue, and Louie's blindness were caused by direct current electrical shock, comparable to a direct lightning hit. The three men are all out of critical condition, at least," Brendan sighed.

"The idiots! They were all armed, all supposed to be professionals. Saxon must have enjoyed watching my hit men lose the game," Damien said.

"So what do you want to have done about Saxon, Damien?"

"I want to crush him. I want him beaten and scarred before they kill him. I want him to know who destroyed him. I want his reputation ruined and his family hurt. I want his home vandalized, the whole works." Damien lifted his feet off his desk and placed them squarely on the floor. "I want you to hire Max Traytur," Damien ordered. He crushed his cigar butt in a black ceramic ashtray.

"Traytur disgusts me," Brendan said.

"The important thing about Traytur is that he has never failed at his work. He is the best at what he does." Damien was vaguely annoyed.

"Traytur doesn't know when to stop. He enjoys his work too much. He's not like other professionals."

"Don't develop scruples on me, Brendan. They don't suit you."

"Why do you hate this Saxon guy so much?" Brendan asked. His voice sounded odd.

"Since when is it any of your business?" Damien snapped. He needed Brendan. He didn't want to feel he had no allies. And so he altered his tone of voice.

"Saxon has Selina wrapped around his little finger and her inheritance tucked in his back pocket."

"Selina gets more beautiful with each passing year. Someone is bound to nab her eventually, Damien."

"Not *this* someone! You know more about me than anyone else, Brendan. And yet this Saxon knows a secret that even you don't know.

He is powerful, and I don't know where he gets his power!" Damien glared at Brendan. He didn't have to explain himself to his underlings.

"I'm on your side, boss. I'll call Max Traitor tonight and get him on Saxon's case." Brendan looked at Damien's desk when he spoke. He would not meet Damien's eyes. Was it because he was groveling or because he was trying to hide his disapproval of Damien? Damien didn't care. Brendan would not forget who it was that buttered his bread.

Damien stood near the window and watched the heavy snow dumping on the city. He wasn't going to try to make it home in this weather. He would go to Christine Carnes, his mistress, tonight. Maybe he would stay with her all week to punish Aleece. He was mad at Aleece. He was mad at everyone tonight, even Brendan. It was all this Saxon's fault. The smell of vengeance was sweet. Max Traytur would take care of everything. That is, almost everything.

Damien knew there was one thing that he could handle himself-- and right away. It would be difficult to reach the University of Ann Arbor president at 8:00 p.m. It was Christmas week, and the University would be closed for winter break. So Damien called a friend with whom he traded favors. His friend was an influential member of the Ann Arbor Alumni Association, and he knew how to reach the University president, Dr. Adams.

IV.

Dr. Adams was in Vail, Colorado, enjoying a ski holiday with his wife when he received an urgent phone call from one of the University's attorneys. He listened carefully to every word the attorney said and then made a few more calls of his own.

Dr. Adams phoned the chairman of the mathematics department, Dr. Anthony Paoli. After some discussion, they agreed to convene an informal hearing on Friday, December 31. They would both be back in Ann Arbor by that date, and the issues raised by Mr. Devon were too serious to postpone handling until after winter break.

Mr. Devon had contacted the University's chief attorney to register a formal complaint against the conduct of Dr. Richard Saxon, a part-time faculty member. Mr. Devon explained that he used restraint in dealing with Dr. Saxon. He did not call the police to file an assault charge against Dr. Saxon on Christmas Eve when Saxon struck him and tried to strangle him. He did not want to disrupt his family's holiday festivities any more than they had already been disrupted. Mr. Devon said that he could overlook Saxon's violent and unpredictable behavior. But he could not overlook the more serious matters. Mr. Devon's only daughter, Selina, was a vulnerable, young AA student in the school of nursing. She was also an heiress. Dr. Saxon knew this and was attempting to use his position as a respected authority figure to secure Ms. Devon's affections and wealth.

And there was still more. The charges only got worse. Dr. Paoli got an earful. He knew the person on the faculty who knew Saxon most closely. Dr. Paoli phoned Dr. Sam Steinberg. It was getting late, and he understood why Dr. Steinberg sounded so groggy when he answered the phone.

V.

"Did someone die?" Sam Steinberg asked. He had tripped when he jumped out of bed to answer the phone. He stubbed his toe and cursed under his breath before picking up the receiver.

I'm an old man, Anthony. I usually go to bed around 10:30 or so, Sam thought, but managed not to say.

"No one died, Sam. But we do have a big problem," Anthony Paoli spoke in a foreboding tone of voice. Paoli described Damien Devon's charges regarding Dr. Richard Saxon. And then he said, "The worst charge of all reflects on the good reputation of the University. Devon fears that Saxon has some sort of strange power over his daughter. He said that Selina's behavior had changed and that his son Mickey would testify to that. Devon believes that Richard Saxon is heading a secret cult and that Saxon is not only exerting a strange kind of control over his own unsuspecting daughter, but that Saxon has been winning groups of other students. Devon claims that Saxon boasted openly about this cult when Selina was absent and that Saxon said he knew how to program the students' minds for their own good! But Devon believes that all Saxon really wants from the students is to get their money once they are initiated into his cult."

"Hogwash! Hogwash! You woke me up in the middle of the night during vacation to tell me this stuff! Is this some kind of a joke?" Sam blurted out. He knew it was not a joke. He only wanted it to be.

"This is not hogwash, Sam. This is terribly serious! Mr. Devon asked whether or not his complaint was the first one lodged against

Saxon by anxious parents. The University attorney is trying to reach Saxon. But no one knows where he can be reached. It is believed that Selina is with him and that he may be taking her out of the country against her will." Paoli's voice became high-pitched as he grew more excited.

"I've never heard such garbage, Anthony! Calm down and think this through for a minute. Why would Saxon confide in Devon about the fact that he had lured Devon's daughter and the rest of the student body into a secret cult?" Sam asked.

"Mr. Devon said Saxon was drunk. It was after all the guests left on Christmas Eve!"

"Wrong again, Anthony. Saxon won't touch alcohol. He says it's a medical condition."

"You are saying that Mr. Devon lied? Could you prove it?"

"Why should I have to prove anything? No one is actually complaining about Richard Saxon. They are *accusing* him! It's outrageous! I've only known Saxon since August, but I've never met a more refined, sane person in my life. He is dedicated to teaching, and his students love him. You told me yourself that you were disappointed that he couldn't teach additional course sections this term." Sam tried to keep the indignation out of his voice. This was a witch hunt.

"Go back to the part about his students loving him, Sam. Why *is* he so popular? Why are students on waiting lists to get into his classes? Do his students seem to relate to him in any sort of odd or unusual way?"

"Anthony Paoli, I can't believe that you are asking me these questions and keeping a straight face," Sam said. Now he was exasperated.

"Damien Devon is a respected businessman with many powerful friends, Sam. You cannot discount his anxieties and observations. He could cause harm to the University's reputation. Anyway, why would Devon make such accusations if they were not true?"

"I have no idea. Listen, I have met his daughter Selina. She is a fine young woman with a good head on her shoulders. She is no more under some cult leader's spell than you are."

"Under what circumstances did you meet her?" Anthony asked.

"You don't have to sound so confoundly anxious about this. If you must know, I went on a double date with Saxon and Selina Devon, and my date was a friend of Selina's. We had a nice dinner together, and then everyone went home."

There was a long pause before Anthony spoke again.

"Sam, you are *never* to mention this to anyone, do you understand? I don't want your good name dragged into this investigation. We have no set policy about faculty dating students, but under the circumstances, this could get messy."

"Under what circumstances?" Sam blurted out angrily. "You sound as though you've already tried and convicted Saxon as a criminal!"

"I'm more interested in protecting the good name of the University and your good name than Saxon's name. You are a tenured professor. Saxon is brand new on the faculty, and we have made no investment in him."

"This whole thing stinks to high heaven!"

"I want to talk with you before the hearing on December 31. You will need to..."

"Hearing? You're having a hearing in three days?"

"I don't want people to think ill of you, Sam. They may think that you have come under Saxon's... influence."

Sam became very quiet. Anthony Paoli was a reasonable man, but he wasn't paying any attention to what Sam was saying. The situation didn't look good for Richard. It smelled even worse. Sam could tell, as Anthony's voice droned on and on, going through a labyrinth of rationalizations, that the phone calls exchanged earlier in the night were the important ones. What several people had said to one another before anyone ever called Sam, those were the things that counted. The truth did not count. The truth was probably lost.

Sam hung up the phone from talking to Anthony Paoli. He tried to reach Richard's private office, only to reach an answering service. It didn't help that Richard had no home phone and that no one, including Sam, even knew where Richard lived, or his home address. Sam tried reaching Richard in the morning. And tried. And tried.

VI.

Maybe there was a Santa Claus, or some such stupid creature. Because on the evening of December 27, Max Traytur received a spectacularly timely phone call from Damien Devon. Not from Devon himself, of course, but from his man, Brendan Stills. Max had only worked for Damien one other time. It was a most confidential project. Max had not actually done the killing that time, he had merely been a consultant and a supplier. Damien needed to poison someone, and Max provided him with a method. Max didn't even know for sure who it was that Damien wanted poisoned. But he did read about the death of Damien's father two months later. Max had been well paid for that assignment. Designer drugs don't come cheap, after all.

Max hung up the phone from talking to Brendan Stills. He went into his den, poured himself a large cognac, and sat beside his fireplace. And thought. He could not believe how fortuitous this phone call was! He was beginning to relax about the Tethra thing. Not that he could truly relax as long as he was impotent and Natas was breathing down his neck. Max started for a minute, sat up straight in his comfortable black velvet chair, and glanced nervously around the room. He half-expected Natas to appear. He half-dreaded the thought. He didn't dare admit to himself how fully he dreaded the thought of Natas' presence.

Lately, every time that Max really felt self-satisfied, really began to enjoy his treasures and his pleasures, Natas appeared and tormented him. It had not always been that way. Max had gone for years and years without a visit from Natas. For years and years Natas had showered him with presents, expecting almost nothing in return. But lately, that had all changed. Now, instead of giving him succulent women to use, Natas had struck him impotent. Instead of continuing to increase his wealth, Natas had allowed Max's stocks to drop. At least, the good ones. And the "visits"--Natas was really putting the pressure on Max about this Tethra affair. It was enough to make Max rebel.

Not that he could rebel against Natas. A sickening wave of fear washed over Max. What if Natas was listening to his thoughts now? Natas could do that. Natas could be anywhere, anytime. Max put the cognac down and paced the floor. Then he went to the little silver box on the mantel of the fireplace, found the key, and unlocked the safe beneath the floorboard by his desk. He pulled out his cocaine and sniffed some. Sniffed quite a bit. He was feeling a little shaky, with all this self-reflection garbage. He needed to feel a little better. Ahh! That's nice. Max put his things away neatly and returned the key to its silver box.

He sat down again. This time he didn't need the cognac. He was on top of the world again, and he knew just what to do. He would kill someone before New Year's so that he could celebrate with a few women. No, wait! He was getting off the track. Max laughed aloud to himself, alone in his den.

Max jumped. He heard a noise near the fireplace! He broke out in a cold sweat and ran to the fireplace. *Thank God! It wasn't Natas! It was simply a large log that cracked in the middle and broke in half. Thank who?* Max thought. What was wrong with him tonight? His hand was shaking. He felt nauseated. And Natas wasn't even here.

VII.

Max Traytur did not want to meet with Damien Devon. He resented having to fly to New York City before New Year's to arrange a confidential meeting that neither Max nor Damien wanted. But Max did not disobey Natas. And Natas had come to him once more, this time babbling about his theology of sin and saying that he wanted more than murders from Max. He wanted Max to secure Damien Devon's soul, to drag Damien into deeper sin. More talk about sin and Selina's destruction. As if Max did not have the message by now.

At least Damien had consented to meet with Max. They had only met each other face-to-face on one other occassion. It was not very pleasant. They had tried to outdo one another in appearing to be self-important empire-builders. This time Max had to approach Damien for permission, as if Max were some sort of hired hand.

Devon removed the locks and opened the door of Christine Carnes' apartment. It was a heavily decorated apartment, rich with ornate French provincial furniture, embroidered everything, and flowers everywhere. It looked something like an expensive brothel. Oh, well! Every man to his own poison, Max thought. Damien Devon was trying to impress Max. He was meticulously dressed in an expensive Italian-cut, imported wool suit. Max knew his own suit must have cost more than Damien's. Damien did not even bother looking in Max's direction once he had closed the door behind him.

VIII.

Damien glanced at Traytur when he opened the apartment door. He remembered Traytur's ugliness from the last time, the transparent white skin, white eyebrows, white lips and white hair. Damien rarely looked people in the eye. But he briefly noticed Traytur's peculiar red eyes.

"I expect this to be brief. We need to finish our business before my associate returns to her apartment," Damien said.

"Of course, Mr. Devon. May I call you Damien?"

"Whatever."

"I need to discuss one point of procedure with you. Something that I believe is rather personal and would be better decided by you than by your assistant, Brendan Stills."

"That's what you told me on the phone. And I told you I don't want to be involved in the details. I'm paying you a big fat fee to get results." Damien deliberately acted indignant. It did not ruffle Traytur.

"It is my assumption that you want your daughter Selina to be spared any unpleasantness as I complete my work with Saxon." Traytur's voice was crusty and slow. Each word sounded too calculated. He was grating on Damien's nerves.

"And?"

"As I have plotted my... strategy, it occurs to me that there is a way in which Selina will forsake this dreadful Saxon person and will see you, her dear father, as a sort of hero."

"Then do it, Traytur."

"It would involve, Damien, pardon my specific description, a little half-willing rape." Traytur's irritating voice became very soft as he said the last word.

"Half-willing rape isn't rape. But I don't see how raping Selina is going to make me look like a hero." Damien felt oddly intrigued.

"You will be a hero because you can console your injured daughter and tell her how you wanted to protect her all along. There is another benefit to this plan. I have researched Saxon, and he will reject Selina if another man violates her." Traytur seemed tense. His left eyelid twitched as he gazed intently in Damien's direction. Then traitor waited quietly as Damien thought. Damien knew that he was crossing some line as he stepped forward in his vengeance. He was fed up with

Selina and her insolence. *And anyway,* Damien thought, *rape is not such a big offense. Women give themselves freely all the time.*

"This is a tricky business. Do what you have to do," Damien said. He reached in his empy breast pocket for a cigar. Not finding one, he felt a little nervous.

Traytur seemed a little too pleased. There was nothing else to discuss, so he hurried away. Damien shut the door and locked it behind him.

Damien could not see the host of two-foot demons scampering in a gleeful circle around him. But he thought that the sun must have gone behind the clouds for a minute, because the darkness fell across him and the place where he was standing.

                                   IX.

That ought to make Natas happy, Max thought. *Maybe he'll get off my back for a while. Natas is becoming a real... pest.* Max was afraid to think the thought. Natas could read thoughts. Max had to be careful. But surely Natas could understand that it made no difference to Max whether Damien Devon wanted his daughter raped or not. Max was going to kill the woman, after all. And Damien couldn't stop him. At any rate, Max had done his duty. And now that he was in New York, he wasn't going to waste the trip here. Max would shop and dine in the great city and then have a meeting.

Max was scheduled to meet with two important U.S. ROSET leaders. They were probably the only leaders in the world underground movement who were not off on some Christmas week vacation and who had responded to Max's urgent call to meet.

Max enjoyed his Italian dinner and then caught a rickety, smelly cab which took him to, of all places, Brooklyn. He and the leaders, a scientist and an Air Force captain, were meeting in the home of the scientist's aged mother. She was deaf, half-blind, and as innocent a person as one could hope to find in Brooklyn. Max hoped he didn't have to meet the mother, but he had to admit it was a clever spot for a secret ROSET meeting.

The little Brooklyn house was exactly what Max expected, quaint and tiny and cluttered with old fashioned things. There were big dark pieces of furniture in the small living room, furniture that belonged

in a larger house. Everything was dusty and looked as though it might
break if a man handled it, instead of a frail old lady. The nice thing was,
though, the old lady was already in bed at 7:30 p.m., and he didn't have
to meet her.

Max was a celebrity tonight. The scientist, Doug, and Captain
Lick expressed their skepticism about Max's supposed "Alien Find."
Being skeptical was the sophisticated thing to do. But then they heard
Max's tape. Max's toes curled with excitement. He was exhilarated as
he watched the faces of his two colleagues. There was no mistaking the
conversation between Saxon and "Frank" in California. They were from
another planet, had superior knowledge, and a starship waiting for them
somewhere.

"My God! This is incredible. Traytur, how did you get this
tape?" Captain Lick stood up as he reacted. He began to pace the floor,
and then he rambled on. "How many of them are there? And why are
they trying to teach our college students? They're trying to control our
minds! This is big, this is really big!"

"Max, do you know where these aliens are at this moment? We
can't just let them run around loose! We have to find out what they want
with us! We have to study them." Doug, the scientist, got out of his
chair and stood up also.

Max assumed the air of a cool intellectual, a patriot who only
wanted to do what was right. He would have them eating out of his hand
before this meeting was over. He would tell them nothing of his plan to
destroy the Tethra Triangle. He would give them no information about
Saxon's whereabouts. He would only use them and use all of ROSET
and its eager resources, its willing, panting paranoia. He would use
them all, when the time was right, to surround and trap Saxon and
Selina. He would use ROSET to locate the priest and help him kill the
priest also.

Max told them very little tonight except that he needed their
help and expertise and dedication. Max didn't want them to know
enough to get in the way. He merely wanted to be sure that he could use
them when he needed them. And not before.

When he left the meeting, Max knew that he had already
become a hero. His stature would increase when the other ROSET
leaders returned from their vacations after New Year's and heard the
news. They would be putty in his hands. They may have laughed at him
behind his back in the past. But in the future he would be a hero and an

idol. It made him feel good inside. When Max was ready, he would present ROSET with the writhing bodies of the male alien Saxon, the female alien Selina and the half-human alien, the Fisk priest.

But Max had a lot of work to do before this achievement. He had to do two things. First, he needed to study Richard Saxon's moves. He would not try to capture him until Max understood what weapons and defenses Saxon could use. For that, Max needed to find out what Saxon was hiding in the fortified confines of his house. Max knew that he could pick Selina off at any time, but he would save her as the perfect bait for Saxon.

There was a second problem worrying Max just now. Saxon had gone somewhere, and Max could not find him. Max had located Saxon's business office and had tapped that phone. But even Saxon's secretary had not heard from him in five days. Was it possible that Saxon knew he had been discovered and was on the run?

Max wasn't going to let anything more bother him tonight. He would simply savor the taste of admiration, the admiration of the two ROSET leaders who would jump the next time they heard Max's voice on the phone. Max relaxed in his first class plane seat and watched the city glittering below him.

Then he saw her! There was a delicious teenage girl sitting across the aisle from him. She was just his type, ripe and young, perhaps 15 or 16 years old, with plump... he forced himself to take his eyes away from her. He wanted one like her, and he wanted one tonight! He ordered a double scotch, and still he could not control his heavy breathing. He heard the girl talking and laughing, and he could feel her under him even when he wasn't looking at her. Lust was a burning torment in his groin. Lust drove his thoughts into a feverish panic! Max would have to kill someone *soon* to restore his sexual abilities. It had to be someone close to Saxon and Selina. "Anyone who helped them," Natas had said. *Anyone,* Max thought. And he realized that the line had just blurred between the lust for sex and the lust for blood. Max realized that he was lusting for blood, like Natas. Max had never lusted for blood before.

CHAPTER
TWENTY-EIGHT
EYE OF THE STORM

Deceiver had been right, and hating her for it changed nothing. Natas could see the monastery from a distance. The angels had cast a light mist around the monastery, fogging Natas' vision. As he came closer he saw the angel guards--they were stubborn and strong and fierce. They waited until he was right on top of them, and then they raised their fire swords above their heads. Their power was like a solid wall of fire. They were entrenched. Entrenched here for more than a hundred years. Before the walls of the seminary had been built, before the ground had even been broken, the angels had been sent here by the prayers of the faithful to clear the ground and guard the spot. The faithful had prayed and fasted and formed a dream for their seminary before a stone had been set. And then, as each stone and each brick had been set in place, the faithful had prayed for it. And each priest and each seminarian who had walked here had asked for grace and asked for mercy. With each prayer, the angel guard surrounding the monastery became stronger, became more entrenched.

Natas taunted and spat and cursed at the angel guard. He swooped down, shooting his black spit, and it landed on a few of their heads. He knew it smelled and that it stung. And then two dozen smaller demons followed his lead and swooped and spat. As the taunting and distraction ensued, Natas threw a dart into the central heating system of the monastery and wrecked it. "Let them freeze as they pray," Natas laughed aloud. Until he felt the sword of the captain angel. He battled the captain for two hours. He and all his demons. But the angels did not yield. And they were not tiring. Soon Michael would find him here if he stayed longer. Deceiver was right about another thing also. The Tethran three could not stay forever in the fortress. Natas fled.

II.

Nothing went the way John expected things to go. There was a pulsing undercurrent of urgency at work. John almost didn't trust the sense of urgency. And yet it flowed in peace, in harmony, gently in the ways of the Holy Spirit.   The Spirit that John not only trusted, but followed.

Richard and Selina had arrived on Sunday, December 26, and had settled themselves at the monastery of Our Lady of Peace. They seemed delighted with the setting, with the peaceful, snowcovered, forest-like grounds and the large brick and stone buildings. The monastery had been built at the turn of the century as a seminary for priests. But as the numbers of priests declined throughout the last fifty years, the buildings had been converted into half-seminary on the west wing and half-retreat facilities on the east wing. Today almost anyone could come here any time, either in groups or as individuals to seek quiet time with God.

Richard enjoyed the ancient architecture of the monastery, with its lanky hallways, its foot-thick brick walls, its elaborate stained-glass windows. Selina loved the view of the Ohio River which could be seen from almost any point on the grounds, since the monastery was perched high on a hill on the eastern side of Cincinnati.

But from the moment of their arrival, John realized that there was little time for leisure and for river-gazing. Everything moved quickly. John talked briefly with Richard and Selina when they arrived on Sunday afternoon. The next day he met with them in a small private dining room in the monastery. He was struck by Richard's eagerness.

"I finished the books you gave me yesterday afternoon," Richard said.

"*All* of them?" John asked.

"You only gave me four. I especially liked the catechism. It made reference to several other texts that I need to get. " Richard's face beamed.

"You're different, aren't you, Richard?" John said, smiling.

"I want to be baptized. I need to be baptized. Could you do it today?" Richard asked.

"Today!   There is supposed to be a period of prayer, contemplation, and instruction before an adult is baptized," John said gently.

"Do you want me to read more books first?" Richard asked.

"No! The four books I gave you were not exactly light reading. The decision to be baptized is not simply a mental thing, it is a matter of the heart and the spirit."

"I know that," Richard said. "It is my heart and my spirit that cannot wait. My intellect is satisfied in reading your books. But my soul has spent a lifetime waiting for the living water and the living flame."

"The living flame?"

"Unless a man be born again of water and the Holy Spirit, he shall not enter the Kingdom of God,"[10] Richard quoted Scripture. "I have already received the Holy Spirit, the living flame. But I have not been baptized with water. For that I need your permission."

"No, you don't," John said. "You don't need my permission when God has obviously already given it to you." John looked at Selina. She had a pleasant, amused expression on her face.

"You must have some questions for me from all your reading," John said, half afraid of what would follow.

"I have a thousand questions. Selina has answered some of them for me. But I saved some of them for you. One relates to my baptism today. In the Apostle's Creed, the prayer that expresses the faith, it says. 'I believe in one, holy, Catholic and apostolic church....' Would you define the word Catholic for me? Does it mean more than a denomination?" Richard asked.

"Catholic means universal, all-inclusive, whole. Catholic means that we are making a contract, an agreement to remain united." John had only begun his answer. He paused to watch Richard's response.

"Yes," Richard said, and he closed his eyes.

"I believe in that. Jesus wanted it like that. He said it at His last supper, 'That they all may be one, even as I, Father, am one in you and you in me.'"[11] Richard opened his eyes, and then he smiled a broad smile and looked at John, then at Selina when he spoke. "I am only an infant Christian. You both have understood these things for a long time, but I am beginning to understand."

The whole thing was highly irregular. It was not wartime, and Richard was not dying. If he had been more of a legalist, John would not have agreed to baptize Richard that same day. But it felt right.

As the afternoon sped by, John experienced a rich outpouring of grace on the three of them. John found the words to answer all of

---

*10
*11

Richard's questions. Not dry answers but answers that almost moved him to tears. John found that he was at his best being with them.

That evening after dinner, Larry returned with John to the chapel of the monastery. Larry agreed to be Richard's godfather.

It was pitch black by 7:30 p.m., and the chapel was chilly and drafty. John felt the December cold penetrate his shoes as he stood on the hard tile floors near the baptismal font. His hands were cold, and the water was icy. But when Richard and Selina entered the chapel, they brought their warmth with them, their vibrancy and their fire.

And the Lord was with them all, there in the tranquility of the delicately lit chapel. The candlelight flickered in the baptismal waters, and John said the words to bring the power. It felt so natural and seemed so simple. Kollann-Richard was baptized.

For a short time after the prayers and the ceremony had ended, no one spoke. Then Richard looked into John's eyes, his hair matted down wet over his forehead,

"Tomorrow," Richard asked, "can we talk about Christian marriage--mine and Selina's?" Richard had a look of delight and mischief in his eyes.

Yes, John thought, *if you don't wear me out before then.*

III.

John Fisk did not look like a priest this Tuesday afternoon. Not like the dignified, solemn man who had worn his priestly vestments and had baptized Richard the night before. Today John looked like a tired man with circles under his eyes. He wore the same flannel, plaid shirt that he had worn the last two days. It had a blend of blue and black fibers, and the colors tended to emphasize the deep blue of his eyes. Today everything about John seemed older and more tired than before.

But whenever he spoke, John Fisk was impressive, and Richard listened to him intently.

"Richard, I know that I need to walk a fine line with you. You are not obligated to answer any of my questions. I don't want to infringe on your privacy or the secrecy required of your trade. But I need to ask you some questions for Selina's sake. The church considers preparation for Christian marriage to be a serious matter."

"I read your three books about Catholic marriage." Richard activated the Sound Distort. He noticed that John heard the faint crackling sound. It seemed to echo in the bare private dining room in which they were sitting.

"What did you just do in your pocket?" John asked.

"I activated a security device to mask our conversation... if there are any bugs hidden in this room."

"Then you are a spy?"

"It is better for you if you don't know the answer to that question. Then if someone asks you, you can answer, 'I don't know.'"

"I don't need to know. Does Selina know?"

"Yes."

"Does she know everything about you?"

"Yes."

"At the airport on Christmas Eve, I saw your skin glow like fluorescent lights. Does Selina know about that?"

"Yes."

"Is there anything... wrong with you that would prevent you from having a normal life?"

"Normal is a relative term," Richard said. He felt appreciative of the sensitive way in which John was questioning him.

"Can you have a normal sex life and children?" John seemed mildly exasperated.

"Yes, definitely. We want to have at least four children. Children are important to Catholics. They are important where I come from also." Richard smiled.

"So you have held back no important secrets from Selina which may influence her decision to marry you?"

Richard folded his hands and looked at them.

"Only one secret."

"Why haven't you told Selina this one secret?"

"It is about my family and our position in... society. All of my life, people who have known our family have perceived me as being either a giant or a worm... based only on my family name. I don't want anything to change the way Selina looks at me. I want her to love me for myself."

"You need to trust Selina," John said softly.

"No one has ever loved me for myself. They saw my family crest before they saw my soul."

"Selina saw your soul first." John reached for Richard's folded hands and placed his right hand on top of them. His hand was big like Richard's. John looked in Richard's brown eyes.

"Do you think that anything could overshadow the wonder of seeing your soul, Richard? The wonder of who you are? I am impressed with you, and I've barely known you for a week. Selina is ready to leave everything and follow you blind, who knows where? But she will wear your 'family crest' with you. And she has a right to understand it, everything about it."

"Yes," Richard said. *You have won me,* he thought. *Christian priest, I would do anything you told me to to do.* "You love Selina, don't you, John?" Richard knew that he was being bold.

"Yes. I love her like a father and a brother. And I love you like that," John said.

"You love us like the Good Shepherd who laid down His life for His sheep. Is that why you are celibate? So that you can love both men and women like the Good Shepherd?"

John paused. He seemed uncomfortable. "Yes. So that there is more room inside of me for loving like the Good Shepherd."

"And will you ask Selina all sorts of questions for my sake?" Richard asked.

"Yes, I will," John said. John's hand felt warm on top of Richard's hands. And his smile was warm.

Richard reached across the table and opened his small Bible. He turned to the last chapter of the book of John and read aloud.

"'Simon, son of John, do you truly love me?' Jesus asked. "He answered, 'yes Lord, you know that I love you.'*[12] 'Take care of my sheep,' Jesus said."

And Richard understood what it was to be a priest. And that this big man with the blue eyes wanted to walk in the steps of that first fisherman named Simon, son of John.

That night Richard and Selina had a private talk alone in the safety of the monastery. He told her his last and only secret and what it meant to be a Sorn. He told her more than Frank Nelson knew. He told Selina what his father told his mother... many years ago.

---

*12

IV.

Deceiver stretched her four tentacles next to John Fisk and tried to stir him from his dreams. She made him sweat with fear and memories and self-doubt. He tossed and turned in his sleep. But he would not wake from the dreams. Deceiver put her fifth tentacle into his wounded shoulder and breathed in pain. And then she leeched herself onto his sleeping body.

John Fisk ached as the pile of high school football players unwrapped their tangled bodies. A tearing pain streaked through his left shoulder and left knee. He wanted to get up and walk off the football field the way he always had. But his time he couldn't get up. He could barely breathe, let alone move. He wanted to scream with the pain, but he knew that hundreds of pairs of eyes were watching him from the stands. All that he could do was groan. And then he felt them lifting him from the muddy ground and placing him on the stretcher. He looked up at the bright white floodlights against the black sky as they carried him off the field. He was eighteen, and he didn't want anyone to see him like this. But they could all see him, and he could feel the presence of the hushed crowd surrounding him.

John slid from the dream state into a half-awake state. There was a new pain in his left shoulder tonight, not merely a memory of pain. The past and the present had been brought together tonight by the throbbing pain in his shoulder. John looked at the clock. It was 3:30 a.m., and this was the third night in a row that he had been awakened at this hour. The doctor told him that the pain should be subsiding by now. But it wasn't.

John lay in the dark for a minute, listening to what the pain in his shoulder was telling him. He remembered his senior year in high school, all the difficulty and all the decisions. He had been forced to give up football and dating girls in the same year. Football because he had injured himself. Dating girls, because he made his decision to become a priest.

John remembered graduation day. He graduated with honors and scholarships. He had his choice of colleges, his choice of careers. His father had wanted him to become a lawyer and a politician. Everyone had flattered and encouraged him, saying that he was a persuasive speaker, full of ideals and energy--saying that he could do anything or be anything. It seemed as if the whole world had been set before him in that year, 1973. As if the future were a ripe plum waiting to be picked. He was eighteen, and everything seemed possible.

But there was this flame in his soul. Burning flame. And it called him to God. It called him "to a life that would not make sense if God did not exist," as someone named Cardinal Suhard had said. It called him. No, it almost seized him. John took one step toward the priesthood and then another step. And then he found that he was totally, passionately, radically committed to Christ. And that there was nothing God could not ask of him. And so God asked everything. Asked him to give up his dreams and his past and the parts of him that held onto other gods. But it took years before John even realized that he was sacrificing in order to become a priest. Because at first John thought that he was taking. Taking from God, hungrily basking in the love which God offered him. Taking from the seminary, all that it could teach him. Sifting through a thousand pieces of nonsense and unfocused learning and hurrying through a maze to find the truth.

People loved to argue in his college and seminary years. People loved to sound scholarly and to take sides. John loved it for a while, and then he hated it. He hated the thinking of the seventies and eighties. He began searching back at the roots of the Scripture, deep into the theology of the doctors of the church and the doctrines and the dogmas, searching, always searching. And then finding.

Like the Pentecost flame, finding answers that burned like hot coals into his mind and soul. Only these hot coals were not painful. They tasted sweet.

John sat up in bed. It had taken Richard and Selina to remind him of the day of Pentecost. It had taken their zeal and fervor to remind John who he was. John had become stale. Stale like a loaf of bread that sat uneaten on a shelf.

These last five years in Rome had made him stale. Maybe becoming a bishop would make him stale forever. The thought pierced him to the heart! He felt achy and weak. He needed another pain pill. John made his way out of bed, and when he reached the bathroom, he tripped clumsily and almost fell on the floor. John did not see the demon who had tripped him.

Deceiver felt twisted in her gut. She cursed the limitations of her powers! She hungered to know what the priest was thinking. But she could not read his mind. All she knew now was that some holy grace was stirring in the priest's mind and that it was repulsive to her.

She felt sickened and she wanted to withdraw. No! She would watch and wait.

Deceiver watched as the Fisk priest gulped his water and swallowed a pain pill. "That pill will never stop the pain I have for you, priest," Deceiver thought. She dug her four drooling tentacles into the priest. He winced and clutched his shoulder. Seeing the pain effect the priest, Deceiver felt stronger. The priest was a worrier and she knew one of the things that worried him.

"You like to beautify your sins and your weaknesses. The Vatican is destroying your missionary zeal. It has made you into a religious bureaucrat--something God never intended." Deceiver shot her accusation into John's mind. She paused. Deceiver knew what the real truth was. That this Fisk priest was becoming a seasoned diplomat and fighter at the Vatican. And so it was crucial that she convince him of the opposite. The best place to attack was at the seat of his own doubt. This time she fed him thoughts as if they were his own.

"I spend all day talking with religious men about religious issues, off in our little cocoons! When was the last time that I preached the Gospel to the poor?"

John sat down on the edge of his bed. "Lord, my God," he prayed aloud. "I really don't like working exclusively with holy men in Rome. But I thought it was what You wanted. All I really want is to do your will, Lord. Please light my path and show me the way to take if I'm not serving you well, not pleasing you," John prayed.

Deceiver felt the prayer like a slap in the face. She changed her tactics. "How can I ever expect to think clearly in the middle of the night? I'm exhausted. No one looks out for *me*! My vacations have been canceled or interrupted for the past three years." Deceiver spat the thought into his mind, speaking the thoughts as if they were John's own.

"This was supposed to be my special vacation time with my family. And then Selina and Richard showed up here and wrecked it! I'm sure that the two of them will go off somewhere and have a lush vacation of their own," Deceiver continued. "But not me. People treat me like trash. The life of a priest is hard. The life of a bishop will be harder. They will drain me dry and throw me out like an empty husk."

John Fisk interrupted Deceiver's thoughts with his own words. "Jesus had the hardest life of all. And the best life. All I can hope for is to live a little like Him," John whispered.

Deceiver twitched at John's words, cringing at the faith and hope and love in them. John began to relax. He settled himself comfortably back in bed and pulled the soft blankets over his arms and legs.

Deceiver sweated and panted. She was almost too sick to go on. But she would not give up yet. Deceiver collected herself. She had to be more cautious.

"Jesus never had to evangelize spies! Who do I think I am that I can get involved with Richard and his secret espionage? I have no idea what kind of danger he has dragged me into. I've put my life and my safety into Richard's hands, and I don't even know the man. I may never live to see the day of my ordination as a bishop." Deceiver spat the thoughts into John's mind then paused to check the impact of her words.

John felt a knot in his stomach, and he sat up in bed, holding his stomach.

"Help me to give and not to count the cost, Lord God," John said aloud.

Deceiver shivered. She held onto John tighter than before.

"Cost! You know nothing about cost. Wait for the coming days. You think that serving Richard cost you a wounded shoulder and a little vacation. It will cost you everything! You know this in your gut. Richard's life will entrap you like fly paper. Everytime you lift a finger to get away, your hand will stick harder than before." Deceiver hissed each thought into his mind.

Deceiver watched John as dim rays of moonlight peeked in through the window. She could not deduce anything from his actions. She continued her attack.

"Maybe this is all some ego trip. Richard and Selina make me feel special and important, and I like that. I like thinking that I am the chosen one, called to help these two strong people. But they are really just distracting me from what God wants," Deceiver added.

"All I ever wanted was to serve you, Lord," John prayed aloud. His voice cracked with emotion. He was hurting.

"No, all I ever wanted was the glory and respect of being a priest. My priesthood is a false god, an idol. I need to give up the priesthood in order to truly be humble, in order to truly please God," Deceiver said.

And John listened. She could see it, each arrow puncturing his heart. She could smell the misery that was entering John Fisk.

John pulled himself out of bed. His stomach churned in knots. He went into the darkened kitchen and poured himself a glass of milk. And then he noticed Larry's cigarettes sitting on the kitchen counter. He wanted one. John had not smoked in four years. And now he wanted one. Deceiver watched as John examined the packet of cigarettes. "Why shouldn't I smoke? I'm not allowed any other pleasures," Deceiver said. And she jabbed John with self-pity. "I need a cigarette. I need something," Deceiver spoke for him. John tapped the filter of the cigarette on the countertop. And then he lit it and inhaled deeply. The instant the nicotine entered his bloodstream, he felt its pleasure. He was hooked again. He was ashamed. He finished the cigarette anyway.

John walked into the living room, sat in a comfortable chair, and turned a small lamp on beside him. He opened the Bible that lay on the table next to the lamp. Deceiver began to sweat.

"Say to Yahweh, 'My refuge, my fortress, my God in whom I trust.... Because he clings to me in love I will deliver him.'"[*13] John read the words silently. They soothed him. They made a promise to him.

"I really do like to make my faults look like strengths. I really do like to feel self-important and special. But I can always repent. I can always ask for mercy, and try again," John told himself. He searched through the Bible for the prayer he wanted, and he found it, Psalm 51.

"'God, create a clean heart in me; put into me a new and constant spirit. Be my Savior again, renew my joy. Keep my spirit steady and willing; and I shall teach transgressors the way to you, and to you the sinners will return.'"[*14]

John read the words aloud three times. He knew he needed this prayer. He felt numb inside. But he knew that God was near.

Deceiver let out a scream of rage and pain. The priest was tired and numb, and yet he had thrown acid on her and beaten her. Deceiver withdrew her tentacles from John's spine and fled. Natas, for all his boasting, was not nearby to help Deceiver. Natas preferred to attack the weak while Deceiver attacked the strong. At least when she, the great Deceiver, lost, she lost to the strong.

John did not hear the demon leave, just as he had not heard her come. But he did go back to sleep. He fell into a deep sleep. Two

---

*13
*14

hours later John's nephews woke him, making breakfast. John wasn't ready for another day. Somehow he was sure the day would be a challenge.

V.

John sought refuge and peace in the chapel. Last night's battle with his motives and his intentions had left him feeling vulnerable and discontent. He knew he had felt honored when they offered him his new position as Secretary to Cardinal Abel. He respected and admired the Cardinal. He respected the work that had been assigned to him. But the other side of the truth was that John did not want to work in Rome, analyze reports, and attend endless meetings. He wanted to be a missionary and not a bureaucrat.

John was wrestling with his thoughts and was thinking about being stale when he heard Selina enter the chapel. He heard her light footsteps and her earrings jingle as she walked.

Instead of sitting several pews behind him, keeping a comfortable distance and showing her respect for his privacy, Selina came right next to him. She genuflected and then knelt beside him in his pew. John was not scheduled to meet with her or Richard for another hour. He needed this time alone. He felt himself defensively pulling inside of himself.

They greeted each other quietly. John went on praying alone. He knelt in the pew, and he folded his hands, but he knew he wasn't praying. He was wrestling with himself. Then Selina startled him. She spoke aloud as though she were reading John's thoughts. Her voice was soft and confident.

"The Lord knows you intimately, John. He knows what you need and who you are, and He is excited about it. The Lord knows where you belong, and He will take you there. He will use you until your hands shake with exuberance and until you are old and used up and burned out with joy. Some of us will be martyred young for Christ's sake. But not you. And you will never be bored." Selina smiled. She spoke as if she knew all this for a fact. And in the instant that she spoke it, John believed it. And he wanted to believe that it was true, every syllable of it. And he wanted to believe that it was God's Holy Spirit who had led Selina to say this. Because at the moment when she said it, his soul felt starved to hear it. Hungry for it. He felt in touch with all his hungers and his frustrations. He wanted to thank Selina and to thank God. But it was hard to say anything aloud. And Selina didn't expect him to say anything. She opened up her Bible and started reading to herself. She had nothing more to say. And now she was leaving him to his privacy. He loved this about Selina. That she knew when to interrupt and when to leave a person alone.

Richard would be waiting to challenge John again, waiting with his brilliant mind and pressing questions. Or maybe it was Selina's turn today. John had come into the chapel thinking he didn't have a crumb to offer either of them. Now he knew that he did--that he could dip inside himself and draw out living water.

VI.

Selina reached the private dining room in the monastery before John Fisk. She looked at the bare, ascetic little room with its off-white walls. If they had just painted the ceiling a deep shade of green, the walls would pull in the color from the huge tree bowing beside the window. It was winter now, and most of the color was gone. But in the spring, summer, and fall, there would be color coming in the window. Selina sat on one of the three wooden chairs beside the dark, wood-stained table. She glanced up at the crucifix on the wall.

Selina heard John opening the door, and she offered him her warmest smile of welcome. John had a Bible in his hand, a tiny silver tin containing holy oil, and a rosary. This meant that John was ready for serious talk and prayer. He wore a red and black plaid flannel shirt and jeans. But he was always a priest. He was *the* priest in Selina's eyes, the man who stood for Jesus and who could be trusted.

John said nothing when Selina activated the Sound Distort and put it back inside her open purse. Selina assumed that he was used to it by now, accepting without question whatever came with serving Richard and her.

"It feels so odd to me, to be holding back anything from you. I have always told you everything," Selina said.

"You don't need to tell me any of Richard's secrets." John looked deep into Selina's eyes. "So you are sure that you want to marry Richard?"

"I have never been so sure of anything, of anyone."

"I believe that he will be a good Christian and a good husband for you. He already knows more about theology than most seminarians. He embraces you and God with commendable passion."

Selina felt too many emotions stirring at one time. *Help me, John,* she thought. *I don't know what I need to ask you.*

"When God asks us to give up everything, He provides the grace to do it, doesn't he?" Selina's voice quivered. She felt embarrassed.

"If God is asking you to give up one thing, He will fill your life with other things," John said.

No, Selina thought, *He is taking too much away from me.*

"The Lord has shown me that He wants me to give up art. Never to paint or sculpt again." Selina felt tears break loose from their dam. She had not mentioned this to anyone. But it had tormented her. It had eaten at her soul. She was created to be an artist who loves art and who is destined to live without it.

"How did the Lord show you that you should never paint again?" John was calm at the sight of her tears. He must have seen tears often. It was safe to cry here. And suddenly the tears came hard and fast. At first it was hard to talk. But then Selina found the words, and she told John everything. She told him about the fever-induced dream. She told him about the arthritis in her left hand. She told him about the image of her crippled grandmother who could have been, should have been an artist. If John had been like most other men he would have fallen apart at the force of her emotions or been disgusted with her. John was relaxed. He smiled at her.

"Selina, does Richard tell you often how beautiful you are, because you should be told? I don't mean physically beautiful, I mean spiritually beautiful. Your soul is as pure as fresh water flowing from a mountain stream. Your desire to please God is a light in the darkness." John's words moved her. They were healing balm.

"I don't know why I'm crying so hard," Selina said, and she crumpled the blue Kleenex in her hand and reached into her purse for another one.

"Then I'll tell you why. The demons have been lying to you. They made you think in some part of your heart, that God Himself was stingy and harsh and demanding like your father Damien. The deceiver tried to make you feel worthless for loving the artistic skills which you were born to use. Remember the parable of the talents. God gave us talents to *use*, in order to return good fruit to Him with those talents.

God loves the talent that He gave you. Even if God permits you to have
arthritis, you will find a way to be an artist. All of us who love you will
help you to find a way."

John spoke gently but with a kind of authority that jolted
something in Selina.

"What is wrong with me that I can be deceived? That I can
think I hear the Lord's voice and hear the opposite?"

"Everyone is deceived sometimes."

"Even you, John?"

"I am often deceived. Sometimes deception starts out as open-
mindedness. Sometimes it starts out with good intentions. Sometimes it
starts out with confusion. In your case it started out with a high fever."

John reached into his pants pocket and pulled out a wrinkled
black stole, the symbol of his priesthood. He put it across his shoulders
and it hung over his right shoulder and his left sling. He stood up and
placed his right hand on Selina's shoulder and began to pray silently.
After a few minutes he spoke aloud to Selina.

"Renounce the curse that came with your fever, the belief that
you would never paint again."

"I do renounce it," Selina said. "And I give all my talents and
all my life to you, O God," Selina prayed, and her voice began quivering
again.

And then John opened up his small silver case containing holy
oil, and he anointed Selina's forehead, lips, and hands. He prayed for
healing of mind and body and protection against evil spirits. Selina
loved John's hands. She watched his hands as he prayed. Because when
he prayed, John's hands became the hands of Jesus.

VII.

Deceiver let out a blood-curdling wail! She leapt across one
city, crawled, gasping and groaning to the Inbetween Spaces. Her head
spun with agony. The Fisk priest had punched her in the gut! She hated
him. She hated all the priests. Some of them were decadent, and some
of them were saints. Some were cowards, and some were brave. Some
were hypocrites, and some were heroes. But she hated all of them.
Because when they prayed like priests, when they put the mantle of
Christ over their shoulders, they were all alike. They stood in the place

of Christ, and the power of Christ flowed through them. Deceiver had
had enough of the Fisk priest for the time being. Let someone else ache
from the anguish of defeat!

Deceiver groaned with despair. They had shattered the power of
her curse with their faith and their prayer and the authority of their holy
oil! Now Selina's festering wrist wound would heal and the arthritis
symptoms would gradually disappear. And Selina would paint again.
Every time Selina made an act of faith, lifting her pencils or her brushes,
she would find that she could paint. And how she would paint! Selina
would stir the souls of her people. Selina's art would soothe and mend
and teach. It sickened Deceiver! It panicked Deceiver! Deceiver ran and
hid. Let Natas find someone else to do his dirty work. Let someone else
go after the baptized Saxon, the strong Selina and her priest! Deceiver
clutched to one hope, that Natas would destroy them all! That the
humans would not live long enough to taste their victories.

Natas would punish Deceiver for refusing to return to the Tethra
three. But the pain Natas would give was not like the sting of the holy
oil. And Natas' pain would be brief. Natas knew that he could not
control the great Deceiver.

VIII.

Richard felt wonderfully refreshed--as if he could face anything
and fight anything. Since he had arrived here four days ago he had spent
his mornings reading and exercising, his afternoons in discussion and
prayer, and his evenings going to bed early. Selina slept in the women's
quarters, and she always slept late and attended noon Mass. Selina
seemed to have recovered both from her strep throat and her post-exam
exhaustion. They felt safe in this monastery, as though nothing could
touch them here. And so it surprised Richard that Selina was sensing
danger on this Wednesday afternoon.

It was Selina who reached into Richard's pocket, removed the
Sound Distort, and activated it. The crackle echoed through her tiny
sleeping quarters.

"Richard darling, would you place John under your protection?"

"What do you mean?"

"Could you give him my watch so that if he finds himself in
danger, he can signal you and the... starship for help?"

"I cannot do that, Selina, it is too complicated."

"Too complicated to save the life of such a good man?"

"I don't think that his life is in danger. We have told him nothing."

"The ROSET people would not believe that. John has spent several days in private conversation with the two of us, mostly you. If they have been following us, they have been following him." Selina's eyes were intense as she spoke.

"I don't believe that any of them know that we came here. You know the precautions I took, making our plane reservations under false names."

"If you don't believe they could have followed us here, why are we using the Sound Distort, darling?" Selina asked. She followed him with her eyes. Those beautiful eyes, and behind them was a mind like a steel trap.

"If you give John my watch, you could have another one customized for me when we get back home to Ann Arbor."

"You don't understand, Selina. I broke all the rules for you. To bring you into my life. I cannot break all the rules twice. If a person activates the homing device on that watch, it triggers a complex chain reaction. The starship itself will... get involved."

"You explained that to me when you gave me my watch and ring," Selina said softly.

"Whoever has that watch can summon my starship. I cannot give another person access to my ship." Richard spoke in a tone of voice that was meant to end the conversation. It was his captain's voice. Selina did not seem hurt or angry. She looked at her watch and touched it with her forefinger.

"Is there any other way we can protect him?" She asked.

"Why are you so concerned about him, Selina?"

"I keep thinking about martyrdom," Selina said. "My own and John Fisk's." Selina twisted a strand of hair around her finger.

"You already have a gun to protect yourself. I will give John a gun to protect himself, Selina. My kind of gun."

IX.

Richard had carefully avoided any subjects which could suggest espionage or ROSET. But there had to be a way to discuss how John would deal with violence.

"Are you a pacifist?" Richard asked. John gave him a puzzled look.

"I have known good Christians who were true pacificists, who believed that killing or bearing arms for any reason was wrong. And God was pleased with them. I have known other good Christians who felt it was a greater good to defend the way of life that stood for Christ, who felt that it was better to kill than to let that way of life be stamped out or destroyed. And God was pleased with them. There are people who have rejected Jesus and His way so completely that they live for the pleasure of defeating and killing those who stand for good," John answered.

"I know," Richard said. He thought of the Greole. John had never heard of the Greole, but he had seen the Greole traits on Earth. "But my question is personal. It is about you, Father John Fisk. Are you a pacifist?"

"I don't know," John answered. "No one has ever tried to kill me. My guess is that I would use any force to stop someone from killing me. But when the moment came to end either their life or mine, I don't know whose life I would choose."

"What if they tried to kill Selina or someone else you loved?"

"I would let them kill me before killing Selina. I would pray in the moment of the danger that God's will would be done for the killer's sake, Selina's, and my own."

"So you have never killed anyone?" Richard pressed.

"No."

"Have you ever used a gun?" Richard asked.

"No," John said softly.

Richard had never met a person, man or woman, who had never used a gun. Until he came to Earth. Perhaps Frank Nelson was wrong about the people of Earth being barbarians. Perhaps the true barbarians were Tethrans.

"Why are you asking me these questions, Richard? What is troubling you?" John looked worried.

"I told you earlier this week, before my baptism, that I had killed before. You said that all my sins would be forgiven, wiped clean at my baptism."

"And they were," John said.

"I am afraid that I will never make a good Christian. With all my soul, I want it. And yet I do not think that I could ever love my enemies."

"It is easier to defeat them, if you love them. Easier to reform them and to win them if you love them. Hate only teaches people to destroy. Love teaches us how to conquer evil, to bind it. To end it." A feeling of peace moved through Richard. Like a fountain flowing in him and through him. He had never looked at warfare through the eyes of a priest--through the eyes of a man who had never killed or used a gun.

Suddenly in his mind he saw a different side to the coin of military strategy. And a dozen options opened to him all at once.

Richard looked at John, at the pacificist who had freely entered into Richard's hidden dangers without ever demanding explanations. Without ever counting the cost to himself. And Richard realized that Selina had been right to want to protect the priest.

"I came not to judge the world, but to serve, [15]" Richard said as he looked at John. As their eyes met, Richard realized how much he had grown to love this man. And how hard it was not to confide in him about everything.

"I have a purpose for this questioning. I would like to give you a gun to use. If you ever found yourself in danger, you could defend yourself."

"I was not in danger before I met you. Am I in danger now?"

"I do not think that you are. But I would rather not trust the lives of my friends to chance," Richard said very quietly.

"Then we are friends, Richard?"

"More than friends. " Richard paused. "The gun I want to give you requires no real training or skill. It is very easy to use."

"It would not be easy for me to use. I cannot accept it," John said.

"Then you refuse to protect yourself?"

"I didn't say that. I said I refuse to accept a gun. Can you tell me anything about the danger that may touch my life?"

"No, I can't."

"Then let's talk about Jesus. Tomorrow is your last day here. I may never see you again."

---

[15]

X.

Richard didn't call his answering service until early Thursday morning. He left the monastery without waking Selina. They had been up late the night before. Richard walked the four blocks to the nearest breakfast restaurant in town. It was a freezing, windy day, and the dark skies looked like they were brewing a winter storm.

Richard huddled in the dimly lit corner at the rear of the restaurant and deposited handfuls of change into the pay phone. He decided not to use his credit card, because his location could be traced if he used a card.

"Dr. Saxon, we have several urgent calls for you, beginning with late night calls on Tuesday, December 28. Your secretary told us to contact her immediately if you checked in with the answering service. She could not refer the callers anywhere because she had no idea where you could be reached."

"Please, tell me who called." Richard's pulse began to race.

"The University Attorney, Paul Kadetz, Dr. Anthony Paoli, Dr. Sam Steinberg, Dr..."

"Was Dr. Steinberg's one of the urgent calls?" Richard asked.

"That's an understatement. Dr. Steinberg must have called four times a day, beginning on Tuesday night. He said his calls were of an emergency nature."

"Dr. Steinberg is a close friend. Please give me his number."

"Very well, Dr. Saxon."

"Are there any phone messages from Donald Cantril or any representatives of Bay Tech Industries?"

"No, Dr. Saxon. But these other callers also said they were urgent. Don't you want their numbers?"

"Yes, of course."

Richard wrote down all the phone numbers, but Sam Steinberg's was the first he dialed. Sam answered his phone on the second ring.

"Samuel, this is Richard Saxon. Are you all right?"

"Richard, thank God it's you! I'm all right. You're the one who is not all right. All hell is breaking loose here. Is Selina with you?"

"Who is asking about Selina?"

"I'm asking. Lots of people are asking," Sam began. And then he talked fast and he told Richard everything. Everything about Damien Devon's charges, about the University's response to his charges, about a scandalous newspaper article regarding a cult leader at the University of Michigan. The newspaper article was in the Thursday morning paper.

"And the informal hearing is scheduled for tomorrow, Friday the thirty-first at 10:00 a.m. Richard, you have to be there," Sam blurted out.

"So that's why you are worried about how and where Selina is?" Richard asked. His pulse was racing, but he knew how to keep his voice controlled.

"*I'm* not worried about her. At least not worried that you've kidnapped her under some cult spell. But blast it, man, you are a difficult person to defend. Are you batman or something that you live in a secret cave with no address or phone?" Sam asked. It was obvious to Richard how worried Sam had been, how involved he was in Richard's defense. "You've got to be here for that hearing tomorrow, Richard. Tell them all where to shove their accusations."

"Let me think about it, Sam."

"*Think* about it? What's to think about? You sound awfully calm!"

"I'm not calm, I'm just trying to sound that way. I promise you that I will give Dr. Paoli a call today and that I will respond to Devon's charges. I just have to think this whole situation through and decide how to handle it."

"Tell me one thing, Richard. Why would Damien Devon say such outlandish things about you and go so far as to call the top brass at the University?"

Richard thought before he answered. The pause probably made Sam nervous.

"The reason for his actions are simple, the actions themselves are extreme. Devon doesn't want me to marry his daughter. He doesn't want anyone to marry her. He treats Selina very badly, and we did clash a bit."

"Clash a bit! The man is trying to ruin you! If you don't prove him a liar, you'll never teach again. And that would be a rotten shame."

"Thank you, Sam."

"For what?"

"For behaving like a friend. Some people talk like friends, but they don't behave like friends. But Sam... watch out for yourself. If hell breaks loose on me, it may also come after my friends."

Richard was angry when he hung up the phone. And he didn't want the anger to consume him.

XI.

"My father did what?" Selina asked. She stood up from her wooden chair and placed one hand on her hip.

"Which point do you want me to repeat?" Richard asked, half-smiling.

"I can't believe that he would do something like this, call the President of U of M, invent lies about you, and try to ruin your reputation!" Selina was aghast.

"It is not important if I lose my teaching position. The only thing that is important is my business relationship with Bay Tech. They produce a product that we need in order to return home. I cannot allow some type of scandal or misunderstanding to affect the delicate nature of my business negotiations. It could be disastrous if the Bay Tech people heard that I had been dismissed from the University because I was a cult leader."

"Let's walk to the Queen City Cafe and use the phone. I need to call my lawyer. He'll know what we should do," Selina said. "I've never told you this, darling. I was advised to keep it secret, but I have my own set of attorneys and some money with which to pay them."

"You have your grandfather's fortune."

"How did you know?"

"I didn't intend to pry into your private affairs, Selina. But I did pry into your father's affairs. I had to know how to fight him if he fought me. I found out about your inheritance while I was looking."

"You didn't tell me."

"It didn't seem relevant."

"I suppose it isn't relevant. But now I'm going to call my attorney for help."

"The same attorney who won the case against your father when you were only twenty?" Richard looked down at the ground when he spoke.

"Is there anything you don't know?"

"Does that upset you, Selina?"

"I'm not sure. But there isn't time to think about it right now. My lawyer's name is Adam West. He was my grandfather's lawyer, and I trust him implicitly."

"I don't want you to get involved in this, Selina. It's my battle."

"My father is the attacker and my future husband is the attacked. How can I not get involved? We'll simply ask my lawyer's advice."

Richard only heard Selina's side of the conversation as she phoned her lawyer from the public phone. But he was impressed. West interrupted a staff meeting for Selina's call and dropped everything for her. Selina hung up the phone and pulled Richard close to her in the small hallway of the restaurant. And then she spoke softly so that she could not be overheard.

"Adam will prepare a case for the University hearing tomorrow. I knew the University president's name, but I didn't know the University's attorney. Adam said that was all right, that he could take care of everything. He is sending his son James West to meet us tomorrow morning before the hearing. Adam advised me to sue Damien for defamation of my character and for libel. He said that Damien's accusations were an attack on my competency as well as yours, Richard. He said if I sue Damien, you don't need to do anything. You will look even more innocent if you say nothing. He said we should approach this matter as a father-daughter feud and asked my permission to make reference to Damien's fight for my inheritance. I agreed that we should do this. After all, it *is* a father-daughter feud. What could Damien possibly have against you, darling?"

"You're going to sue Damien? I have not seen this side of you before."

"Four and a half years ago, I was devastated when my grandfather's lawyers fought my father in court for the inheritance. I cried for two weeks, and I told the lawyers that I didn't want the money..."

"I don't want you crying over this. I have my own ways of fighting Damien."

"I'm not crying this time. I feel resolved and sure of myself. I wasn't ready to stand up against my father when I was younger. I'm ready now. He stepped over the line in coming after *you*, Richard. I won't allow it."

"Is the gentle lamb turning into a lion?" Richard asked. And he put his face close to Selina's face.

"Maybe I am. Maybe your love and your presence in my life are giving me courage." He put his arm around her.

But when they walked back to the monastery from the pay phone, Richard felt the anger rising in his soul. He wanted to tear

Damien Devon's heart out for the ways he had hurt Selina. For pretending to be a father but never giving Selina the protection and the love of a father. Damien had belittled her, attacked her, hurt her, again and again. It would have been so easy for Richard to put an end to it. To send one order to the starship for the termination of the life of Damien Devon. It felt right. But then it felt wrong. Richard was changed now, even if Damien Devon had not changed. Richard now carried in his soul the cross of Christ, the one who had died in a state of love and mercy for the sake of sinners. Even for Damien Devon. Richard would have to fight Damien, but he would have to use his new morality in his fighting. As he walked back toward the monastery of Our Lady of Peace, Richard paused. Damien Devon would never know that his life had just been spared because of the mercy of Jesus Christ, set in the heart of Richard Saxon.

XII.

John didn't want to say goodbye. He was feeling a wave of holiday loneliness. John doubted that he was supposed to be feeling lonely. In a better world there would have been many kinds of support for being celibate and for being radically committed to Christ. But there wasn't a lot of support. Celibate people didn't know much about taking care of one another and giving to one another while they went on living in a secular world. While they were involved and interacting with all the non-celibate people who had their ways of bridging the loneliness. Ways that John could not use. And so loneliness was a factor in being a priest.

Richard and Selina were leaving today and returning to Ann Arbor on sudden business. John had grown attached to them. They were both gifted and dynamic people, and they made him feel gifted and dynamic as well. They lapped up John's pastoring, and they served his needs in turn. When they left today John didn't know if he would ever see them again. And when John left Cincinnati in another four days he would be leaving the only family he had. Leaving for a more sterile, more ethereal, more lonely life.

Years ago John realized that these waves of loneliness could be very strong. He knew that the loneliness had the power to drive him either away from God or closer to God. And so he prayed that the loneliness would drive him closer to God. Every time he felt the need for the intimacy of that human touch and it was missing, he leaned on God the Son, who was His brother. And every time he hurt inside because he felt misunderstood or just alone and separate, he leaned on God. And every time he found himself disappointed by humans because they didn't love him, didn't extend themselves to him in the intimate gestures that he needed, he leaned on God. And it drew him toward God and into tangible intimacy with what could have been an intangible God.

John watched Richard and Selina throughout this week, perfecting each other's nature by the bonding of the love between them. John was glad that he had faced his celibacy years ago--before he ever met this couple.

It happened in those first years after seminary. It hurt a lot in those early years. He was in Peru, and everyone there was so poor that they had nothing material, except their wives and children. John wanted what they had. He watched the men and women holding each other in the hot sunshine. He watched the children being nursed on love and family. John found himself longing for a wife and children of his own. And so he talked to God about it. He cried out to God.

Gradually, like a gentle rain falling on the dry earth, a rain that came so softly and so consistently that the dry earth was transformed and drenched in health and water until it forgot its thirst. Gently like that, God came to him with grace. And God changed his soul and his need for a wife and children. And the Lord sewed up that need inside of him so that he became truly celibate. And celibately at peace.

The Lord God loved John in that intimate, exclusive place in his heart that needed to be loved back, for all the love he gave. In that place, the love of God began to satisfy.

John knelt alone in the empty chapel. It must have been below zero outside, or the antique heating system in this building wasn't working well. The wooden pew was hard and curved uncomfortably behind his back. His praying wasn't going well. John heard the heavy creaking door open and a man's footsteps enter the chapel.

It was Richard. He sat next to John in the pew and smiled.

"May I disturb your prayer? Selina and I have to leave a little earlier than we thought. We'd like to say our goodbyes now. After that, we won't disturb you anymore."

"I don't mind being disturbed. Undisturbed lives are usually lonely."

"Is a man like you ever lonely?" Richard asked.

"A man like me?"

"Strong, self-sufficient, married to the church."

"I am not married to the church. I have heard other priests say that they were married to the church. But I wouldn't say that."

"But you love the church, don't you, John?"

"I love the church. But the church is a thing, an institution. I love her like a patriot loves his country, only more. I love the church for what she is and for what she is not. I love her for what she does and what she stands for. I would die for the church because I love her. I would give my life to make her one ounce stronger, one ounce better than she is. But the church cannot love me back. Not the way I need to be loved as a man.

"Only God can do that. Only God can love me in that personal, intimate way in which one person loves another."

John's voice had become louder as he talked. And he realized that he had answered much more than he had been asked. He looked at Richard and then down at his prayer book.

"I have heard it said that to live for the one you love is even better than dying for the one you love," Richard said. He had followed every word, had absorbed every thought that John had shared. And it made John feel less lonely, less separate.

"Thank you for everything, Father John Fisk," Richard said.

Selina had entered the chapel so quietly that John did not hear her come. She was carrying a heavy, attractively wrapped package.

"This is our Christmas present for you, John. Four videotapes of National Football League Championship games. You can study the plays. And there's an adapter device so that you will be able to play these tapes on your Italian VCR."

John was thrilled! Thrilled because of the gift and thrilled because they loved him. He was not a porcelain pastor in their eyes, not someone who prayed and preached and had no other loves, no other needs.

"We have one last request of you, John. Please pray with us together before we leave," Richard asked. They looked around the chapel, and it was empty. John stood up, and Richard and Selina knelt in the pew. John placed his right hand on Selina's head and leaned his bandaged left arm and hand on Richard's head. He prayed and asked God's blessing on them. And as he prayed, John felt a knot in his stomach. John sensed it very clearly, almost concrete enough to touch. John prayed that he could give the "sense" a name. He knew its name was danger and that it was coming after these two. John prayed hard, while they were with him in the chapel. And after they left, he prayed even harder. Prayed against danger.

CHAPTER
TWENTY-NINE
MAX'S WAY

$\mathbf{M}$ax Traytur's left eye twitched. He tapped his long fingernails against the thin crystal of his glass. The sherry wasn't helping. He hated to admit it, but nothing was helping. The last few days of tense waiting had felt like months! He couldn't bear the waiting. Waiting for a clue as to the whereabouts of the alien or his woman or their friends! Max couldn't find out one thing, and his whole precious future hung in the balance. The alien Richard had vanished! Neither the phone tap on Selina's home phone nor the one on Richard's office phone had given Max a shred of information. He felt impotent in more ways than one.

Richard's answering service hooked up to his office phone had been busy enough. The calls were intriguing but unrevealing! There was a flurry of urgent phone calls coming from the University. None of that nonsense helped Max.

And Selina's phone calls were equally dull. The only calls coming for her were from some squeaky-voiced art dealer in New York who had tried to reach Selina at her Ann Arbor home and her parents' home. Something had to break for Max! It just had to!

And then it did. Max reached his long arm from the steaming tub of lilac-scented bubbles and answered the cordless phone. Stan and Bobo were excited!

"Saxon called! Saxon called his answering service. We taped it all!"

"Where is Saxon now?" Max asked the only relevant question.

"We don't know."

"From where did he call?"

"We couldn't trace it."

"Idiots." Max hung up the phone. He dried himself gently with the soft red towel. Max could feel the adrenaline begin to flow. He could feel the excitement. Stan and Bobo would be here in fifteen minutes.

Richard's voice on the tape was music to Max's ears. It was the nectar of the gods! It was the turning point.

Richard was in trouble with the University. Maybe he would have to come home to Ann Arbor now. Or maybe he would have to run away! At any rate, Richard had a "close friend" named Samuel Steinberg, and here was Steinberg's phone number! At last Max could satisfy Natas' lust and his own. Max could make a kill.

Only three hours later, even as he plotted Steinberg's murder, Max got his second prize. As he listened to Selina's phone line, Max discovered that Selina also had a friend. The friend left a message on her answering machine:

"Selina, this is Todd Weako. I'm calling you on Thursday morning, December 30. I haven't heard from you since before Christmas. I trust that your strept throat is better. You sounded pretty sick, doll. Let me know how you're doing when you get back in town. I'm never home these days, so give me a buzz at the hospital at 555-7810. Happy New Year!"

Max felt sexually aroused. And his left eye stopped twitching. *So you helped Selina, Todd Weako. What a dear friend you are. And you have given Max a number where I can reach you.*

Max wouldn't kill that Steinberg person right away. Steinberg might lead Max closer to Richard and to valuable information. But Todd Weako...

II.

The plane rose above the clouds and into the face of the golden sun, and then it descended. The flight time between Cincinnati and Detroit lasted barely forty minutes. And then Richard and Selina walked to his car in the long-term parking lot and drove home to Ann Arbor. They arrived in Ann Arbor just before 5:00 p.m., as the winter sun was setting. Richard felt refreshed and serene. He could see that Selina was glad to be back in her home, and he wanted to stay with her there. But he was too cautious to rest just now. He hadn't made any contact with his computer or the starship in ten days. He ought to check with Jenxex and Frank Nelson.

Some premonition was nudging him in the back of his mind. Something that felt like dread. He pushed the sense aside. Was he becoming too paranoid? And then he reached his home and his front door and he found the source of his dread. Yes, the sense he had was dread, he told himself. His home had been broken into, not once but twice! This was not supposed to happen!

Richard examined the tampered security system. The first time the system had been activated, it must have electrocuted the burglar. But, in spite of this, the burglar returned a second time. The second time he came with a friend and a calculated plan to absorb the shock waves of the system. And to step through them. The second time the burglars made it inside Richard's house and delicately rummaged through each room. They obviously stopped exploring at the more complex security lock to his computer room.

These were no ordinary burglars. They stole nothing and tried to hide the evidence of their intrusion. So what did they want here? What were they looking to find? Richard felt the dread like a heavy weight leaning against him. Someone was stalking him! Perhaps Damien had already hired someone to come after him. Perhaps not. He hoped the stalker had been hired by Damien. If not, the danger was worse. If not Damien, then his enemy was ROSET. But how would he have aroused the suspicion of ROSET? When had he given anyone a clue as to his alien identity? Or even a clue as to where he lived?

Richard hurried into his computer room and fingered the keyboard in the language of Eetan. Immediately he felt connected, he felt at home, he felt strong! He had grown up, lived, learned, and thought with a keyboard like this one throughout his life. It was the one constant. Through his keyboard and its computer he teamed his own intelligence, intuition, and all his need with the vast resources of the machines. As he communicated with the starship and began to think once more in the Eetan language, he felt his sense of well-being return. He felt his cold self-confidence and his assurance of power return. He was a starfighter, not a hunted alien. He could devastate whatever enemies crawled on the earth and blast gaping holes in this troublesome planet if anyone came after him.

And then he felt some new thing stirring inside of him. It was the conscience of a Christian. He heard his own conscience speaking to him in the language of Eetan, and it brought his new Christian heart and his old skills together. Fighting his enemies was going to be complicated. Being Captain Sorn was going to be complicated.

"Jenxex, give me a full report since my last communication."

"Captain, where have you been? I will send you transmissions from Nelson first."

Frank Nelson Transmissions:
    date: December 24
"Richard, note your own log for recent ROSET activities. I came home to England today to find ROSET computers busy showing new activities all across the world. None in Michigan or England. Respond, brother."
    date: December 26
"Why no response from you, Richard? Where are you? The ROSET computers are falsely reporting activities. Jenxex cross-checked two of ROSET's reported incidents with other records. Either these incidents never happened or they were *so* well hidden that no other sources noticed or reported them. Respond ASAP."
    date: December 27
"Respond ASAP, Richard. You're worrying me, old chap."
    date: December 28
"Respond ASAP. More reported ROSET activity, this time in Germany, Poland, Canada, and New York City. Respond ASAP."
    date: December 29
"Jenxex and I did a thorough investigation on each of these newly reported activities that ROSET claims. Nothing, not one of these incidents checks out as having really occurred. I can only hypothesize that ROSET is playing games with their computers. The question is why? Who are they trying to fool?
    Please respond ASAP. I'd send out a search party for you if I had one."
    date: December 30
"I am scheduled to leave for China on January 1, 2000. But I am not going anywhere until I hear from you. This is enough to drive a man to prayer. Respond ASAP."
    Richard sent an immediate transmission to Nelson through the starship:
    date: December 30
"I'm home, Frank. Your prayers worked. Detailed transmission upcoming."
    Richard reviewed all the reports from the ROSET computer files and Nelson's cross-checking of information with other sources. Why

was ROSET making it appear that they were busy doing things that they weren't doing?

Richard Saxon Transmission to Frank Nelson.

date: December 30

"Burglars broke into my house when I was away. They bypassed my secondary security system and broke in a second time. They stole nothing. The cautious course of action leads me to assume that ROSET is stalking me. I will go underground for two weeks. You do the same. Go to China incognito. Agreed?

Respond ASAP."

Richard's second transmission had barely left his screen when Frank responded.

"Brother, am I relieved to hear from you! Are you going into hiding alone or with Selina?"

"With Selina. You are invited to our March wedding. I was baptized a Christian last week. What's new with you?"

"Give me time to absorb all this."

"I am leaving soon. We must keep Bay Tech happy in the next two weeks. You are in a better position to be in contact with them, Frank. Agreed?"

"I will contact Bay Tech from China. When will you be back at your computer, Captain?"

"January 13. God go with you, Ont."

Richard felt a tinge of grief and loss. He wanted to hear more from Frank. There were no more transmissions. He wanted to see his Tethran friend. He wanted to stay here with his keyboard and with the civilized language of Eetan.

Richard ordered the ship's computer to prepare a message to send to Damien Devon's mistress, Christine Carnes, in New York City. He ordered the ship to delay the message and not to have it appear on her home computer until January 1. He wanted to make sure that Christine would be home when the message arrived.

Richard was barely finished with his task when a sense of foreboding gripped him. He hurried out the door toward his car and to Selina's home. He had left her there alone nearly forty minutes ago! If ROSET was after him, then they were after Selina also. And Selina may or may not use the gun he had given her.

III.

The freezing air stung Selina as she opened the front door, and she gasped in surprise! For just an instant, all that she could see on the pitch-black front porch was the white hair and white face of Max Traytur, smiling at her like a disembodied head. He was wearing a long black leather coat which was practically invisible against the black night. All she could see was his face, absorbing the indoor light of her home. Just the sickening white face.

Selina had opened the front door when she heard the doorbell. She hadn't bothered to check who was there. She expected it to be Richard. No one else knew that she had come home. No one but Richard and Max Traytur. She didn't want Mr. Traytur to come in. She didn't even want him on the porch. He hadn't said or done a thing to provoke her fear. Why was she feeling like this?

Selina didn't have time to decide. Max Traytur pushed himself through her front door with such ease and suddenness that he caught her completely by surprise. He stood close enough to touch her, towering over her in his cold black leather.

"Mr. Traytur... I don't understand what..."

"Ms. Devon, I was crushed that you were unable to attend my holiday party. I decided to come by and deliver these get-well flowers to you in person. But you seem to be in excellent health."

Selina noticed the large bouquet of flowers wrapped in pink tissue paper. They seemed irrelevant.

"Your party... that was eight days ago. Why?"

"Do you have a vase for these flowers, Selina? Something sweet to decorate your little home."

Selina had lost her composure, and he had taken charge. How had this happened? Traytur began to walk around the living room, examining the furniture.

"And what a luscious home it is! But you must pardon me, all this luggage strewn everywhere, it looks as though you are getting ready to leave for a trip."

"Actually, I was just returning from a trip. And I'm afraid that I don't have time to visit right now, Mr. Traytur."

"You can call me Max, precious."

Traytur stopped looking at the furniture and glared at Selina. Selina found herself backing away from him as he stepped closer and closer to her. Suddenly, she felt the touch of his hand grasping her hand. His skin had a tough, dead, non-flesh texture. She backed away once more and bumped into her dining room table. There was no more space to back away from him. He placed the bouquet of flowers in her arms. When she glanced down at the flowers she saw that Traytur was wearing black leather gloves. It was the gloves and not his flesh that she had touched. Why did she feel relieved at the thought?

Selina placed the flowers on the table as Traytur moved one step closer to her, jamming her next to the table. He reached his gloved right hand and held her chin firmly in his snake-like fingers. Selina jerked her chin away from his fingers.

"My dear, I didn't mean to frighten you. I was just adoring your sensuous mouth. You really are something to behold.... But never mind, my sweet. I only wanted to ask you to have lunch with me sometime this week so that we could discuss the fund-raising needs of the hospital. We have a little... unfinished business, you and I."

Selina knew that his eyes were focused directly on her. She could almost feel those eyes but she could not look into them. His raspy voice was slow and succinct, carrying a disgusting note of eroticism in each word. She felt vaguely dizzy. She was nowhere near her gun or her purse. Why was she even thinking about that right now? *Angels of God, protect me!* Selina thought. And she noticed Max Traytur twitch slightly. *I'm trapped in the corner of the dining room. Traytur is standing between me and the front door, several yards away! Relax, Selina, calm yourself.* And then she knew what to say to him.

"If you would... just leave me your phone number, I could call you later about lunch. But I do have to ask you to leave now so that I can finish my unpacking and get settled." Selina started to move around Traytur, taking a small step toward the front door. She concentrated on looking composed.

"You're being very inhospitable!" Traytur bit the end off each word. And then he grabbed her left arm and stopped her. His fingers felt like clawed bones, and they dug into her muscle. His grasp was hurting her.

"You should be flattered that such an influential man as me is offering you my... attention." Traytur's voice had a new sound to it. Selina knew now that she was in trouble. That sort of voice wanted to draw fear. Selina hid her fear. She did not try to withdraw from him.

He was stronger than she was. Very strong. She did not mention that he was hurting her. He already knew that.

"That's better, precious. Just relax and be a little nicer." Traytur reached for something in his breast pocket. Selina bit her lip. And she tasted the drop of blood on her tongue. In that instant she heard the doorknob quietly turning behind Traytur.

Richard stood in the doorway, stone-like. Instantly, the hot pink color was emerging beneath the surface of his skin. It was subtle, and Selina saw it.

No, Selina thought, *not now! Don't let this Traytur see you glow.* Her pulse raced. The blood rushed out of her head. And Traytur noticed. Noticed everything. Or so she thought. Because Traytur too became very still, and he seemed to smell her agony like animals smell human fear. And Traytur smiled a cruel smile and he dug his fingernails into her thin sweater until they bruised her flesh. *He is enjoying my agony,* Selina thought. And the thought stunned her.

"Who is this, Selina? A friend of yours? Richard asked. His voice was ice cold. *Richard knows what to say, what to do,* Selina thought. *And so do I.*

"This... is Max Traytur, a former patient. The man who is interested in donating money... to the hospital." Selina's anxiety was on the surface, in the speed of her voice, in the dryness of her throat. She had done her best. And it was all she could do.

"And you are?" Traytur asked Richard, as politely as if they had just met at a cocktail party. *Maybe it is working. Maybe Traytur saw nothing and I imagined it. Maybe Traytur did not see Richard's skin glow and did not sense my agony.*

"He is a friend of mine," Selina said quickly.

"Doesn't your friend have a name?"

"Why do you want to know it?" Richard asked. His face was stoic.

It occurred to Selina in one of those concious seconds when you feel everything and understand everything at once. It occurred to Selina that neither of the two men in the room could move. As if they were both frozen in some chess-like stalemate.

Richard would kill Traytur if Richard dared to allow himself to move a muscle. Selina could sense the pressure of his self-control. Traytur was frozen also, in some peculiar state of awe as he gazed at

Richard. Why in awe? But it was awe. Traytur was frozen as though he were beholding the ninth wonder of the world!

"My, my, but your friends certainly aren't very friendly," Traytur said. He could not take his eyes off Richard. He paused. Then Traytur released his grip on Selina's arm and waved his hands. Selina noticed for the first time that Traytur was wearing a large ring on his right hand. He wore the ring on top of his glove, and the ring had an occult symbol on it.

Go away, she thought, repulsed, and she moved away from Traytur. Moving in small steps, trying to retain her poise--or regain her poise.

"His name is Richard." What was next? "But Mr. Traytur, I really would like it if I could call you later."

"So you're throwing me out?" Traytur asked in a childish tone of voice.

"Yes, she is." Richard had barely moved, barely breathed since entering the house. Now he moved quickly and stood in front of Selina, shielding her from Traytur. As Richard moved, he left the front door clear for Traytur to leave.

"Mr. Traytur, how did you know that Selina would be home this evening?" Richard asked.

"Just a lucky guess, just thought I would drop by." Traytur waved his right hand and his ring good-bye. "Selina dear, you be sure and call me, okay?" Traytur smiled a freeze-dried smile and turned toward the door. But as he walked away, he moved slowly and deliberately, creating a defiant tension.

Richard stood by the door and watched Traytur get into his car and drive away. Then he handed Selina his gun and went outside to search the perimeter of her house and yard to see if there was anyone else hiding in the shadows.

Richard locked Selina's front door when he returned. He activated the Sound Distort. "Why did he touch you?" Richard asked, his look piercing Selina.

"I don't know. You could tell that he had frightened me, couldn't you?"

"I had an unusual response to Traytur," Richard said.

"What kind of response?"

"I wanted to kill him the instant I saw him. I had hoped that I had become a Christian like you and John Fisk. But I am still a killer at heart."

"You are not a killer. You are a fighter. Something is wrong with Traytur. We could both sense that, sense that he's... evil. You wanted to fight the evil you sensed."

"I wanted to end it," Richard said, and he looked at the floor.

"But you have changed, Richard. The other time when I saw your skin glow, it was when you were questioning Rock, the kidnapper. You wanted to kill him, too. And he was not repulsive like Traytur is repulsive. That time your skin glowed instantly, hot and fluorescent and out of control! When I prayed for you that night, the Lord's power calmed you. Tonight the Lord's power calmed you again. But this time God's power was inside of you, not outside of you."

"I did feel God's power in me. I felt Him here with us." Richard put his arms around Selina.

"You noticed my skin beginning to glow. But you notice everything about me. Do you think that Traytur saw my skin warming?"

"I wish I knew," Selina answered.

"We need to go away again. We need to go into hiding for a while. Get your passport and any cash you have. We will need lots of cash."

"Where are we going?"

"We will decide that tonight. Let's get into my car and talk... where it's safe."

"It isn't safe here?" Selina tried to hide her disappointment.

"No," Richard answered her. And she knew that he was hiding more than she was.

IV.

Natas hissed wildly as he swung his sword, missed, and swung again. This time his sword met its target, and he felt the exhilarating crunch of the angel's form as he saw the angel fall. The defeated beauty dimmed.

Natas spat wet fumes into Max Traytur's face as Traytur started his car. He watched as the pathetic human choked on the fumes, then drove away from Selina's house. Traytur had failed!

It would have taken Traytur only seconds to grab Selina tighter, to hold his gun to her head and to wait until Richard came to rescue her. It would have taken only seconds for Traytur to blow large holes in Richard's body while using the woman as his shield. And then Traytur could have raped and killed Selina. It would have taken only a moment! It was in that moment when the clarity of this plan came into Traytur's mind, that Archangel Gabriel reached the spot. Gabriel was the messenger. And Gabriel filled Traytur's mind with a different plan, a plan of grandeur that confused and baffled Traytur. Traytur had never listened to the thoughts of an angel before. Traytur's humanity was decayed, almost deadened. But the remnant of his soul that could hear the angel's voice leapt at the sound. Gabriel swooped near Traytur and spoke into his mind.

"ROSET will never make you a hero, will never believe you, if you tell them that you killed two aliens in Selina's house. You need witnesses that these are aliens, and you need proof."

The angel could only speak truth. And the truth was perfectly timed. Traytur wanted grandeur and recognition and admiration. He wanted it so much that he could taste it. And so Traytur fumbled from the perfect plan and in doing so delayed the murders of Richard and Selina. Instead Traytur took photos of Richard and Selina with his ring finger camera. Photos to send around the world! Traytur chose photos before choosing blood!

Natas growled with a raging curse! Natas swung his sword to the left and to the right, crushing bodies and spitting flames! He lost track of the time, and the blood-letting failed to ease his hunger or his hatred or his pain. But he wanted more anyway, and he thirsted for more battle. Natas swung as the light began to change. And the light brought Michael one-on-one. Natas poured everything into the blow directed at Michael's perfect face! Michael seemed to vanish before the blow reached him. And then Natas felt an excruciating force behind him, throwing him toward the ground. Natas saw the dreaded white net settling over his limbs. Michael and Gabriel together were the only ones with the power to throw the net. He moaned as he watched the net cover his form and stick to his fingers and his toes and his slimy hair. Natas knew that Michael and Gabriel were together here, fighting as one. And he knew that he was beaten. Beaten, tied, and bound. Cursing, drooling, raging, defacating in the net which would drag him back to the Inbetween Spaces.

V.

Archangel Michael inhaled deeply and paused to catch his breath. His right arm was weak enough for the moment that he dropped his sword, placing it in the waiting hand of Archangel Gabriel.

Gabriel turned to face the seven hundred and seventy-seven panting angels behind him. He lifted Michael's sword and his own sword high above his head and placed the swords together to form a cross. At the sign of the shining white cross, the seven hundred and seventy-seven warrior angels let out a mighty cheer. Michael and his honor guard had dispeled Natas from the Earth for the final time in the century of the 1900s.

Michael smiled, refreshed by the angels' cheer. Gabriel handed him his sword, and Michael raised it, touched it on his forehead, and replaced the sword in its sheath. The other seven hundred and seventy-eight angels followed his actions, raising their swords, touching them on their foreheads and replacing them in their sheaths. Michael, still facing his forces, raised his left hand above his head and spread out his wings. The angels flew as one flock and returned to the Inbetween Spaces, dragging Natas and his shrieking demons in the silver-white net.

Michael watched Natas and his bands of demons reluctantly withdraw into the dark craters of the Inbetween Spaces. And when he was sure that the demons were too weak to cause harm on Earth, Michael called all his angels, except for the permanent guardians. And he and the angels began a time of respite and peace together.

They would rest and wait. Tomorrow was the last day of the old century, and the following day was the first day of the new century-- January 1, 2000. It was during these days and perhaps for a whole week that both the angels and the demons withdrew from Earth as the changing of the centuries brought with them the changing of the tides of good and evil. When the clash of the waves came, it would cause both good and evil to happen.

As the twenty-first century dawned, the good humans would stand without the angels, having only what good power they carried in their souls. And the bad humans would have only the evil in their hearts with which to act. Michael had seen it in the past, and he knew that he would see it in the future. These were the most noble and good of human hours, and the most potently evil as well.

VI.

Selina was clearly shaken as she rubbed Traytur's claw marks on her arm. If she could read him at all, this was as close to shaken as she had seen Richard. He gave her five minutes to cram new items into a suitcase, and then he loaded her new and old suitcases into his car. He drove quickly to his house and did not bother cloaking his car before he turned into his driveway.

It was dark and there were no street lamps shining through the trees on Richard's property. Selina could barely see him as she waited in the living room of his house and loaded one piece of his own luggage into the car. When he had finished, he locked his front door behind him and turned to face Selina.

He walked toward her, still wearing his overcoat, then held her tenderly.

"I haven't told you a thing about what is happening. And yet you stand here trusting me." He surprised her with one of those kisses that should have been a prelude to other kisses. But wasn't. He reached into his pocket and activated the Sound Distort, and he held her hands in his as he spoke.

"My starship computer can connect with all the computer networks and computer systems around the world. It informed me that ROSET is planning something. But I don't know what. My house was broken into while we were away. I have to assume that ROSET could be stalking me. That is why you and I need to go into hiding for a short time, perhaps two weeks."

"When do we leave?"

"That depends upon who Max Traytur is. If he really is some acquaintance related to the hospital, we will leave tomorrow after the University hearing. If he is someone else, we may need to leave tonight. Do you know his address and the correct spelling of his name?"

"His party invitation said he lived in Barton Hills. I don't remember anything else."

"That's sufficient. We'll ask the computer to tell us about him. The computer will also make new passports for us, with false identities."

"Is there anything your computer cannot do?" Selina asked.

"It cannot go with me when I leave this house. It is my link with the starship and its power. When I am away from it, I feel like a three-handed man who has only two hands." Richard took off his coat and threw it on a chair.

"Can I see the computer?" Selina asked.

"You can see it right now. We have work to do."

Selina didn't like what she saw. Richard stretched out his hand and pressed his palm against a red panel near the ceiling of the door to his den. The panel blinked in recognition of his five finger-print identification. A white light shot down on Selina and scanned her. Richard quickly keyed a message on the red panel and the scanning beam disappeared. Selina had been granted permission to enter the computer room. The door opened automatically, and they entered the room.

"What would happen if someone tried to get in this room without your permission?" Selina asked.

"First the person would receive an electric shock. If he stayed past that, the scanning beam would make his heart stop."

Selina choked. "You Tethrans don't play games, do you?" she asked.

"This is no game. It is access to a warship. My starship is a warship."

"Where is the... starship hidden?" She was beyond the point of return, and she wanted to know everything.

"It is hidden in a time zone, four minutes in the future," Richard said matter-of-factly.

"You mean that you and... your people can actually travel in time?"

"It is scientifically possible to move through time. But it is forbidden by law to move back into the past. And movement, or travel into the future as you put it, is tightly restricted by law. Time is a delicate dimension, and it is possible to rupture its well-hemmed seams."

"This all sounds like magic, not science!" Selina knew she must have sounded ignorant to Richard.

"Two-thirds of Tethran science will sound like magic to you, darling. But if you look back only two hundred years ago on Earth, two-thirds of what you take for granted about daily life would seem like magic to your ancestors. How could you explain to a woman from the 1700s that she could touch a switch on the wall and turn lights on throughout her house? Or that she could pick up a phone and talk to someone 3,000 miles away?   Or watch living humans on a television set? Or travel to the moon?"

Richard seated himself next to a computer terminal.   Selina stood by uncomfortably and looked around the room. The window was boarded up with metal strips, and the walls were bare. The door of the den was coated in metal on the side facing the computers, and the door closed automatically once she and Richard were inside the room.

"Does all this frighten you?" Richard asked.

"Will I be like some relic from the past who doesn't understand how to use a telephone when we are... among your people?"

"My people are proud of their technology. But they are also slaves to it. You are no one's slave. You understand things my people do not understand. And you will teach them as much as they will teach you... maybe more."

"It is hard to believe that I have anything so special to teach."

"Who is your favorite writer in the English language, Selina?"

"Shakespeare."

"And did he understand electricity, telephones, and space shuttles?"

"Of course not."

"But he teaches you things today, and you value him.   My people need you like you need your Shakespeare."

Richard turned away from Selina and began pressing keys on his keyboard. Selina looked lovingly at him. Only his love for her could see such a thing--could compare her to Shakespeare. She knew that she didn't need to be great like Shakespeare in order to have valuable things to offer the Tethran people. But she had needed his reassurance at this moment. When she first laid eyes on the hook-up to the warship, she needed to know where she fit in.

Selina still did not sit near him in the second chair near the second computer. She studied everything. She was intrigued as she watched Richard's fingers race across the wide keyboard with the foreign symbols. And then she started! Richard's terminal lit up, and a three-foot holographic figure appeared, hovering above the computer screen. At first she didn't know that it was a hologram. She didn't know what it was! Instinctively she jumped behind Richard's broad shoulders.

The hologram was a bald, pale-skinned man dressed in a one-piece navy uniform. His face was utterly expressionless.

"Selina, this is Jenxex, my friend and android crewmember. Jenxex, this is Selina, my future wife."

"Greetings, Selina, in the name of..."

"Jenxex, we are in a hurry. Find everything you can for me about this man." Richard keyed what he knew about Max Traytur into the computer, and as he did so the hologram vanished.

Selina was fascinated. She could not decipher the symbols on the computer screen. They moved so quickly that it was hard to believe that Richard was reading them. The search lasted for twenty minutes. Richard concentrated so intensely as he studied his screen that it almost frightened Selina. He was an alien, and he not only understood this alien language on the screen, but he read it faster than anyone she had ever seen. She was intimidated. But only for a minute, because soon he turned and faced her. And his big brown eyes had not changed.

"No luck, Selina. I cannot make a clear connection between Max Traytur and ROSET. He is a disgusting human being, powerful, wealthy, and well-connected. He has done things that I would rather not describe to you. But he does not appear to be closely related to ROSET. He attended two legitimate ROSET conventions ten years ago. But he attends dozens of different conventions every year. And he did not carry his participation in ROSET any further than that. Or if he did, he has hidden it so well that even my computer has not found it."

"What do your instincts tell you?"

"That's my little artist. Forget the technology and use your soul. My instincts tell me that he is dangerous to us. But if I cannot prove it, logic tells me not to run away from him. What do your instincts tell you?"

Selina knit her brows and looked around the room. "My instincts tell me to run away from him. But the University hearing tomorrow is important, and I don't think that we should miss it. Let's wait until tomorrow to leave town."

"There are a few more things about Traytur that I want to cross-check on the computer. I can dig deeper, but it will take more time."

Richard turned to the keyboard and fingered instructions into it. A metal tray opened on a thing that looked like a FAX machine and swallowed the two passports that he placed on the narrow tray at its outer edge. He removed his fingers quickly as if it were hot.

"I'm hungry. Let's have some dinner while they make us new passports. You can shower and relax when I come back here and do more Traytur research."

Selina could only find canned food in Richard's bare kitchen. But they enjoyed the hot vegetable soup. The tiredness hit them both when they sat down. They kicked their shoes off and melted into Richard's comfortable couch. Selina found herself longing for one missing ingredient. She wanted normalcy. She wanted to sleep in her own bed and to call her friends on the phone. She wanted to hear Nana's sqeal of delight when she announced her engagement. She wanted to plan her March wedding.

Richard reached to hold her. There was nothing normal about this man. His hands reminded her of this. There was a starship hovering above their heads waiting for his command. Selina smiled at the thought. Maybe she didn't want normalcy after all.

"You gave up your Sanibel Island vacation so that I could take a retreat in a frozen monastery," Richard said softly.

"We both had a retreat. It was great!"

"Tomorrow night is New Year's Eve. We need to do something special to celebrate." Richard moved his mouth close to kiss Selina. And then he jumped! So quickly that Selina's head banged against the couch. Selina heard the strange whistling sound, but she didn't know what or where it was.

"Get your gun from your purse and stay here," Richard said. He pulled his own gun out of the coat pocket lying on the chair. And then he practically leapt out the front door into the black night. He didn't even bother to put his shoes on.

VII.

Richard heard the footsteps moving in the front yard. It was too dark to see the form, but he had deliberately neglected to turn the porch light on. Richard assumed that he could find a man in the dark better than most Earthborn humans. Unless they also had military training. Richard knew that his security alarm would not have sounded unless something the size of a human had entered the front or back porch or leaned against a window. He wanted to capture and question whoever the intruder was. He hoped that there was only one of them.

Richard paused in the middle of his yard. He stood very still and listened. He heard nothing. And then something. Hard ice breaking in the grass, crunching under the weight of heavy footsteps. Richard lunged toward the sound. He shot his foot high in the air at the source of the sound, heard a groan and a body fall. Richard paused. There were no more sounds. Richard found the arms and subdued the intruder. He felt a flashlight in the intruder's hand, and he grabbed it, leaning on the man's heavy arms with his knee. Richard shined the light in the man's face.

"Akram Kasab? So Damien Devon sent you!"

"No, Mr. Saxon. I come here alone. I mean no trouble. I come to warn you of danger."

"Selina and I never told you where I lived. How did you find this house?"

"I know where Selina lives. I watch for her to come home, and I saw you drive here."

"Were you the one I saw in Selina's backyard earlier tonight?"

"Yes, I saw the other one come, too. Mr. Max Traytur. He is the one I wanted to tell you about, he is a terrible man. Mr. Devon hired him to hurt you. But Max Traytur hurts bad and kills people. He will kill you and hurt Selina."

"Do you mean to tell me that Damien hired someone to hurt his own... daughter?"

"No. Mr. Devon hired Traytur to kill only you. But Traytur, he always hurts women. He is a pervert. He will hurt both of you. Akram knows."

"Are you trying to convince me that you have come here to betray your own boss? You work for Damien. How can I believe what you say?"

Richard asked the right questions. But already he believed Akram.

"I do many things for Mr. Devon. I work hard and get paid good money. But I hear things. I hear all Mr. Devon's business. Mr. Devon thinks Akram is like furniture, that I do not hear things, do not feel things..." Akram moaned.

"My arm doesn't move right. Something snapped when you hit me with your foot, Mr. Saxon." Richard lifted his knee from Akram's chest and arms. He moved the glaring flashlight from Akram's face. He turned the light toward the ground so that it cast only a portion of its light. Akram moved to a sitting position.

"I heard Mr. Devon talk to Mr. Stills. He says, 'Hire Max Traytur. Crush Saxon.' Selina is good, I told myself. And Richard is good. I thought all these things, and I could not sleep with myself. I told Mr. Stills that Akram needs to take a vacation. Mr. Stills looks into my eyes, and he could see in me that I was coming to warn you and Selina. Mr. Stills says, 'Go on, Akram, take your vacation. Stay away as long as you need!'" Richard felt deeply moved as he listened.

"I'm sorry that I hurt you, Akram. Why didn't you just come and knock on the front door?"

"I started to knock. And the whistle sound happened. I thought I was in big trouble."

"Come inside. Selina will know how to splint your broken arm."

"No. I go now, Mr. Saxon. I go back home right away." Akram took his flashlight back from Richard and smiled broadly in its light.

"Tell Selina that Akram is good. Akram thinks about things, how everything I do is between Akram and God."

Richard thanked him and listened as Akram's footsteps disappeared in the darkness. The computer had failed to give him the answer about Max Traytur. His instincts had failed him. And so God sent him a messenger to guide him. An unlikely messenger. Richard ran into his house from the cold. They would leave tonight. They would take their false passports and their luggage and go far away.

They had seen Max Traytur over an hour ago, and for some reason Traytur had made no move against them. But he would make his move, and Richard was not sure how or how soon. Traytur had pursued Selina and invited her to his party before Damien had hired Traytur. Or so it seemed. If only there were time to use the computer and find out if there were some connection between Traytur and the burglary to his house and ROSET. *Is there time to have the computer track and kill Max Traytur?* Richard asked himself. *No, there isn't time!* He and Selina needed to go far away, and they needed to go fast. This, his instincts did tell him.

VIII.

Stan and Bobo watched the figure in the shadows walking away from Richard's driveway. They looked at their watches. The others would not be arriving for another ten minutes. It was up to Stan and Bobo to capture this man, lurking in the darkness. They followed the man slowly as he walked to a car parked near Selina's house. It was the same car that had been parked here for the last two nights and two days. Traytur had ordered them to watch the man and not to lose him.

Stan and Bobo flashed the headlights of their car on the man just as he was entering his car. Stan jumped out of his car. "Identify yourself," Stan said.

"Akram Kasab. And who are you?"

Akram was big and strong, and he fought hard. Stan was badly beaten, and Bobo didn't want the same to happen to him. And Bobo didn't dare let this Akram escape Richard's property ten minutes before Traytur's arrival. Bobo pulled out his gun. He warned Akram to stand still. Bobo looked at Stan's blood splattered on the hood of Akram's car. Akram paused, and then he lunged toward Bobo. Bobo pulled the trigger twice. He watched as the bullets tore through Akram's chest.

Bobo had never shot a man before. He stood there looking at the body of the large Arab. He had worked for Mr. Traytur for several years. He was a surveillance expert, not a hit man. Bobo didn't know what he felt or what to do next. It was Stan who took charge. It was Stan who wiped the blood and fingerprints from Akram's car. It was Stan who ordered him to stuff the Arab's body in the backseat of their car and to take the body to Traytur.

Bobo watched everything else through a dazed fog. Six cars arrived, silently and swiftly. They parked in Richard's driveway as if they were going to a party. Except they all turned their headlights off. Twenty people surrounded Richard's house. They were electrocuted right and left as they tried to enter his house. Eventually some of them got inside. Once inside, they manned his house as if they had just confiscated an enemy fort, talking to one another in whispers on their cellular phones.

These ROSET people were real fruitcakes. Bobo wished that he were not here tonight, not on this job. He kept seeing the look on Akram's face when he had shot him. Bobo felt terrible that he had actually killed a man. Until a few hours later. Bobo realized that Akram was better off dead before the ROSET doctor did the autopsy on him. Bobo heard them talking about how they could have learned more from the Arab's body if Akram had been alive for the dissection.

IX.

It was 1:30 a.m. before Max left Richard Saxon's house. Max could no longer maintain his composure. By the time he reached his car he was sweating and trembling. He had to be alone before all his circuits blew at once. Max had convinced the ROSET leaders that the siege of Richard's house was a triumph. Even now the ROSET security team was examining every detail of Richard's house, studying a possible way to enter the secret locked room. They had autopsied an alien who looked like an Arab. ROSET felt sure that they were on the right track.

But Max knew that he had failed. Richard and Selina had escaped Richard's house in the few minutes during which Stan and Bobo left their surveillance post to capture Akram. Max knew the make and year of Richard's car, but he knew nothing else. Max had no idea where they had escaped or how they knew when to leave. Or what to do next. Max would not admit it to himself, but he was losing his grip! No, he wasn't! Max had the whole international ROSET organization at his fingertips. Max had photos of Richard and Selina that he had taken with his ring-sized camera today. Max had the bloodthirsty, the stupid, and the powerful waiting to capture the couple. Their escape was only temporary! Max was feeling better. The cocaine was helping.

Max accepted the first call when it came. A ROSET security expert had just died! Dropped dead tampering at the door of Richard's locked room! Max was delighted, although he acted dismayed. ROSET was sure now that they were onto something big. They had siezed an *alien's* home. A home that shot silent beams of light capable of stopping a man's heart. This was exciting! Max let the news buzz through ROSET's new computer system. It would reach everyone, everywhere.

Max was ready for a little selfish gratification. He would have an opportunity to kill Todd Weako tonight.

Max pressed his home intercom button, his hand slightly shaking.

"Get me two girls tonight. As young as you can find them.
Bring them to my room and have them wait for me here. I'm stepping
out for a while. I want them here when I get back."

Max went upstairs to his attic where he kept his private things.
And then he took his scalpel and its metal sheath in the leather pouch
and he drove to University Hospital in one of the servant's cars. And
waited.

X.

They found Todd Weako's body face down in a pool of blood
when the day shift arrived at the hospital on Friday morning. The victim
had barely been dead for three hours. The police assumed that Todd had
been robbed, because his wallet and watch were missing. Todd must
have been alone in the dark parking structure, taking the steps instead of
the elevator, when the assailant mugged him. But whoever the attacker
was, he used a scalpel, and he used it skillfully, driving it twice into
Todd Weako's heart. There did not appear to be any signs of a struggle
preceding the murder. There were no other clues. No witnesses.

The police decided to keep the details of the mugging quiet. It
had a spooky feeling about it.

XI.

Sam Steinberg woke up early on Friday morning, December 31.
He remembered watching the sunrise. He thought it was the most
beautiful sunrise he had ever seen. And then a day of heavy worries
followed. Such a strange day. Soon the sun would set.

Sam went for a drive to think things over. The University
hearing of Richard's case and Damien Devon's charges had been a
fiasco. Richard and Selina did not show up! That could have been a
disaster. But a well-dressed, soft-spoken New York attorney did show
up for the hearing. The attorney operated like a velvet power-saw. He
was prepared to sue the University and Damien Devon for challenging
Selina Devon's competence. No one was prepared for this man. There
would have to be another meeting. There always had to be more
meetings to settle things.

And then there was Richard's long-distance phone call in the
middle of the night. Richard wanted to tell Sam himself what was going

on. He and Selina were fine, but they had sudden business to take care of out-of-town. Richard was mailing his formal letter of resignation to the University this week. Richard intended to fight Damien Devon in court, but he did not want to fight anyone else. Richard said that he would see Sam in two weeks. Richard tried to sound normal. But something was wrong. Everything was wrong. Sam could smell it.

Sam drove to a pay phone on Main Street. The cold wind whipped at him as he stood outside. He waited for five rings before Nana answered.

"This is Sam... the baldish one. Would you meet me for a spontaneous little rendevous before the sun sets?"

"I suppose I could fit you in, short-bald-and-handsome. Where and when?" Nana asked.

"In about half an hour. Meet me at the place where you like to jog."

"Why there? It is below zero today, or perhaps you haven't noticed," Nana said.

"I guess I'm just a wild and crazy guy."

"Yes, and I'm prim and proper."

"Tell me you'll meet me, and I'll hang up the phone a happy man."

"I'm getting ready for a big New Year's Eve party... the one that you said you're too old to attend! I'll meet you in forty minutes."

"Okay. And Nana... don't tell anyone where you are going or who you are meeting."

"The tone of your voice is a little weird."

"Yes. Do what I say, Nana. I'm counting on you."

Sam drove to a small Jewish restaurant on the other side of town. He warmed himself up with a cup of hot tea. Sam would spend New Year's Eve alone tonight. It was a tradition that he and his wife had always followed. They used to take time together to reflect on the last year, have a quiet glass of champagne, and go to bed. Tonight he would reflect alone.

Sam drove near the Arboretum and parked his car a few streets away. Sam looked at his watch, then hurried to the entance of the Arboretum. Nana was waiting for him, dressed in a long black coat with an even longer red scarf wrapped in layers around her throat. The subzero wind howled through the tall trees in the park.

"So, wild and crazy guy, I guess you want to take a walk through the frozen Arb, maybe have a picnic?"

"I'd love to. But I'm too old," Sam said, grinning broadly. Nana was one of those rare people who could always make him laugh. He had dated her three times, and each time they had both laughed the entire evening.

"Why did you want to meet me *here*, if not to prove your rugged manhood?"

"Nana, I think that Richard Saxon is in trouble. And I think there is a way that you and I can help him."

"I'm all ears." Nana's eyes opened wide.

"I don't have much to tell you. And I might be overreacting to something." Sam leaned his face close to Nana's, as much for warmth as confidentiality. His feet and hands were cold, and he wanted to keep moving.

"Let's walk," Sam said, and then he asked, "Do you know where Selina is right now?"

"I haven't the foggiest. She and Richard were supposed to go to Florida for the holiday, but I thought they would be home for New Year's."

"If you find out where Selina or Richard is, don't tell anyone. Don't even tell me. If anyone, including her father asks, tell them a lie. Can you do that?"

"You're being awfully serious, Sam."

"That's because I'm Jewish."

Nana frowned.

"My grandparents were hunted and killed by Nazis in Germany a long time ago. The only reason I was born is because someone smuggled my mother into England. My mother was pregnant carrying me. I've heard that story all my life. About how careful Jews have to be. About how careful good people have to be about taking care of each other.

"I smell a rat, Nana. And the rat is after our friend Richard."

Nana was very quiet. She rubbed Sam on the shoulder with her hand in a consoling gesture.

"You said to lie to anyone, including Selina's father. Damien is no prince!" Nana said. "But I've known him since I was in high school."

"Yes, and my grandparents were betrayed by people they had known all their lives. There were people in Germany who betrayed my grandparents. And there were other people who saved my mother's life. Let's side with the rescuers."

"I'll be the best liar you ever saw," Nana said.

Sam moved his gloved hand gently across Nana's cold cheek. He expected Nana to see it as a fatherly gesture. But something in her eyes told him that she had not. And then she leaned close to him and kissed him. Sam was taken aback. Nana had never kissed him before. In fact, no woman had kissed him like that since his wife died. He stood there in the snow not knowing what to say. *Don't fail me now, unfailing wit,* he thought. And then the clever words were on his tongue.

"So, you want to bring out the hidden macho streak in me?" Sam asked.

"Hidden only to yourself."

"What does a beautiful woman like you want with an old man like me?"

"That's easy. No one else has ever called me beautiful before," Nana said. And then she repeated in a whisper, "No one."

And they warmed each other in the snow. "I need to go home, beautiful. The sun is going down," Sam said, smiling, feeling young inside. But something deeper knawed inside of him. Some kind of premonition. And he wanted to go home.

XII.

Max Traytur's adrenaline was surging through his veins, and he was eager, hungry for blood. Blood had a distinct smell, and it was exhilarating! He didn't know why he hadn't noticed it before. But now he noticed, and he wanted more of it. And he wanted the sexual pleasure that it would bring. And Sam Steinberg would give it to him once more.

The back door to Sam Steinberg's house was easy to enter. The lock was a simple design, built fifty years ago with the rest of the creaky old house. It was almost too easy. Max was ready for more of a challenge.

Max was wearing his disguise, complete with dark wig and the casual student-looking denims and ski jacket. Youngish, low-class garb that Max Traytur would not be caught dead wearing except in a disguise.

Steinberg lived in one of those family neighborhoods where people were always coming and going. If it had not been for the rows of trees and the shrubbery around Steinberg's house, neighbors may have noticed Max as he slunk into the back yard and fiddled with the lock.

Max wore his buttery soft black kidskin gloves. They fit comfortably like a second skin. But unlike skin, they left no fingerprints.

Max walked gingerly through the empty house, cluttered with photographs of a wife and children and grandchildren. A home full of memories and smells and dust and old books. Max explored it all until he knew exactly how the layout of the house would fit into his plan. And then Max went into Steinberg's basement and he waited.

Max caressed his gun, and he screwed and unscrewed the silencer several times as he sat in the dark. Max crouched on a damp old chair in the dark basement, breathing in the cold, moldy air. And he listened intently.

Max listened as Sam Steinberg came home and talked with someone on the phone. Max listened as Sam made himself a simple dinner. Max heard the wooden floor creak as Sam went through his evening routine, rocking in a rocking chair, reading after dinner. Max heard Sam turn on the seven o'clock news. Max heard the muffled news report coming through the creaking floors. And when Max was sure that it was pitch black outside and was sure that Sam was alone in his living room, he tiptoed up the basement stairs. He tiptoed through the kitchen and paused. Sam did not stir. Sam did not seem to hear him. And then the moment Max had waited for arrived.

The gun was ready and the silencer was ready, and Max was ready. Max walked softly into the living room, pointing his gun at Sam as he walked. Max relished the look of dread, the look of horror on Sam's face.

"What I'm going to do won't take long."

Max's voice was mellow. "Come, sit here at the dining room table." Max nudged Sam, pointing to the dining room with his gun.

Sam was silent. He lifted himself carefully from his chair. The muscles around his mouth were tightly controlled.

"No questions? Don't you want to know who I am or what I want with you?" Max almost whispered. He leaned his face close to Sam and let Sam take a very close look at his face and his gun.

Sam was silent. The silence angered Max. He wanted Sam to plead for his life, to grovel and to weep the way Todd Weako had wept before Max killed him.

"You passive, worthless piece of garbage! Don't you care whether you live or die?" Max raised the butt of his gun as if to strike Sam in the face with it. Sam flinched and closed his eyes, expecting the blow to come. But he didn't utter a sound.

Max lowered the gun. He was losing his temper, but he couldn't cut or bruise the victim. It would ruin his plan.

Slowly Sam opened his eyes and looked at Max. Sam looked into the cruel red eyes, and he saw murder in them. Sam knew that he had been right about the rat. The rat that was after Richard had found Sam. In those eyes Sam saw the same rat that had murdered his grandparents and had tried to murder him in his mother's womb.

The rat thinks that it has won, Sam thought. *But it is wrong. I die tonight a happy man who has lived a good life, who has borne good fruit. I leave behind four children of my own and a stadium full of children to whom I taught important things about math and about life. The rat has lost.* Sam heard his own thoughts, and he did not hear Traytur's obscene insults lashing against him.

Max saw dignity, and he wanted to destroy it. But he could not have Sam's dignity. Even if he beat Sam to death.

Max calmed himself. If he didn't he would wreck the plan. Max pressed the cold gun against Sam's right temple. Max lifted Sam's hand and he pushed the gun into Sam's right hand. Max used Sam's own finger to move the trigger. And then Max pressed the trigger, and he smelled the blood.

Sam's body and mangled head slumped against the dining room table. Max washed the blood from his coat and put a clean pair of gloves on. Max left the room and the house in perfect order. Max would celebrate tonight. It was New Year's Eve. And in the morning Max would read about Samuel Steinberg's suicide in the paper. And then Max would plan his most important kills. Wherever they were, Saxon and Selina could be found.

CHAPTER
THIRTY
BLUE-THREE

Captain Lohnarks remained impassive as he watched the data move across his screen. Impassive, but aware of the excitement of his crew. The excitement had cut through the starched discipline of their manners. Today's new discoveries continued to astonish them.

Ever since they reached this solar system five weeks ago, the monitors had been feeding them intriguing information. Sorn's directions had been perfect. Follow the eye of the cosmic vortex, follow the jump through hyperspace, follow until you reach the coordinates pointing to the third planet from the sun. And there it was, the phenomenal third planet from the sun. They named it Blue-3 because of its color on the monitors. And they watched it, studied it, analyzed it because it was emitting the noises of a technological civilization through the silence of space.

Evimator had theorized that the planet had blue oceans. But it was not until today, until this hour, that they could confirm his theory. They had come close enough to do a full analysis of the planet's terrain, atmosphere, and composition. The planet was not only teeming with life forms, but the atmosphere was perfect for supporting human life. No one had ever discovered a planet so similar to Tethra! Not in 4,000 years of space travel. No one. Nowhere. But even these new discoveries would not be reported to Tethra by ansible. Until he was sure why Captain Sorn had kept the discovery of Blue-3 a secret, Captain Lohnarks would do the same.

Lohnarks held his post until the end of First Watch, and then he left the bridge as he always did. But this time he went to his private quarters to have dinner alone.

Lohnarks sat on the edge of his bed and rubbed his eyes. He was grateful for the excitement that was passing like a wave of energy through his crew. Because until recently, morale had not been good. The war news that poured in through the ansible was not good. Lohnarks was deeply depressed.

The truth was, Lohnarks didn't care about anything other than finding Sorn and his ship. He didn't care if they had made the discovery of the century! Finding some new planet would not save Tethra and the Free Worlds. Their mission here had failed.

There had been no trace of the *Stealthfire*. There had been no response from all their signals. No response even today when Lohnarks sent an emergency SOS signal. It was not ethical to use a phony distress signal to get the attention of another starship. But Lohnarks did it anyway. And when Sorn did not respond, he knew that Sorn was dead. If the *Stealthfire* was anywhere within two quadrants of this solar system, Sorn would have heard and would have responded to the distress signal. Lohnarks was one of the few aboard his ship who knew how much was really at stake. The lieutenant in charge of the Royal Guard also knew.

Lohnarks saw the violet-blue lights blink across the entrance pad of his door. He did not respond. The visitor did not leave. Lohnarks addressed the light panel to turn the lights on inside his room so that no one would know that he had been sitting in the dark.

"Enter," he heard himself say.

The doors parted, and first officer Lieutenant Abthulzar walked through them. She stood quietly, showing a dim hint of concern.

"What are you thinking, Captain?" Abthulzar asked.

"I was just thinking that perhaps we made a mistake. Perhaps we should have followed Captain Sorn's second message to us instead of the first message. He warned us! He told us in his second message not to come here, not to come after him."

"It was not your choice which message was to be followed. You and Qeeswick merely decoded his messages. It was the Hegemon who decided which message to follow. We are merely obeying her orders," Abthulzar said.

Lohnarks looked at Abthulzar. In her own cold way, she was trying to be consoling. She stood there looking tall and trim and muscular, the way the warrior class was supposed to look. She had small dark eyes and a small mouth, her long black hair tied stylishly behind her head. She was sometimes too much a warrior and too little a woman. Only now she was trying to be a woman.

Lohnarks offered her a cup of Sui. He didn't mind her company. His thoughts were burdening him. Abthulzar couldn't know all his thoughts. She did not realize that Lohnarks had been involved in the decision to seek and rescue Captain Sorn. She did not realize that

Lohnarks' life had been turned upside down and that he had already suffered just to be here today.

Lohnarks was silent for a long time as he thought about the past. He was not a politically-minded man. Nor a hero. He was just a soldier. All he had offered to do was to help another soldier, to help in the search for Captain Sorn. For that crime, High Command had imprisoned him. They held him in secret, jailed him like a criminal, and kept him jailed even when his wife Freepar died. Even when they buried her. Everyone forgot Lohnarks. Until the King's assassination. After that, everything changed. The Hegemon Ishpenar sought out Lieutenant Lohnarks. She commissioned a journeyship to rescue Sorn. She made Lohnarks a captain so that he could lead the mission. And she put her trust in him. Now he had more responsibility than he had ever wanted. And he had to make a terrible decision.

"I don't like our situation, Abthulzar. We are 1,000 light years away from Tethra in the same solar system that swallowed up the *Stealthfire*."

"We don't know for sure that the *Stealthfire* was swallowed up. We only know that we lost communications contact with it."

"If the *Stealthfire* was not destroyed, what other possible explanation could there be for its silence, its unresponsiveness to our communications, even our distress signal?"

"Theoretically, if the ship were cloaked and its communications system inactive, it would not respond to us."

"Cloaked--you mean hiding. If a Chadran warship like the *Stealthfire* is hiding, then there is an enemy. Then this journey ship should be hiding also."

"Captain, I agree with your concerns. But we have been in this solar system for five weeks, and we have encountered no starfleet, no patrols, no space stations. The evidence seems to point to the fact that there is no interplanetary defense system in this solar system," Abthulzar said.

"None that we recognize. But space is full of unknown factors. We think that we know so much, and yet we know so little. Each new discovery seems to defy the laws of the universe. And then we find that nothing old was defied but something new was found.

"Abthulzar, you are younger than I am. I know you have seen the videos but you weren't alive when the actual thing happened. When the Dreyens were discovered forty years ago. I was an eleven-year-old student in battle school. I remember sweating with horror as we watched the newscasts of the first encounter with the Dreyens.

"The Dreyens are so completely different than humans that we could barely detect traces of their existence in the galaxy. Until it was too late. Until the Dreyens had crashed their two-dimensional matter disrupters through the hulls of our exploratory ships and torn the insides out of them. It took the Dreyens months to detect our three-dimensional carcasses and more months for us to find the math to use to communicate with them."

Lohnarks paused. He had allowed too much of his fear to seep into the texture of his explanation. He would lose Abthulzar's respect if this continued.

"We are at the turning point, Abthulzar. We have come close enough to Blue-3, to the point of Sorn's disappearance to conclude that there is no trace of him or of his ship. But we are still far enough away from the planet so that nothing has destroyed us. We are one week away from achieving orbit around the planet. If we approach it any closer, whatever seized and destroyed the *Stealthfire* could destroy us.

"There are 800 lives aboard this ship, hand-picked star travelers who are needed to defend Tethra. It is time for us to turn around and go home."

"So you have given up hope of finding Captain Sorn?" Abthulzar asked. She looked sad. In spite of her training, the sadness was visible on her face.

"What is left to do? A ground search of the planet? Yes, I have given up hope."

"I gave up hope long before you did, Captain. But I wanted you to keep hoping for all of us."

"Do you want me to keep risking all our lives? Do you want me to keep wasting precious time while we could all be used in planetary defense?" He didn't mean to sound angry.

"Starfleet will not consider our journey to this solar system a waste of time. The discovery of Blue-3 is a once in a lifetime event! After the war has been won we will send Chadran ships to explore every inch of this planet," Abthulzar said.

"Yes, after the war has been won, Abthulzar."

"We must send the probes to Blue-3, to continue to collect data."

"We will send the probes. After we have backed away from the planet a little further. The probe ships will alert the inhabitants of Blue-

3 as to our presence in their solar system." Lohnarks looked at Abthulzar. He wanted to be alone. Somehow she sensed it. "I support your decision to consider the search ended and to return to Tethra. Captain Sorn would have made the same decision." Her voice was calm and reassuring.

Lohnarks rose from his seat as Abthulzar left his quarters. *What decision would Sorn make if he were in my place?* he asked himself. He looked out the porthole window in his quarters, and he stared at the stars. A wave of grief passed through him. And with it came sobs and wrenching tears. Captain Lohnarks watched the tears dripping onto the chest of his uniform. He watched the droplets as if they were coming from someone else. He had not wept like this in twenty years. He wept because he was turning back and the mission had failed. He wept for the loss of his friend Kollann Sorn. He wept for the Hegemon. And he wept for the future. Sorn was supposed to have saved them all.

CHAPTER
THIRTY-ONE
ROME

"We don't smell like Europeans, Selina. Europeans smell like perspiration and other body odors. Americans smell like sweet soap and deodorant. If we are to fit in here, we need to smell like they do." Richard made her laugh. But he wasn't joking. They were only twenty minutes away from Fiumicino airport and in a taxi headed for Rome. And already Richard had started observing, adapting, mastering his new environment. He was always gracious, always cautious, always cool. At least on the outside. And Selina found herself trying to be like him. She had tried hard, through the tense drive to Chicago's O'Hare airport, through the long flight to Rome, through everything. But now she was alone in the hotel room adjoining Richard's. And Selina knew that she was anxious and afraid.

Selina tossed and turned on the too-soft mattress. The lumpy down comforter was too heavy, and the room was drafty. Selina wanted to be home. Her bed at home was hard and comfortable, and the heat worked well. Home was quiet. She could barely hear the wind blowing through the two large pines on her property. Selina heard a loud bang. She sat up in bed, then hurried to the window. It was only the noise of an old car backfiring on the narrow street.

Selina turned the light on and climbed back into bed. Maybe she could sleep with the light on. Her thoughts were still racing. She remembered their conversation yesterday evening as they drove to Chicago.

"Why are we running away?" she had asked Richard.

"We know that Traytur intends to kill me. If Traytur is only working for your father and I make it difficult for him to find me, he may give up. I sent your father a message warning him to get rid of Traytur. Maybe he will. Then you and I can return safely to Ann Arbor. But we don't know enough about who Traytur is. If he is working for ROSET, then he will chase me with a vengeance if I try to escape. And he will chase you. If I am forced to fight Traytur and all of ROSET, people will die."

"How would you fight the whole ROSET organization?"

"You and I would transport to the starship. From there I would fight ROSET with the ship's computer and its weapons. My goal would be to disable ROSET without attracting the attention of the police or the... armed forces.

"I don't mind fighting ROSET, but the timing for it right now is bad. I want to avoid any conflict with ROSET until after I have secured the uranium cargo that I need from Bay Tech. I need to remain visible and reputable in order to complete my business negotiations. Securing the uranium peacefully is crucial." Richard looked grave when he explained all this.

"What if you cannot secure the uranium peacefully?"

"Then I will confiscate it. And that will be dangerous. I could end up killing many people. It is the one thing that we have tried to avoid since coming to Earth. We decided to hide ourselves and our ship and our weapons. We knew that your people would be afraid of us if they knew about our superior technology. Your people would attack us, and they would start a war that we would have to finish.

"You and I would be safe. But the people who would try to stop us from confiscating the uranium would be destroyed."

Selina remembered cringing at this point. Richard's manner was coldly calm.

"My starship has shielding devices, speed potential, and weapons that your technology cannot touch. Our weapons are capable of disarming all and destroying most of your planet. But even the disarmament phase would cost hundreds of lives."

"You always say we. Are you the only Tethran on Earth?"

"That is the one thing that I cannot answer for you. The ROSET fanatics would torture you unmercifully if they thought you knew about other living aliens. So it is better that you do not know." Richard paused. "I should not have said that. I will never let ROSET lay a finger on you." Richard spoke in his most gentle voice. But the fear was implanted, and the gentle words had not reached to the core of it.

Now she was alone, and the thin walls seemed to offer her little protection. It was 4:00 a.m., and she could still hear too many noises. It was New Year's Eve, and she wished that everyone would stop celebrating and go to bed.

A sudden thud banged against her hotel room door. It sounded as if someone had just thrown his body against the door. As if someone were trying to get in. Selina almost screamed. She felt paralyzed for an instant. And then she heard a woman laughing, and a man joined in. She could only translate a few words from their rapid Italian. "Drunken fool... go home now." The few words were enough. Selina calmed herself. But she could not sleep. Danger was a presence, and even when it wasn't touching her, she could feel its claws.

II.

Richard sat up in bed alarmed. He had been in a deep sleep, and for a second he did not remember where he was. The room was dark except for a small panel of moonlight in the corner across from his bed. Italy! He was in Italy! He heard Selina's voice and her knocking on his bedroom door.

"What is it, Selina?"

"Can I see you for a minute?"

He didn't like what he heard in her voice. He slipped into his jeans and opened the door between their adjoining rooms. Selina was standing there in the full light of her bedroom. She was wearing one of those acutely modest nightdresses of hers. The soft, flannel kind that covered every inch of her. It hung loosely, making her look like a shapeless child.

"I've been tossing and turning for two hours. Every noise scares me." She spoke timidly, and her tired eyes were red-rimmed.

"That's not like you."

"I know. Everything hit me at once. The realization that my father is a murderer. That he would try to murder *you*... The fact that ROSET would murder you and torture me. The... ship heavily armed with weapons..."

"Shhh!" Richard put his finger to his lips. He reached into the pocket of his jeans and activated the Sound Distort.

"Do you need to talk?" he whispered.

"No. I need to sleep."

He put his arms around her. His chest and back were naked, and he felt her soft fingers against his flesh.

"Would you hold me until I fall asleep?" she asked softly.

Richard reached his arms to her knees and picked her up. He put her next to him in his bed. He kept his jeans on. Selina pulled the covers over both of them as he turned out the light.

"I just need to get through this first night. Everything is hitting me at once."

"You have more to face than I ever had to face," Richard whispered close to her face.

"I do?"

"I never had to face the fact that the man who raised me was a murderer."

"I have another Father, Richard. One who has always loved me."

"Ohh?"

"God, the Father."

"He is very real to you," Richard said.

There was a long silence. Richard could feel the shape of her body next to his. Every soft curve. He could feel her hair brushing against his naked chest. A thin mist of perspiration rose on his forehead.

"I asked God the Father to give me the courage I need for everything that lies ahead," Selina whispered.

"Even wanting more courage is an act of courage."

"I don't like the fact that we are sitting around waiting for ROSET to make the first move. Couldn't we just transport to the ship tonight and find out through your computer what ROSET has in mind?"

"Transporting spends the valuable energy resources of the ship. There is also an element of risk. We can be seen transporting back and forth to the ship. We would look like tiny meteorites flashing through the sky. We will save that move for the right moment."

Selina was still. He could feel her breath on his bare chest.

"Don't let anything bad happen to you," Selina whispered.

"Nothing will."

Richard moved his hand to touch her face, and she kissed his hand. She fell asleep quickly. He noticed her breathing change, and the soft hand on his chest went limp.

Every time that he thought he could not love her more, he found that he was wrong. His love for her was growing. He hadn't realized that it would work this way. That love would multiply itself in quantum leaps. That there would not be additions and subtractions that you could count. There would be multiples. And you couldn't count those either.

He hadn't realized that anything would go the way it had gone. Tonight as he lay in the dark, with her resting on his chest, trusting him with her life, he felt a wave of doubt. What if his decisions were all wrong? What if when he decided to transport to the ship, it was too late? He had even forgotten his starfleet training--never to think about the "what ifs." He was surprised when he felt the sleep pulling him under its power.

III.

Father John Fisk felt the contentment of a man who was in exactly the place he wanted to be on New Years Eve. This time tomorrow night he would be headed for Rome and his ordination as a bishop. But for tonight he was happy being with his brother Larry and his wife and children. They had found a good viewing space on the grounds of Our Lady of Peace Monastery. There, perched high on the hill overlooking the Ohio River, they would be able to watch at least two fireworks displays. One was to the west of them coming from Cincinnati's Riverside Park, another would be clearly visible south in Kentucky across the river.

Cars were parked everywhere along the narrow streets of Mount Adams. People clustered everywhere that a hillside view could be found.

The fireworks started slowly. John Fisk looked up into the clear sky filled with stars. He felt excitement in the air. And then the sky went wild with color and surprises. *What are we celebrating?* John asked himself. *And why?*

And then he felt it in the cold night air, something moving like an unseen wind, something pulsing like a living breath. Some metaphysical tidal wave was breaking across the earth, shattering time because it was a part of eternity. Here on the hillside in Ohio, there in the blue grass of Kentucky, in New York City, in Alabama and across the seas in Rome, in China--wherever humans lived, the forces of the past were meeting with the tides of the future. Fireworks, the excitement of the crowd, the church bells that began ringing as the clock struck twelve--these were the physical actions of the present--but they bubbled up from the past and flowed into the future.

John understood it all in a flash without the fumbling fingers of his reason. He watched as a beautifully coordinated display of fireworks formed the number 2000 across the night sky. The crowd began to cheer. And then he clapped and cheered with everyone else. Not because of anything his mind understood but because of the way in which he flowed with the massive tidal wave of grace that God was pouring out on him and on all of them this evening. And then John cried. Perhaps they had all been secretly afraid of the future, expecting suffering. Expecting the worst. Until this moment. Until the grace came.

Little Lauren sitting on her father's shoulders looked over at her Uncle John. She reached to touch him and so he grabbed her tiny hand in his. Then he caught the look in Lauren's eyes. Lauren who was barely three years old and should have understood nothing of what John felt--in her eyes he saw the truth. Lauren, in fact, understood everything. Along with suffering, days of wonder lay ahead.

IV.

The message appeared on Christine Carnes' home computer at 11:00 a.m. on New Year's Day. She did not hear the computer turn on by itself. What she did hear was the noise of the printer as it transferred the message from her computer screen to a sheet of paper. Christine jumped out of bed and hurried to her den. She stood there horrified, reading each word.

"I know all about you, Christine Carnes. You illegally handed insider trading information to Damien Devon in exchange for favors and financial reward. I have documentation regarding these illegal exchanges which occurred on 2/11/99; on 6/20/99; on 7/26/99 and on 8/14/99. I am sending this documentation to Damien Devon's rival, Abel Schwartz.

"Tell Damien not to make one more move against me. Not through Traytur. Not alone. Or I will make another move against Damien. Damien will understand.

"Richard."

Christine hid the print-out sheet from her lover. He had followed her into the den from her bedroom. Christine ordered him to leave her apartment right away, because she had sudden business that needed her attention. She did not even give the overnight guest a chance to shower. She wanted him gone before she called Damien. Damien was allowed to have other women, like his wife. But Christine was expected to be faithful to Damien.

Christine was in tears when she reached Damien. She was not supposed to call him at home, but this was an emergency. Damien reached Christine's apartment twenty minutes later. Twenty minutes after that he called Max Traytur.

Traytur's butler said that Mr. Traytur was still partying away from home. That Mr. Traytur was not expected home any time during New Year's Day. Damien insisted that it was an emergency and that he would have the butler fired if he failed to locate Mr. Traytur within the hour.

Five hours later Max Traytur called Damien at Christine's apartment. Damien was fit to be tied.

After spouting a paragraph of obscenities, Damien was able to articulate his thoughts.

"You really screwed up this time, Traytur. Saxon knows that I hired you. You're off the case, you incompetent fool. I intend to ruin your professional reputation. To drag your name through the mud."

"I have not completed my assignment, Devon. Before you threaten me you should exercize an ounce of patience."

"Complete your assignment fast, and we'll talk. But remember, you're no longer working for me." Devon hung up the phone so hard that it hurt Traytur's ear.

Traytur's hand trembled with anger. He hurried into his bedroom and took out some of his anger on the teenage girl who waited obediently in his bed. Then he felt better, and he told her to clean herself off in the bathroom. She could still walk. Max couldn't party any longer. New Year's Day or not, the mood was broken! He didn't have to take that kind of verbal abuse from Devon. He didn't have to take it from anyone!

Max went to the bathroom to wash the girl's blood from his knuckles. He felt a quick rush from the smell of her blood, and then he was depressed. Max stood in front of the mirror. The room was spinning. All this anger was not good for his blood pressure. He had to calm himself.

As he looked in the mirror he felt a wave of self-pity. There were dark circles under his eyes, and he looked gaunt and thin. He didn't like what his life had become. Pleasure used to be the refreshment and the delight of his life. Sexual pleasure, sadistic pleasure, drinking and getting high pleasure. The pleasure of power and the pleasure of money. Now pleasure was something that he had to squeeze into stolen moments. Although pleasure had also intensified. Now when he experienced pleasure, he felt his body shudder and sweat with the intensity of it. The delirious smell of blood after a kill and during sex after a kill.

Now pleasure could be spelled with a capital "P"; it had gained an identity all its own. It was his new god, his new obsession. And he would do anything to serve it. Perhaps that was how mighty Natas had always experienced pleasure. Perhaps Max was moving to a higher spiritual plane. Max washed his naked body in the shower, and his mind turned to the teenage girl showering in the next room. He wanted to kill her in the worst way. But it would only be disappointing. She was not a friend of Saxon or Selina. There would be no orgasmic reward.

Max walked into his private den to work. And he locked the door. He had regained his composure and his self-discipline. Just the knowledge that he could kill when he wanted to soothed him. He was a powerful man. Max was ready to hunt now. Hunting made him powerful also. Stenroos of Interpol was slow thinking, compared to Max. But they worked well together. They knew how to use one another. Max needed to stir up the slow-moving Europeans and get their juices flowing.

Max drove the forty minutes to Southfield where he kept his hidden ROSET files. The security guard accepted his ID card and let him pass through the entrance to Mother Nature's Baby Formula Company.

The photos of Richard and Selina had turned out well. He sent the photos through the company fax machine. They reached three ROSET locations in the United States and then on to Stenroos. Stenroos would send them all over Europe. Wherever the long fingers of Interpol's underground went, there would be people watching, searching, and finding.

IV.

Aldo Martini showed the photos to his wife.

"This is the British couple who came to the restaurant last night. Don't you think?"

"Those sweet darlings! So polite! And such good tippers, too. The man loves our food so much he eats like a horse. But he doesn't touch our delicious wine, just gulps down mineral water."

"Antonio says they are dangerous criminals, spies! Look at the pictures, Maria. It is them!"

"Spies?! Garbage! Last night they came in here with a priest. A priest, Aldo! The priest was their friend, and he spoke perfect Italian. Dangerous spy criminals don't eat dinner with priests. You tell Antonio and his sleazy friends to go away! They kicked Antonio out of the police academy. He's not good enough to be a real policeman, so he pretends to be a spy with those spy-policemen. They are good-for-nothings! Always trying to act like big important men. You stay away from those good-for-nothings, Aldo."

But Aldo didn't stay away. He knew a good thing when he saw it. Antonio would pay him 1,000 American dollars if Aldo could lead him to the place where the British man and the American woman were staying. The ones in the pictures.

Aldo set the tables and tended to his business as always. He watched as his wife pampered and mothered each guest. He set the tables, smiled, and took the customers' money. But Aldo watched carefully when the handsome foreign couple came to the restaurant for the second time. And when they left after a late lunch, Aldo left also. He followed them as they walked, winding through the streets of Rome, winding through the park laid out around the ruins of Trojan's Baths and down to the Colosseum. They stayed at the Colosseum for a long time, the woman sketching and the man walking and slowly studying each and every stone. Aldo followed them as they left the Colosseum and took the Metro to their hotel. To the Hotel Campidoglio.

Aldo paused and waited outside of the hotel, and then he hurried inside.

"My friends, I lost my friends. The tall British man and the blonde woman. What room are they staying in?" Aldo asked the hotel clerk.

"Don't your friends have a name?"

"Yes, but... of course I can't remember it."

The clerk shot Aldo a look of angry indignation.

"You don't know their names, they're not your friends. Out of my hotel!"

Aldo left. Maria would be hot with unforgiving anger that he had been gone for such a long time. He wouldn't go home to Maria just yet. He would go to Antonio's house and collect his 1,000 American dollars.

V.

Richard stood in the center of the Roman Colosseum. He could feel the soul of the past seeping through its pores, the soul and the stories of the rise and fall of the Roman Empire. It all intrigued him. In his visit to Earth he had lived in one of its newest democracies. And now he stood in the ancient heart of western civilization.

The sky looked cold and gray, but the air was warm and muggy and heavy. The day had a foggy, mystical quality about it, and it was not hard to use his imagination and step into another time.

He could imagine the Colosseum filled with mostly white-robed multitudes cheering for the barbaric sports and the gruesome killings of the gladiators. Richard knew how savagery could grasp you in its power and hold you. How savagery could master you and keep you thinking that you were the master and not it. Richard knew the pleasure of hand-to-hand combat, the excitement of combat and the terror of it. Today he was not proud of his understanding. But he understood.

He understood too well how the ancient Roman crowds must have cheered for the thrill of combat, bravery, and death. As he walked around the base of the Colosseum and climbed its crumbling, weed-ridden steps, it reminded him of something. It reminded him of Chadra and of the Stadium of Xenocon. Except that the Stadium of Xenocon on the planet Tethra was not decaying. Today it stood clean and polished. And three times a year it was filled to capacity for the war games competitions.

Richard was shocked at the similarity between ancient Rome and modern Chadra. Chadra, his homeland, his first love. Chadra with its long line of kings. A dynasty started by a warrior-king 2,500 years ago. If the king had not fought well, he could not have ruled well.

Selina interrupted his thoughts. He had noticed her putting aside her sketch pad and coming toward him. Now she was close enough to speak.

"They fed the Christians to the lions because the Christians refused to fight one another." Selina paused. And then she went on.

"The Christians committed one crime because they refused to worship the emperor as a god. Then they committed a second crime because they would not fight and kill one another in the arena. They would not entertain like the gladiators."

Richard turned and looked directly at Selina. Her face was silhouetted against the late day sun, as if she wore a halo.

"'Christ has died. Christ has risen. Christ will come again. And I will rise with Him!' That is what each of the martyrs said with their blood." Selina spoke loudly. And the acoustics of the Colosseum carried the sound. The words sent chills down his spine.

"Come home with me, Selina," Richard whispered. "Home to Chadra." And he kissed her ear.

As they passed the exit of the Colosseum and walked to the Metro, Richard noticed someone following them. Seeming to follow them. It was indeed time to go home.

VI.

Max Traytur found himself pacing nervously across the length of his private jet. In only two more hours he would land in Rome. He would trap the unsuspecting Saxon and Selina in the Hotel Campidoglio. And no one was going to deprive him of their blood! No one! Stenroos had some nerve! Telling Max to stay on the other side of the Atlantic and let the Europeans of ROSET handle "the matter of the aliens." No way, Max consoled himself.

Max sat down in his leather recliner and gulped some scotch. It tasted bitter. There was no good Macallan Scotch aboard the jet. The glass clanked as he smacked it on the table.

Max told himself that he should be feeling excited and optimistic. His photos of Saxon and Selina had brought him results in less than a week. Stenroos couldn't prevent him from assuming control of the capture and the kill. Stenroos was merely trying to steal the limelight. But he had no more authority than Max had in this situation.

Max picked up the scotch once more. It had spilled on the table, and the smell of the alcohol was strong but oddly soothing. Max laid back in the leather recliner and closed his eyes. He would meditate on success, and he would make it happen.

In two hours he would land in Rome. The city would be closed in celebration of the national holiday, January 5, The Feast of the Epiphany. No one would notice Max or the others as they crept in their clever secret ways.

The ordination of Bishop John Fisk was scheduled for the next day, January 6. Saxon and Selina were bound to attend the event. Why else would they be in Rome? Stenroos said it would be complicated trying to kidnap the bishop on the day of his ordination. But it would not be impossible. Stenroos said it would be easy nabbing Saxon and Selina in the crowd near St. Peter's. Stenroos had little imagination. Max had plenty. Max's plan would impress the other Europeans.

Max sat up suddenly in his chair. The chair jerked awkwardly under him. Max couldn't relax enough to meditate. He poured more scotch. Then put it down. He couldn't afford a hangover. Max opened his briefcase and searched through it. Just a little snort of cocaine was all he needed. Just a little more than the last time.

VII.

Richard's tense muscles ached for release. He needed to clear his head. He wanted the rain to stop. The persistent gray drizzle saturated everything, seeping now into his mood. He decided to jog through the wet streets before Selina woke up. The rain would drench him. But he didn't care.

And so he jogged. Jogged in the pre-dawn mist, swiftly in a measured pace. He jogged over the cobblestone and the cement and the gravel paths. He jogged as the heavy rain blurred his vision and slowed his pace and he kept on jogging as the rain stopped and his sighting became clear. And his thinking became clear. Lack of exercise always fogged his mind. Today the fog was lifting, and the sweat being released from his pores was cleansing the pathways to his mind.

Today his instincts were telling him to leave Rome. He could hear the voice inside of him speaking clearly. It was not the usual rational voice that guided him. This time it was his battle instinct stirring. That same battle instinct that flowed from the reservoir of all his experience, intuition, and reason. It was the part of him that could sense the center of a danger before it arrived. Something had awakened his instinct, and he had not heard the instinct nor obeyed it until now.

It was becoming more and more difficult to hear the rhthyms of his soul, living on Earth, pretending to be something that he was not. He had been thinking too much like the cautious Richard Saxon. But no more. It was time to go home.

Richard turned a corner. He headed back toward his hotel room and Selina. He increased his speed. It was time to stop restraining himself, time to stop running away from unseen enemies. Time to stop worrying about Selina's safety every time she was out of his sight. Selina had been right when she had asked him six days ago, "Why don't we transport to the ship? I don't like waiting for ROSET to make the first move." Selina had been listening to her instincts, and he had not.

Richard bristled at the sight of a man who moved in and out of the shadows of a nearby building. He had seen that man before! He would end this paranoia today. He and Selina would transport to the ship today. They would contact Frank Nelson and get the uranium one way or another. They would hasten the repairs on the ship, and they would go home.

Richard could feel the sunrise. The rain clouds blocked the direct rays of the sun but the chill of the night air was gone. He was leaving Rome today. Leaving Earth. And he was ready to fight hell to make it happen.

VIII.

Selina won the argument without even arguing. "I want to attend Mass one last time. I want to see John Fisk ordained as a bishop today."

Richard didn't make her use a lot of words to explain herself. He could sometimes read her as if she were of Chadran blood. Selina's eyes sparkled. Her eyes pleaded gently, filled with the sadness of saying goodbye to Earth. Filled with trust in the man who was to take her away. Filled with longing to be with him at the cost of everything else. For all these thoughts he loved her. And he yielded to her. And he told his instincts that they could wait for four more hours before transporting to the starship.

They would be ready to transport immediately after the ordination. They would stay within the safety of the numbers of people surrounding St. Peter's. ROSET would never make a public spectacle of itself. It did not work that way. ROSET hid itself in shadows. Richard would keep himself and Selina in the sunlight and in the chapel light of the Sistine. And then they would transport to the ship in broad daylight. It was a safe plan.

Richard armed himself and Selina. And as they entered the richly ornate cavern of St. Peter's, as Selina lost herself in its beauty, Richard watched. He was on the alert, like a warrior ready to strike. He did not feel safe. He did not want to be here. What was wrong with him?

There was so much of the presence of God in this place. Would Richard never learn to rest in the knowledge of God's presence? Was his conversion only a flash of glory in a darkened place, his soul?

He looked at Selina, and her face was radiant. Her God was holding her close to Him, and Selina could feel it. She turned her head and smiled at him. She was wearing the gold pendant necklace which he had given her on her birthday, December thirty-first. He had explained to her that in Chadra, engaged couples or bonded couples do not exchange rings, they exchange pendants. Pendants were always symbolic of love and allegiance. There were two halves of this pendant. He wore one on a chain around his neck, and she wore the other half. When the two halves were placed together they read: "The Lord watch between you and me while we are absent one from the other."

It was his Chadran way of claiming her. She was bonded to him now. But it was also his Christian way of claiming her, of putting her in God's hands. It was hard to put her in anyone else's hands, even God's.

And then something caught Richard's attention. His eyes fixed on one frame of Michelangelo's great artwork on the ceiling of the Sistine Chapel. The series of paintings told the history between God and man. The painting that caught his eye was the depiction of Abraham tying Isaac to a rock and lifting a knife to sacrifice his only son. Richard felt himself freeze. *Selina is my Isaac.* The voice inside his heart spoke. *She is the one thing that I love before all else. I cannot imagine my future without her. And I would never raise a knife to sacrifice her. Even if... but God would never ask me to do such a thing.*

Selina belonged to Richard. But she also belonged to God. And so did Richard.

The Lord gives, and the Lord takes away. Blessed be the name of the Lord. A thought spoke in Richard's mind. *Get out of Rome today,* his instinct told him. And the music in the huge Basilica began to swell. It flowed everywhere. It echoed. And it soothed. Selina called it Gregorian Chant. And it sounded like the lullaby a great God might sing to His children. And it sounded like a cry of longing of the children for their Father. And in the music Richard sensed the deep pulse of God's patience. God was eternal, and He was patient with His children. God accepted Richard. Accepted his selfish grasp on Selina. Accepted Richard's impatience and anxiety. Loved Richard. And for one moment Richard felt God pass near him, and for one moment he was at peace.

IX.

Max Traytur moved carefully in the shadows of St. Peter's. He wound his way to the spot outside of the Sistine Chapel where he could watch from the entrance. He could still supervise and control without going inside the Chapel. And he was glad not to be going inside. The place filled him with contempt. His disgust was strong enough to distract him from his anxiety about the details of today's abduction. He hoped that the stupid ROSET Europeans would not miss their cues. The slightest error in timing could ruin everything.

Max rehearsed today's plan in his mind, savoring his sense of triumph. But his concentration was being interrupted by something stirring inside of him. Something was upsetting Max. It was the music of the seminarians choir. It was moving him, agitating him. There were horns as well as an organ accompanying the strong male voices. The baritones and tenors flowed in delicate harmony. Each verse of their song was in a different language. And then there was English, and Max could understand the words:

"Come to me. Come to me. To the house of God, to the House of your Father; for my love is sure. Come to me. Come to me. I will forgive your evil doing. And your sins I will remember never more."

The words meant nothing to him! Why was he moved by them? Moved until he felt a hard lump deep in his throat. Mesmerized by the caressing words, glued to the spot. Why was he leaning like some stone statue against the hard chapel wall? And then a terrible picture flashed into Max's mind. A picture of his tall, blonde father reaching to pick him up after he fell off the swing and hit his head. Little Max was only six, and he buried his face in his father's white shirt. He could feel the comfort of the white cotton. Max smeared his bloody nose and tears on his father's shirt and tie. Max wanted to be there. He wanted to be held in those protective arms. And then he pushed away from his father, like all the other times.

And then there was another terrible flash! Because Max knew what the music meant. What the memory meant. That God the Father was reaching to him. That God himself loved Max and wanted him. This sort of thing had happened before. But today it hit Max with such clarity--such clarity that it startled him. It terrified Max that he understood. And for one splitting second, it filled him with sadness. But only for that second. And then it filled him with rage!

"You want me to give it all up, God? Forget it! You want me to need you! Forget it! Max needs no one! You think that you are strong! Max is strong without you! Wait and see!"

Max noticed that the music stopped abruptly. As if someone had turned the handle of a faucet and the water stopped flowing. Max felt powerful. He could shake his fist at God. He could rebel! And make things happen.

X.

Selina felt the sudden jab of the needle in her right arm! Someone had thrust it hard enough to penetrate her clothing. She remembered turning her head, and everything went blank. Had she dreamed it? Wasn't she still walking down the aisle from Communion? A blurred picture came into her mind, a picture of Richard sitting in his pew and of her being a long aisle away from him. That's right, Richard did not leave his seat to go to Communion. And she did. But she couldn't hear the music anymore. The Gregorian Chant. Everything went blank again.

Now as she slowly opened her eyes, she was aware of a dizzying nausea. And intense white lights hanging directly over her head. Like in an operating room! Selina's heart raced. Anesthetic, formaldehyde, she could smell it everywhere! In one horrified sweep she recognized the lab equipment, the test tubes, the lights! She was in a clinical lab, and she couldn't move her arms or legs. Selina struggled. Both her hands and her feet were restrained. She was strapped to a stretcher!

No, dear God. No! Selina watched as two figures in lab coats came near her. Her vision cleared, then blurred, then cleared again. One of the figures was tall and pale. He was coming closer and closer.

My God, it's Max Traytur! For the first time in her life Selina felt terror. Cold terror!

Richard, where was Richard? Was he next to her on another stretcher? Was he safe? *My signet ring. I need to push it off my finger. That's all I need to do to get away. Get away!* Selina moved the trembling thumb on her left hand to push the ring off her middle finger. She pushed one side, then the other. The ring wouldn't budge past the knuckle. Her hands were sweaty and swollen. She kept on struggling, trying to move the ring. She felt hot. Then cold.

"It seems to be awake, Dr. Ungad." Traytur's hand looked massively large as it reached for Selina's face. He held her chin in his hand and turned her head from side to side.

Selina was paralyzed with fear. Perhaps it was because of Traytur's ugliness. Perhaps it was because of what she saw in his eyes.

"Sweet little specimen, you have no idea what torture you are about to undergo. We have the drugs to make you insane. But pain will do that job first. I am the only one in this room who cares about you. You do what I say, and I'll take care of you. The rest of them are animals. Say 'Yes, Max.'"

Nothing was working right in Selina's brain. He couldn't be saying the words she thought she heard! This couldn't be happening!

Selina saw his hand coming toward her face and then she felt a wave of dizziness and pain as he struck her.

"I ordered you to say, 'Yes, Max!'" He lifted his hand once more.

The eyes. The horrible eyes!

"Lord Jesus Christ, Son of the living God, help me," Selina whispered.

"Stop that!" Max went into a rage. Selina felt another pain, this time the left side of her jaw. She thought she had passed out. But she wasn't sure. She knew her eyes had closed. But she could still hear voices. And she could still feel pain. Voices speaking in German or French. The hitting stopped. And the voices seemed to get louder. And then she couldn't hear them anymore. Couldn't hear anything.

XI.

Richard knelt beside his bed alone. Alone. His hands covered his face, and he tried to pray. But he wasn't praying. Almost two hours had passed since Selina's abduction at the Sistine Chapel. And he had no idea what to do. How to find her.

The Italian police refused to help him. They said he could come to headquarters to file a missing person's report. But that he should wait for twenty-four hours before panicking. Had Richard been arguing with his woman before her disappearance? Maybe she needed time alone, they had said condescendingly. Even bribing the police did not help.

Why did ROSET take Selina and not him? Perhaps they knew more about him than he realized. Perhaps they knew that he was strong. That he would fight them all barehanded or armed. Perhaps they knew he would kill them in an instant if it were not for Selina's sake. And he wanted to kill them all.

How meticulously they must have planned her capture. Clearly they knew where Richard was now. Why didn't they come for him? Why were they making him wait like this? If they were watching him, they knew where he was. Waiting in his hotel room like a trapped animal. He could not transport to the ship without Selina. How would he ever find her? Did they know him well enough to know that?

Why didn't Selina slide the ring off her finger? *Do it now, Selina. Do it now. It takes no effort. Just use your right hand to slide the ring off your left hand. My ring will alert me that you have transported. And then I'll come too.* Even if they had her hands tied together, she could still slip her ring off. Unless...

The helplessness began to overwhelm him! *I cannot even help her from my great warship if I do not know where she is.*

He thought that everything had changed when he gave his life to God. That he would never feel powerless again. But now he felt powerless. He would rather die than feel powerless. He would rather die. But he couldn't die, not yet. Not until he had helped Selina. Only one prayer formed itself in his mind.

"Save her, O Lord. You who command the seas and the skies. You who made all things. Save her, O Lord."

And Richard thought of Jesus weeping in the Garden of Gethsemane. Weeping for all mankind. And weeping for Selina.

The sound of the phone jarred him and caused him a moment of hope and pain. Hope and pain. He had lost his cool. Even in battles where many lives had been at stake he had not lost his sense of cool control, his ability to win. But now he had lost his cool. Just for an instant. His voice was not steady when he answered the phone.

"We have Selina. If you want her you will obey us." The voice was foreign, the English labored.

"Prove to me that you have her and that she is well. She is wearing a large signet ring on her left hand. Remove the ring and read the inscription inside the ring. Then I will believe that you are holding Selina."

"We have no need to prove anything."

Richard hung up the receiver. He began to sweat. They did not call him back. His skin began to glow as twenty minutes passed. He paced the floor, praying to God that Selina's kidnappers would give him one more chance. He had made a mistake. He would demand nothing from them. He was their victim. Their pawn. They held all the cards.

The phone rang. He answered it during the first ring.

"We can wait for your cooperation forever. Can you wait for Selina forever? She may not live that long." It was an American's voice this time.

"Describe to me what she is wearing."

"A floral dress. Black stockings. And a gold chain around her neck. With a crucifix and half a circle. If the broken circle were placed with the other half it would read, 'The Lord watch between you and me while we are absent one from the other.' Touching. Is the Lord watching now?" The crusty voice taunted Richard. Richard was losing control.

"Let me talk to Selina."

"No." Pause. "Shall I hang up the phone this time, Saxon?"

"What do you want me to do?" Richard's voice was calm. But he felt something breaking inside of him.

"Come when we say come. No tricks, or Selina is dead." The American voice paused. "We choose the time. You obey."

Richard listened as the dial tone returned.

No. No. He could not take this waiting. They were trying to break him. It was working. What had he learned in battle school? *Never break. Die first, but never break. Where is your mercy, Lord? Where is your power?*

The phone rang once more. Richard let it ring three times. With each ring he thought his heart would break.

"We are in charge. Are you ready to obey?"

"I am ready." Richard said the words coolly and mechanically. He would say anything and mean nothing. That was the way a man could be a hostage without breaking. All he needed was to get close enough to Selina to remove her signet ring. He could do anything for that moment. First her ring, then his. He would take torture and humiliation. But he would live for that moment. And he would not break. God's grace was loosed like power in him, and Richard knew that he was ready to fight against hell. Fight ROSET. Ready to fight.

"A small black car will pull up in front of your hotel. A man will come for you and say, 'Your car is ready, Mr. Saxon.' He will search your room for weapons. Then you will get in the car and come to us. Do you know who we are?"

"I will do anything you say."

"Do you know who we are?"

"No, tell me." He would say anything. Do anything.

"The Research Organization for the Study of Extra-Terrestrials... And we have waited for you for a long time."

Silence.

"No tricks, Mr. Saxon. Selina will live if you obey. Die, if you do not."

"I will obey."

The car arrived half an hour later. Wherever they were, the ROSET people were half an hour from the heart of Rome. Richard needed to know where they had Selina. He would activate the homing device on his watch the instant the car stopped, the car that would take him to Selina. That way the ship could find her. Find both of them.

Richard was stoic as the hefty, bald stranger pushed him against the wall and searched his body for weapons. He was stoic as the man tore apart his hotel room, found his tubular gun and Sound Distort and kept them both. Richard walked obediently toward the black car. Everything that he had learned in battle school, he needed now. But the grace of God he needed more. He wanted to break their necks. He wanted to release his anger, his fear, and his pain.

The hefty man pushed him in the back seat of the car and sandwiched Richard in between himself and another man. The other man was Max Traytur. Richard did not express surprise at seeing Traytur.

"I am holding a hypodermic needle." Traytur held the needle close to Richard's face as he spoke. "Put your hands on your knees so that I can see them, and do not move a muscle, Saxon."

"If you drug me, it is the same thing as killing me. Your drugs will kill me." Richard fought back his pressing fear. He calmly placed both hands on his knees. The bald man slapped handcuffs across Richard's wrists.

"You can learn from me if I am alive. You can find out where the starship is located. You will lose everything if you kill me with your drugs," Richard spoke quietly.

"Thank you for telling me that! I didn't know it would be so easy to kill you." Traytur stuck the needle under Richard's nose.

"My people have traveled through space for 4,000 years. I have many secrets to trade for my life."

"Put the needle away, Traytur! Do you want to ruin everything?" the bald man suddenly shouted in his heavy accent.

"He's lying, Pendergast," Traytur said to the bald man.

"You will lose everything," Richard repeated softly.

"No, my friend. It is *you* who have lost everything. You are our prisoner. And so is your Selina." Traytur spoke slowly and deliberately.

Richard felt his anger like a pain in his gut. *Stoic. I can hide anything. I am a Chadran captain.*

"Selina knows how to defend herself," Richard said, keeping his voice calm and steady.

"Selina is so drugged that she doesn't know who or where she is, let alone how to defend herself." Traytur laughed to himself.

Panic dug its fingers into Richard's spine. *Stoic. I can hide anything. Say anything. Mean nothing. That is how not to break.* "Selina is waiting for the right moment," Richard said calmly.

"We have the priest, also. It wasn't easy snatching him from his 'celebration.' The police are looking for him even as we speak. But they won't find him. Because the head of Interpol is on our team." Traytur leaned close to Richard's face. In the dimming light of the dusk sun, Richard could see the horrible red eyes of his captor. "Nothing shakes you, huh, my prize alien? It will perhaps shake you to know that we have confiscated your home and its... weapons system."

"My home is not important."

"Your weapons system is."

"My home will self-destruct if you tamper with the security system."

Unconsciously, Richard rubbed the band of his wrist watch. The dial of his watch would light up if his computer self-destructed. Traytur was lying about having confiscated his home. Perhaps Traytur was lying about John Fisk as well.

Say anything. Mean nothing. Lie, Richard.

"You cannot capture all of us, Mr. Traytur. There are hundreds of my people on Earth. Even now, they await my signal to seize and destroy you and ROSET... unless you are kind to me and Selina and the priest."

Richard studied the frightened look that passed between Traytur and the bald man. His lie was working.

"If you kill, even hurt any of us, you will see a thousand kinds of fury come against you," Richard continued.

"He's lying, fool," Traytur said in answer to the expression on the bald man's face.

Suddenly, fear caught Richard off guard! The dial on his watch lit up, flashing once, then three times! Someone had just attempted to blow open the door of his computer room in Ann Arbor. And the computer and his whole house had just self-destructed. Everything was gone!

Traytur must have noticed the fear that registered on Richard's face. And then he noticed the dial on Richard's watch, flashing on and off.

"What's that?" Traytur snapped.

Richard did not answer. He had had enough. He was going to summon the starship. He couldn't wait until he reached the facility where Selina was being held. He was going to activate the homing device now!

Richard moved his right hand toward the watch on his left wrist. In that instant Traytur slapped his own hand on top of Richard's watch.

"He has a weapon!" Traytur shouted. Traytur pulled a knife from his long sleeve and slashed it across Richard's right hand. The pain and the spilled blood shocked Richard.

Traytur's hands were quick. He struggled to unlatch Richard's watch beneath the handcuff and to pull the flashing watch from his wrist. Richard grapped Traytur's wrist with his bleeding hand and almost snapped the wrist. Until he felt Traytur's knife slash through his right arm near the elbow. And then Traytur slashed Richard's left hand with his knife and grabbed the wrist watch. He tore the watch off Richard's bloody hand and threw it under the seat of the car.

Richard bent toward the floor and the bald man grapped him by the neck. "I..I have a needle too. I will... drug you if you get violent," the bald man said. Richard became very still. He let his arms go limp. And complied.

Traytur's knife had cut deep into the palms and underneath the thumbs on both his hands. His thumbs were numb. He realized how deep the wound on his right arm was, as the blood was sucking the shirt and coat into the wound. There was blood everywhere. The bald man released Richard's neck and fumbled with something in his pocket. He handed Richard a white hankerchief.

"Wr..wrap... bandage your wounds before you bleed to death," he said. "Traytur, p..please put the knife away."

The car stopped suddenly. It had turned its headlights off and was jammed inside a narrow alley between several buildings. The sun was setting, and it was dark in the alley.

I have lost my homing device. I cannot summon the ship. I cannot tell Frank or Jenxex where I am. I need to remove Selina's ring and my own, and we'll be safe. I can do this. Say anything. Mean nothing.

Traytur seemed to have gained some new vigor in his slashing of Richard. He shoved him through the alley and up four steps. Traytur was suprisingly strong. Or was Richard becoming weak because of losing blood? Richard struggled to appear calm and compliant. He was dying inside.

Someone flung a door open. The white fluorescent lights of the laboratory hurt Richard's eyes. He stood at the entrance of the room. The room was long and filled with people. He saw two stretchers in the end of the room farthest from him. John Fisk was tied to one. And then he saw Selina. She was strapped to the other stretcher. Her face was stark white, cut and bruised. Her dress was torn. She seemed to be miles away from him. He needed to get near her. He could not feel his thumbs.

Richard froze. *Think like a warrior. Think. Calm. Cold.*

"Don't drug me," Richard said in a loud, cool voice.

"Don't drug him!" the bald Pendergast ordered. He stood close behind Richard. Three men standing near the open door pulled guns from their pockets and pointed them at Richard at once. The sight of the loaded guns turned him into the warrior that he needed to be. *Guard your back. Count the enemy. Count their arms. Strike.* The Rule of Battle had its own clear voice in his mind. He counted thirty men and women. He could see two needles and three guns. There may have been more. He turned his head to look behind him. As he moved his head, Traytur bashed it against the cement wall. It stunned him. *Don't react, Sorn. Not yet. Choose your moment.*

"Someone bring me bandages for his hands immediately! Unless you want him dead within the hour!" Pendergast shouted.

Sorn stood still. He watched as the thick white gauze was wrapped tightly around his hands. Someone was covering his signet ring with the bandage. Reflexively, he pulled his hand away. In the same instant Traytur hit his face with the butt of a gun. Sorn winced at the pain. But he did not fight back. He did not want them to see his strength until he was ready to strike. Survival depended as much on the element of surprise as strength. He tried to push the pain out of his mind. The burning pain of the three knife wounds was distracting him. The pain of seeing Selina... like she was. *Forget the pain. Forget Selina. Get ready to attack. Three lives depend on you.* Sorn noticed a drop of sweat trickle into his eye from his forehead. No, it was blood, not sweat. More pain. Traytur hit him again with the butt of his gun. This time it was in the head. He was dizzy this time. He realized that he was breathing hard. He remembered how he had been trained, to steady himself after a blow to the head. Roll with the dizziness, and it would pass. He suddenly felt very cold. His mouth felt dry.

"Stop it, Traytur," someone said.

Sorn focused his eyes carefully on the face with the authoritative voice. A short, dark-haired man wearing a pony tail and a worn brown leather jacket grabbed Traytur by the shoulders and shoved him so hard that Traytur fell on the floor.

"We want this one to talk before he dies." The short man had a very young face and dark, cruel eyes. Now he stood between Sorn and Traytur.

"Why no drugs for this one? Drugs did not kill the other two."

"Because I am an alien. Drugs will kill me. The other two are not aliens. You should let them go."

"Traytur says that you are all aliens."

"If you give me drugs I will die instantly. If you keep me alive I can share a thousand secrets with you! A thousand wonders that you will never learn any other way." Sorn looked directly into the cruel, dark eyes of the young man. This man was in charge. Traytur did not order him away.

"We intend to cut your gut open to see if there are any wires or machines inside you."

"Ask Traytur about that. He cut through the flesh on my hands and arm. But aren't you asking the wrong questions? I can tell you how the stars change when you are traveling near the speed of light. I can explain anti-gravity to your scientists. My planet is 1,000 light years away from here. And every cubic inch of space between there and here is filled with mystery." The room had become very still.

Good, Sorn thought. *I have them. Their guard is down.* He was ready to strike.

"He is trying to catch you off guard, you fools! Don't listen to his ramblings until you have him restrained," Traytur shouted at no one in particular. At everyone. Sorn looked in the direction of Traytur's voice. Traytur was moving toward Selina. Traytur was holding a gun.

Sorn had lost his perfect moment. He had to try again.

"Four thousand years ago my people began to explore our galaxy. It was slow at first. But then we discovered something amazing..."

Sorn paused. They were listening to him. They were more intersted in his voice than Traytur's. More curious than afraid. He would have only one chance. He inhaled deeply. And made his first move. His right arm pulled free of his captors, and he reached for the neck of the cruel young leader. Sorn snapped his neck and watched as his gun fell. He jabbed his left elbow into the chest of the one standing nearest to him with the needle. He held nothing back. He flattened everyone who interfered with his path to Selina. He swung and he kicked, and his skin glowed. He shot bolts to knock the guns and needles from their hands. His feet were working well as he kicked. His hands were not.

The bandage on his right hand loosened as he delivered blows with it. Blood was soaking through the gauze. His head throbbed. He was losing strength with his blood loss. He would not have long to fight. But he was winning. And then he heard a gunshot.

"The next bullet goes into Selina's brain!" Traytur shouted, standing only inches from Selina's head. So Richard had missed Traytur's gun when he had thrown a bolt at him earlier! Traytur grabbed Selina by the hair. And looked very calm.

Som paused and focused on Traytur. He could not pause more than seconds, or he would be dead. Traytur's hand was shaking slightly. He had not yet cocked the lever of his gun. Som could kick the gun out of Traytur's hand before Traytur could pull the trigger. It would have to happen that way! Som's anger gave him strength. His anger was like a spring inside of him, coiled tighter and tighter and waiting to be released. He sprang toward Traytur and kicked. The gun flew out of Traytur's hand. And then Som swung with his right arm. The force of the blow pushed Traytur's nose into the front of his brain. Traytur did not even scream as he fell. Richard reached for Selina's hand and barely brushed against it. Someone grabbed him. And then he felt the needle in his shoulder. And he knew the drug would kill him. Everything went black.

XII.

Captain Som was dying. There was no time for caution or courtesy. To hell with all the aliens! Abthulzar gave her order as she and two of her team aimed the guns at each of the Earth humans in the laboratory. She sprayed the paralyzing rays into their bodies as they stood with stunned expressions on their faces. The stun would not kill them. Lohnarks' anger might. Lohnarks had at first been gentle in removing only the roof of this dwelling so that the Rescue Team could transport inside quickly.

"Som's vital signs are failing fast. They injected him with something lethal. We have the needle for analysis. I'm taking him on ship." The chief medical officer did not look up when he addressed Lieutenant Abthulzar. Abthulzar watched as the three medics worked on Som. Nothing else mattered.

The medics rubbed the bands on their wrists, summoning emergency transport. Then the three of them shielded Som with their bodies, feverishly injecting him with fluids and oxygen. A tiny swarm of air bubbles formed a thick cocoon around Som and the medical team. Then the wire mesh of copper-colored metal fabric formed a thick cocoon around the four. The cocoon craft shot up like a bullet into the night sky, headed for the Journey Ship *Horizon*.

Abthulzar was anxious. She looked around the room. Som had put up a fight before he went down. Why did they attack him? The thin Albino lying on the floor was very dead. So were three others.

Evimator rushed toward Abthulzar. "Lieutenant, we must also take those two humans with us, those who are restrained on the tables. When our weapons froze the others, I saw two angels shielding them from the spray. Observe, they are not frozen." Evimator pointed excitedly.

"I have no interest in taking aliens aboard the *Horizon*," Abthulzar said.

Abthulzar had not seen the angels. All she had seen in those first seconds was a half-dead Sorn. But Evimator was trustworthy. And the two restrained humans had indeed not been affected by their weapons.

Abthulzar walked toward the woman on the stretcher, scrutinizing her face for clues. The woman was young and delicate looking. She had been beaten, as had the man on the stretcher. Abthulzar noticed the neck chain on the woman's chest. She lifted the neck chain into the palm of her hand and examined it.

"She is Captain Sorn's woman. Sorn was wearing a medallion like this one," Abthulzar said.

"What is she babbling about, Lieutenant?"

"Who knows? I can't understand their language any better than you, Evimator." The other Tethrans drew near Selina and studied her. Abthulzar stiffened for an instant and listened to Captain Lohnarks' voice in her earring.

"The Captain orders us to return to the ship immediately. So that he can destroy these people and their facility. He does not want even one of them to escape," Abthulzar said.

"The woman and the other? We cannot leave them to die, Lieutenant," Evimator said. Abthulzar looked again at Selina's medallion.

"Transport Sorn's friend. I will transport his woman," Abthulzar ordered.

The man on the stretcher fought his rescuers. Once they untied him from the stretcher, he kicked and shouted. It took two Tethrans to hold him.

Abthulzar turned her attention to the woman. She found herself being gentle with the beaten woman. The woman did not struggle once she was untied. She looked up drowsily at Abthulzar and touched her own medallion.

"Sorn," she said with a funny nasal emphasis. Her green eyes were sad.

"Sorn," Abthulzar acknowledged, and she pointed toward the sky.

The green-eyed woman said something to the frantic Earth man. It calmed him. He relaxed just as the first cocoon began to enfold him. Abthulzar pulled the young woman close to her so that the second cocoon craft would form around both their bodies. She watched the Earth female with intense curiosity. As the transport craft formed around them and started its ascent, she saw not fear but relief on the young woman's face. And then the green-eyed woman began to cry.

XIII.

Max Traytur did not scream. Not at first. The pain was so intense that he could do nothing. Pain everywhere, in his head and eyes and tingling up and down his spine! Pain so excruciating that it shattered reality into chunks of rationality and flashes of light. And then the intense pain ended abruptly, and all he had was a pulsing memory of pain. Suddenly, it felt as if a wind sucked him out of his body. He found himself floating, hovering near the ceiling above his own twisted corpse.

No. This cannot be happening. No. No! Max thought wildly.

But "it" was happening, and he watched it all. Watched as the aliens shot into the room in their copper pods and paralyzed everyone. Watched as the aliens rescued the Tethra Triangle. Max watched, and he could do nothing, and he was consumed with hate. Max tried to scream. But his scream was silent. Then he watched as a white hot flash erased the clinical lab and everybody and everything in it. Erased his own body from the face of the earth.

Max felt a cold dread creep through him. Then fear. Then panic. "I cannot be dead! I'm still alive. When you die you die. There is no life after death. But I'm still alive! What the hell is happening to me?"

"You chose the correct word, Max, hell. Hell is both a place and a state of mind. They are both yours." It was Natas speaking. His voice was soft and close. Too close. And then Max screamed, and he heard his own scream, and he felt his own scream. He was falling down a tunnel, being sucked by a terrifying blizzard. Natas swirled like a gust of wind around him. Natas was all that he could see. Natas was everywhere and everything. As if Natas were a red-speckled blizzard and he, Max, was a tiny animal caught in the storm. Nothing seemed real. The colors were all wrong. Everything was wrong. Max wasn't sure whether he was still moving or standing still. Then he seemed to sway back and forth. Natas didn't look right. His facial features were all mixed up, floating in the deep red blizzard. Max thought that he was going insane! Natas' facial features floated together in one place and stared at Max and spoke to him.

"No, Max, you are not going insane. You will never go insane. Insanity is an escape that will evade you. But you will always thirst for the kind of sanity that you knew on earth. That kind of sanity will torment you. The memory of what it used to be like will never leave you. But you are here with me now. You have entered a dimension of chaos and pain that humans were never meant to enter. You chose it. You chose yourself as your god. And you chose me.

"You served me on Earth, and you will serve me in hell... eternally. Except it will not be like it was on Earth, Max. On Earth there was a cord connecting you to the Triumphant Christ. You could have taken that cord at any time and used it to pull yourself toward God. You could have gotten away from me at any time. And so I was limited in how I could torture you. Now there are no limits. No limits to the pain that you can take. No limits on how I can torture you. And torture you, I will."

"You lied to me, Natas, you repulsive, vicious, drooling savage, you lied to me! You said there was no heaven and no hell. You said there was no God and no such thing as sin. Only energy and power. And that everything was relative!"

"You knew that I was lying, worthless one. The law is written on your hearts. You all know that I am lying in the beginning. Your pride tells you that you are the only god who should be served. After accepting that fact, it is your own lies that bind you. You betrayed yourself, Traytur. In the latter days of your life I told you about sin and about how I covet sin. By then you thought that I, Natas, was a fool." Natas spoke in a cold, disembodied voice. And then he vanished.

Everything grew frighteningly still. Miserably silent.

Natas is gone! I must escape! Max turned and looked around for an escape. He saw nothing but a vast flat gray emptiness surrounding him. And then he saw a huge mirror floating toward him. Max ran to it. He looked in the mirror, hungry for the consolation of seeing his own familiar face. As he looked, the mirror changed, and Max saw his whole life flash before his eyes. Everything. He saw with a searing clarity who he really was and what he had done. He saw that he had no one he could blame. The mental anguish tore through him, and he wept. He wept until he could not bear any more of it. His weeping made him ravenously thirsty. And he knew that what he thirsted for was God. His thirst repulsed him. But still it lingered. Thirst without end.

"Stop this! Stop this! Give me a drink. I cannot stand any more! I'm going to die!" Max screamed. His scream was a prayer, and the one he prayed to answered him.

"You cannot die. You already died," Natas said. He reappeared out of nothingness. This time he was not the blizzard. This time he looked like the Natas of Earth. Natas raised a huge claw and dug it into Max's right shoulder and severed the arm from its dripping, throbbing socket. Max fainted from the pain. When he woke up, he found Natas chewing on his other arm, tearing him apart into agonizing, twitching pieces. Max thought he fainted again. But he wasn't sure. He did not know how long he was unconscious. Time did not exist. He craved the sanity of order and time. Max tried to stay unconscious. But it didn't work. The terrible pain woke him.

"What are you going to do to me?" Max screamed.

"Whatever I want," Natas answered.

This time the poisonous claw headed for Max's groin. It leeched and tore. Max fainted for an instant. Or maybe it was for an hour. But when he awoke, he saw Natas' hideous, dripping claw. And it started all over again.

CHAPTER
THIRTY-TWO
HORIZON

Selina had trouble catching her breath. She gasped for air! When the cocoon craft reached the wide loading dock of the ship, it cracked open like a chicken egg. Immediately the pressure and oxygen changed. Selina lost her balance and fell into the tall woman's arms. Selina couldn't understand a syllable of her language. But the Tethran treated her with courtesy. Selina couldn't see her face or any of their faces until they peeled the gray film of clothing from their bodies. The film was like a second skin clinging to them, probably for protection from Earth-born bacteria. Underneath they wore one-piece Navy uniforms like the one Jenxex wore in the hologram. The Tethrans were tall and vigorous and efficient.

The rescuers half-carried Selina and John through some sort of chemical shower before taking them off the loading dock. The shower felt like icy air that penetrated their cells and quickly disappeared from their senses. It had a tart piercing smell, which also disappeared quickly.

And then Selina felt someone's hands gently push her into a chair and scan her with what must have been a diagnostic medical instrument. Selina's emotions were crowding her reason. The new atmosphere was overwhelming. Everything was colorless and sterile and noisy. The Tethran woman lost interest in Selina and left her.

"Sorn," Selina said, looking into the face of the medical officer. The medic peered at Selina without expression. He touched a swollen sore spot near her eye. Selina winced. "Sorn. Sorn. Take me to Sorn. Is he all right?" Selina insisted. She tried to pull herself out of the chair. It seemed they were all ignoring her. Selina could see John Fisk, a few yards away.

John was so weak that he was barely conscious. The medical team hovered over his body, talking softly to one another.

In the next minute, Selina realized that her chair was moving. Some sort of gravity had pushed her back into the chair, and she found herself moving passively through high metallic corridors. Richard had prepared her for the *Stealthfire*. This was not the *Stealthfire*. This was the size of a city. There were winding hallways, doors, and uniformed people everywhere. The familiar woman hurried toward Selina and caught the side of her moving chair. They passed into a clear glass elevator and traveled two stories, looking down on the sprawling city. Selina's head was spinning, and everything looked like a blur.

"Take me to Sorn," Selina said, and her voice sounded weak and hoarse.

The doors of the elevator opened. Selina felt a wave of relief when she saw Frank Nelson standing there in street clothes.

"Richard is being treated in the hospital unit. We are taking you to him," Frank said.

"Is John Fisk all right?" She asked quickly.

"John Fisk?" Frank spoke to the Tethran woman in their language. They talked for what seemed a long time. Selina interrupted them.

"Please have John brought here, too. He is terrified. He has no idea what is going on."

"And you have, Selina?" Frank asked. He gazed intently at her. "You don't seem surprised to see me here."

"Can I see Richard now? I was afraid that the ROSET people... had killed him." Selina felt her eyes filling up with tears. She deserved an answer.

Frank did not answer her. Instead he continued talking to the tall woman. Selina was miserable. She couldn't understand their language. She couldn't even read their strange facial expressions. She tried once more to get out of the chair, but the gravity held her back.

Frank moved ahead of her and touched his hand on the corner of a huge white double door. It opened at his touch.

Frank leaned close to Selina and spoke. "Abthulzar is second in command of this ship. I told her that you are Captain Sorn's future wife. The Chadrans are... cautious about bringing you close to him. Be patient."

"Is he all right?" Selina asked.

"I don't know. They don't know."

Selina felt dizzy. None of this seemed real. Richard had to be all right. He had to be.

A set of white doors opened on Selina's left side. Another tall uniformed Tethran came through the left doors. He was gray-haired and had large, dark, kind eyes. He stared at Selina as he spoke to Abthulzar and Frank. *Why don't any of these people ever smile or frown or look surprised?* Selina thought.

"She is the one, Captain Lohnarks." Frank started speaking in both languages so that Selina would understand. Frank lifted Selina's wrist and flipped her watch to reveal the homing device. "The enemy must have captured Selina first. She activated her homing device alert system thirty-five minutes before Kollann arrived at the place. That is how you found Kollann in time."

Selina listened as they spoke more Chadran. Then she interruped Frank.

"I want to see Richard now."

"Please be patient. He is not conscious." Frank leaned close to Selina again. "Captain Lohnarks told me the story of Kollann... Richard's rescue. The Journeyship was going to turn around and return to Tethra a week ago. They were only one week's distance from Earth! Lohnarks couldn't bring himself to give the order to leave. A day later they had come close enough to Earth to discover satellites orbiting the planet. The satellite technology showed them that Earth was populated by humans. Humans with unthreatening technology. Their curiosity was too intense to turn back.

"It would have been impossible for them to find you and Kollann because the *Stealthfire* was hidden. But when ROSET captured you and you activated your homing device, it set off the chain reaction. The *Stealthfire* came out of hiding, Jenxex pinpointed your location, and Lohnarks sent a rescue team."

Selina began to relax. Richard's life must not be in danger. Otherwise all these people would not consider their rescue a success. She was suddenly aware of all her aches and pains. Traytur had not raped her as he had threatened. But he had hit her repeatedly. And the drugs they gave her were making her weak and nauseous. She must have looked like a wreck. But they were safe now.

Frank had been speaking Chadran to Captain Lohnarks. Then he turned toward Selina.

"Captain Sorn is asking for you, Selina. Your name was the first conscious word he spoke. The crew is quite impressed that he asked for you."

The gray-haired Captain Lohnarks looked hard at Selina. And then he did an odd thing. He bowed to Selina by bending at his waist. He did not move his mouth, but he smiled through his eyes. Then he escorted Selina in her chair through the white doors to the "hospital." The room was filled with medical equipment. Rows of uniformed people stood on both sides of the hall and into a long room. Richard was lying in the center of the room, pale and bandaged and very still. The people stood silently with their stiff posture and unmoving faces. Selina sensed the tension in the room. Every eye was on Kollann-Richard. She fought the gravity of her chair and stood next to him. It would worry him to see her sitting. She reached for one of Richard's bandaged hands. He did not move. She brushed the sweaty hair from his forehead, and this time he responded to her touch. He opened his eyes and looked at her.

"You meant it when you said that you would never leave me," he said weakly.

"I will never leave you."

"The Lord God has given us a miracle, Selina. Let's use it well."

Selina nodded. She did not try to hold back the flow of tears. Richard closed his eyes again.

Lohnarks came next to Selina and gently nudged her into the chair. He escorted her out of the hospital and back to the area where Frank waited.

"I want to be with him," Selina insisted, looking directly at Captain Lohnarks but speaking to Frank.

"Richard is doing well but he needs to sleep. Believe me, Selina, he is in good hands. Everyone aboard this starship is sworn to defend him with their lives. To all of us, your Richard, Kollann Sorn, is the most valuable person in this or any other galaxy," Frank said.

"Because he is the Hegemon's brother?" Selina asked.

"No, because Kollann Sorn is the Hegemon."

II.

Frank Nelson made Selina wait for a full explanation. The medics were impatient to "regulate Selina's system" and to heal her wounds. Frank stayed with Selina while the medics examined and tested and pampered her. Frank translated for the medics and showed them how to get the medical data and background from the computers of Earth, so that they could understand and care for the alien humans. Six hours later, Frank had John Fisk brought to Selina. And then Frank stayed with Selina for the next twenty hours while Kollann was sleeping. Frank hovered near Selina like a loyal guardian. He was blunt and impatient. But Frank loved to talk, and this served Selina well.

"Kollann's father was the Monarch of Chadra. He died almost three years ago, and Kollann's older brother Jarn became the new monarch. For the past two hundred years the Monarch of the nation of Chadra has also been the Hegemon for the United Alliance of Planets," Frank began.

"Kollann's brother Jarn was born and bred to assume the throne, although few thought that he would do so until he was an old man. Kollann's father died at the age of 65. That is young for a Chadran.

"Eight months ago the Greole assassinated Jarn. It was a shockingly clever maneuver. They assassinated their own ambassador in order to kill Jarn at the same time. Jarn's death threw the free worlds into a panic. Kollann's younger sister, Ishpenar, dutifully assumed the throne. But Princess Ishpenar does not have a stomach for war. She immediately commissioned this journeyship to seek and find her brother, Kollann. Kollann is next in line to the throne after Jarn.

"But Kollann is more than that. He is the perfect wartime ruler for the people of the Alliance. He is more of a natural leader than Jarn. Kollann is competent and shrewd when it comes to military thinking and planning. The fact that he entered starfleet as a commoner and earned his commission as an officer gained him uncanny public respect. So much so, that after Jarn became King, some of Jarn's closest advisors saw Kollann as a threat to Jarn. They manipulated things so as to have Kollann shipped to a worthless region of the solar system, a place called the Red Ice Quadrant. When the Greole attacked Kollann's starship, some even thought that the Greole had a little help from Chadran high command--to get Kollann out of the way so that Jarn could rule. Of course, this would be high treason. But Lohnarks told me that he has been putting together the pieces one-by-one in these last months." Frank paused. He looked at Selina and sipped his cup of hot Sui.

"Kollann didn't know any of this, Frank, did he? And he did not know that his brother Jarn had died," Selina asked.

"Kollann and I have had no communication with Tethra for the past sixteen months. We are learning these things at the same time that you are. Kollann probably won't accept the possibility that we were chased from Tethra by his political enemies. He's too good-hearted," Frank said.

"Perhaps Kollann has too much faith in God," John Fisk said. John had been sitting silently, listening, evaluating everything that Frank said.

"I think it was the sovereign hand of God that brought Kollann to Earth. Kollann found Jesus Christ, not only for himself but for all of you on Tethra."

Frank said nothing.

John continued anyway. Selina knew that no one could discourage John once he had decided to say something.

"Kollann also found Selina. And he found his homeland Earth, your homeland. Like the Changelings promised long ago. 'When the separated brethren are united, it will be the joy of the right hand finding the left hand!'" John looked squarely at Frank.

"It is treason for me to be impolite to Selina. But I can argue with you, priest," Frank snapped.

"Does it offend you to have me quote your sacred mythologies? I meant no harm. I know that you think of me as an alien. But a strange thing has happened inside of me," John said. "I don't feel like an alien to your people. I feel like a brother."

"You have been here for less than twenty-eight hours, and already you have read our classics? Nothing has been translated into English!" Frank glared at John as he spoke.

"One of your crew, Evimator, has been exceptionally kind to me. It was he who gave me this Deist Changeling prophecy. He has been working with Jenxex to translate other things also," John said.

Frank smacked his cup hard on the table and stood up.

"There is something that you need to understand, John." Frank paused. He looked at Selina, and she knew that he was addressing her also, whether he used her name or not. "We Chadrans are nationalistic and proud of who we are. The Monarch, the Hegemon, is as close to an idol as you will ever know. He epitomizes everything good about us, our self-respect, our dreams, our values. And you people, you are aliens and yet you are intimate with him. There will be some resentment for a while. We can't... we won't accept you... for a while."

Frank looked guiltily at Selina, then at the floor. There was a quiet pause.

"But Frank, it is you who are the bridge. It is you who must take us across from one land to the other. You and Kollann are the only ones who speak both languages and understand both sets of hearts." John said it gently. There was another pause.

"You people are impossible to hate!" Frank said in an angry voice. "Selina makes me feel like a member of the royal family. And you make me feel like the Apostle to the Lost Children." Frank looked exasperated, and then he started laughing. He laughed hard, and when he was finishing, Selina noticed the entrance pad to her quarters blinking.

"Come in," she said.

Kollann stood at the entrance as the doors parted for him. It was the first time she or anyone had seen him standing on two feet since ROSET's assault. He was a beautiful sight, standing there in his navy starfleet uniform with its simple style and flattering lines. His face was still flushed with a vanishing fever. But he looked younger, stronger, and ready to lead.

A medical officer stood on his right side, and a stoic member of the royal guard stood on his left.

"I wanted to come home to you, Selina. They wanted me to stay in the hospital. So we compromised. They came too."

Selina glanced around the wide, colorless room without lamps, instead with glistening panels of light that responded to voice commands. Without windows, but only portholes like on an ocean liner. Without an ocean, but only the stars. The leather-like gray furniture was not really leather, and there were no paintings nor works of art anywhere--only the Ytar plant that Selina saw and loved and asked them to bring to her quarters. But Kollann called this "home," because she was in it. And she knew that she could make it that for him. And for herself. "Welcome home, darling," she purred.

III.

Abthulzar watched attentively while the King addressed them. King Kollann sat at the head of the narrow, long, charcoal-colored table. Selina, his future wife, sat at his side. He held her hand, a gesture that was obviously a habit of Earth-origin. And King Kollann did it for a reason. He was showing them, all of the top-ranking crew as they sat before him, that many of the ideas and some of the culture of the Earthwoman would be adopted, would be respected for her sake. He was the King, and he could change the very texture of Chadran culture if he chose. They knew him, and they trusted him. Whatever he changed he would change carefully, respecting Chadra, its people, and the values it held dear. But he would make changes for the Earth woman's sake. Big ones and small ones. He was already telling them that, by the holding of her hand. No doubt the hand-holding thing brought Selina a type of comfort. Abthulzar thought that she could read it in Selina's eyes.

Although it was not easy to read this Selina. So many of her gestures and her facial expressions were strange. It would be hard to understand her--if one could not read her facial expressions easily and could not speak her oral language.

And then Abthulzar put herself in Selina's place in her mind. It was the thing the Ytar empaths had trained her to do, to study new species or to understand another human better. Abthulzar imagined sitting next to King Kollann and being his future wife. She imagined being Selina's size and age. Smaller and younger. Selina had left everyone to be with him. And now she sat at a table looking at a group of aliens. She could not read their facial expressions or their gestures. She could not speak their language and would not speak it well for some time. Selina had no female companions as friends. Her only companions were the King, Ont Zejen, the priest from Earth, and an android named Jenxex. Selina must be very brave, must have a deep courage within her, to love a man like Kollann Sorn. Kollann was a genius, and this did not frighten Selina. Kollann was the King, and it did not frighten her. And Kollann was an alien, and still she was not afraid.

Abthulzar smiled as she looked at Selina. The Earthwoman was small and looked fragile like a child. But she was the most couragous female aboard the Journeyship *Horizon*. Abthulzar would try to be her friend, would try to help her to become a Chadran. Would try to learn from Selina about courage. Selina would need at least one woman friend, just as all women need women.

IV.

"Qeeswick was the one who finally figured out the code. He has no position or status, but he is gifted, and you have always known that. No one would have paid any attention to him except another Sorn. Your sister Ishpenar had him relieved of his regular duty and well compensated in pay to break the coded message you sent from Earth. It took him nearly seven weeks. I helped Qeeswick, but I am not so skilled in decoding as he is.

"You put a twist in it, Your Majesty. If you had only used the one language and set of numbers we agreed on. But you had to put this twist of illogic in the code that drove us mad." Lohnarks smiled. He sat in the privacy of his conference quarters, where the walls would absorb and distort all sound.

"Thank you for not giving up, Lohnarks," Sorn said.

"I almost did. Thank Qeeswick when you see him." Lohnarks nearly reveled in the joy he felt being with Sorn.

"I resisted sending a message to Ishpenar and the Hegemonic Body telling them that you are alive and that we have found you. I leave the honor of that move in your hands, King," Lohnarks said, and he lowered his voice.

"You are wise, Lohnarks. For now, no one outside of this ship must know that I am alive. No one except the Commander-In-Chief at the Prime Ansible."

"Princess Ishpenar?"

"Even Ishpenar must not know, not at first. Ishpenar has the power to keep our secret well hidden. Everything that you have told me about the progression of the war shows me that the Greole's strength is in their continued surprises. I want us to master the element of surprise," Kollann said.

Kollann stood up from his chair and walked across the room. He touched the wall of the starship, gently exploring it like some foreign object. Lohnarks sat in respectful silence.

"Love your enemies. Pray for those who persecute you," Kollann said softly, talking to himself.

"Sir?" Lohnarks asked.

"Do you have security clearance to know the location of the Commander-In-Chief and the Prime Ansible?" Sorn asked.

"As far as I know, no one on board has that level of security clearance."

"Someone does. No Journey ship is ever missioned without the knowledge of Central Command. Central command always retains a hidden link to itself aboard each ship."

"I did not know that. And I have been an officer for eighteen years."

"You know other things that I don't know," Sorn said.

"Then you know the location of the Prime Ansible?"

"I knew it 24 months ago. It may have changed. That is our destination, Lohnarks. The Prime Ansible and Central Command. Once we journey there, no one from this ship will ever leave it. Not until the war has been won and all security clearances have been lifted. But when we go home, Tethra will be free and the war won."

"So be it, King Kollann."

"Have you decided to follow my recommendation to bring the *Stealthfire* with us?" Sorn asked.

"Yes, Your Majesty. It will fit into the loading dock of my ship if we get rid of two probes. I wanted to leave the probes behind anyway, to continue their exploratory data collection."

"The probes must be disconnected from the ansible."

"Of course, sir. Earth will remain our secret," Lohnarks said.

"One last thing. I have asked the priest, John Fisk, to come with us. Selina and I need him to bring the gospel and the sacraments to us and to whoever else wants to share our faith."

"So you have made your decision, King Kollann."

"Yes. And John Fisk has made his."

"Then we must wait another week orbiting Earth while he goes to seek permission from his commander," Lohnarks said, looking anxious. "The crew resents having to delay departure for the sake of..."

"An alien," Sorn finished. He walked closer to Lohnarks and looked directly at him.

"John Fisk is a lifeline for me. I need his help."

"You are the Hegemon. Why must you ask anyone for that which you need?"

"I have no authority over John Fisk's commander. It is as it should be."

"I understand none of this. But I trust you. I am your servant, and I will keep my ship here for a week--or forever--to serve you."

"Thank you, Lohnarks."

"You have picked up this habit of saying 'thank you' while you were on Earth. It honors me."

"You are right, Lohnarks, I learned to say 'thank you' on Earth. I was arrogant before."

"If John Fisk's commander refuses to send him out with us, I will want to rain down missiles on him," Lohnarks said.

"I know that you will want to. But we will hold back our missiles."

Lohnarks did not understand why King Kollann smiled broadly and patted him on the shoulder.

V.

John Fisk placed the tiny yellow tablet under his tongue and raised his hand to signal the transport back to Earth. Rowing a splintery canoe in Peru had been much easier than this type of missionary travel. Within minutes, the copper-colored craft cocooned his body and shot him from the orbiting Journeyship through the atmosphere, landing him smoothly on the surface of the Earth. He marveled at the cocoon shuttle! Such speed and such precision and a buffered landing that left him only vaguely shaken. The yellow tablet had indeed made a difference with this trip. There was no loss of breath or nausea when the craft opened in the Italian breeze. In fact, John felt invigorated. Even euphoric. In only the last three days he had witnessed wonders and had adapted to changes that he had never dreamed possible. And he had also found the place where he could live out his call to serve God. He was to be the first Bishop for the nation of Chadra. He felt excited when he thought about it.

But as two days of tedious anticipation passed, John found that he was already losing heart. The Vatican bureacracy turned its painsaking wheels in response to his urgent request for a private, confidential audience with the Pope. John had been arrogant enough to request it immediately and without giving an adequate explanation to the Cardinal and his other superiors.

The experienced members of the papal staff were annoyed with John. And then they were shocked when his urgent request was granted. None of them understood why it happened so fast! Only two days after his formal request, Bishop Fisk found himself waiting for his meeting with the Pope in the papal offices.

John fidgeted nervously. He was not easily intimidated. But he was intimidated today. His stomach was tied in knots. He felt healthy and strong like an ox. The Tethrans had begun to work their medicine and their vitamins on him. In some ways he felt like a new man. But his stomach did not know this yet. He stood up and began to pace the elegant waiting area. Its towering ceilings echoed when he sneezed.

It was not the thought of talking with the Pope that made him nervous. The Pope was only a man, and a kind one at that. What made John nervous was the business that he had to discuss with the Holy Father.

John had rehearsed his speech several times. He had arranged and rearranged the order of his sentences. But the story always came out the same. John Fisk had recently been aboard a starship filled with unbaptized humans who needed a priest to come and stay with them. To preach the gospel to them. John would work hand-in-hand with a Christian married couple. Would the Holy Father send John to be a missionary for them?

Hopefully, the Pope would not send John somewhere else, like to a hospital for a long involuntary rest.

John started when the papal aide tapped him on the shoulder and escorted him through the hall and into the wide, clean room with its bare white walls. The Pope stood up from his huge mahogany desk with the dark green marble top. He walked quickly toward John and greeted him in English. It was the Pope's way of showing John respect, telling him that he was coming to John on John's terms. John bent on one knee to kiss the ring of the beloved Polish Pope. But the Holy Father shook his head to forego the courtesy of kissing his ring.

"Could we walk in the garden, Your Holiness? So that no one will overhear us?"

The Pope smiled warmly and nodded. And then they walked. And John told him everything. About having known Selina for nine years, about Sorn and his conversion to Christ. And then about the Journeyship *Horizon*. John talked fast and furiously. He made no apologies. He gave only facts.

And the Holy Father said nothing. It was only when John reached the part of his story where he told the ancient myth of the Changelings, and how the Changelings told the murderer's children a prophecy. That one day "the separated brethren would be reunited. It would be the joy of the right hand that had found its left hand." It was only then that the Holy Father stopped walking, stopped frowning, and stopped listening. He looked directly into John's eyes.

"It is well past the time when the lost children of Cain should receive the gospel of Jesus Christ." The Holy Father said softly. And there was a heaviness and a sorrow in his voice when he said it.

"The Lord spoke to me many years ago and told me that before I died I would commission a bishop to serve the Lost Children of Cain. Those children of God who had no hope for 2,000 years but the seeing of the Star of Bethlehem in the heavens." The Holy Father spoke softly.

"They did see the Christmas Star. They named it the Angel Fire," John said. He was awestruck, and he did not know what else to say.

"God the Father has never forgotten. Not one of us. Not one hair on any of our heads," the Holy Father whispered. And as he spoke, John noticed that his lip was trembling and that a large tear had trickled down the wrinkled face of the old Pope.

There was no need to say much more. They both knew who they were and what to do. The young bishop knelt at the old Pope's feet and bowed his head. And the Pope placed his hands on the bishop's head and prayed. He prayed for John Fisk, commissioning him, sending him out to Tethra, so far away and yet not too far. And as they prayed the young bishop felt new waves of emotion rolling through him, he reached and grabbed the papal robes and he clutched the Pope, like a child might hug his father for comfort. Or perhaps out of habit because it felt good. And the Pope embraced John and called him "my son." And they both wept.

This time they wept for joy. In that unique way of two people who had sacrificed many times and made all their choices and placed all their hopes and dreams in one place, for the one purpose, the coming of the Kingdom of God. And now, as they witnessed themselves as being at the center of that great coming, there was no greater joy. And in their celibate hearts and in their celibate souls which had been cleansed to channel grace, they were cleansed with joy. The joy of the Lord, which had been, was and always would be, their strength.

It was a windless day. The overcast winter sky cleared only for a moment. And John saw a wisp of sunlight as it made its way through a cloud to shine on the two men in the garden. And in the still, windless moment of sunlight, they both knew deep in their souls that something new had just been born. And they could barely take it in.

VI.

Archangel Michael and his warriors stood vigilantly and watched the two men in the garden. There were seven thousand angels surrounding the men. The angels were poised over them, under them, and on every side. The warriors had braced themselves for a major battle with Natas--a battle that never came. Natas would wreak his vengence on the weak today. Somewhere in the exposed, lost corners of the world there would be suffering. But for now, in this moment past the Turning Point, the Angels guarded the Pope and the bishop. And the angels could feel their joy.

"They have won, and we have won with them, in establishing the perfect triangle, man and woman and the clergy, joined as one in Christ. We have gained a foothold in these first days of the new twenty-first century," Michael said.

"It burns me to think of the wrath that came against these humans! Not only the Tethra Triangle. But all the Triangles who have fought to find their place in this century. I remember the pain and the paralyzing confusion they have felt," Gabriel said.

"I remember the day each of them was born," Michael said. And his smile brought the sun back into the winter sky.

"We will send seventy legions with the journeyship *Horizon*. The legions that have been waiting for this day." Michael turned and faced his armies. And the angels sang a victory song.

VII.

Captain Lohnarks wanted the uranium, and he wanted it badly. He had shown great restraint in not taking blatant advantage of the defenseless Earth. There were a thousand treasures he could have taken. And didn't. But he could not restrain himself from going after a healthy quantity of mined uranium capable of nourishing a warship. Especially since there was time to act now, while the priest met with his commander in Rome.

Frank Nelson remembered last night's strategy meeting. He felt honored to be included in the meeting between King Kollann and Captain Lohnarks. Frank listened and said nothing.

"We can limit the killing to twenty night personnel staffing the uranium storage area," Lohnarks said.

"The system of defense and security is more complex than it at first appears. A hostile disruption to this plant's security would arouse a response from the powerful armed forces of the United States," King Kollann said.

"We can disable all military communications while we seize the uranium. We can return their communications to normal when we are finished, approximately ninety minutes later."

"Lohnarks, how do you think our Chadran military leaders would react if all their communications were disabled for ninety minutes while an unknown enemy seized a uranium cargo and killed twenty citizens?"

"They would panic! They would find out which enemy did this and how."

"And if they could not find the enemy responsible for it?"

"The military leaders would find an enemy. They would create one."

"And start a war?"

"Probably."

"Let's not start a war on Earth."

"I want the uranium," Lohnarks said. His annoyance was just beneath the surface.

Frank concealed his own impatience with Kollann. It was not easy having a Christian King.

Kollann stood up from his seat and paced. He asked the computer a few more questions, and then he said, "The *Horizon* has resources to secure the uranium peacefully that the *Stealthfire* did not have."

The King proposed a plan that required the same number of Chadran personnel, was slightly more costly, and was decidedly more peaceful than Lohnarks' plan. And Frank had to admit, the King's plan might even be fun.

Frank felt warmly smug today as he headed for this, his last trip to the Earth's surface. This time he was not intimidated by the suntanned California executives. This time Frank brought a military escort with him. The "escort" of four waited quietly in the van while Frank and his "associate, Mr. Ezners" went into Donald Cantril's office. Ezners' haircut was not quite right for his role, but he did wear one of Frank's business suits. Ezners could not speak one word of the English language, but he was a Chadran telepath, and he could clearly read Donald Cantril's mind. Frank was jovial and overly confident. Both traits seemed to annoy Cantril. Cantril seemed a little less polished and cool today than the last time Frank had seen him.

"Trust me, Frank, we are bending over backward to please you. We rushed our production deadlines to meet your needs. And this morning I canceled a meeting with an important client in order to fit you in... on the spur of the moment."

"I, too, am an important client, Mr. Cantril," Frank said. *You have no idea how important*, he thought. "I appreciate your efforts. I would not inconvenience you if it were not necessary. But I need to move my uranium cargo today. I have made arrangements to oversee its safe transport and delivery myself, and I do not need Bay Tech's assistance."

"Today! You can't be serious. Our contract clearly specifies that Bay Tech Industries will deliver the cargo to your plant. We have signed shipping contracts with air and ground transport companies--contracts that are binding. Didn't you receive my fax emphasizing these terms, Frank?"

"I cannot wait a week for your contracts to be renegotiated and then several more days for your transporters to lumber through the air with my cargo. All I am asking of you now is to authorize release of the cargo into my hands and my shipping agents'."

Cantril was angry. Not just annoyed. But he quickly turned his face away from Frank and looked out the window.

"Sir," Ezners interrupted, "Cantril has been debating in his own mind whether he should hand you over to military authorities or continue his business dealings with you. Nine days ago he read a disturbing newspaper article about Richard Saxon... being a cult leader. This and the urgency of your demands are arousing his fears. He fears that you may be political enemies to his people, manufacturing dangerous weapons. His only defense is a button under his desktop that can summon security officers. I have been watching Cantril's left hand near the button." Ezners spoke softly in the Chadran language. Cantril fidgeted nervously as he heard the foreign tongue. He moved his hand closer to the button. Instantly, Ezners pulled the tube gun from his sleeve and shot it into Cantril's chest.

"He will sleep for ninety minutes, sir."

"We will make them all sleep," Frank said. "We can do our job without Cantril's help, but we must move quickly." Frank felt an odd sense of satisfaction. And then he realized that since coming to this planet, he had wanted to flex his Tethran muscles. Now he could do it in a magnanimous fashion. He and his crew did not need to hurt anyone. They could put all the Bay Tech people to sleep and transfer the uranium aboard the starship cargo shuttle, freshly disguised with a U.S. Air Force insignia. After that, everything Tethran would disappear. When Cantril awoke, his bank account would be full, and he could not complain of theft. When the others awoke they would be frightened. But all they would really have was a hangover. And barely a clue as to where and how their uranium disappeared.

And so it was that they left the Earth behind them.

CHAPTER
THIRTY-THREE
CANDLES FOR THE LIVING

Bishop John Fisk choked back his tears as he sensed the powerful presence of God's Holy Spirit with him. With them. With all of them. Tonight he stayed up most of the night with his ten converts, the ten who had asked to be baptized after Kollann and Selina's wedding Mass.

The wedding itself was Selina's story to tell one day. No one would ever forget how stunning and queenly Selina looked. She was distractingly beautiful in a full-length gown made of a fabric that John had never seen. It poured like liquid gold around her body and was a tad immodest in John's eyes. But this dress had been made for Sorn's eyes. Although he carried himself with the dignity of the Hegemon and dressed like the King, he was a man in love that day, and he did not hide his show of love. Sorn broke tradition for his Earth-born wife and married her before the public eyes of all the four hundred crew members who were able to cram themselves into the Assembly Room. John was grateful for the breach of royal privacy, because it gave him his first opportunity to expose the Chadran crew to Christian prayer.

Tonight he was working with the harvest. Eight weeks into the journey, John could only speak to them through his translator attachment. But it worked well, translating even the subtleties of English into Chadran. And the converts were patient with John, in their hunger to know. He read them the story of Cain and Abel from Genesis.[*16] Then he read them the story of the Prodigal Son from Luke's Gospel.[*17] Then he told them about Jesus and how Jesus was the Truth, and spoke the truth which set them free. He explained that they were all the sons and daughters of the Most High God, and that their true identity and their worth was in that. And that alone.

John drank his coffee as they sipped their Sui. And he looked into their faces, and he saw the future.

[*16]

[*17]

II.

Sorn woke up at 4:00 a.m. because he felt her fingers doing effleurage on his naked back. Ever so gently, ever so alluringly her fingers moved. He pretended to be asleep, secretly delighting in her touch. She withdrew her hand, leaned over, and kissed him on the ear. Then she moved away from him and lay very still.

Sorn had been sleeping on his stomach. He turned around to face her and began kissing her. He kissed wherever his mouth felt like going. And her body welcomed him.

"It is the middle of the night. Are you too tired?" he asked softly.

"Do people actually get too tired for this?" Selina whispered.

"Maybe not us," Sorn said. And he relished the sound and he relished the feel of "us."

III.

Kollann Richard KurKuk Adrens Seege Sorn made the announcement of his ascendance to the throne of Chadra and his acceptance of the role of Hegemon for the United Alliance of Planets. He made the ansible announcement on the day that corresponded to the Greole's greatest, if not only, holiday: the New Year. And he stunned the Greole.

Three days later Sorn was in conference with the crew of the *Horizon* when they heard the news. No one wanted to believe it.

"Greole forces swiped at the outermost region of the Red Ice Starbase. They destroyed the Space Station and massacred many personnel. We do not have a casualty figure at this time."

"And Greole casualties?" Sorn asked.

"No figures at this time," Admiral Bidwhy replied.

"How could the Greole act so quickly, masking their approach and making such a devastating strike?" Sorn asked in a cold, authoritative voice. He addressed the Council of Admirals through the ansible. And he studied each of their faces. Some knawing intuition told Sorn that one of the admirals did not want the Greole to be defeated.

"We do not have an answer for you at this time, Your Royal Highness," Admiral Bidwhy replied.

"The main Greole fleet will reach our solar system in another three years. How will we be prepared to beat them if we cannot even suppress sniper squadrons?" Sorn asked, this time angry. And his anger shot itself through space and across the light years.

"We have been successful in destroying sniper squadrons, your majesty. This was... an oddity," the admiral said. And the King was not pleased.

Those among the admirals who saw the King's anger that day would not forget it. They would not forget his brilliance either, nor the questions he asked and the orders he gave. This King clearly grasped military strategy and had been doing his homework in the months he had spent traveling from the "hidden nowhere" back to Tethra and its solar system. And although no one was satisfied with the conclusion of the afternoon's military briefing, everyone had more hope than before. Because this was the Sorn who could win the war. Everyone had hope, they thought, except the King himself.

IV.

Sorn went to bed that night with a heavy heart. He waited until night watch. Until Selina was asleep. Until the chapel was empty. And he tiptoed quietly away from Selina's side and went into the chapel alone. The Royal Guard was silent as they stood outside the chapel, permitting him his privacy but never leaving him unprotected. The chapel door closed behind him, and he knelt on the floor beside the rows of candles which had been lit to remember the dead. They were not real wax candles like Selina knew on Earth; they were simulated, smokeless, safe candle lights that flickered occasionally and warmly from their tiny encasements. Sorn kept the other lighting dim so that he could barely see the silhouette of the altar, its cross, and the golden candles.

Sorn thought about all the dead. Those who died today at the Red Ice Quadrant. The young and the old of both sexes. He thought about his dead brother Jarn, and he thought about his father. All dead. *Where are you, Lord God, in all of this?* Sorn asked.

And then the answer came.

"Why do you seek the Living One among the dead? He is not here. He has risen, as He said."*[18]

He is risen, Sorn thought. And then the truth grasped him and upheld him and strengthened him. It was only the present that he feared, and not the future. The present in which tragedy was temporary and death was partial, and life went on. He could serve the present with all his heart. He was at peace. Because he would inherit the future. The future that belonged to the Risen Christ and to all the sons and daughters of God. The only future that could ever satisfy the hunger of the children of Adam and Eve--the victory of Easter, eternal life, and the rising of the dead.

---

*18

APPENDIX

All footnotes in this novel refer to Scripture passages taken from The New American Catholic Bible or the Revised Standard Version, 1971 Edition.

#1   "...you will know the truth, and the truth will set you free." John 8:32

#2   "Blessed are those who hunger and thirst for righteousness (sometimes translated justice), for they shall be satisfied." Matthew 5:6

#3   "Lamb of God, you take away the sins of the world, have mercy on us." Taken from the Canon of the Mass; also John 1:29

#4   "Yet in all these things we are more than conquerors because of Him who has loved us." Romans 8:37

#5, #6   "...but God chose what is foolish in the world to shame the wise, God chose what is weak in the world to shame the strong..." 1 Corinthians 1:26-30

#7   "Yes, God so loved the world that He gave His only Son, that whoever believes in Him may not die but may have eternal life." John 3:16

#8   "In the beginning was the Word and the Word was with God and the Word was God..." John 1:1
     "But to all who received Him, who believed in His name, He gave power to become children of God..." John 1:12

#9   "You are the light of the world..." Matthew 5:14

#10   "Truly, truly, I say to you, unless one is born of water and the spirit, he cannot enter the Kingdom of God. That which is born of the flesh is flesh and that which is born of the spirit is spirit." John 3:5-6

#11   "...I pray also for those who would believe in Me through their word, that all may be one, as you, Father, are in Me, and I in you: I pray that they may be one in Us, that the world may believe that you sent me..." John 17:20-21

#12   "...'Simon, son of John, do you love Me? 'Yes Lord,' Peter said, 'you know that I love you.' Feed my sheep.' Jesus said..." John 21:16

#13   "Say to the Lord, 'My refuge and my fortress, my God, in whom I trust... He shall call upon me and I will answer him'..." Psalm 91:1-16

#14   "A clean heart create for me, O God and a steadfast spirit renew within me...I will teach transgressors your ways and sinners will return to you."
Psalm 51:12-16

#15   "...for I did not come to judge the world but to save the world." John 12:47

#16   The story of Cain and Abel. Genesis 4:1-16

#17   The parable of the Prodigal Son. Luke 15:11-32

#18   "Why do you search for the Living One among the dead? He is not here: He has been raised up. Remember what He said..." Luke 24:5-8